P9-CAX-648

DETROIT PUBLIC

3 5674 00755335 8

DETROIT PUBLIC LIBRARY

BL

DATE DUE

A PRIDE OF PLACE

ALSO BY WILLIAM P. McGIVERN

THE ROAD TO THE SNAIL

SEVEN LIES SOUTH

SAVAGE STREETS

A PRIDE
OF PLACE

WILLIAM P. McGIVERN

DODD, MEAD & COMPANY

NEW YORK

c. 2

Copyright © 1962 by William P. McGivern
All rights reserved
No part of this book may be reproduced in any form
without permission in writing from the publisher

Library of Congress Catalog Card Number: 62-17925

Printed in the United States of America
by Vail-Ballou Press, Inc., Binghamton, N.Y.

BL
DEC 14 '82

FOR RAY BOND
GENTLEMAN AND PLAYER

                                        'Tis unnatural,
Even like the deed that's done. On Tuesday last,
A falcon towering in her pride of place
Was by a mousing owl hawked at, and killed.

                                         MACBETH

The characters, places, incidents and situations
in this book are imaginary and have no relation
to any person, place or actual happening

A PRIDE OF PLACE

Community solidarity is threatened in an exclusive Pennsylvania suburb when an Italian restaurateur tries to buy an old estate there.

CHAPTER 1

THE alarm clock rang at seven-thirty that morning, and its gentle chimes terminated a dream which Ford Jackson (awake now and reaching for a cigarette) found himself examining in a mood of pleasurable nostalgia. In the dream he had been driving along a winding road in a country he knew was France; chestnut trees marked like palominos whizzed by on either side of him, and the sunlight, breaking through nets of brilliant green leaves, danced about on the surface of the road like shiny new pennies. That was about all there had been in the dream, but he knew it was France because of the wind in his face, the calm, solitary countryside, and the chestnut trees posted like sentinels along the gray, winding road. There were no people in the dream.

Ford Jackson didn't look for revelations in dreams, in fact he put no significance in them at all, but this one puzzled him slightly because he hadn't particularly liked France the two times he had been there. It must have been dreaming about a fine sunny countryside that had put him in a good humor, he thought, as he pulled on his robe and walked barefooted across the thick wool carpeting to the windows on the east side of his bedroom. This was the third week of December and while there hadn't been much snow in Darby County so far, or all of Pennsylvania for that matter, Ford Jackson was already restless for spring. He loved the look and texture of the countryside then, with Black Angus cattle standing in sharp relief against the rolling green meadows and the farm ponds shining like glass in the morning sun.

1

From the east side of his bedroom, however, there was a view which satisfied him in all seasons of the year. The two hundred acres of sloping meadows and winter-black forests were unmarred by houses or barns, silos or chicken coops. From where he was standing he enjoyed the sight of perfectly open country, with the lake in the low meadow winking in the sunlight, and beyond that, the thick stands of beech and locust which marked the northeast line of his property. The fields were brown with crab grass now, covered with a slick of frost, and the sun flashed and sparkled on slivers of ice.

Something flawed the usual pleasure this view gave him, and he realized he was frowning faintly, and trying to isolate a vague anxiety flickering on the edge of his thoughts. Finally he pinned it down: Wiley Poston's telephone call last night. The Henderson place had been sold, and Wiley was upset about it, furious rather, his emotional tones ranging from solemn self-pity to savage belligerence within the confines of a single sentence. It was a waste of energy, Ford Jackson thought; the Henderson place was gone, and that was that. Wiley's wounded cries wouldn't change matters.

Ford showered and shaved quickly and efficiently, rubbed his body down with a coarse, warm towel, scrubbed his teeth, brushed his hair, weighed himself, and then looked critically at his body in the full-length mirror on the back of the bathroom door. At forty-four his stomach was flat, his shoulders square, and there were smooth firm muscles in his long arms and legs. His hair was thick and dark, with patches of gray at the temples, and (although this never occurred to him) these signs of age were a flattering counterbalance to his youthfully fresh complexion and a certain vulnerable look about his eyes and mouth.

Smiling at the results of this physical inventory, Ford Jackson walked into his bedroom and called the tack room in the barn. There was no answer so he pressed the intercom button that rang the kitchen. The cook answered immediately, and her smooth, rich voice, benign and contented as always, added to his good humor.

"Good morning, Mr. Jackson," she said.

"Good morning, Catherine. Have you seen Jones around?"

"Yessir. He here now. In the kitchen. He brought the eggs up."

"Good. I'm riding this morning. Would you ask him to tack up the Blackbird for me?"

"Sure, I tell him right now. And how about our breakfast?" She laughed pleasantly. "Number One or Number Two?"

This was a ritual joke with them, satisfying as any tradition in its predictability. Ford's normal breakfast, which Catherine called Number One, consisted of fruit juice, oatmeal, bacon and eggs, toast, coffee, and a glass of milk. As long as his weight remained under 170 pounds, this menu was as inflexible as the wheel of the seasons, but when he went over that mark Ford cut down to soft-boiled eggs, black coffee, and one piece of dry whole-wheat toast—breakfast Number Two.

"Oh, it's Number One today," he said. "And I've got some margin to play around with."

"Well, wait'll after the holidays, Christmas and all. I'll bet it's Number Two all through January."

"We'll see. Is Mrs. Jackson up yet?"

"Yessir. She already called for her breakfast. She's going out. Philadelphia, she said."

"Thanks. Tell Jones I'll want the Blackbird in half an hour."

Ten minutes later, dressed in boots and breeches, a flannel shirt and hacking jacket, Ford crossed the second-floor hallway and rapped on his wife's door. There was no answer but he heard the water running in her bath so he turned the knob and walked into her room. The shades were still drawn and the lamps on either side of her bed threw graceful circles of light on the soft beige carpeting. The décor of the room was supposed to be restful, he knew, and all of Janet's friends were excited about it, but the effect just made him restless.

Everything here was in shades of pink and white, the blankets and wallpaper, dressing tables and lounges, pictures and curtains, even her collection of china birds followed this bland motif, the hundreds of tiny white figures frozen in attitudes of song or flight behind the glass doors of two rosewood cabinets which stood on either side of her writing desk.

He saw that her breakfast tray was untouched, the food protected by napkins and silver warmers. There was a fragrance of perfume in the air, and fresh cigarette smoke, and the aroma of strong coffee. Ford took the morning paper from his wife's tray and looked at the weather report. It wasn't encouraging: colder tomorrow, with snow. As he was turning to the financial section the bathroom door opened and Janet emerged, or materialized, it seemed to him, through a cloud of scented steam.

"Do you have the right time?" she asked him, as she crossed quickly to her dressing table.

"Yes, it's five of eight."

"There's no crisis then, thank Heaven," Janet said, as she sat down and snapped on the soft lights above the triple mirrors of her dressing table. She wore make-up, earrings, a slip over her girdle, and high-heeled pumps. As she began vigorously brushing her gray-blond hair, she said: "I'm picking up Jane Calloway at eight-fifteen. If she's ready, we'll make the nine o'clock Congressional all right."

"Catherine told me you were going over to Philadelphia," Ford said, replacing the morning paper on her tray. "Shopping expedition?"

"Oh, no! We're being very virtuous, angelic actually. The County Hospital asked us to do a room for their Fair next week. They'll show it for a fee to lines and lines of little women they flush up from God knows where. We're using a Spanish theme, castanets, bullfight posters, and two of those old chests the Calloways liberated from a convent in Seville last summer. And Wiley Poston's lending us a Spanish policeman's hat, one of those black, patent-leather things that look like typewriters. He claims he stole it from a customs booth in Biarritz, but I imagine he bought it from a proper little shop in Madrid with a proper little traveler's check."

4

She talked in a steady, forceful flow which seemingly defied the customary conventions or restraints of respiration. But it wasn't an unattractive mannerism, Ford thought; her voice was low and husky, and she dramatized its lack of inflection with vivacious posturings and exaggerated facial expressions. She would be forty next month, he thought, looking at the thin ropy muscles bunching in her arms and shoulders as she brushed her hair. He wondered—and wondered at the direction of his thoughts—if men found her attractive; if any of the men on the Congressional, for instance, would bother maneuvering for a seat that would give them a view of her long slim legs. She had kept her body in shape with tennis and riding, and except for the extra highball or two after dinner, which was a recent habit, she lived a nearly Spartan life, with appropriate diets for all seasons of the year, plus massages, beauty aids, and a great deal of cold-creamed, eye-anointed sleep.

She had a round, youthful face, a high, clear forehead, and the blond streaks in her hair were always kept in flattering proportion to the gray ones, but something about her clear, cool eyes, it seemed to Ford, didn't match her vigorous body and rosy complexion. They were very good eyes, alert, clever, and direct, but lately they never seemed to focus on anything with very much interest.

"Will you be back tonight?" he asked her.

She turned around quickly, widening her eyes dramatically and letting her mouth fall open; the grimace froze her face into a mask of astonishment. "Did you forget Mother's coming for supper? I'm collecting her at six at the station."

"No, I hadn't forgotten," he said. "But I thought you might have to stay over in Philadelphia. Should I ask anyone for cocktails?"

"Please don't," she said emphatically. She had turned back to the mirror and was inspecting her teeth with the impersonal care of a horse trader. "You know how queenly she gets if she thinks we're fussing for her. Who are you riding with?"

"No one. I promised Wiley I'd take a look at the Henderson place this morning."

"When did you talk to Wiley?"

"Last night. After you'd gone up. About ten-thirty, I guess. Did you know that George Delucca bought the Henderson place?"

She spun around again, putting the back of her hand to her mouth in a theatrical gesture of alarm. "You're not serious! You're joking!"

"No, I'm not joking," he said. "Wiley told me last night. He was pretty high and he wouldn't hang up until I promised him I'd ride over this morning to look at the place."

"And a promise is a promise," she said. "Even to Wiley when he's tight as a tick."

"I had planned to ride this morning, so it doesn't make any difference whether I use the bridle path, or go up to the meadow to look at the Henderson place."

"What possible good will it do to ride over and *look* at the Henderson place? It's sold, isn't it?" She walked swiftly over to her closet and took a black suit from a hanger. "I think it's perfectly ridiculous to ride all the way over there and *stare* at it. It's maudlin and undignified. The whole business is hysterically funny, if you ask me." She zippered her skirt and twisted around to inspect her stocking seams in the closet mirror. "Do you imagine Mr. Delucca will hang neon signs on the gate to advertise his restaurant? And use that wonderful old barn for church suppers? Can't you just see it? Spaghetti dinner for the Sons of Italy, bingo games for St. Mary's hot-lunch fund?"

"I'm sure Wiley would find your light approach consoling." Ford said dryly. "And so would Tony Marshall. He's boiling, too."

"It's a silly, ridiculous business and that's my last word on it. Wiley or Tony should have bought the Henderson place when it went on the market last month. Or you and your brother should have. But you did nothing about it, nothing at all, and now George Delucca has it and it's all over, finished, kaput, and I'm not going to waste any sympathy or wring my hands over you all-knowing, all-seeing men."

"Do you care that much about it? That Delucca bought the Henderson place, I mean?"

"I know what you mean. Well, let me see." She adopted one of her standard comical poses, cupping an elbow in one palm, resting her chin on a fist, and wrinkling her forehead into a brooding frown. "Do I care?" she said, raising her eyes to the ceiling, and speaking in a deep, throbbing voice. "Do I really care?"

"I'd like to know," Ford said, stifling a tiny but resolute surge of irritation.

"I suppose not really," Janet said, abandoning her pose and hurrying across the room to pour herself coffee. "I don't imagine Mr. Delucca will exactly be lionized here, do you? What do you suppose he'll do about his daughters? Keep them in Consolidated Public, or try to get them into Miss Crane's?"

"He's probably thought about that," Ford said, as he walked to the door. "Well, you have a good day now. I'll see you about seven?"

"Yes. What time is it now?"

"Ten after eight."

Damn it! I've got to fly."

The morning was cold and the wind stung Ford's cheeks and made his eyes water as he cantered along the headland of the meadow above the Henderson place. The Blackbird wanted to run but Ford held her to an easy canter, for he had no intention of risking a fall on the frost-slick ground that was ringing like seasoned timber under the big mare's hoofs. At the top of the field he reined her in and turned in the saddle to look at the Henderson place. The Blackbird blew once, then shifted comfortably under him and lowered her head to tug at the clusters of stiff grass growing along the fence line.

Ford stared down at the Henderson place. The house stood sturdily against the far slope of the valley, rising darkly through the morning mists, a rectangle of weathered old field-stone brightened with white trim at the windows and doors.

Curtis Henderson had done over the original structure forty-five or fifty years ago, and Ford remembered his father telling him several times that the old man had been foolish not to add another wing back in the days of cheap labor and materials. It was a small house, really, with four rooms downstairs and four upstairs, and its style was typical of the area, typical of southwestern Pennsylvania, with foot-thick field-stone walls, and hand-hewn beams, huge fireplaces, and narrow windows. With the house there was a sound horse barn, with ten box stalls, forty acres of high pasture land, a kennel run, and a one-car garage. There was an old pump behind the kennel run, Ford remembered, and they'd always been warned to keep away from it, for the stone crown was cracked and broken away in parts, and you could push rocks through these openings and hear them land—ominous seconds later—with a soft cool splash in the bottom of the well.

The house had been empty for three or four years. Old Mr. Henderson had gone down to Aiken to live after his wife died and a colored man had looked after the house, and the land had been rented out to a farmer for grazing. When the old man died these arrangements had been continued for almost a year, but eventually the lawyers and heirs had got around to putting the place on the market. That had been, as Janet had reminded him, just a month ago, and the asking price had been sixty-five thousand dollars. According to Wiley, Delucca had got it for a flat fifty thousand. It would have been better, Ford thought, if Wiley or Tony Marshall had bought it. Or—as Janet had said—he or his brother, Clay. The Henderson place was part of the Downs.

Ford shifted his position and looked out across the valley. The sky was gray and heavy except for the brown smudge of sun in the east. To his left was a stand of timber, the crowns of trees rising and falling with the sweep of the land, and all the trees stiff and hard as iron now, except where the dappled trunk of a beech or sycamore flashed whitely against the winter blackness. On his right the meadows rolled like massive waves toward the low gray sky. Homes and barns stood firmly against the horizon, and herds of beef and dairy cattle dotted the brown crab-grass fields like children's cutouts.

What Ford was looking at now, this thousand-acre roll of meadowlands and forests, was the southern corner of an area known in Darby County as the Downs. As his eyes traveled over the familiar houses and landmarks, a scene he could draw from memory, he was thinking that he had spent considerable time and energy over the years worrying about just such problems as the one presently raised by George Delucca's purchase of the Henderson place. Or more accurately, why such problems should exist in the first place. And that brought him back to the peculiar character of the Downs, an area he probably knew as well as anyone else, but which still seemed to him full of bewildering fiscal and social contradictions. You might say, for instance, he thought, that the families who lived in the Downs were wealthy, but that wouldn't include Sam Harris, whose family had owned land here since the Revolutionary War, but who had very little money and whose children went to Miss Crane's nevertheless (turned out in patched coats like waifs from a Dickens novel), and who hunted with the Derby Hounds, and belonged to the Downs as firmly and as inevitably as Tony Marshall, who probably paid his grooms and huntsmen more in a month than Sam earned in a full year from his logging business.

In prep school, which had been St. David's in Massachusetts, Ford remembered he had once devised a negative definition of the Downs which had seemed to him to embrace all the peculiarities of the area. He had told his roommate that the Downs was a place where you wouldn't put up barbed wire, but that hadn't impressed Master Joseph Thomphson, he recalled, a stocky, red-haired boy from Detroit, with dead-white skin and turned-up nostrils which were aimed at the world like the muzzles of a double-barreled shotgun. "Who'd stop me?" Joe Thomphson had shouted at him, and Ford had disliked him from that moment on, and would dislike him all his life, although Joe Thomphson was no longer around to like, dislike, or have very strong feelings about one way or the other, since he had completed his short life in the hold of the *Lexington*, where he had been directing the work of a fire-fighting team, unaware apparently that the order to abandon ship had been given and that the bridge of the stricken carrier was already under water. Ford had read about Joe Thomphson's death, sitting at his desk in the Navy Building in Washington, and the news had been brought to his attention in a manner ironical enough to satisfy all the bittersweet theatrical standards of that or any other war. His WAVE secretary had placed a carton of coffee on the bulletin sheet, and when Ford had raised the carton a bit later there was Lieutenant Joseph Thomphson's name staring up at him, circled and signified by a ring of muddy, brown coffee.

And how had he answered young Joe Thomphson's hooted, derisive question? *Who'd stop me?* Lying in their bunks, with the faint scream of the Boston and Maine's night express beating against the frost-slick windows of their room, what had he said to Joe Thomphson? He couldn't remember just now; probably he hadn't answered him at all, but had just turned on his side and listened to the howl of the night express going down the grade into Providence, thinking angrily and ineffectively that Joe Thomphson was a fool, that only a fool would ask a question like that, that only a fool would want to string up barbed wire where it could ruin a hunter.

About the only way you could describe the Downs, Ford thought, as he turned the Blackbird toward home, was in physical terms. There you could talk with some precision. It was roughly twenty-five thousand acres of rolling country in southwestern Pennsylvania which had been originally settled by Quakers, whose descendants still lived there and preserved a way of life based on mutual interests and advantages. But those interests were trickier to explain than the physical properties of the Downs. Of course, there were activities with no mystery attached to them, such as fox hunting, horse shows, golf, tennis, sailing, cockfighting, gunning; such as the production of more-or-less mannerly children who were slated from birth to ride certain prescribed escalators in the exposure to, if not the pursuit of, higher eduaction; such as the shrewd and careful management of homes, land, stock, and all other investments.

The Quaker faith had lost out to the Episcopalians over the years, although some families still went to Meeting on Sundays, rather than High Mass, and it was still possible to hear the occasional bits of plain speech, the "how are thee's" at cocktail or dinner parties, although this custom was pre-served chiefly by women who used the old forms with a larkish inflection to indicate they were no more than sprightly little jokes. But the Quaker tradition lived on in the shrewd, impersonal approach to business matters; Tony Marshall bought locust posts from Sam Harris and though Marshall was a millionaire and Harris worked energetically and anx-iously for a bare living, Marshall drove tight, tough bargains with him, and neither man regarded this as anything but normal and proper.

In college Ford had once discussed the Downs with a thin, articulate young man named Schuman, an economics major from Chicago who had been one of the few Jews in his class at Princeton. That had been 1939 and everyone knew that the war was coming, that President Roosevelt would push the country into it somehow, since he was already giving England everything short of full tactical support, and one incident now, a sinking, a boarding, anything at all, would be enough to plunge the United States into it. In Ford's class, which was graduating, the consensus was that it would be wise to get into the Navy right away, on the theory that when the shooting started there would be no opportunity or time to choose your branch of service. How the Downs had been introduced into this tense and gloomy background, Ford didn't remember, but he did remember that Schuman

11

had said to him, "You've got a romantic notion about your section of the country, and it's charming, I'll grant you, quaint and sturdy at the same time, and just chock-full of pioneer values, but it's a very funny notion all the same, and damned unrealistic. You've got real-estate values confused with religion, money with some kind of a mystique. I'll tell you what money is, it's a way to express privilege. Take your fox hunting, it's merely a way to advertise a privileged condition in a highly public, highly conspicuous way. But there's nothing wrong with that in our society, and I'm sure lots of your friends get a kick out of it without analyzing it beyond the point of saying it's good healthy exercise in the open air. The same thing goes for swimming pools, indoor tennis courts, the whole rigamarole of conspicuous consumption—it's a way of defining and advertising privileges based on money. But it's the blindest kind of snobbery to imagine that the good things of life attach themselves to people with special talents for enjoying them."

Schuman had gone on at considerable length, quoting Veblen, Marx, Max Lerner, and Bertrand Russell, and he had smiled wearily when Ford had insisted that the Downs represented a collective will and a cohesiveness of interests which had nothing to do with material matters. Challenged by Schuman for an example, Ford couldn't think of any, but he recalled that he had said: "They've got emotional strength that comes from both belonging and contributing to this country in a special way. They have a continuity of family and money, and that's given them confidence. They're insular, I guess, stuffy, reluctant to change their ideas—anything you say. But they've also got a passive unselfconscious pride in their place in the scheme of things, and that's what gives them their own kind of inevitability."

Schuman had smiled and said: "I'll bet there were chaps in wigs sitting around the court of Louis the Sixteenth saying just about the same thing—while Marat and Robespierre were out oiling up the tumbrils. Let me tell you something: this is 1939, and we're going to war, make no mistake about that.

12

And when it's over I doubt very much if there'll be any such place as the Downs left in America. It's going to be broken up and put to better use, and in the process some heads may get broken up too, but that's an inevitable historical process. And let me make another guess: after the war, when you've finally got out of this Eastern-Ivy cocoon, you'll find what's left of the Downs an irrelevant and silly place to spend the rest of your life in. You want to bet?"

Ford hadn't gambled on it. He had missed a chance to make an easy dollar, he thought, looking out across the wide valley, the morning mists thinning now, turning gray and white as they climbed up the black trees on the horizon. Schuman had been a damn poor prophet, he thought: here, twenty-five years later, the Downs was still unchanged, intact. He had read only two weeks ago in *Newsweek* that Schuman had been appointed to a housing commission in the Kennedy government. "Volatile" and "brilliant" had been two of the adjectives used to describe Schuman. They should have added, Ford thought, smiling faintly, that Mr. Schuman would bring to Washington a very cracked and very clouded crystal ball.

And how would George Delucca fit into the pattern of the Downs? Not very smoothly—if at all. But why should he want to, why should he try? Ford wondered. Why butt his head against this particular stone wall? Why push in where he knew he wouldn't be accepted? The Downs people would be blamed for this, of course, called snobs and bigots by the locals, because Delucca was a Catholic, an Italian, and owned an eating place, three strikes against him right there, although Ford had to admit that dismissing the White Hackle as just a place to eat would be a bit like calling the Pavillon just another French restaurant. But these weren't the important things; it was more subtle than that, Ford knew, though he couldn't quite pin down what these subtleties were, only that they were related to what was old and what was new, to distinctions between tradition and experimentation in living, to the peculiar, hard-to-learn, hard-to-understand shadings and tintings that gave a certain correct color to social and

13

moral behavior.

Once, in a Navy bull session, Ford had been talking of his home and background, and, in trying to clarify it, he had attempted to draw a verbal portrait of a typical male resident of the Downs. He remembered, in a splintered fashion, some of his comments. "Forty-eight, married, three children, probably two boys and a girl." Yes, he had started that way, rolling a thick white china mug of hot coffee between his hands, and searching for the words that would make this composite figure come to life. "He's healthy, solid as a tree," he'd gone on, because that's how his father's friends had always impressed him—thick, sturdy men with calloused hands and cheeks hard and shiny from the winds of all seasons. "Keeping fit, keeping in shape, that's a big thing with him, because he's grown up with stock, and the need to take care of it, so he's the same with himself, sensible and temperate and cautious. Work's another big thing with him, whether he needs to or not. He wouldn't just sit around, he'd hunt, shoot, help make hay, things like that." And because he'd seen a certain skepticism, or more embarrassingly, a certain lack of interest in his listeners' eyes, he had tried to give his portrait more color, more sophistication. "He drinks, don't think he doesn't, but he holds it well, and he doesn't horse around with other women, not because he's prudish or anything but because the women he knows are the wives of his friends and he wouldn't touch any of them, even if they were ready for it—although that wouldn't be very likely either. If he travels, it's probably to Ireland or England or France to buy horses. He wouldn't know what the Abbey Theatre was, I don't guess, and he wouldn't go if he did becuse he'd consider them just a bunch of malcontents or socialists biting Mother England's generous hand. In Paris he'd put catsup on his pâté de foie if he wanted, and he wouldn't use a pissoir if his bladder was up like a basketball, but he'd shock hell out of the people he was buying horses from, he'd be tough, I mean, and when he got home he'd feel as lucky and grateful as a man who'd just got back from Mars."

14

The callowness of these judgments made him smile now, but he remembered that, at the time, he'd felt very worldly in his pronouncements, but also a bit disloyal at making fun of his father's friends just to elicit a tolerant smile from men he would probably never encounter after this interlude in his life was tucked away in mothballs with his dress uniforms.

They were within sight of his home now and the Blackbird pulled hopefully against his hand, ready to run if his knees told her to, but Ford held her in the easy canter all the way down the meadow. This was a view he loved, the house with the lake behind it, and hundreds of acres rolling away on either side of the tall pines which flanked the winding, graveled road leading to the house. Three generations of Jacksons had enlarged and improved the original structure, a sturdy old farmhouse with thick fieldstone walls, random-width floorings, and great open fireplaces staring into all the rooms on the first floor, and most of the bedrooms on the second and third floors. Ford's grandfather, Peter Jackson, had taken off the wooden shed which housed the laundry and kitchens, and replaced it with a fieldstone wing which extended at right angles from the main structure. Twenty-five years later, Ford's father, John Jackson, had installed new plumbing, heating, and electrical systems, and had added a second wing to counterbalance his father's. This was the present exterior shape of the house, a smooth unbroken expanse of white-trimmed windows and doorways facing the meadowlands, with the twin wings extending back from this toward the lake. Ford's own contributions had been minor: a terrace off the dining room, a balcony on the second floor of the older wing. The house suited him perfectly as it appeared to him now, nestling between open country and the small lake, the white trim shining and clean, the beautifully pointed fieldstone glowing in mellow shades of brown and beige and gray and white.

As he walked the Blackbird up the graveled driveway, he saw his brother's car parked in the lot behind the paddock, and after the first reaction of surprise and pleasure, he won-

15

dered uneasily what Clay was doing here at nine in the morning. He turned the Blackbird into the paddock and by then Jones was hurrying up the driveway from the stables, a twisted, shrunken colored man with one hand holding the lapels of his jacket together against the wind and the other tugging at the peak of his tweed cap.

"Morning, Mr. Jackson," he said, bobbing his head in rhythm with the words. "She behave herself this morning?"

"Yes, she's coming along nicely. After you water her, put her down in the low meadow. She needs to run off some energy."

"I'll do that. I'll do that for the young lady," Jones called over his shoulder, as he started across the paddock for the Blackbird.

Ford entered the house by the side door. The short back corridor which led to the main foyer was lined with jackets and overcoats and sweaters hanging from wooden pegs, and formations of overshoes and stadium boots standing beneath them on the floor. The room smelled warmly of leather and fur and rubber. As Ford hung his cap on a peg, draping his gloves over it, Catherine pushed open the swinging doors from the kitchen. She was large and tall and plump, brown features shining with health and humor, and she regarded Ford with a head-shaking disapproval, which was one of her cherished privileges in the household.

"I've got to scramble you some more eggs, I guess," she said with a sigh which implied that burden, and others too onerous and numerous to mention, might just be the straw to break the camel's back. "You gone so long the other got cold and I give it to the dogs."

"I'm sorry, but we just couldn't make any time on that frozen ground."

"Why you mess with horses anyway, more than I know. One end kicks, other end bites. Your brother, Mr. Clay's in the living room. I brought him some coffee with a cup for you but breakfast's in twenty minutes, you hear?" She let the swinging door close on her solemn face, but Ford heard her

16

chuckling as she turned back to the kitchen, and he knew she would have a happy moment explaining to Jones and Emma, the maid, just how she laid down the law to him that morning.

He crossed the red-tiled foyer and went down three broad steps into the large living room, which, when the sun streamed though the wide bay windows facing the meadow, glowed in vivid, tawny colors, the light gleaming from the pale yellow wallpaper and copper sheathing around the fireplace. Even on this leaden morning, however, there was a soft pearly glow in the long room, as the shafts of gray from the windows were quickened and brightened by the beige carpeting and the warm, oatmeal shade of the draperies.

For a second or so he didn't see Clay, then he saw his feet, shod in dull brogues, propped against the arm of the sofa that faced the bay windows. Ford walked to the sofa and looked down at his brother, who lay with a covert-cloth topcoat pulled up to his chin, and a green velours hat pulled down over his eyes. He seemed to be asleep. One of his hands trailed from the sofa, almost touching a coffee tray which rested on the floor alongside a bottle of Irish whisky.

Ford shook his shoulder and Clay lifted the hat from his face slowly and deliberately. He hadn't been sleeping; he was grinning at Ford. "Okay, officer, I'll move along," he said, in a thin, quavering voice. Laughing then, he raised his feet high above him and shouted "Geronimo!" as he swung his legs down and rolled forward, catapulting himself onto his feet. "Catherine, your dark lady of the pots and pans, brought me coffee," he said, patting Ford's shoulder. "The touch of Irish was provided by yourself, sir, and may God reward you for it." Ford smiled indulgently at his brother. He knew this was wrong but he couldn't help it; Clay must have been drinking all night, he realized, which meant he was in trouble at home, and probably other places as well, but instead of feeling appropriately stern and disapproving, he felt nothing but a good-humored (and nearly envious) respect for Clay's ebullient high spirits.

Clay was thirty-five, as fair as Ford was dark, with thick, gold-blond hair, brilliant blue eyes, and skin which remained smooth and pale and delicate despite all the hours he spent on horseback or on the golf course. He had always been wild, impulsive and irresponsible, and since these were seemingly permanent, immutable characteristics, people forgave him for them, dismissed them as something instinctive or glandular, and even those who were directly embarrassed, chagrined, or disappointed by his outbreaks or outrages, even they didn't really give a damn, for being around Clay Jackson was like being around an open fire on a dreary winter day, and no one seemed able to hold a cold front for long against the warmth and excitement of his personality.

Ford was no exception to this, Ford least of all, but now, for propriety's sake, he said: "Isn't it a little early for whisky?"

"Well, I haven't been to bed yet, you see, so this qualifies as a late nightcap. Would you get solemn and censorious if I had another?"

"No, go ahead. Then we'll have some breakfast."

Clay winced slightly. "You drive a sadistic bargain." He placed the tray on an end table and filled his cup with coffee and Irish whisky, measuring out the liquids with elaborate care.

"Now here's the trick to drinking," he said, smiling at Ford. "Inconspicuous drinking, that is. It's a dead giveaway to be sloppy about making drinks. Sure sign of the alcoholic inclination. Ever notice Wiley Poston? Acts like he's in heat when he gets around a bar. Grabs the neck of the bottle as if he's afraid someone's going to wrestle him for it. Then splash, splash, splash! You'd think he was trying to drown something in the glass. No talent for dissembling there! No subtlety. But note my detachment, my scholarly deliberation. I create the illusion that if the drink isn't perfect I'd rather not bother with it. Clever, eh? Cheers!" He raised the cup to Ford, still smiling at him, then took a small sip from it and sighed gratefully. "Lovely concoction, isn't it?"

"What were you celebrating last night?"

"No celebration, I'm sorry to say." Clay finished the Irish coffee in two deliberate swallows and put the cup back on the tray. He began to pace restlessly, a frown gathering on his forehead. "I wasn't celebrating a goddamn thing, Ford." He was subdued now, the frown shadowing his face, pacing restlessly with the covert-cloth topcoat slung like a cape about his shoulder.

Still, Ford thought, no amount of carousing or dissipation seemed to have any effect on him physically; there was, now, a strand of hair falling over his forehead, and his black, wool-knit tie was pulled down away from the collar of his shirt, but his skin and eyes were fresh and clear, and, as he drifted about the room, occasionally slapping the back of a chair or sofa with a suggestion of pointless exasperation, all of his movements were precise and graceful, as if he were following patterns and rhythms expressly designed to supplement his slender, supple body.

"If you weren't celebrating, what were you doing?" Ford asked him.

"Christ, I hardly know." Clay stopped pacing and looked at him with an odd, awkward smile. "Ford, do me a favor. I'm going to New York for a few days, to play squash, see some old pals and unwind a bit." He shrugged and rubbed a hand over the back of his neck. "Alicia and I had a large brawl last night, and I think the best thing for me to do is clear out for a while. Don't ask me what the row was about. I'll be damned if I remember. We started out with some pleasant Martinis before dinner, gracious living to the hilt, and after a while we were shouting about her father and mother, about something I either did or did not do at the club last night, why the Kennedys don't get their damned hair cut, and Christ, I don't know what else. Eventually, in the best, old-family tradition I—" Clay sighed and looked away from Ford. "What's your position on wife beating, by the way? Do you knock Janet around as a regular thing?"

"No, I don't," Ford said slowly, but this sounded so censorious, so self-consciously literal, that he added: "I've been tempted, of course,—every man has, I imagine." This wasn't true, of course; he had never had any inclination to strike Janet. Even considering it made him uncomfortable, for he could imagine her exaggerated reactions to any such theatrics.

Clay was smiling faintly, still staring at the backs of his hands. "I had a funny notion coming over here. Wife beating was a husband's legal prerogative in England for centuries, but with all this relish at touching up Madam's buttocks they still manage to give us Magna Charta. While in our own dear Southland, where the women were placed on pedestals and treated as if they were carved by master sculptors out of whipped cream and raspberry ice, the men compensated by cutting darkies to ribbons. Any moral there?"

"I don't know. If you hit Alicia, I imagine you were pretty stoned."

"That I was, that I was," Clay said wearily. "But it's a pretty middle-class excuse, don't you think? Look, here's what I want you to do. Go see her tonight, will you? I don't know what you can say, but maybe you can cheer her up, and try to convince her I'm not a reincarnation of the Marquis de Sade."

"Perhaps you'd better not go to New York."

"No, I've got to. Please, Ford. Will you go to see her?"

"These trips to New York are becoming pretty regular." Ford hesitated, feeling an uncomfortable warmth in his cheeks. "Your private life is your own business, of course, but do you have a girl over there? Is that the reason for these excursions?"

"I don't have a mistress, if that's what you mean. Sometimes there's the accidental roll in the hay. You know how that happens, you go to a party with the purest motives in the world and you meet someone you dated in school and pretty soon you're talking about what fun you had skiing a thousand years ago and then you're sitting around some place in the Village listening to good jazz—" He grinned and rubbed the back of his neck. "That happens if you're lucky."

"Let me ask you a big fat cliché," Ford said. "Do you think

this tomcatting around is fair to Alicia?"

"Hell, she doesn't know anything about it."

"She's very special. Have you thought about how she'll feel if she does find out?"

"Christ, I know she's special. She's a doll. A sweetheart. Intelligent, gracious, sensible, temperate." Clay let out his breath explosively. "But try living with that year in and year out. I sound like a bastard, don't I. But to get that special, exquisite, attenuated quality of Alicia's means you got to breed something else out. Hell, I don't just sound like a bastard, I am one. She's wonderful, and if she had any sense she'd tie a can to me. Will you see her, Ford? Tell her I'm sorry? Tell her I feel like a first-class heel?"

"Yes, I'll do that," Ford said. "But I think it would be better if you told her yourself."

"No, I trust my intuition. You can do more for her than I can just now. She thinks you're great, you know, all ready for a niche at Mount Rushmore."

Ford was warmed by this. Alicia was only twenty-seven, which seemed almost girlish to him, and he was pleased that she liked him. But he wished she were more tolerant of Clay's needs. His brother simply wasn't made for hobbles or restraints. Maybe if she accepted that and gave him head, he'd surprise her by settling down.

Clay picked up his hat. "Thanks for the moral support," he said, almost as if he had sensed Ford's thinking.

"I'm not taking sides," Ford said. "I want things to work out for both of you."

"They will, don't worry."

As they walked across the foyer, Ford remembered Wiley Poston's call, and he said: "You hear about the Henderson place?"

"Yes, Harvey Shires called me last night. Delucca bought it, eh?"

"What do you think about it?"

"That's what Harvey wanted to know. What difference does it make? Do you mind?"

"In a way, I'm afraid I do," Ford said. "I don't know why exactly. I'm not as concerned as Wiley, or Tony Marshall. But I understand how they feel."

Clay grinned at him. "End of an era, carpetbaggers crawling around the stately old mansions?"

"I just don't know," Ford said.

"Listen to your kid brother for once. Wiley and Tony are stewing because the Henderson place got plucked out of their itchy little fingers. You know, I can listen to this talk about the sanctity of the Downs just so long. Then I begin to sniff the bright green smell of money. O.K., O.K.," he said, grinning and putting up both hands in a defensive gesture. "I know how you feel. But look at it this way: in the past, when a property in the Downs was up for sale the real-estate dealers made damn sure they showed it only to approved clients. You know that's true, Ford. Go down the list of dealers, Moran and Son, the DaBundo brothers, John Wilson, Jerry Corcoran—name any dealer you want, they all asked around nice and discreetly before they closed a deal in the Downs. And who did they ask? Wiley, Tony Marshall, Tom Calloway, and maybe half-a-dozen others, including you and me. And they wouldn't even show a property to clients who didn't pass that social litmus paper test. This did more than keep the land in congenial hands. It kept prices down by eliminating bidding. And that's what I told Harvey Shires last night. Hell, maybe that's why I got drunk. I got fed to the gunwales with his whining. 'It's not that he's Italian, and of course a man can worship God in any fashion he chooses . . .' I don't know what the hell he expected from me, a medal for tolerance maybe. Anyway I said to him, 'I know you don't mind that he's an Italian and a Catholic, but you mind like hell that you got screwed out of a good real-estate deal,' and then I hung up on the silly bastard."

"You shouldn't have said that."

"Why not?"

"You don't know what his motives are. Second, if you want another reason, you were drunk. And you shouldn't discuss anything serious when you're drunk."

"Well, I wouldn't classify his bleats and whines as serious," Clay said. "So I'm excused on one count anyway." He laughed then, and patted Ford's shoulder. "Hell, maybe Delucca will liven things up out here. Do you remember the night he turned poor Alicia away because she was wearing slacks?"

"Yes, of course," he said, and added dryly: "I still don't find it a laughing matter."

"Come on. It was three years ago. Actually I admired him for it."

Was it that long ago? Ford thought. Three years? Yes, at least. It had been in the fall, a month or so after Delucca had opened his new place, the White Hackle Inn, on Powder Mill Road. Ford remembered the incident clearly.

They had decided that night, on impulse, to go to the White Hackle for dinner. Just the four of them, Janet and himself, Clay and Alicia. Ironically, they had had to talk Alicia into it, for she had been shooting skeet and didn't want to change, but they had insisted she come along as she was and she had given in. But at the White Hackle they were stopped by the headwaiter, who told them with what seemed genuine anguish that he couldn't seat Mrs. Jackson because she was wearing slacks.

Clay had been amused at first, Ford recalled; he couldn't believe the man was serious. Alicia had been irritated, and had wanted to leave, but Clay's temper was up by then and he was in no mood to retreat. And while he was arguing with the headwaiter, George Delucca had come down the wide stairway from his office, moving quickly and confidently toward the disturbance, a bland, unrevealing smile on his lips and his dark, shadowed eyes taking in the situation with an alert glance. He came toward them through the softly lighted foyer like a sleek, powerful animal, moving silently over the thick soft carpeting, his dark pirate's face shining above the immaculate expanse of his white dress shirt. He had listened gravely to Clay's angry complaints, his big dark head tilted to one side, thoughtfully and judicially, but the gentle and

23

sympathetic smile on his full lips somehow reduced Clay's indignation to the level of a schoolboy's bluster. His expression was kindly and understanding, as if he were saying: "Now, now, young man, this really isn't so terrible," and while he listened patiently to Clay's loud protests, nodding slowly so that the light moved and flickered on his wavy black hair, his eyes had gone from Ford to Janet and Alicia, as if begging their forbearance for their spokesman's intemperate outbursts. There was a message of consolation for Alicia in his rueful appraisal of the offending slacks, but his faintly cynical grin suggested that she probably knew better than to come to the dinner table straight from the back of a horse.

It had been an exasperating experience, Ford recalled, because, while they knew they were in the wrong, they still couldn't believe that any restaurant in the area would take a chance on losing their good will over such a trifling matter.

Alicia, who was pink with embarrassment by then, had turned on her heel and walked out, leaving Clay in the middle of a harangue which included, among other irrelevancies, the charge that Delucca obviously wasn't equipped with enough taste or judgment to run anything more elaborate than a pizza joint or trucker's diner. Janet and Ford and Clay had left too, of course, followed by Delucca's compassionate, head-shaking smile.

"I don't see why you admire him for that," Ford said to Clay. "Any more than you'd admire a policeman for stopping traffic. Delucca was simply doing his job—there was nothing else for him to do."

"No, you're wrong," Clay said. "Delucca could have done several things. He might have wrung his hands, suffered our annoyance with a hanging head. Or he could have stood us a drink in the bar and ushered us out with humble bows. Or he could have appealed to Alicia's sense of fair play. Would she want him to break a rule which would cause all sorts of embarrassment when others demanded the same privilege? Or he could have winked at his own regulations by giving Alicia one of the waitress's aprons which would have technically satisfied

24

the rules of dress. But he was too shrewd to make any concessions. And his choice was a stroke of business genius. He knew the White Hackle would get a blast of favorable publicity when the news spread that proper little Alicia Jackson had been turned away at the door just as casually and firmly as if she'd been a hillbilly's wife wearing blue jeans and an army fatigue jacket. Remember, it did cause a lot of talk. Our phone rang all the next day. Alicia's dearest friends calling to tell her how terrible it was, but how hilarious too, and to avoid giving them any satisfaction, she had to pretend it couldn't matter less, and that she wasn't angry at all, and that she'd be back at the White Hackle as soon as she could persuade me to buy her a dress, or anyway a wraparound cotton skirt."

"I never thought of all those angles," Ford said. "You may be right. But I still don't think it's particularly admirable. I'd admire him, I suppose, if he'd made the decision on principle, without all this tricky psychology."

"Principles are a luxury," Clay said. "They're a form of conspicuous moral consumption."

"Well, I couldn't agree less," Ford said. "What does a principle cost? You can't put price tags on them."

Clay grinned at him. "I could paraphrase Mr. Morgan on yachts. If you have to ask what a principle costs, then you probably can't afford it. Well, I'm off, trailing epigrams." He suddenly became serious. "Do your best with Alicia, will you, Ford?"

"Yes, of course. Now watch yourself on the Turnpike. We're due for some snow."

After Clay had gone down the lane to the parking lot, Ford closed the front door. The sun was gaining strength and a soft, hazy light slanted through the windows of the foyer. This room always gave him pleasure. It was the core of the original structure, snug, low-ceilinged, with exposed beams and wide pine floorboards that were as glossy as satin in the sunlight. The grandfather's clock ticked with a thoughtful sound from its position beside the fireplace, and the apple logs burning there filled the air with a sharp, winy fragrance. He rubbed

25

his hand gently over the curved back of a cockfighting chair, and smiled as he thought of Clay's comments on George Delucca.

He was stimulated by Clay's visit. Things always looked different, assumed odd, fresh shapes, under Clay's examination. He had a remarkable mind, Ford thought, subtle and perceptive. Who else would have worked up this elaborate analysis of Delucca? Perhaps this flair for hidden motives, for the truth behind the surface of things, was the clue to his fascination for women.

They must like this sinuous streak in him, he thought, for it probably complemented their own mysterious and well-publicized intuitions. Whatever it was, it was catnip to the ladies. As Ford went in for breakfast he felt animated and cheerful. The day seemed to hold all sorts of vague and pleasant promises. As he sat down and shook out his napkin he wondered, smiling, what complicated and silky-haired girl his brother might be speeding toward on the Turnpike.

CHAPTER 2

IT was ten o'clock when Ford drove into the village of Rose-dale to drop off Janet's letters. The town was gay and bright with Christmas decorations, red and green lights strung above the main street and holly wreaths and lighted Christmas trees sparkling in shop windows. Rosedale had once been as pretty as its name suggested, with the village fanning out from Mr. Giorgano's general store, a two-storied frame structure stocked with slickers and boots and hunting clothes, barrels of strong yellow soap cut like paving bricks, glass-fronted bins of beans and chick peas and coffee, racks of axes and hoes and shovels and sledges, and a tantalizing case, made of heavy mesh wire and always kept securely locked, where Mr. Giorgano kept his deer rifles and shotguns. There had been a saddle shop in the town, and a bootmaker who lived and worked in the basement of a red brick boarding house, and the railway station with its breath-taking, daytime clangings and hissings from the long passenger trains, and, at night, the heavier, graver, more excit-ing rumble of the freights rattling through to Oxford and Messala and Kentucky and Virginia, with brakemen swinging out from grab irons, their lanterns signaling mysteriously and importantly in the darkness.

Now Mr. Giorgano's store was gone, and so was the saddle shop and the bootmaker, and the trains no longer roared and puffed through Rosedale. In their place was a supermarket, three gasoline stations, two diners for truckers, and two bars, one for whites, the other for Negroes.

Ford parked on the main street and went up the steps of the

small, white-clapboard post office. He gave Mrs. Fegin his letters, exchanged a comment with her on the weather, and was turning from the counter when he noticed a girl in blue jeans and a red jacket standing beside the door with a piece of paper in her hands. For some reason she made him uncomfortably aware of his muffler, his Chesterfield overcoat and dark suède gloves. She looked cold, and her expression was confused and sullen. He wasn't sure why he stopped, but he did, and he said: "May I help you?"

She looked at him and shook her head.

"I'm sorry," he said, a bit stiffly, and was reaching for the doorknob when she touched his arm with fingers that were light and hesitant as a child's. She held the piece of paper toward him, and he took it from her thin brown hand and read what was written on it: Maria Ruiz, General Delivery.

"You're Maria Ruiz?"

She nodded slowly, carefully. She was young, twenty-two or twenty-three, he guessed, with a thin, spare body and long black hair pulled straight back from her forehead and temples. The planes of her face were too sharply angled for beauty, but her eyes were quite amazing, large, clear, and brown as cordovan leather. She wore no make-up, and he saw that her lips were chapped.

"You're expecting a letter?" he asked her. "A letter addressed to you, care of General Delivery?"

Again she nodded, slowly and carefully.

"Una carta, eh?" he said, and smiled as he dredged up these words from the mental ravine into which they had settled after his freshman semesters of Spanish.

"Yes," she said, and looked away from him.

"Just a minute. I'll see if there's anything for you."

Ford turned back to the counter and saw that Mrs. Fegin had been listening to his conversation with the girl. She was smiling patiently. "I explained to her there's nothing, Mr. Jackson. They're hard to convince. It's probably a relief check, though, so I can't blame her."

Ford glanced at the girl and realized that she understood

28

what Mrs. Fegin had said; a touch of color showed in her cheeks behind the smooth, light brown skin.

"There's nothing for you today," Ford said, and without knowing why, added: "I'm sorry. Maybe it will come tomorrow."

She looked uncertainly at him and then turned toward the door. He held it open for her, and she went down the stone steps ahead of him, and walked away from the post office toward the center of the village. Ford stood beside his car and watched her as she passed under the black branches of the locusts that lined the street. She had no gloves and the thrust of her hands in the pockets of her red jacket pulled the fabric tightly across her thin, square shoulders. He knew she was cold from the way she was walking, with her face turned sideways to the wind and her elbows hugging her body. She wore black loafers with white wool socks, and her blue jeans had been laundered thin; the material was faded white where it stretched against her narrow hips.

He wondered where she was going, and what she would do with herself on this cold, gray day. Something about her stirred a curious nostalgia in him. It was fanciful, he knew, but she reminded him of the loneliness of winter, the feeling you had when you saw wild ducks wheeling against the sky, or a single hawk high in the branches of a tall tree, scanning the meadows with savage vigilance.

The thought made him uncomfortable; it was the sort of romantic foolishness he had no taste for. Mrs. Fegin's estimate was probably closer to the mark; a Puerto Rican girl waiting for her unemployment check, which she probably shared with a mushroom house worker.

Ford climbed into his car and drove down the pike ten miles to Cottersville, where he kept an office in the Merchants Building. As a lawyer, he spent most of his time taking care of his own investments and taxes, but he also looked after Clay's interests, and since they both ran dairy farms and leased part of their land out for grazing, the operations were complicated enough to absorb his full time and attention. After a routine

29

morning, he lunched with Tom Landon, president of the Cottersville National Bank, with whom he shared the responsibility of raising money for a new library.

Cottersville had tripled its twelve thousand population since the war, and every facility in the city, including the old library, was straining to contain this lusty expansion. To Ford it seemed odd that most people thought this was a good thing, a grand thing in fact, as if it were a matter of pride to live in a city that became steadily less functional and more disagreeable with every unit added to its population figure. But everyone accepted the disastrous consequences of this unplanned growth with shudders of relish. They predicted happily that in five years you wouldn't be able to park within a mile of the town square. They shook their heads with spurious alarm at what the schools would be like in the next decade, day and night shifts, all instruction by television or teaching machines, juvenile delinquency rampant, switchblades for sale in the principal's office. The rising prices, thickening belt of slums, the rationing of water in the summer, the sporadic collapse of the municipal electrical and plumbing systems, all of these crises, which might be extended to areas of feasible lunacy within one generation, and which Ford imagined any rational person would view with distaste, were, on the contrary, regarded by the shopkeepers and professional people of Cottersville as boons from the Almighty and proof of the magnificence of the American way of life.

At lunch, Tom Landon was complacent at his role in helping Cottersville burst at the seams. He had coined a slogan for Rotary—The Bigger the City the Bigger the Citizen—and he asked Ford what he thought of it.

"Well, I don't quite understand it," Ford said, after a polite pause.

"The point is simply that a native of New York is more significant, in an intangible way, than a citizen of, say, Oshkosh, or Broken Knee, Iowa."

"How does that follow?"

"Well, being part of something big and growing gives people a sense of importance and identity. And that feeling of excitement is good for a community, and good for business."

"Perhaps," Ford said. "Perhaps it's true in relation to quantity. But what about quality? Aren't we concentrating on making things bigger, without trying to make them better?"

"Quality, in certain areas, is just something we can't afford any more. The grandson of the man who made saddles by hand is now turning a lathe making automobiles. And if you have to go to New York you want a car, not a hand-made saddle on a sound horse, right?"

"Unfortunately, you have a point," Ford said.

Tom Landon smiled at him, and it wasn't altogether a friendly smile. "Your viewpoint is different from the people we're talking about. You're part of a successful community. The Downs, I mean. But a good many others take their civic pride where they can find it. Or invent it any way they can."

Landon paused to light a cigarette, and his smile changed slightly; it was good-humored now, but touched with an innocent malice. "I read in the *Courier* that George Delucca bought the Henderson place," he said. "Did you see the piece?"

"No, but I heard about it."

"It's quite a step up in the world for George, isn't it?"

"It's a good house and a good property, if that's what you mean."

"You know that's not all I mean," Tom Landon said, laughing comfortably. "But that aside, George Delucca is one of the people who's putting Cottersville on the map. You know he borrowed a hundred thousand dollars from us, as cool as you please, last week, and he's not worried about it and neither is the bank. The White Hackle's a gold mine, but he's not resting on his oars. He's betting on the growth of this community and we're betting on him—and dozens like him in the area."

"Did he put a mortgage on the White Hackle?"

"No, it's a demand note. With the cash business he does, that seemed best. Well, let's get to work and see who we can blackmail into building our library, O.K.?" . . .

In his office that afternoon Ford found himself thinking

31

about his talk with Tom Landon. Landon seemed to agree with his brother, Clay. One said that principles were a luxury, and the other that quality was too expensive to strive for in this day and age.

Landon's mild needling about Delucca hadn't escaped him, and he wondered if this would be a typical reaction in the area. Satisfaction that one of their own had made it, plus the enjoyment of watching the reaction in the Downs. Ford hadn't been irritated by Landon. Tom Landon had come to Cottersville from Chicago after World War II, and had married a girl from Philadelphia. With that background, he wouldn't understand the Downs. He undoubtedly respected the land and money controlled by the families there, but Ford suspected he regarded the activities of the area as tiresomely affected; the fox hunting, the point-to-points, the clannish loyalties, the English tailoring, the cool indifference to change and progress, all this Landon would consider old-fashioned at best, and, at worst, a foolish attempt of contemporary Americans to pose as figures in English hunting prints, landed gentry wistfully distressed that labor unions had replaced their grandfather's retinue of forelock-tugging peasants. What Landon didn't understand was that people in the Downs weren't aware of themselves as special or insular or snobbish or clannish—they had no flair for analysis, no need to dig into themselves in a quest for identity. They would probably be surprised to know that Landon thought of them as social curiosities; surprised, that is, that he thought about them at all. For they spent no time thinking about him.

But was this accurate? Ford thought. It hardly squared with the concern over Delucca. Wiley Poston was thinking about Delucca, and so was Tony Marshall and Harvey Shires, irritably and unhappily. You couldn't pretend these men were just hearty, red-cheeked country squires, happily indifferent to everything but horseflesh and whisky punches.

Ford wondered then if his own comparative indifference to Delucca stemmed somehow from the fact that the roots of his family had been planted originally in Iowa and not Pennsylvania. Ford leaned back in his swivel chair, frowning faintly at his thoughts. He lit a cigar and put a foot against the roll-top desk which bulked so incongruously in his carpeted, book-lined office, with its bucks' antlers shining whitely on either side of his law diploma, and the old Parker shotgun snugly encased beneath his class picture from Princeton and framed Navy discharge papers.

But he liked the old desk because it had belonged to his great-grandfather, after whom he had been named, and he liked the old Parker because it had belonged to his grandfather.

His great-grandfather had farmed corn around Marengo, Iowa, for almost forty years, and had retired at sixty-five with a sound body, a clear mind, and fifteen thousand dollars in hard cash. Instead of settling down in Sioux City or Davenport where he had relatives, the old man had surprised everyone by going east and buying a farm outside of Rosedale, Pennsylvania. No one understood this lemming drive of his, for he had been born in Iowa and knew no other part of the country, but some tales and recollections of his parents about the east must have inflamed his youthful heart, just as stories of Indians and buffaloes had caused dreams and desires to start up in the minds of youngsters growing up in the eastern states. He had been a one-man revolution against the movement west; he had wanted to go east, and had nursed this dream through forty years of hard winters and worse summers, and when the dream came true, when he arrived spry and alert in Rosedale, a wonderful change had come over the old man, and, through a weird alchemy, which was part of the family folklore, old Ford's spirits were revitalized, and his ambitions sprouted sky high. He bought a stone quarry and a lumber yard, became partner in a feed and grain business, went into construction and logging, and picked up scraps of land all over the county with the undiscriminating zeal of a pack rat.

He lived to be eighty-two, and at his death presented his two sons (who were still farming the old homestead in Marengo) a formidable complex of business and agricultural interests in his adopted state of Pennsylvania. The sons came east to manage this small empire, thus starting the Jackson line in Darby County, from whence it had spread to South Carolina, New York, and New Jersey, with all its members deriving benefits from the strange, piratical enthusiasm which had infected old Ford when he had come east from Iowa. But the Iowa part of his saga, which had made all the rest possible, was played down by many of the Jacksons. It always amused Ford to hear his uncle Peter, for instance, refer to the "land out west" rather than "the Marengo farm," as if old Ford's axes and plows had bitten only into romantic frontiers, instead of the homey black earth of America's bread basket. And the Jacksons in Philadelphia and on Long Island, third and fourth cousins whom Ford saw at occasional funerals or board meetings, had become so social and suburban that they ignored the fact that the original source of their money was lumber and feed, preferring to think only of land, and not the black soil of Iowa, but the rolling, patrician acres in and around Darby County. It was a harmless deceit and necessary to their self-esteem in a sense, for old Ford wasn't deeply enough embedded in the past for their comfort, and the stories which still circulated about him couldn't be dismissed as good, earthy folklore in the best American tradition.

No, old Ford had lived long enough to own an automobile and vote for Teddy Roosevelt, and there were still elderly parties about who had been eyewitnesses to his drinking and wenching, who had seen him bite the heads of snakes at county picnics, and had seen his Apperson streaking along dusty back roads with the old man drunk at the wheel and laughter like the cackling of hens rising from the colored girls in the tonneau of the car. Of course, these eyewitnesses had been children at the time, but this only made their recollections more lustrous and vivid.

He must have been quite a boy, Ford thought, grinning. He'd kept women in Wilmington and Philadelphia, on a formal, courtly basis, but it was said the old man would bed down with a snake if he could find someone to hold both ends.

Ford's excursion into the past was checked by the telephone, and he was caught up in the routine of business for the rest of the afternoon. At four-thirty he signed his mail, and gave the letters to Mrs. Simpson, his secretary, and left for Wilmington where he had an appointment with a director of Inter-Allied Chemical. The meeting lasted until five-thirty, and he called Mrs. Simpson before starting for home.

"There's nothing you need to bother about, I don't think," she said. "Your brother called from New York to remind you you're seeing Mrs. Jackson tonight. *His* Mrs. Jackson, that is, although I don't have it on your calendar."

"No, but would you call Alicia and tell her I'd like to stop by after supper?"

"Yes. And Mr. Marshall called twice. He asked if you'd be home tonight, and I said as far as I knew, yes."

"He didn't say what he wanted?"

"No—just whether or not you'd be home. Oh, and one other thing. Someone by the name of Maria Ruiz, as nearly as I could make out, called just a little while ago. She asked if you could come to see her and she left an address—just a second—116 Green Street, in Rosedale. She seems to think lawyers make house calls like plumbers."

"She needs a lawyer? Did she say that?"

"Honestly, Mr. Jackson, I'm not sure exactly what she wanted. Yes, she mentioned needing a lawyer, but she didn't seem to understand when I suggested she make an appointment. I didn't know whether you'd care to see her, but I took the address just in case."

"I don't imagine it's anything important," Ford said. He remembered the girl as she had walked away from the post office, her face turned away from the wind, and her elbows pressed tight against her body. His cheeks were suddenly warm, and this reaction confused and irritated him. "Good night," he said to Mrs. Simpson and replaced the receiver quickly, cutting off her pleasant voice in mid-sentence.

When he started for Rosedale it was dark and there were flurries of snow in the air, swirling like moths in the yellow beams of his headlights. The traffic was heavy, and, as he moved along carefully with it, leaning forward for a clearer view of the highway, he thought of Maria Ruiz's call with some detachment. How had she known his name? By asking, obviously; anyone in Rosedale would have told her who he was. But what did she want? Help, obviously. But what kind? He couldn't imagine, beyond assuming she was in trouble. That was the only reason poor people turned to a lawyer.

In Rosedale he turned off the highway and drove slowly through the residential section of the village, following a route which would bring him to the curving road that led upward into the Downs. There were some good homes here, large and solid, with gingerbread trim and wide porches, but in a few blocks the character of the streets changed rapidly; first were smaller houses, frame bungalows pressed close together but showing care in the tidiness of paint jobs and lawns; then poorer homes, with garbage pails and ash cans permanently on the sidewalks, and cars with the depression look of crumpled fenders and torn or patched upholstery; finally the village seemed to give up the fight, the last touches of pride and respectability dwindling and disappearing in the colored section, with its church in the basement of a shoe shop, and its name (The Mount Zion Congregation of the Ascension) in flaked gilt on a smudged window, and alongside this a body-and-fender garage, and then a grocery store, and then nothing but a straggling collection of unpainted, crazily angled shacks.

This was where the girl, Maria Ruiz, lived; for 116 Green Street was somewhere in this section of Rosedale. Ford drove slowly through the unlighted streets, unable to make out any house numbers. Finally he stopped and asked a colored man pushing a bicycle where 116 Green Street was, and the man, after scratching his head and looking about uncertainly, said he thought it was down the hard road a piece, out toward the edge of town.

Ford thanked him and drove on; in a few hundred yards he came on the place by luck. The house was on a curve of

36

the road leading to open country, and when he made the turn his headlights flashed across the green-glass numerals that were tacked to the wooden door at irregular angles.

He stopped on the shoulder of the road, his motor idling softly, and studied the house in the darkness, unable to pick out any details at first, but finally seeing that it was a two-storied frame house with a single light showing through a window on the first floor, and a wisp of smoke being whipped away from a brick chimney. The wind was blowing hard and he saw electric wires swaying between the corner of the house and a pole beside the road. In his headlights the snowflakes flew about frantically.

Well, there's a fire and electricity, he thought, which meant some protection against the weather. Then as he sat there in the warmth of his car, the motor humming gently and his cigarette reflected in the windshield as he drew on it, Ford saw the girl's shadow cross over the lighted window. He had an impulse to get out of the car, knock on her door, and ask what she had wanted of him, but it was a weak and flickering impulse, short-circuited instantly by common sense. If he saw her at all it would be at his office, but then he wondered why he had stopped there in the first place. Suppose someone recognized his car and pulled up alongside to ask him why he was waiting here in the darkness—what would he say? Cleaning the snow from the rear window, getting a pack of cigarettes from the glove compartment—anything would do, of course, but anyone who knew him would grin if he told the truth; if he explained this hard, sullen lonely girl had caught his interest, and that he had stopped here with the intention of talking to her. This would get him credit for a hitherto undisplayed talent for leg-pulling, he knew.

Ford rolled the window down and the winter air blew sharply and cuttingly against his face. Then he saw her again, more clearly now, crossing in front of the window, and he recognized the silhouette of her thin body, and the long hair falling to her shoulders. Again he was tempted to knock on her door, to talk to her, but the cold, pinched look of her body checked him for reasons he didn't understand except that they were related subtly to the look of his own hands on the steering wheel, firmly and snugly protected from the cold in supple, hand-stitched suède gloves.

Why this contrast affected him Ford didn't know, but a faint stir of apprehension accompanied it, and he rolled the window up quickly and started home, relieved to be rolling smoothly once again toward his own familiar, substantial world.

As his lights swept up the curving approach to his home, he was surprised to see a cluster of cars in the parking lot behind the paddock. Janet's convertible was among them, which meant he was later than he had planned to be, for she had picked up her mother at six in Wilmington. It was after seven, he saw, glancing at his watch, and he wondered a bit uneasily just how long he had been sitting in the darkness in front of Maria Ruiz's home. It had seemed like seconds; but in fact it must have been fifteen or twenty minutes.

As he was hanging up his hat and coat in the foyer, Janet came quickly down the wide stairway from the second floor. She wore black slacks and a white blouse, and a blue ribbon held her gray-blond hair in a childishly neat bun at the back of her neck.

"Who's here?" he asked, nodding toward the sound of male voices in the living room.

"Tony Marshall and Wiley Poston. Harvey Shires is on his way over, and mother is upstairs combing tons of Pennsylvania Railroad dust from her hair." She locked her hands over her slight bosom and widened her eyes slowly and solemnly. "Tony's here about the Delucca business. Mother thought they'd all come to see *her*. Poor thing wanted to get into a long dress and gobs of make-up, but she's taking it bravely." Janet sighed and raised her eyes to the ceiling. "It seems odd that one of the few nights I'm here, Ford has to have a business meeting." She took off her mother perfectly, Ford thought, and he had the unhappy realization that in time the mimicry would probably become both unconscious and constant.

"I'll try to wind this up quickly," he said. "I've got to see

Alicia after dinner—Clay asked me to this morning—but I'll be back early and have a good long talk with her. I'll tell her scare stories about the market—that always gets her adrenalin spurting."

"You're nice, Ford," she said, and touched his cheek with the back of her hand. "I mean that, you really are."

She was quite nervous, he saw; it was always this way when her mother was here, out came the epicene slacks and blouses, the girlish hair ribbons, and the pert, sprightly posturings. He felt a stab of pity for her as he saw the faint rash that was beginning to flame on the soft white skin beside her mouth. Yes, it was always the same, he thought, even after twenty-odd years of marriage she turned to him like an anxious child when her mother was in the house.

"Well, I'd better see what Tony and Wiley want," he said.

"Try not to be too long—I'll anesthetize mother with the television."

"Yes, I'll try."

Ford patted her arm, and then crossed the foyer and went down into the living room where a cedar log fire burned fragrantly, and the glowing lamps cast soft reflections against the warm beige colors of the room.

"Excuse us for dropping by this way," Tony Marshall said, as he smiled and stood with easy grace, a tall, wiry man with hair like well-polished silver, and bold, bushy, black eyebrows. "I called your office earlier, and Mrs. Simpson said you were probably going to be home tonight."

"I'm glad to see you," Ford said. "What's up?"

"This Delucca business," Tony Marshall said. "I thought we'd better have a talk about it."

Wiley Poston was standing at the bar making a drink. He looked over his shoulder and grinned at Ford. "Mind if I help myself? Help myself again, to be accurate. I already had one, but I couldn't persuade Tony to join me. He insisted we wait for our host, but hell, you might have run off the road, so I went ahead on the theory that a bird in the hand is worth two in the Bushmill's, and that's a joke, son."

Tony Marshall smiled faintly. "I don't pour liquor in another man's home."

"Now that's a fine old sentiment," Wiley said. "Only thing is, it costs you a lot of booze in the long run." He grinned as he said this, for everyone grinned as a rule when sparring with Tony Marshall. Watching him fill his glass, Ford remembered what Clay had said this morning about Wiley's drinking, and he saw that Clay was right; Wiley held the neck of the bottle the way a boy would grasp a baseball bat choosing up sides, and he splashed out the liquor as if he were putting out a fire in the glass. No subtlety there, as Clay had said; Wiley wanted his drinks strong and frequent, that was obvious.

Carrying his glass in a big hand, Wiley crossed the room to join Ford and Tony at the fireplace. He moved with short, pigeon-toed strides, and despite the easy grin on his red, beefy face the forward thrust of his round, balding head and huge shoulders gave him the look of a man advancing on enemies. "You ride up and look at the Henderson place this morning?" he asked Ford. "You promised to, but I had an idea you might just be humoring me."

"No, I took a look at it. Tony, what would you like?"

"Whisky, please, a little water and no ice."

As Ford was making a drink for Tony and himself, Harvey Shires came down the stairs into the living room. He said hello somewhat breathlessly, and smiled and held up both hands at Ford's offer of a drink. "No, please," he said, and this briskly virtuous refusal hinted that he had been called here from a variety of sorely pressing problems, while the quick smile indicated that was all right, perfectly all right, but let's get down to business, please.

"I talked to Clay last night," he said, rubbing his hands briskly as he joined the group at the fireplace. He looked solemnly at Ford, who was handing a drink to Tony Marshall. "Clay wasn't much help, I'm sorry to say."

"He told me you'd called him," Ford said, repressing a smile as he remembered Clay's vividly irreverent account of the conversation.

"I'm not blaming him, mind you," Harvey Shires said. "He can take either side of the issue, that's his privilege. But there's no reason to be flippant about it. I think he might at least pretend to be serious about this matter."

There was nothing dearer to Harvey's heart than seriousness, Ford well knew—seriousness of all kinds and shadings, real or pretended, lugubrious or appropriate. Harvey was in his early forties, but he always gave the impression he wished he were a lot older than that, venerable, in fact, white-haired and patriarchal, the grand old man of the tribe. He was trimly and stockily built, with smooth unlined features, pleasantly unobservant eyes, and black hair that was thinning a bit toward the back of his head. Everyone knew he parted his hair to make the bald spot more conspicuous. "A skull honorably denuded by the heat of the brain within," was the complacent way he referred to it. His earnestness, his righteousness, his cunning entrapments of the glaringly obvious, and his total lack of humor were fortified stoutly by a great deal of money. He pictured himself as the good, long head in the group, Ford knew, the man who would listen thoughtfully and quietly to all areas of the problem, pipe held in a rock-like hand, and only the barest trace of a smile about his eyes to indicate that while the solution was already apparent to him he would delay its announcement for a while in deference to the slower wits in the company. And then, when discussion was stalled in wrangling and confusion, the pipe would be taken slowly from that good, square jaw, the silent lips would part, and (with a shrug at the obviousness of it all) Harvey Shires would put the problem and its solution into one tidy nutshell.

Now, turning to include Tony Marshall and Wiley Poston in his remarks, he said quietly: "Clay was drinking last night, I think. That's why I'm not making any judgment on his attitude. When a man is drinking he frequently takes a position or makes a statement, if you will, which doesn't reflect his true feelings. To put it another way, I'm not sure he was serious at all."

Tony Marshall cleared his throat. "Let's see what we're up against." He stood with his back to the fireplace, and this central position and the casual and instinctive authority in his manner established him as the chairman of the group. "George Delucca bought the Henderson place from Tom Moran, as you all know," he said, his eyes moving alertly from Ford to Wiley Poston. He didn't look at Harvey. "Last Tuesday he made a down payment of five thousand dollars against the full price of fifty thousand."

Harvey Shires took the pipe from his mouth before Tony could go on. "Leaving an unpaid balance then, I gather, of forty-five thousand dollars."

"My feeling is we should do something about this," Tony Marshall said, still looking at Ford and Wiley. "I think we've been screwed, to put it bluntly. We have a permanent, continuing stake in any Downs property that goes on the market. We have a stake that's more valid, let's say, than that of some prosperous mushroom grower who spots a place out here while tooting around in his Cadillac on a Sunday afternoon. Until now the dealers in the area seemed to understand that. We were always advised when there was outside interest in a property."

"The fish eaters ganged up on us this time," Wiley Poston called over his shoulder, as he went to the bar for another drink.

"But the place was on the market," Ford said to Tony Marshall. "There wasn't any secrecy about it. There was a For Sale sign on the front gate, and there have been ads in the *Courier's* real-estate section for the past month."

Marshall looked at him closely. "Yes, I know all that, Ford," he said. "But George Delucca picked up a phone and said I'll buy it, and Tom Moran said sold—sold to the Italian gentleman in the chef's hat. I'm convinced we had a right to be advised of Delucca's interest before the deal was closed."

"What do we do about it?" Wiley said, as he rejoined the group. "Let's cut the ifs and the ands and the buts. What do we do?"

42

The pipe came out of Harvey Shires' thoughtfully clamped jaws, and he said: "I'd say the point is, what *can* we do? Except to lodge a protest with Moran, request his cooperation in the future, I don't quite see . . ."

"We can do a goddamn sight more than lodge protests," Tony Marshall answered, in a deceptively mild voice. "And we'll have only ourselves to blame if we don't. Our first mistake was in assuming that George Delucca would have sense enough not to try to buy a place in the Downs. Our second mistake was in assuming that Tom Moran would have sense enough not to sell it to him. So I propose we set about correcting those mistakes right now."

"It's the fish eaters against us poor ole white Protestants," Wiley Poston said, and while he grinned as he said this, there was a deliberate, almost sensual roll of belligerence in his voice. This was one of the Poston family characteristics, their flaming and dangerous temper, and Ford saw it leaping in Wiley now, as hot and consuming as the flames spurting from the logs in the fireplace. The Postons, themselves, regarded this streak of temperament variously; the women, who displayed it in shrewish, intoxicated outbursts, were complacently smug about it, feeling, it seemed, that it went well with their deep-south connections, their love of whisky and horses, and their wild extremes of stinginess and generosity; the men were calmer about it, knowing violence was a law of their natures, they accepted it as matter-of-factly as they did the genetic peculiarities of their coloring and bone structure.

Harvey Shires frowned, and said, "Wiley, I think we should leave religion out of this. I told your brother last night, Ford, that I don't object to the fact that Delucca's a Catholic or an Italian. My feeling is—"

"Harvey, I just don't give a damn what your feeling is," Wiley said in a weary voice. "Anyway you're winding up to make a speech that's going to put you squarely on both sides of the fence, and we don't have time for that kind of twaddle now." As Harvey stiffened and affixed a wounded elder-statesman expression to his face, Wiley grinned at him and said:

"Now don't get upset and touchy, we ain't got time for that either. I say this: Delucca and Moran both go to Saint Patrick. They work together on fund raising for the church; they're out every year selling ads for the Catholic school's graduation book, that sort of thing. They're close to each other, it's part of their religion actually to help each other out, and I think Moran saw a chance to do Delucca a favor and he jumped at the chance. And who's to say Delucca won't give the property to the church some day, or will it to them when he dies?" Poston was almost shouting now, and Harvey, the irrelevant stimulant to his anger, shrugged and said sonorously: "I don't think we'll accomplish anything by losing our tempers—" probably, Ford thought, because he knew Tony Marshall would back this position. And he wasn't wrong, for Tony looked irritably at Wiley, and said, "Yes, for Christ's sake, calm down, Wiley," and Harvey returned his pipe complacently to his mouth as Wiley accepted this rebuke with a sheepish wag of his big head. "O.K., O.K., I'll unsimmer," he said, sighing, "but don't think it's easy for this old redneck."

"Here's what I propose," Tony Marshall said. "Together we run a sizable amount of business through Moran's office. Insurance on stock and property, plus the 5 per cent he collects on sales in the Downs. I wouldn't be surprised if it doesn't add up to around 25 or 30 per cent of his annual gross. My proposal is this: one of us, chosen by lot, will go to Moran and use what pressure is necessary to persuade him to return Delucca's down payment. At the same time he'll accept a check in full for the property dated a week or ten days ago. Moran can explain this to Delucca any way he chooses. Misunderstanding, office snafu, clerical mistake." Tony Marshall inquiringly glanced at Ford and Wiley. "See any bugs in it?"

"You think it would work?" Ford asked him.

Tony Marshall nodded and said calmly, "I know it will work."

Yes, he was right; it would work, of course, Ford thought. The men standing here represented money and power, and it was evident in the cut of their tweeds, their expensive shoes, the casual confidence of their manner.

"Well, if you want what's probably a minority opinion," Ford said at last, "I don't like it. I'd prefer to go directly to Delucca and buy the place back from him."

There was an instant of silence. Then Tony Marshall shook his head slowly and said: "I don't think that will work, Ford. He'll know he's got us in a bind then."

"He'd put a price on it that would make us look like fools," Wiley Poston said.

"You asked me what I thought," Ford said, shrugging. "I've told you I don't like it."

"If you're not with us, I hope we can assume you're not against us," Tony Marshall said quietly. "Is that right?"

"No, I'm not against you," Ford said.

"You're neutral, is that it?"

"Call it that, if you like," Ford said.

"Oh balls!" Wiley Poston said irritably, but Tony Marshall raised a hand in a gesture that confined Wiley's outburst to those two words. Then he frowned at Ford. "What's the difference between this matter and the steps we took to prevent that six-lane highway from running along the southern edge of the Downs? You and I went to Harrisburg and threw some weight around, and I don't recall that you had any ethical objections then. We didn't quite blackmail Tom Hughes but we put it to him pretty clearly that we had made a state senator out of him, and that we could make a used-car dealer out of him again if that's the way he wanted it. We were within our rights, I think. And we're still within our rights now."

"There was an alternative route for the highway," Ford said.

"Oh hell, let's get on with it," Wiley Poston said. He took a notebook from his pocket, ripped out a page, and tore it into three pieces. Marking one of these with an X, he crumpled the three pieces into tight little balls and dropped them into an ashtray. "Let's draw," he said.

"One second," Tony Marshall said, raising his hand again and glancing inquiringly at Ford. "Do you mind if we settle it here?"

"No, go ahead," Ford said. What difference did it make, he thought. Here in his bright glowing living room, or at Wiley's or Tony's or Harvey Shires' home. But as Wiley picked up the ashtray and held it out to Harvey Shires, Ford suddenly felt as if something personal and important had just drifted past him, slipping forever beyond his reach. It was a bewildering sensation, but before he could analyze it, or do anything about it, it was too late, it was all over, and Wiley Poston was staring with a pleased smile at the cross-marked slip of paper he had drawn from the ashtray.

CHAPTER 3

AFTER they had gone Ford walked down the hall to his study. Janet and her mother sat in a marine gloom facing the glaring rectangle of the TV screen. The two women seemed disembodied to Ford: their faces, glowing with phosphorescent light, floated whitely in the murky darkness, like heads drifting sluggishly in an aquarium tank.

He kissed his mother-in-law on the cheek, and apologized for being late.

"It doesn't matter, Son. Do turn off the television, Janet. I would have liked to say hello to Tony Marshall, of course. But Janet wanted to see the news and we were quite content back here out of everyone's way."

"I thought you wanted to look too, Mother."

Mrs. Marsten smiled vaguely. "Oh it didn't matter to me. I wonder why you thought it did."

Janet rose and snapped off the TV set, catapulting an inoffensively handsome announcer into its swiftly darkening depths, then switched on the two lamps beside Ford's desk. As she moved about the room, angular and clumsy in her mother's presence, Mrs. Marsten followed her progress with a look of vague concern, and when Janet sat down at last, tucking her feet beneath her childishly, Mrs. Marsten nodded approvingly, as if congratulating her daughter on the completion of this trying social obstacle course.

Then she said to Ford: "And how is Tony? I've always liked him, you know. We always seem to find a great deal to talk about."

"He's just fine," Ford said. "But he was in quite a rush to-night. This wasn't a social call—just a business matter." You had to explain every goddamn thing to her, he thought with a surprising twist of anger. And he realized then that he was disturbed and worried about the decision that had been made here tonight.

"Did you tell him I was here?" Mrs. Marsten asked.

"No," he said. "No, I didn't."

He sensed the leaden weight of her disapproval. God, he thought, it's so eternally boring, and he realized that he wanted a drink, that his irritation was growing, and that his hands felt tense and prickly. Instead of getting a drink he lit a ciga-rette. Mrs. Marsten sat straight in her chair, lips pursed, hands clasped in her lap, a tall, imposingly proportioned woman in her early sixties, with blue-gray hair and shining blue eyes, the luster of which, Ford knew, resulted from myopia rather than any inner force of conviction or spirit. He had known her twenty-odd years and in that time he had never heard her ex-press a thought of her own, initiate a course of action, place the responsibility for her boredom and frustration where it belonged, which was squarely on her own two shoulders. She was lonely; she was weary; she was unhappy; she was reaping a bitter harvest for having borne without resentment or re-proach the full weight of what she referred to in mysterious accents as "Mr. Marsten's ways." What this meant no one knew; it had never been explained. But there was the impli-cation that Mr. Marsten, in slaking his feverish thirsts at the springs of her soul, had left her drained, arid, depleted, squeezed dry, burned out—in short, unable to do anything at all for herself, a pathetic victim of "Mr. Marsten's ways."

To Ford this was simply tiresome, but it wore Janet into nervous exhaustion. There was no way she could please her mother, for there was nothing her mother wanted for herself; she didn't want to watch television, return to New York, stay for Christmas, or not stay for Christmas, choose lobster over steak, or soup in favor of the shrimp cocktail. Wanting noth-ing, having no preferences, she couldn't be pleased; Janet's

48

plans, arrangements, and conciliatory overtures were accepted by Mrs. Marsten in a spirit of stoic indifference. There were times when Ford took a certain relish in accepting Mrs. Marsten at her word, and not coaxing her into doing something he knew she had her heart set on, but Janet didn't have the strength or confidence to stand up to her mother in even such trivial areas, and so, Ford thought, maybe the old girl has good reason to feel that life had been a waste, and that nothing mattered much anymore. Janet was her only child, there couldn't be much satisfaction in having produced this one tremulous hostage to fortune. She'd probably like it a lot better if Janet hit back—if she'd tell her to go to hell occasionally, or make plans without consulting her, or brag about the children instead of obliquely apologizing for them—yes, that would be the basis of a more rewarding relationship, but all that presumed a new and different sort of Janet, a secure woman who didn't break out in rashes when her mother came to her home, and who (Ford thought, irritably but still clinically) slept with her husband instead of lavishing her affections on a collection of white china birds.

"Are you hungry?" Janet asked him brightly. "We can have dinner any time. I didn't know how long your oh-so-solemn meeting would last."

"Whenever you like," Ford said.

"Mother, would you like a sherry?"

"No, thank you. It doesn't matter."

"If you want a drink, there's certainly time for it."

Mrs. Marsten looked at her coolly. "What a curious way to put it—if I want a drink. Certainly, I don't want a drink."

"We'll have dinner then," Janet said, and left the room with awkward haste. Alone with Mrs. Marsten, Ford knew he was expected to chat with her, to mollify her vaguely injured feelings, to coax her into a passive good humor. This was his customary role; after Janet had put her out of sorts he was expected to smooth her ruffled feathers. But he had no interest in talking to her now, and he sat staring at the book-lined wall, almost enjoying the tension created by the silence.

"When are the children coming home?" she asked him at last, stiffly and sharply.

"Peter gets in day after tomorrow, I believe. Ginny, too."

"I'm sorry I'll miss them."

"You aren't staying over?"

"No—Janet asked me to, but the house will be busy enough without me. And quite frankly, I can make out nicely in New York. I'm afraid I hurt her feelings, Son. She was so eager for me to stay on, but it's just not a practical idea."

"Fine." Ford said. "I think you're wise. It's going to be a madhouse here." He kept his face straight with an effort, ignoring her sharp, unpleasant stare of surprise and annoyance. Now he realized what had created the tension between Janet and her mother, and what had been expected of him; to override the old lady's objections, of course, thus placing her in the satisfying position of having refused Janet's invitation but still getting what she wanted in spite of it.

"I think it's the best thing all around," he said, standing as he heard Janet in the hallway. And as Janet entered the study, he said: "Janet, your mother tells me she's not staying over to see the children. I think she's being sensible. It might be a good idea if everyone split up at Christmas time. These family involvements can be a bore. I'd like to go down to Palm Beach with my golf clubs, and Janet, you could go skiing. Then we'd all meet again about the middle of January when the whole silly business is over." He grinned at their anxious, disapproving expressions. "I'm not serious. Let's have dinner. Mrs. Marsten, may I take you in?"

She said grimly, "I think you've already done that, Son."

Wit didn't become her; it went badly with her tight lips and cold eyes. But her comment, though sharp and clever, had been unintentionally revealing and Ford was touched by it.

"Come on now," he said, taking her arm. "You were cheated out of a sherry, so we'll open a good bottle of claret for dinner."

"Not for my sake, please."

"Then you'll have to watch me finish it by myself."

After dinner (during which Mrs. Marsten perked up surprisingly and drank three glasses of Château Margaux), Ford excused himself and drove across the Downs to his brother's home. As he turned into the long driveway, and his lights flashed over the glass and chromium wing that Clay had added to his farmhouse, he remembered the stir this architectural heresy had originally caused in the area. What head-shakings, what conclaves and resolutions at the Darby County Historical Society. But none of this had mattered to Clay.

He disliked the heavy fieldstone walls and narrow windows of the original structure, which gave it (and most of the big homes in the area) the look of a well-landscaped fortress. Local architects were dismayed by his proposals, so he imported a young man from New York, who was intense and bearded, and who talked feverishly of "nature's anxieties" and "integrated imbalances" while poring over Clay's sketches and listening to Clay's plans. The sketches became blueprints eventually, and were ultimately translated into a sixty-foot rectangle of aluminum and glass which jutted out from the good gray Quakerish farmhouse like the gleaming prow of a space ship. At first the result looked hideous. People drove for miles to catch a glimpse of it through the woods. But now, with oatmeal-colored draperies, a hanging fireplace, and modern paintings on the inside, and boxwood, yews, and dogwood trees on the outside, the two styles of building had blended together in an effect that even the purists conceded was oddly charming and graceful.

Clay's pair of merle collies swarmed around Ford as he went up the front steps. The colored maid told him Alicia was in the "summer parlor," which was as far as she seemed able to dignify the glass wing on the southern side of the house.

The first impression of the addition was breathtaking, Ford thought, as he came into it from the short hallway off the foyer. The beige draperies were drawn across the glass walls on two sides of the room, but the third was open to the night. A fireplace hung in the plastered panel dividing this window and the flames leaped and spurted against a background of sky and stars. The huge room was floored with hand-kilned, blood-red tiles, each irregular square gleaming with reflections of fire and moonlight. Modern paintings, as vivid as the fresh flowers on the coffee table, were spaced along the single wall which formed a background for the three glass sides of the room. The couches and chairs were all of rosewood and black leather.

From the long sofa in front of the fireplace, Alicia turned and looked up at him with a quick smile. "Hello there," she said, and stood to kiss him on the cheek. "I was so glad when Mrs. Simpson told me you were coming by. How's Janet?"

"Just fine. Mrs. Marsten's with us for the night."

"That's nice." She grinned at him. "Or is it?"

"So far, everything's serene."

"Let's sit down. Look, I'm all ready for you." She pointed proudly to the coffee table on which there was a tray laid with tiny coffee cups, slices of lemon peel, an espresso machine, and a bottle of brandy. "I've even got cigars. I hope you're not in any rush."

"No, of course not."

He sat and watched her with a smile as she made coffee and poured two glasses of brandy. Clay's wife was small and slim, with bright, good-humored eyes and the sort of narrow, sharply angled face that people usually thought of as "well bred"; the bones were delicate, the cheeks hollow, and the line of the throat sharp and clean. Usually she wore her brown hair in a sleek page boy, but now it was fluffed out in the current mode, and Ford didn't think it was right for her; she looked like a chrysanthemum on a windy day, he thought.

But this fragile look was deceptive, he knew. For all the cashmere and pearls, the firelight shining on slim wrists and ankles, she rode and shot expertly, and, in their summer water-polo matches, was forever surprising overconfident males with her strength and stamina. Wiley Poston had once caught her from behind in a bear hug, and the two of them had disappeared for a long time in a whirlpool of threshing arms and legs, for Wiley played water polo only for the pleasure and opportunity it gave him to wrestle around with attractive girls who were usually too caught up in their sport, or too water-logged, to realize they were being handled with a lecherous familiarity masquerading as a boyish enthusiasm for fun and games. But this time, Ford remembered, his pleasure had been violently interrupted, for Alicia had got an arm free and smashed her elbow into Wiley's nose, and he had back-pedaled furiously away from her with blood streaming from his nostrils and a thoroughly phony smile on his lips. He must have made an unusually obvious pass at her that time, Ford thought, for she hadn't spoken civilly to him in months.

"Did you talk to Clay this morning?" she asked as she gave him coffee.

"Yes, he stopped by the house. Do you mind my acting as an emissary for my idiot brother?"

"He told you about our row then?"

"What he could remember of it."

"Well, the details aren't—I don't know." She sighed faintly and looked into the fire, a frown coming over her face.

When she didn't go on, he said: "Aren't what? Edifying?"

"That's not what I meant to say. They aren't—well, they don't explain very much, that's all. He got very tight before dinner and wouldn't eat. He didn't want to go to bed when I did, so I went up alone. That was about ten, I think. Then he started wandering around the house. The maids came into my room, I don't know, about one o'clock. They were upset, so I put on a robe and came down here. The place was a mess. He'd tipped over a table of drinks, and so forth. But he wasn't drunk anymore. You know, he gets deliberate and judicial after he's had enough to drink—he actually drinks himself sober. He explained all my shortcomings and inadequacies—and those of my family—in great detail. He dropped a cigarette during his lecture, so I brought him an ashtray. He knocked it out of my hand, and claimed I threw it at him. And that was it. He fell asleep, and I went back up to bed."

"He said he hit you. Weren't you going to tell me about that?"

"I didn't know if he'd told you or not. Anyway it wasn't much of a punch. Earnest, well intentioned, I'll admit, but miles off course."

"Let's not dismiss all this as whimsical, frat-house behavior," Ford said. "I admire you for taking it calmly, but don't overdo it. He behaved like a louse. Can you tell me what's wrong with him?"

She twisted her hands together and he saw the knuckles whiten with the pressure of her grip. "I don't know, I just don't know, Ford. He drinks too much, but I don't know why. When he starts he can't sleep, can't rest, can't talk reasonably. I don't know what he wants from me, or what he wants from himself."

"Well, in spite of his childish behavior, he obviously wants you," Ford said.

She raised her head and looked at him steadily. "Have you wondered why we don't have children?"

The question caught him off balance; and its implication brought a blush to his cheeks. "It seemed to me that it was your own business when you wanted to start a family." He smiled awkwardly. "Maybe that's what he needs—that sort of responsibility."

"I want children, it's about all I do want," she said, and he was startled by the bitterness in her voice. "If I talk about it I'll puddle up and sound like a fool, so just accept my word for it. Clay wanted to wait a while after we were married. Why tie ourselves down? Et cetera, et cetera. Plenty of time for kiddies in footed pajamas crawling about the hearth. So we just never did get around to it." She stopped and looked down at her hands. "Now, as I totter toward my twenty-eighth birthday, I think back to the birds and bees lectures at Miss Crane's, and I seem to recall—although my memory's probably slipping along with everything else—that sleeping together was a sort of first step in the human creative process. As things stand, we aren't going to add one bit to the population explosion." She turned away from him suddenly, but not before he saw the flash of tears in her eyes. "You're his brother," she said, in a hard,

54

steady voice. "Don't you have any answers? Why does he avoid me? Am I a sexual incompetent? Why don't I interest him? Why does he treat our home like a pigsty? And why does he roar off to New York every week like a stud in rut? Are the girls there so desirable? Do they know tricks we country mice never heard of? What does he want, why can't he let—" Her voice broke then, and she began to cry, the tears spilling down her cheeks. "Oh, damn it, I'm sorry, Ford," she said, shaking her head helplessly. "I didn't mean to do this."

He went to her and held her hands. "Now now," he said. "It's all right. Cry it out. You'll probably feel better."

"No, it won't help," she said wearily. "Give me your handkerchief. You're nice to put up with all this."

"Now don't talk nonsense. I want to help you—and Clay." But, he thought, as he released her hands so that she could dab at her eyes, what can I say? She's turned to me for advice, for wisdom or understanding, and I have no idea what to say to her, or to Clay. They see the gray in my hair and think it means something besides age.

"These things run their course," he said awkwardly. "Believe me, Alicia, they do. Clay just hasn't settled down yet. It takes some men longer than others, that's all. You've just got to roll with the punch a bit."

She sighed and gave him his handkerchief. "Hope and pray, is that it?"

"You still have some good times, don't you? It's not all grim, is it?"

"Yes, he's sweet and repentant occasionally, and he swears he's going to turn over whole volumes of new leafs. Get back to that short story he's always threatening to write, play golf and squash regularly, give small suppers for people who know how to talk, start his French lessons again—and so on and so on."

"Oh there's hope galore, Alicia," Ford said, smiling at her. He felt better now; as long as Clay was thinking along these lines things would work out all right. "You still love him, don't you?" he said, patting her cheek.

55

"No," she said shortly. "I don't. I haven't done anything about a divorce because I feel I could love him again—if he cared that I did. But I can't fall back in love with these spoiled-brat explosions. I know I sound inconsistent. Wanting him here, wailing because he's having his fun in New York, but making all sorts of qualifications instead of accepting him the way he is. I'm the villain in the piece, at least with Clay's friends. Prim little Alicia, so stuffy and difficult. Can't cut loose and have fun herself, so she wants Clay to suffer with her. But there's nothing to admire or love in destruction."

She held up a hand as Ford started to speak. "Please—I know they don't think of it that way. He's considered a great treat at the club; Clay, the joyboy. The way he drives and rides, even the trips to New York, that's all admirable in their opinion. True to the best Virginia gentleman tradition." She put her thumbs to imaginary galluses and assumed a deep-south, mushmouth accent. "Suh, Ah been gettin' elegantly laid and elegantly drunk since Ah was a boy of ten, and Ah just naturally aim to continue on that way." She sighed wearily. "Ford, I can't stand it. It embarrasses me, and it enrages me. When Wiley Poston goes into his cackling hillbilly act, and talks about how he's 'gonna whop him some niggers 'fore sunup' it damn near makes me sick at my stomach. And even worse is to sit there and watch Ellie smiling indulgently at him, as if he were some great big baby showing off before company.

"So maybe it's all my fault because I don't chortle over Clay, and pretend he's just a naughty little boy. Oh damn!" she said explosively. "I'm mixed up. My pride is hurt, I want him and I don't want him, I hate whoever he sees in New York, but I won't take him on any terms but my own. Do you wonder we're having trouble? I don't make sense to myself, so how can I make sense out of our problems?"

"I think you've made a step in just being frank about the whole thing," Ford said. "Let's call it a good night's work, and enjoy some more of your brandy. O.K.?"

He saw that she was relieved to change the subject. As re-

56

lieved as I am, he thought. They were going in circles, getting nowhere, but he hadn't missed her use of the word "repentant" when she had described Clay's attitude during one of their "happy" times. Could that be what she really wanted? Breast beatings, tearful admissions of guilt? Supposing Clay performed like a virtuous puppet, turned himself into the worthiest of burghers, would she miss the old days when it had been her priestly role (and pleasure) to hear his confession and forgive him his sins?

They chatted for a while and when he mentioned that Wiley Poston had been at his home this evening, he smiled at her moue of distaste.

"How *did* you tear yourself away from the dear boy?"

"You know, I always figured he made a pass at you in the pool last summer, but I never figured out where he got the nerve."

"It wasn't a pass, technically. It's what you lads call a 'horse bite' I think. On the inside of my thigh, and he really squeezed for keeps." She winced at the memory. "Good God, did it hurt! But he had to let go one of my arms to do it, and I caught him with a lucky swing right on the nose. You know what made me so furious. That he was getting a kick out of making me squirm. He wasn't after the ball, he just wanted me to ship some water and hit the panic button. Doesn't that disgust you? I mean, using muscles and weight to scare people with?" She smiled cheerfully at the fire. "I tell you, when I saw that blood spurting from his nose, I felt like I'd just won the Nobel Peace Prize."

And about now, Ford thought, Wiley would be using that muscle on Tom Moran, hammering away with the weight of the Downs behind every blow. And driving home later that night, he realized that he was ashamed of the meeting in his house, and of the decision that had set Wiley in motion. Even the view from Lowry's hill failed to raise his spirits. The homes of his friends, with lights streaming from their windows, stretched out across the black meadows like a flotilla of luxury liners. Tony Marshall's place was closest to him, a stately flagship at the head of a staggered column of lesser vessels, a formation that dipped out of sight in the valley and rose again on the far slope, with the homes at that great distance twinkling like skiffs on the horizon.

He knew these homes as well as he knew his own. He knew the dogs that guarded them, the horses stabled in their barns. As a rule this view gave him a calm and comfortable sense of well-being, but tonight it only added to his depression. The fabric of his life seemed so tightly woven, so strongly enveloping, that he wondered what would happen if anything ripped the tiniest part of it. What kind of winds would they face then?

The foyer of his home was lighted, but the other rooms on the first floor were dark. Trouble, he thought, sighing. It was only nine-thirty, but Janet and her mother had already gone up to bed, which meant they must have bickered and quarreled until the emotional climate became so raw that it had driven them to their rooms at opposite ends of the house. He could have prevented this, he realized, with a flicker of remorse. If he had insisted Mrs. Marsten stay over, things would probably have gone off peacefully, and the two women would now be waiting to have a nightcap with him. Well, he would ask her tomorrow, and she would stay, of course, for she had no intention of going back without seeing the children.

But that wouldn't solve tonight's problem. Tonight's problem was Janet. She would come to him tonight, for sex had become the only specific, the only antidote against her mother's venom. And Ford was finding it increasingly disagreeable to be used for medicinal purposes—for that's all it amounted to, he knew. The male member as aspirin tablet, he thought, as he went as quietly as he could up the stairs to his room. Something you ordered, a prescription from the drugstore.

He showered and brushed his teeth, and stood for a moment at the mirror, rubbing his jaw and studying his face. His flesh was firm, his color good, his eyes clear. Only the patches of silver at the temples of his thick black hair gave any sign of age. I'm not riding much lately, he thought, but I still play

58

off a four handicap. I don't look forty-four, he thought. Then he realized that there was no serious point to this examination. He was simply killing time, hoping Janet would fall asleep (if she'd heard him come up) and that was one hell of a note, he thought wryly, one hell of a note to be forty-four, with a hard body and well-muscled arms and legs, and the appetites (you could hope) of a healthy male animal, and with all that to be standing here stalling for time, postponing the inevitable moment when he would be asked to go to bed with his wife.

Turning out the lights, he put on his pajama jacket and got into bed. He stretched out gratefully and relaxed for a moment. The house was silent. He fumbled around cautiously for cigarettes and matches, found them, lit a cigarette and blew smoke at the ceiling. With one hand under his head and his long legs stretched out comfortably, he waited, smoking his cigarette in the darkness.

Before long—he hadn't finished the cigarette—his bedroom door opened and closed with a pair of soft clicks.

"Ford? Are you awake?"

"Yes, just finishing a cigarette. Sorry I was late."

"It doesn't matter. As long as you're here. Can I come in with you?"

"Yes . . . yes, sure."

He heard the soft whisper of her robe as she threw it across the foot of the bed. Then she slipped in beside him, and he felt her body straining against him, her arms clinging to him, and her cheek wet against his shoulder, and he thought, She's been crying, this will really fix her rash.

"I can't stand it anymore," she said. "Not another minute. She kept *at* me, *at* me, *at* me! Why does she hate what I have? Why can't she be happy for me?" The words were a blurred whisper; her mouth was pressed tightly against his arm. "She's got to stop it—she's got to go away, Ford. Oh help me, Ford. You're all that matters to me, you and our home and children." The words came in spasmodic gasps, and the sound was pathetic and ugly, as if it were being forcibly torn from her throat.

"Now, now," Ford said gently. "Try not to be surprised by these blowups. They're bound to happen!" She lay on her side, breathing unevenly, and he put his arm around her and rubbed her bare shoulder. "If she weren't your mother, you'd simply stop seeing her. But she is your mother and you've got to go on seeing her. Tomorrow I'll ask her not to go back to New York. I'll insist she stay and see the children. That's what she wants, of course, and it's natural enough."

"No, don't, don't," she said, the words straining in her throat. "It's my home. Let her get out."

"You don't really mean that," he said. "You wouldn't be happy if she went back to New York tomorrow. She wouldn't write or phone—you'd have to call her sooner or later, you know."

"I don't want her. I don't need her."

This was what she couldn't say to her mother, Ford knew, or dare to admit to herself except under this present anesthetic of pain and desire.

"You're very sweet, very patient," she said with a childish catch in her voice. "You're tired, too, aren't you?"

"No, of course not."

She laughed softly. "That's hardly a growl of animal impatience." She moved her legs against his and drew her fingertips lightly over his flat stomach. "I think you are tired," she said, and kissed his shoulder.

This was the oddest part of it all, he thought, as he swung his arm out to extinguish his cigarette, and the most irritating; this playful aggressiveness of hers. He wondered, with an uneasy pang, what would happen when her estimate of their relationship became a fact; when he was truly the pursued, truly tired, truly unable to meet her demands. Fortunately that time was not on him yet, for now he could feel the mingled emotions of pity and desire warming his body. She was fragrant in his arms, her flesh as smooth as ivory, and the tears were over, and she pressed against him with her eyes closed and a small happy smile on her lips. She moved her hand slowly and caressingly, touched him, and laughed softly: "Oh, the man isn't so tired after all."

Later she began to chatter in her flat, unaccented daytime voice. "You might just as well ask Mother to stay over, since she'll go sulking off if you don't, and if you can stand it, you poor, dear man, it's the least I can do. Actually, it won't be too grim, because Peter likes her, he really does, and Ginny will keep her amused with all sorts of bitchy gossip about her friends at school. If you just tell her at breakfast that we'll all perish if she rushes off, I think we can have a real fun weekend. O.K.? O.K., Ford? Oh—good night, dear."

For Ford Jackson, after a day in his life that had been typical in many ways, but oddly disturbing in others, had fallen asleep.

CHAPTER 4

WHEN Ford's son and daughter came home for the Christmas holidays, the phone began to ring immediately; it was as if some extrasensory agency had alerted their friends to the exact instant of their arrival.

Ford had little chance to talk with them, beyond a flurry of words about the trip home, the crowded coaches, and so forth. Peter was taller and huskier, his sensitive, adolescent face hardening into sharper lines, and, with his blond hair and slim quick body, reminding Ford of a smaller, less volatile edition of his brother Clay. He looked tired, but he was on the phone instantly, long legs sprawled in front of him, a cigarette in his mouth, making arrangements to play hockey after lunch with Tony Marshall's sons. Ginny, at sixteen, was cutely plump, with her mother's round face and blond hair. She was also beginning to ape her mother's mannerisms, Ford noticed with mild distress: the low, flat voice, the exaggerated gestures, the little-girl expressions of mock horror, the grimaces, muggings, humorous posturings—all these props had been added to her arsenal of communication.

Ford had coaxed Janet's mother into staying for the weekend, which meant, he knew, she would probably stay on through the holidays. But he didn't really mind, for with Peter and Ginny as distractions, she and Janet would get on amiably enough.

That morning he drove to his office later than usual, but he took the long route across the Downs, skirting the village of Rosedale. Mrs. Simpson was on the phone when he came in, and she smiled at him, and said into the telephone: "Here he is now, Mr. Poston."

Ford took the call in his private office.

"Wiley, how are you?"

"Great, just great." Wiley was chuckling. "You are right now talking to the proud new owner of the Henderson place."

"Well, well," Ford said. He stared at the wall of his office, at his framed law degree, at the antlers of the buck he had shot one morning from the steps of his home.

"It was like silk all the way," Wiley said. "Hell, we were worrying about nothing, about nothing at all. You should have seen Moran crack. Man, he couldn't hardly have been happier to straighten out my little problem."

"He returned Delucca's check?"

"Tha's right," Wiley said, in cackling hillbilly accents. "He was mighty pleased to do 'at little ole thing."

"How will he explain that to Delucca?"

"I just naturally left 'at up to Mr. Moran, hisself, to figure out. He's a shrewd mick, and Mr. Delucca, why he-all a shrewd wop. They can fuss it out, they own selves. I don't have interest one in they squabbles, 'ary one."

"Well, congratulations," Ford said. "But I don't think we've done anything to deserve it."

"Don't talk that way," Wiley said, dropping the hillbilly accent. "It's all done, it's over. But we'll be more careful after this, I can promise you. Is that rutting brother of yours still over in New York?"

"Yes, I think so."

"If he's back by Sunday, how about trying for nine holes before lunch? You and me, Clay and Harvey?"

"O.K., if he gets back, and if the weather's all right."

"We can't miss. The iffier a foursome is, the better chance you got. You get everybody signed and sealed, and swearing on their sacred manhood to be on time, and by Jesus nothing works out. I'll see you now, Ford."

Ford replaced the receiver and walked up and down the length of his office for a few moments, groaning and rubbing the back of his neck. Tony Marshall had called it. It had been just as smooth and uncomplicated as he'd assured them it would be. Put the pressure on Moran, let him figure out a story to satisfy Delucca. And that's how it had gone, smooth as silk.

Ford sighed and walked into the outer office. He had planned to start working today on Clay's income tax, and he decided he had better get at it. There was nothing urgent to be done, but he found himself wishing it were a matter of fiscal life and death, some problem so devious and desperate that he could lose himself in its complexities and dangers. He realized that he didn't want to think about Wiley Poston or George Delucca.

He said to Mrs. Simpson: "By the way, that girl who called the other day—Maria Ruiz. Did she call back?"

"No, Mr. Jackson, but I have her address. I could drop her a note, and ask her to come in."

"Never mind, I was just curious."

He didn't ask for Clay's tax files, which was why he had gone into Mrs. Simpson's office. Instead he returned to his desk and lit a cigarette. He saw that his fingers were trembling slightly. Why had he asked about the girl? It had been very odd, and embarrassing as well, to blurt out her name that way, and feel a guilty warmth rising in his cheeks as Mrs. Simpson looked up at him and answered his question with her comfortable smile. Maria Ruiz had been on his mind, obviously. It was very odd. He hadn't been aware of thinking about her.

That evening he drove home through the village of Rosedale. He had avoided it this morning, although he hadn't been aware of doing so at the time; but now he realized that something had caused him to skirt Rosedale, and take the longer route across the Downs. Deliberately, he slowed down as he turned into the colored section of the village, and brought the car to a stop in front of her house. He wondered if his interest in her was based on pity. In the gray-black winter light, the house was bleak and cheerless. Unpainted, sagging awkwardly on its foundation, a cracked windowpane stuffed with a wad

64

of paper, no lights showing now, broken front steps, refuse littering the yard, a tire with its treads worn off, beer cans and bottles, a leg from a pair of overalls, a few lengths of rusted pipe.

It would have to be pity, he thought. You'd pity your worst enemy if he lived here. There was a movement behind one of the first-floor windows, and Ford started nervously. The reaction was so undignified and uncharacteristic that he swore irritably at himself as he put the car in drive and stepped on the accelerator.

He thought about the incident for several days, trying to analyze and make some sense of it, but then he forgot all about it, and forgot all about Maria Ruiz, for the Christmas excitement was sweeping through the Downs, and he and Janet were caught up on the seasonal treadmill of dinner and cock-tail parties. A four-inch snowfall gave the countryside an ap-propriate Christmas-card look, and all the homes glowed at night with big Christmas trees. In the middle-income housing developments near Cottersville, Santa Claus himself appeared on roofs and housetops, twinkling in red and blue neon lights, and the more boisterous displays were enlivened by prancing reindeer with neon whips cracking rhythmically about their antlers.

In the Downs, the season was launched by Tony Marshall's first cockfight, which was held in the third week of December. Usually Tony's fights were stag, and a bottle of liquor was con-sidered even more offensive than the presence of the police, but everyone was invited to the Christmas fights, women, children, grooms, and stableboys, for cockfighting cut through most of the social and racial and sexual divisions in the county, and it was the one fight of the year at which liquor was served, a great steaming bowl of hot rum punch which was ladled into pewter mugs by a colored groom, who wore for the occasion gleaming white breeches and an old pink hunting coat.

The cockfights were held in a red-brick dairy barn which Tony Marshall had converted into an arena and stable for his fighting chickens. It was as clean and functional as a hospital, with coops for hens and chicks, segregated walks for cocks being readied for battle, and an office lined with bound copies of *Feathered Fury* and *Steel and Grit*, and stud books and performance charts on the Marshall hens and cocks.

When Ford and his family arrived that afternoon, at least a hundred cars were already there, and they could hear shouts from the crowd inside at they walked up the graveled road to the double doors of the barn. Wiley Poston was fighting a main with Bart Chamberlain from New Orleans, Ford knew, matching his Irish Grays against Chamberlain's Swamp Foxes, which had been flown up to Darby County earlier that week.

There were several hundred people in the smoky, brightly lighted barn, the bulk of them crouched in the tiers of black leather seats which surrounded the main ring. At one end of the barn were two drag pits where badly hurt or dying birds were taken after their first slashing encounters in the main ring. Here they fought on sluggishly, with a referee ready to count over them, and owners or trainers watching their last twitching movements, with narrowed, speculative eyes. There was a ring of observers at each pit now, and scattered about the barn were groups of men and women in tweeds or riding clothes, sipping mugs of hot rum as they listened to old darkies or hillbillies recounting tales of famous fights, and refurbishing the ancient lore and techniques of the sport—the intricate composition of a fighting chicken's keep, the porportion of whisky to mash, the need to warm and squeeze a cock's testicles during a fight, the right way to suck encrusted blood from its eyes—for all this gossipy recapitulation was as vital to cock-fighting as the roars of the crowd, the fear of the police, and the gamy smell of liquor and chickenshit and rank cigar smoke.

Ford walked over to the main pit where Wiley Poston, red-faced and sweating, was handling one of his Irish Grays. He wore a blue denim shirt open at the throat, and strands of his thinning hair were plastered over his damp forehead. The stub of a black cigar was clamped in his mouth, and he was talking around this to the cock he was holding. The Gray twisted its head about, straining and bucking against the gentle pressure

66

of Wiley's big hands. Across the ring, a colored trainer held one of Chamberlain's Swamp Foxes. The chickens were ready to fight.

Someone called: "I have ten for the Gray." Ford looked around and saw old Mrs. Mareau waving a bill above her head. But a colored man named Long Johnson had turned sooner than Ford, and he raised his hat and called back: "I'll take it, ma'am. Ten on the Brown."

Ford grinned at Long Johnson, who shook his head and chuckled softly.

"It's a good bet," Ford said. It didn't look to him as if Wiley's Gray could see very well; it was still twisting its head to find something to fight, while the Swamp Fox had zeroed in on him, beady dark eye fixed and glittering.

All you'd lose was your shirt betting against old-timers at chicken fights, Ford thought, smiling. As a boy he had raised fighting chickens, and he still had an eye for their points, but these darkies and hillbillies had seen every strain in the country at work, and their old heads were stuffed with the records of a thousand generations of cocks and hens.

The cocks were released, and there was a shout as they came together with wings beating, spurs pounding, and a sound like an electric fan gone wild inside a bass drum. Their wings scattered the dust in the ring, and there was the *whomping-plonking* noise of steel spurs on rib cases before they fell back to the ground.

Someone bellowed, "Twenty on the Gray!" and before the words were out of his mouth Long Johnson had wheeled around and snapped up that bet too. Ford watched the Gray. He flew up four times, battering the Swamp Fox with wings and spurs, and then he fell on his side. A roar went up. "Wing off!" The Gray's wing trailed helplessly. The Swamp Fox strutted around the Gray, which lay on its side breathing heavily. As deliberately as if he were nibbling corn in a barnyard, the brown cock arched its neck and pecked out one of the Gray's eyes. The Gray came up to fight again, but after two bitter collisions it fell over with its left leg hanging from a thread of muscle. "Leg off! Leg off!" Everyone was shouting, standing now, and Chamberlain's colored trainer grabbed the referee by the arm, and said: "Count for me, count for me." The referee began the first count of twenty over the dying bird. There would be two more counts, these of ten each, and if Wiley's Gray didn't move in those forty seconds, that would be it. But Wiley's chicken raised its head, breaking the count, and the colored trainer, after watching tensely for an instant, tugged at the referee again and said: "Count for me!" The count was started but Wiley's cock broke it at sixteen with a convulsive kick of its good leg.

There was no chance for the Gray now, but the counting might go on for another half hour before an unbroken forty was reached, or the Gray died, so the cocks were carried down to the drag pits and another pair were matched in the main ring.

Ford saw his brother Clay then, and waved until he caught his eye. Clay waved back to him, but stopped to collect a mug of hot rum before crossing the barn and joining Ford at the main pit. He looked very good, Ford noticed with relief: clear-eyed and alert, and swinging along with the easy confident grace that seemed to make wherever he was, and whatever he was doing, the center of interest and attention in any group. He wore tweeds, and a dull yellow waistcoat that matched his blond hair.

"A nip against the weather," Clay said, holding up the mug of rum. "Don't worry, my sodden days are over."

"You're old enough for a nip, I guess," Ford said smiling.

"Look, I want to thank you—I mean it," Clay said seriously. "Whatever you told Alicia, it helped. It's a miracle—no modest disclaimers now. That's what it was, a miracle. I've been good, and she's been angelic, and we owe it all to you."

"There's nothing wrong with you two," Ford said. "Keep that in mind. You tear around a little, she gets upset, and you both act like it's the end of the world."

Clay placed a hand solemnly on his breast. "I ain't tearing around no more, no more," he said. "Don't worry about that."

68

The afternoon put Ford in an amiable mood. As he was leaving, he saw Mrs. Mareau paying off Long Johnson, and this added to his good humor, for it seemed to make a perfect circle of his day, testifying in some fashion to the continuity of his life. He was pleased that things were going smoothly with Clay again, and he was pleased to have his children home for Christmas.

The house was clamorous with their comings and goings. Peter's friends banged in and out importantly, trailing exciting scraps of conversation. "Janey's got the wagon, we'll meet her at Lowry's." "You dress, I dress, period!" "She won't be there, don't worry." They sprawled in the study after riding, or playing hockey, drinking beer and laughing at the soap operas on television. They talked constantly, coursing streams of comment, opinion, and reminiscences, which flooded the house with the impact of their noisy personalities.

Ginny's friends clattered up and down the stairs in high heels, slight bosoms jogging demurely under cashmere sweaters, and they ate all the time, it seemed to Ford, and when they weren't doing that, they sat in mysterious silences behind the closed door of Ginny's room.

He had known these friends of Peter and Ginny's since they were children, and he was pleased to see them all coming along so well. These were the sons and daughters of his oldest friends, and he had been to their christenings, had watched them at their first Hunt meetings, kicking the flanks of their Shetlands in excitement, trailing behind the field with colored grooms, who smiled indulgently at their childish efforts. The boys usually went to St. David's, and the girls to Miss Crane's. As children they spent weekends in one another's homes, playing in the big dairy barns, staging wars with corncobs, bulldogging the yearling heifers, splashing about in pools of farm ponds. They were trundled through the countryside in station wagons, booted and jacketed, taken from home to school, from doctor to dentist, from church to horse shows, occasionally by attractive, and not infrequently hung-over, mothers, but more often by grooms or handymen or gardeners.

They had been raised as Ford had been raised, learning to ride and hunt and shoot, to play golf and tennis correctly, and with neatly compartmented slices of time set aside for dancing class, music lessons, and summer trips to Palm Beach, Long Island, Aiken, and so forth, places where they always felt at home because they always stayed with relatives.

It was a good way to grow up, he thought, a good way to live your life. Everything about his children and their friends gave him confidence, for their good health and good manners, their poise and assurance, buttressed and supported his own background and convictions.

The only thing he regretted was that he had no opportunity to sit and talk with them. They always seemed to be on the wing—hopping up from the table, talking with a hand on the doorknob, waving good-by from a car. A sense of time running out made him feel mildly gloomy. Soon they would be gone from whatever influence he might exert on them; Ginny would marry early, that could be inferred from her maturing body and squirmingly coquettish manner with young men, and Peter would be doing his army service next year, unless he elected to seek a deferment for graduate work.

Ford wanted to leave a mark on his son, a trace of his own values and convictions. He wanted to give him something worthwhile and permanent, an attitude, a mental or spiritual posture, a touchstone to evaluate himself and others by—something which he would cherish and be grateful for all his life.

Ford wanted to be quoted by his son—it was that simple. He daydreamed about this occasionally, imagining Peter gray and solid with years, at the fireplace in his own home, or sitting with friends at the Princeton Club, saying quietly and forcefully: "My father always maintained that . . ." Or: "The old man let us think for ourselves, but one thing he insisted on was . . ."

Ford was always at a loss to finish these sentences, for he couldn't imagine just what it was that he maintained or insisted upon with enough force to make his son refer to it at some imaginary future time.

The day after Christmas Ford rose early and joined his son at breakfast. Peter was leaving for the Thompsons in Rose Valley, and would be there for the rest of the week. Ford knew this was his last chance to talk with him before he went back to school. It was impossible to talk to him with Mrs. Marsten around, for she insisted on complete biographical sketches of anyone he happened to mention, and exhaustive explanations of even his most casual social activities. If Peter said: "We were on our way to the Wards'—" Mrs. Marsten would interrupt gently but firmly. "Are they the Michael Wards, dear?" or "When was that, Son?" and "What was the occasion?" Peter always answered her in polite detail, by which time whatever he'd been planning to say had usually lost its relevance and point. But Ford knew Mrs. Marsten wouldn't be up at this hour, even to see Peter off.

Peter was alone in the dining room. He was eating bacon and grilled tomatoes, and reading a copy of *Newsweek* which he had propped up against the Lazy Susan.

"Well, where are you off to?" he said, smiling up at Ford. "I thought I was the only one on the dawn patrol."

"I wanted to have breakfast with you. We've hardly had a chance to say hello this trip."

Peter smiled ruefully. "There's been a lot of action. I'm sorry we didn't get in some golf, at least."

He looks more like Clay's son than mine, Ford thought, with the quick smiles, the blond hair, the easy grace of his body. And there was something else that reminded him of Clay —an obliqueness, a reserve that made it necessary to guess at the meanings behind his words. Ford helped himself generously at the sideboard, with the half-realized hope that a large breakfast might prolong their visit. Outside the sky was heavy and gray, but the long dining room was cheerfully snug, with the silver serving dishes on the sideboard sparkling in the lights from the chandelier.

As he shook out his napkin, Ford said: "One reason I got up at this ungodly hour, was to ask if you'd made up your mind

71

yet about military service."

"I keep hoping I'll wake up and find the whole thing was just a bad dream."

"You feel that strongly about it?"

"I don't know. I'm kind of neutral. At least I don't get my kicks listening to the Marine Hymn."

Ford laughed, although he wondered if that was the appropriate parental reaction. "It isn't all that bad," he said. "You'll meet different sorts of people, assume new responsibilities. Depending on what you put into it, it can be a valuable experience."

"Yes, I guess I'll learn how to clean a machine gun, or make up a company payroll." He sighed. "Dad, it's a waste of time. Mine and theirs."

"What do you suppose would happen if everyone had your attitude? I'm not being critical—I want to know what you honestly think."

"You mean, what would Ivan do? If nobody got his kicks from the Marine Hymn? Well, he might attack and wipe us out. On the other hand, he might not."

Peter wasn't being flippant, and this irritated Ford. He was stating an opinion, coolly and matter-of-factly, with no more heat or emotion than he would put into the choice of a necktie.

"I see," Ford said, pointlessly. "Then you'd be willing to take the chance that they wouldn't attack? Is that it?"

Peter sighed again. "I don't want to take any chances at all, if you want my honest opinion. Not in a war nobody can win. I'm sorry if that disappoints you."

"I'm not disappointed, but I don't understand you. Do you think this isn't your responsibility? That we—my generation, that is—bungled things at Potsdam, not to mention a dozen other places, and you don't want to take the consequences of our stupidity?"

"No, it's not that." Peter put his napkin aside and lit a cigarette. For an instant he was silent, staring at the burning match in his fingers, then he shrugged and dropped it into the

72

ashtray. "No, I don't think a generation has any collective responsibility. The troubles of this world, it looks to me, stem from excessive profit taking, of one kind or another. One group does in another, and that's about all a war amounts to, I guess. But we're going to do each other in for good this time. We've got the terminal destructive power, and the terminal insanity to use it. Don't people realize that? You'd think they'd look at the world around them—whether it's Kansas or Kiev— and say to themselves: 'This is the target—the whole damn planet.' But they don't. They talk about bomb shelters and survival kits as if they were band-aids. I was talking to a rich hysteric the other day—my roommate's father—and I swear to God, he has the whole thing confused with the Civil War. He's got a buckboard and a mule ready, and he's 'heading back for Virginia' when Conelrad gives him his terminal goose. Do you blame me for not being enthusiastic? For not borrowing your old squirrel rifle and heading up Lowry's hill to protect the homestead?"

Ford was disturbed by his son's attitude, but he could think of nothing to say that might temper or modify it, and this bothered him even more that Peter's cloudy thinking. "Terminal this" and "terminal that." "Rich hysteric"— That would be Davidson Carter, who was rich without a doubt, and about as hysterical as a good T-formation quarterback.

As Ford was thinking of what he might say to him, Peter continued to talk, his breakfast forgotten, his lean, healthy face flushed with excitement. But Ford was lost in his own thoughts, gloomily surveying his stockpile of values and convictions with the hope of finding some trusty old saw that would help his son hack a pathway back to the clear grounds of common sense. But he was jolted uncomfortably from the inspection of this mental warehouse when Peter said: "It's one reason the Catholic viewpoint attracts me. I feel—"

"Now, what's all this," Ford said irritably. "What have they got to do with it?"

"With the problem, or my feeling about it?"

"Now let's just try a little plain talk."

"Well, the trouble is the problems aren't little and plain."

"You've made some Catholic friends? Is that what you're trying to tell me?"

"No, that's not what I was telling you. But yes, I've a few Catholic friends at school."

"They're pretty good salesmen. You want to watch that, Pete."

Peter looked amused. "They couldn't care less. Seriously, I mean it. But I've met an interesting man—he's a French priest who's doing some work on Joyce in the graduate school. He's a very worldly guy, and vain as hell about little things, like digging American slang, which he doesn't, and not liking French food, and so forth. But he's got a mind that's all function. 'War is the health of the State!' Do you know who said that?"

"No."

"Randolph Bourne, an American."

As Peter went on talking, a thought had occurred to Ford, and it seemed so simple and obvious that a confident excitement stirred in him as he searched for words to give it a frame. This might be it, he thought, a distillate of his experience which would provide his son with one touchstone, at least, to use in evaluating his ideas.

"Now see here, Pete," he said. "I hope you know I'm not saddled with stupid prejudices. I have nothing against Catholics, or Jews either, for that matter. How they worship their God is their own business. But we don't go through life on our knees. We spend most of our time involved with practical, everyday matters. And here's a thought that may help you in making up your mind about your Catholic friends—or help you to understand them, at any rate." He paused a moment, pleased and excited by the interest in Peter's face. "It's this, Pete," he went on. "Catholics live in a twilight world—Jews do too, for that matter—and this afflicts them with something you might call social astigmatism."

Even as the words left his lips, Ford knew they didn't represent what he had been thinking; somehow, his idea had become

74

blurred and lost. And he wondered, helplessly, just what he had been thinking about. He had been on the trail of something profound and significant, and the phrase "social astigmatism" had struck him as clever and perceptive. But what had he meant? And he saw now—in his son's face and eyes—a reflection of his own confusion. Peter smiled then, and his expression became closed and polite.

"It's a point," he said. "Social astigmatism?" He grinned faintly. "It might be a job for a combination psychiatrist and —what do you call them? Ophthalmologist, I guess. Look, I've got to barrel out of here. The eight-ten waits for no man —after about eight-thirty, anyway."

When Peter had gone, Ford went upstairs to Janet's room. She was in bed, a long, epicene cylinder underneath pink blankets and an eiderdown quilt, and Ford thought she was sleeping but when he snapped on the light at her dressing table, she said thickly, "Oh dear, must you do that? What time is it? Is Mother up?"

"It's seven-thirty. Pete's just left."

"Oh, that's good. Is he leaving the car in Wilmington?"

"Yes. Listen to me, Janet. I just had the damnedest talk with him. He's picked up a hatful of cockeyed ideas since last fall, and I'm worried about him. He doesn't want to do his army service. I think he wants to be a conscientious objector. Also, I have an idea he wants to be—well, not a Catholic perhaps, but he's awfully interested in their ideas."

"Oh dear God," Janet said. "He didn't mention any of this to me." She had turned on her side and was fumbling for the cigarettes on her night table. "What's got into him?"

"I was hoping you could tell me."

"Please don't say anything to Mother. *Please!* You know how she'll fume."

"She doesn't need an excuse for that."

"Now Ford," Janet said, in her little-girl's voice. "That doesn't sound like you."

"Of course I won't discuss it with her," he said.

As he went back downstairs, Ford was thinking, *And that's*

her only concern—what will her mother think about it, how she'll react. Unfortunately, Mrs. Marsten didn't need this crisis to sour her spirits; her mood had been worsening for days now, in a direct relation to her impending departure. She would appreciate the additional stimulus, of course, he thought; it would give her a fine opportunity to chill the house with icy disapproval. She could leave quite complacently then, with Janet shaken and miserable, and her own emotions intact. Christ, he thought.

After supper that night, Mrs. Marsten announced in a low voice that she had decided to return to New York the following morning. Janet, who sat curled up at one end of the sofa, protested quickly and automatically. "Why don't you wait until Peter gets back?"

"No thank you dear. Although I would like a chance to talk to him. There wasn't much chance this trip."

Janet rubbed her fist against her chin, in a nervous awkward gesture. "You know how it is at Christmas—they've got thousands of friends to see."

"Yes, I know," Mrs. Marsten said, looking at her over the top of her glasses. "I realize that quite well."

Janet smiled brightly. "Ford, don't you think Mother should stay to say good-by to Peter?"

Ford put his newspaper aside deliberately. "Janet, your mother's the best judge of that. I'll have Jones drive her over to the station in the morning." They both stared at him sharply and unpleasantly. "I don't see any need to make such a production out of these things," he said. "Your mother's not off to Mars. She's taking a two-hour train ride to New York. If she didn't have a chance to talk to Peter in the last ten days, she'll have no better luck while he's packing to get back to school." This wasn't what had been expected of him, he realized, and, in the strained silence that settled over the room, he could hear the grandfather's clock ticking calmly and thoughtfully in the foyer, and he wished that both women would go up to bed and leave him alone, for he was suddenly weary of them, tired of placating Mrs. Marsten, tired of assuaging his wife's bruised emotions.

"I take it then, the plans are made," Mrs. Marsten said. "It's nice to have such things arranged for one."

"I have the dreariest headache," Janet said. "'Would you all forgive me if I dashed up to bed?" She stood awkwardly and gracelessly, one hand touching the faint rash on her cheek, the other fluttering to them in a perky farewell.

They heard her high heels clattering above them, and Mrs. Marsten followed the sound with her eyes. "I don't wonder she has a headache," she murmured, and glanced with pursed lips at the brandy snifter beside Janet's coffee cup. "I expect I'd better go up, too."

"Yes, you'll need a good night's rest for the trip."

After she had made her straight-backed, resentful departure, with a last quiver of indignation at being reminded that she was leaving, Ford went into the living room and made himself a drink he didn't really want, and stretched out in a deep chair before the fire. The apple logs were cherry red and the heat flowed smoothly from the brass facings of the fireplace, but he felt depressed and lonely, as if he were a stranger in this large, silent house. He didn't understand Janet, and he didn't understand Peter.

It must be my fault, he thought. But why was it his fault? Why should he feel guilty because he was puzzled by Pete's irrational views? They *were* irrational; he had every right to be puzzled by them. And why should he feel it was his duty to understand Janet? She behaved like a simpleton with her mother. Her timidity was beyond understanding. Why not let it go at that? Did they worry about understanding him? Ginny, with her giggling foolishness, did she know that he had never birdied the long, par-four, fourteenth at the Cedars? And that this rankled the devil out of him? Or that he still thought occasionally of a red-haired girl he had slept with twice in New York during the war?

No, none of them knew much about him at all, and when he died the verdict would probably be that he had been a good man, a kind husband and father, and that would about do it. He had earned a portion of love and friendship, but he knew with gloomy certainty that he had never inspired a strong passion in another human heart. Wiley Poston would get drunk at his funeral and weep for his old hunting companion, but the tears would be for himself, for the reminder that he, too, was mortal, and not for Ford Jackson who had marched off into time to join the endlessly receding lines of his dead clansmen.

Ford finished his drink, and walked aimlessly up and down the room. Finally he went upstairs. Janet was in his bed, crying softly. He sat beside her and took her hand, and she clung to him like a grateful child.

"Please come to bed," she said, in a broken little voice.

He felt trapped by the pressure of her hand. "I've got to go out," he said. "I won't be late."

"What?"

"It's something I'm working on with Tony Marshall, the fund raising for the new library."

"Oh, Ford. Can't it wait?"

"No, I'm sorry. You try to get some sleep. I'll only be an hour or so."

She had stopped crying, and had raised herself on an elbow. As he left the room a bar of light from the hall fell across the bed, and he saw, in that instant, the sharp, surprised frown on her face.

CHAPTER 5

FORD found himself thinking about George Delucca as he drove away from his home. What sort of a Christmas had Delucca had? And then he thought of Maria Ruiz. How had she spent the holidays? She had been in trouble and he had been afraid to help her. But for some reason he wasn't afraid now; he felt reckless and solitary and despairing. What did it matter? "Social astigmatism. Work for a combination psychiatrist and ophthalmologist?" Would it matter to Peter? Would *what* matter?

Ford realized that at the center of his confused feelings was a need to park the package named Ford Jackson somewhere, and walk away from it. The shacks at the outskirts of Rosedale appeared in the long beams of his headlights, the gray wooden sides looking as hard and cold as iron, and wisps of smoke streaming away from stovepipes that swayed in the gusting winds. He parked in front of Maria Ruiz's house, and got quickly out of the car, slamming the door to prove (to himself? he wondered) that there was nothing furtive or sly in his seeing this girl. All right, he thought, walk away from Ford Jackson, leave him sitting motionlessly at the wheel of his expensive car, gloved and hatted and booted against the cold, secure and warm in his complicated cage of steel and leather and glass. Walk away from him. . . .

He remembered the refuse that littered the yard, the worn-down tires and beer bottles, and he picked his way carefully across the dirt yard and rapped decisively on the unpainted door. The wind was noisy in the branches of the big dead locust tree beside the house, and the sound of it rose and fell like the wail of mourners through the darkness. A light flashed against the glass transom, and the door creaked open. A short fat colored woman peered up at him, one hand gathering a shawl at her throat. There was a look of pointless, stupid alarm on her face.

"Yeah, what you want?"

"I'm an attorney," Ford said. "I'm looking for a girl named Maria Ruiz."

"She ain't here." The woman moved forward to get a better look at him, but Ford retreated a step into the darkness. "She called my office," Ford said. "She needed a lawyer."

In the shadows cast by the light behind her, the woman's face was like a shiny chocolate cake into which children had poked eyes and nostrils, and had drawn a mouth into a down-curving arc of fear and suspicion.

"She ain't here," she said.

"Well, when will she be back?"

"Ain't coming back. Leastways, she say that. She gone, mister."

"She's gone?" Ford repeated the words stupidly. Surprise stripped away the virtuous anger, the self-pity which had sustained him thus far; there was nothing left but a sense of shock and disappointment. "Do you know where she's gone? This is important."

"She say something about going to the trailer camp."

"Which trailer camp?" There were a dozen in the area. "Did she say?"

"It was near Beech Road, she say." The woman peered around him toward his car, which, fortunately, was only a shining anonymous bulk in the darkness.

"Thank you," Ford said, and touched the brim of his hat. When he returned to the car and got behind the wheel, it was as if he were slipping into a familiar, comfortable jacket, settling once again into the smoothly worn niche of his personality. Now he shook his head incredulously at the behavior of the stranger who had gone up to knock on the door of this shanty, as guilty and dry-mouthed as a schoolboy facing for the first time the callous impersonality of a whorehouse. You plain damn fool, he thought. But he hadn't been gone more than fifteen or twenty minutes. Janet would still be waiting for him. He wondered if he had better call Tony Marshall to cover the story he had told her. Then he remembered that Beech Road ran through a section of Tony's farm. But there was no trailer camp there. He was sure of that. There was a camp in Lambryville, and several outside Cottersville. They were all watched carefully by the police. At night a squad car was parked at their entrances.

The camps were trouble spots, with racially mixed populations, and on Saturday nights they usually exploded in drunken brawls and knife fights. Ford had once been on a committee which had looked into the problem. There hadn't been anything to do about it, they had decided, except to increase the police surveillance and to investigate the possibility of training guard dogs to work with the troopers. The hillbillies were the worst of the lot, red-necked and sensitive, swollen with belligerent memories of God-ordained caste systems in the red-mud towns of Mississippi, Tennessee, and Alabama. They didn't mind working with the Negroes and Puerto Ricans and Mexicans. They all worked together in the mushroom houses, pitchforking manure in a steaming, subtropical atmosphere, clambering about the latticework of mushroom beds which were stacked from floor to ceiling like bunks in a troop ship. That was all right, apparently.

The trouble started at night, in the touchy areas of protocol: who used the community toilets or showers first, who drank from what cup or bottle, whose children were quickest on the draw with the taunt of "nigger" or "spic" or "white trash." On Saturday nights everyone got drunk, and on Sundays they slept it off, in their trailers, or in jail. The Mexicans and Puerto Ricans went to Mass on Sundays in Rosedale. They did this because—it was taken for granted—the Gospel was read in Spanish and reminded them of home.

But Beech Road ran across the Downs itself, and Ford was

certain there was no trailer camp on or near it. He decided to drive over there anyway, as a simple test of his knowledge of the area. Beech Road was about four miles from his own home, a curving strip of macadam running through woodlands at the southern end on Tony Marshall's property. It served no community need, since wider and straighter roads ran parallel to it, but Tony had kept it open over the years because it provided an artery for his logging operations and a means of access to his woods in the event of fire. There were several small frame houses on Beech Road, which Tony had tried to buy a half-dozen times, without success. They were owned by an old man in Rosedale named Simon Powell, who seemed to relish Tony's irritation more than he coveted money. The houses were empty, and had been for years, but still he wouldn't sell them to Tony.

As he drove into Beech Road, which was only about four hundred yards in length, Ford was surprised to see several trailers parked back in the woods behind one of these old frame houses. His view was a hasty one; his headlights picked them out for an instant, a glitter of glass and steel in the trees, and then swept on across the black woods. This wasn't a trailer camp, of course; these were squatters, Ford guessed, who had tucked themselves into this isolated tip of Tony Marshall's property where, with luck, they might live for months before they were run off. Stopping the car, Ford backed up slowly until he saw the trailers again, strung out in a line like the coaches of a train. There were three of them, thrusting into the woods from the yard of the old frame house, and he saw, too, that a narrow, corduroy road ran up to this bootleg development.

Ford took a flashlight from the glove compartment and started up the road, deciding that as long as he had gone this far there was no point in stopping a few dozen yards short of his goal. As his torch cut through the darkness, a half-dozen dogs came snarling out from the trailers, and circled him with wild, excited yelps. Ford kicked at them irritably, and sent them flying out in wider circles, their eyes glowing green in the beam of his flashlight. Their lack of manners gave him confidence; he was beginning to enjoy this odd adventure. For that's what it was, he realized, something strange and funny and bizarre. The yapping mutts lent it a nice touch. All it needed was a Chic Sale, some scratching hillbillies, and a bottle of white lightning.

Ford could imagine how Wiley Poston would relish this story. He could hear himself saying, "Now keep this under your hat, but let me tell you a funny one." And he could see Wiley's moist, glittering eyes, his reddening cheeks, and imagine his huge, cackling bursts of laughter, his back-slappings, his choking, breathless gusts of mirth. "You did? Oh no! Ole Ford! Goddamn! Goddamn, 'at's perfect! Perfect! Ole Ford pussy-footin' around a nest of coons."

He rapped on the door of the first trailer, and it was opened immediately by a man who looked past Ford and called sharply: "You dogs, you hush! You hear?" And to Ford's surprise the dogs slunk off silently.

Then the man looked at Ford. "They make enough racket to drive you simple. Can I help you, buddy?"

"Perhaps you can," Ford said. "I'm a lawyer and I'm looking for a girl named Maria Ruiz."

"A lawyer, eh? Well, there's a Spanish or Mexican kid in the last trailer. She in trouble?"

"I don't know. She called my office."

"If it's the same one, she's down there in the Clarks' trailer."

From behind him a woman called softly: "Who is it, Roby?"

"Man looking for that Spanish kid. Or Mexican. I can't never tell. Lawyer, he says."

The woman appeared in the door, and the man turned and put an arm companionably about her shoulders. She was young, with curly blond hair and a soft plump body. In turning, the man called Roby had moved under the light, and when Ford saw his face, and the blue birthmark that ran from his temple to his chin, as corrugated as a stream of hardened lava, he felt a sudden constriction in his stomach. The disfigurement was particularly ghastly, for it was the only flaw on a young and powerfully built man, whose face was friendly and handsome, and whose body looked as resilient and durable as a slab of whalebone. He had thick, black hair, a boyishly snubbed nose, and gentle but alert blue eyes, which were now taking an inventory of Ford's covert-cloth topcoat, heavy brogues, and softly shaped tweed hat.

"You a lawyer, eh?" he said amiably.

"Yes. Thanks for the directions."

"I hope she ain't in trouble. She seems like a good kid. See you now." The man moved back to close the door, an arm still resting comfortably on the young girl's shoulders, but as Ford started down the line of trailers, he knew from the light behind him that the man was still watching him from the partially open door. The dogs crept out from under the trailers and snarled timidly at the sucking noise Ford's brogues made in the soft, spongy ground. The middle trailer was dark, but light gleamed from the windows of the last one and coal smoke swirled above it, acrid and tangy in the whipping wind.

Ford knocked on the door of the trailer, and footsteps sounded after a short wait, and a voice murmured something he couldn't make out. Then the door was pulled open by the girl he had seen in the post office in Rosedale. She wore a white dress, and a dark sweater, and her hair was wrapped in a white towel. Holding the sweater at her throat, she leaned forward, frowning faintly at him through the darkness.

"Yes? Who is that?"

"My name is Jackson, Ford Jackson. I'm a lawyer. You called my office, and left your name."

She moved her shoulders and he couldn't tell whether it was a shrug, or an involuntary reaction to the cold wind.

"It was a long time ago," she said.

"I'm sorry. I was busy. If you still need any help, I'll be glad to talk to you."

"O.K." She rubbed her arms with her hands, and her voice was impatient. "Come on in, O.K.?"

The trailer was surprisingly spacious. In the middle of it was a studio couch, two upholstered chairs, a lamp, and a coffee table. At one end was a bathroom, at the other a Pullman kitchen. The girl took his coat and hat and hung them in a closet. Ford sat down in an upholstered chair, and she sat facing him on the studio couch. There was a black, pot-bellied wood stove in a corner, and a pipe angled through a sheet-metal aperture in the ceiling, but the trailer was chilly and he was glad he was wearing a sweater under his tweed jacket. He saw that her hair was damp, and that the few strands escaping from the towel about her head were molded smoothly to her temples, as slick and glistening as the feathers of a fighting cock.

"Aren't you cold?" he asked her.

"No, I have—had a bath. The water was hot."

"You've got running water here?" he asked, and regretted the question at once, for she shook her head and looked sullenly at the backs of her hands. "No—it's from the house. We take it in—" She frowned and made a circle in the air with her index finger. "In pots, buckets."

"It's very nice here."

"Yes, it is good."

"The man in the first trailer told me this one belonged to someone named the Clarks. Do they live here too?"

"They are going—they went to New York to work. They say I could stay here until they come back."

"I see. That's a pleasant arrangement."

"I don't have much money. When I called you I had some. Now I got—have got—" She shook her head irritably as she corrected herself. "I have got twenty-five dollars."

"Supposing you tell me what you want before we worry about money," he said.

"I want to pay you first."

He smiled at her. "That's not the usual procedure." Ford regretted this remark too, for it brought an expression of confusion and defiance to her face. He had meant to be reassuring, but he must have sounded patronizing. "If you want to pay me now, that's all right," he said. "But lawyers generally arrange a fee after they've found out how much or how little work is expected of them. Do you understand?"

She nodded uncertainly. "Yes, I will get it." She rose and opened the closet where she had put his coat and hat, and took down a shoe box that was filled with letters and bills. As she seated herself and began to poke through these, Ford had a chance to study her without any of the odd tension that affected him when she was watching him. The white towel about her head emphasized her dark complexion and brown eyes, and the harsh clean lines of her face. She was too lean and spare for beauty; the angles formed by her chin and throat were exquisitely sharp, almost painfully so, and her cheekbones seemed to be straining against her smooth clear skin. He had thought of her as thin, remembering the way she had looked walking away from the post office that bitterly cold morning, her head turned away from the wind and her arms hugging her sides, so that the red jacket was pulled tightly across her shoulders. But in the white cotton dress she was wearing now, her body was slim and smooth with firm breasts and gently curving hips. She had on white wool ankle socks and black loafers, and her bare legs were shadowed with a fine down that glinted in the lamplight. But it was her eyes that made him feel tense, and curiously apprehensive; they were dark and hard and bright, and they gave her lean, harshly sculptured features a suggestion of secretive contempt and defiance.

She took two tens and a five from the shoe box and looked at them hesitantly. "How much is it? How much do you want?"

"The five will be enough."

"No." She held out one of the tens. "Take this."

"I'd rather you keep it until I know whether or not I can help you."

She narrowed her eyes. "You think you should be paying me? Is that why you came?"

"No, it's not," he said, but he was suddenly and nervously aware of her tense smile and the light gleaming on her bare legs.

Ford cleared his throat, "I went to the address you gave my

secretary. The woman there told me you had moved to a camp on Beech Road, so I drove over here."

"It's a lot of trouble. You must want to earn ten dollars bad. You need it?"

"No. I came here to help you. Don't you believe that?"

"Why should I?"

"Why did you call me?"

She shrugged and made a face, but his question seemed to deflect her antagonism. "I asked at the gas station who you were, and they say you were a lawyer. So I thought you could help."

"All right, I'm here. Now what's the trouble?"

"All right, you're here. I'm here. You can earn some money. Take it!" She held out the ten-dollar bill.

"Very well, if you insist."

When he took the bill from her, she pulled a pillow from beneath the cover on the couch and propped it against the wall. Pushing herself across the couch with a twist of her hips, she made herself comfortable with the pillow behind her and her slim legs crossed at the ankles. Then she put the tip of one finger to her forehead in a childish gesture of concentration. "Well! Last month, no, this month, it was December the second, a friend of mine got in a fight. He was fighting in a bar, and the police came and took him away. He was drunk."

"You were there?"

"Yes, there were lots of people. Hillbillies, with hair down like this." She touched her cheek below her ear lobe. "They were drunk too. They called me a spic, and Buddy laughed at them and they got mad at him laughing. Then they started to fight. The police came and took them away."

"What's Buddy's full name?"

"Taylor, I think. Buddy Taylor."

"You're not sure?"

"I think it's Taylor."

"What's his first name?"

"Buddy, I told you it."

"Where's the bar he had the fight in?"

"Well, near Cottersville."

"He didn't mind that they called you a—spic?"

"No, it didn't hurt anybody. It was funny, they just got mad at him laughing. Then the police came, and I don't know what they did with Buddy. That's why I called you. Can you find out?"

"Yes, I can find out in the morning."

She looked impressed; and Ford realized with embarrassment he was flattered by the respect in her eyes. "It is easy for you?" she asked him.

"Well, it's not difficult," he said smiling. "I'll call the Magistrate's clerk, and he'll tell me what happened to Buddy."

"Maybe I paid too much."

"I told you to wait, Maria."

"Can I have my money back?" She looked at him defiantly. "I'll pay you—tomorrow. It's all I got—have got now. Twenty-five dollars."

"Of course," he said, and returned the bill which he had been holding in his fingers. Their hands touched briefly, and her skin was cold and hard and rough, unlike his wife's or daughter's, unlike the skin of any of the women he would know or meet in his normal environment.

Ford got to his feet and she went to the closet for his coat and hat.

"Is there some place I can phone you?" he asked her.

"You can give a message to the gas station in Rosedale. The Esso place. Joe there will take it."

"I see. The Esso station in Rosedale."

As he put on his heavy covert-cloth coat, and drew on leather gloves, he remembered the cold hard feel of her hand, and he said impulsively: "It's cold here—that fire isn't doing a very good job. I have a flask of whisky in my car. Do you want a drink? It would warm you up."

She leaned against the wall of the trailer, and folded her arms over her small breasts. She put her head back and smiled into his eyes. "You want to have a drink with me? Because I took back the money, eh? That gave you an idea?"

"No, I don't want a drink," Ford said. He felt ridiculous; his cheeks were hot, and he nearly stammered out the words. "I'll leave the flask for you, if you want."

"Maybe I would give it to Roby. Maybe we have a party and drink it all. You lose all the whisky for nothing." She was still smiling, but her deep brown eyes had narrowed slightly.

Ford was suddenly irritated with her; she seemed young and crude, now, savoring her cynical bitterness. "You can do anything you want with the whisky," he said. "Yes or no?"

She looked at him strangely. "No—I don't drink whisky. But—" She was speaking slowly, studying his face as she formed the words with an effort. "Thank you."

The next morning Ford called Magistrate Harding's clerk, Joe Kelly, and asked for the disposition on Buddy Taylor. He had the facts in a few minutes. Buddy's name wasn't Taylor, it was Tatnall. Clarence (Buddy) Tatnall had been slated December second for disturbing the peace, resisting arrest, and committing A & B on the persons of divers police officers. Fined one hundred dollars and shipped off to the County workhouse for ninety days in lieu of payment.

"I'd like to talk to him," Ford said to Kelly. "Would you call Warden Thomas and notify him I'm representing Tatnall? I'll be out there in an hour."

"You representing him, Mr. Jackson?" Joe Kelly sounded surprised. "Well, sure. I'll call the warden."

The Darby County workhouse was a mile outside Cottersville, and, in keeping with most of the area's facilities, was overcrowded, understaffed, and antiquated; crime was celebrating the booster spirit of the community, too, Ford thought, as he drove into the parking lot beside the grimy, red-brick building. Everything on the go, onward and upward! Rape and robbery, mopery and dopery, muggery and buggery, all booming.

Warden Sam Thomas was a tall, stout, bald-headed man with veined cheeks and eyes so watery that they seemed to be defying a natural law by remaining fixed in their sockets. The warden had two complaints about the business of law enforcement, and he voiced them regularly at Kiwanis and Rotary luncheons: one was the evil effects of crime shows in television, and the second was the fact that the whipping post had gone out of favor in the county. The warden had powerful shoulders and hamlike hands, endowments from his semipro football career, and when he spoke of "touching up these punks and sex maniacs" his audience had an almost too vivid picture of a man strung up by his wrists, and the warden's thick arm causing a whip to snap and whistle in an ominous crescendo.

Now, as he ushered Ford into a visitor's room, he said heartily: "It's fine of you, Mr. Jackson, to take an interest in this white trash. Not that he'll thank you for it. He's a smart and sassy one, Tatnall. Oh, he talks like butter won't melt in his mouth, he's a sly one. You take this chair, it's the only decent one." Warden Thomas dusted the seat with a dirty handkerchief, like an usher working the box seats in a ball park. "No, he won't thank you, not that one."

"You'd better bring him in," Ford said, glancing at his watch.

"Yes, sir, right away. And if you don't mind, would you send my kind regards to Mrs. Jackson? She helped us out wonderfully on our drive last fall. She and her friends were just wonderful, I mean it."

"Yes, I'll tell her."

Ford sat down and lit a cigarette, wondering what the warden's reaction would be if he knew the reason for his interest in Buddy Tatnall. But that was a moot consideration, for Ford wasn't sure himself why he was here, or what his interest was in Buddy Tatnall. Did he want to see the girl again? Yes, he thought, I do. I'd like to know her, he thought. It would be interesting to know someone so completely removed from his own background and values. But maybe there was no reason for what he was doing; maybe, for once in his life, he was simply drifting, letting things happen to him.

The room he sat in was small and close, with a barred window beyond which a steady rain drew thin lines on a patch

90

of gray sky. There was one table, scarred with the narrow black imprint of countless cigarettes, and two straight-backed chairs.

Buddy Tatnall came through the door with Warden Thomas. The warden held his arm firmly. "Now you tell this gentleman anything he wants," the warden said. He shook Buddy Tatnall's arm. "You hear?"

"Yes, Warden, yes sir," Buddy Tatnall said quickly.

When the warden had gone (closing the door so softly that it was impossible not to imagine him outside with his ear against the panel), Ford nodded to the empty chair, and said: "Sit down, Buddy."

"Thank you, sir."

"Would you like a cigarette?"

"I'd appreciate that, sir, I surely would."

Ford gave him a cigarette, and watched him as he inhaled the first sulphur-tainted mouthful of smoke with a gasp of relish. He was handsome, Ford thought, there was no doubt of that, with carefully waved blond hair, blue eyes, a good complexion, and a body that was springy with the health of youth. But he was vain, Ford guessed, and his humble courteous manner didn't ring true; it was just a private joke between his inner and outer selves.

"You know a girl named Maria Ruiz, I believe," Ford said.

"Maria? Sure!" Buddy's smile was cheerful and unrevealing, and Ford suspected he might be facing a fairly clever poker player.

"She was with you the night you got in trouble, I understand," Ford said. "She was curious to know what happened to you."

Buddy sighed humorously. "Wasn't no mystery about it. I got locked up, as you can plainly see."

"You'd like to get out of here?"

"Lordy, would I? I ain't made for cages, Mister—" He paused, leaning forward politely.

"My name is Jackson. I'm a lawyer."

"I'm pleased that she wants to help. I really am. But that kid ain't got no money. Unless some rich relative died and left her some since I knew her."

"What was your relationship with Maria?"

"What's that, Mr. Jackson?"

"Were you sleeping with her?"

Buddy chuckled and rubbed the back of his neck. "Well, you're plain spoken, Mr. Jackson, I must say that." He grinned at Ford, studying him with a new interest. Buddy's smile was faintly mocking but Ford saw what he had been looking for, the glint of speculation in his eyes. "I'll help myself to another of your cigarettes, if you don't mind," Buddy said. "Maybe this is my lucky day, if Maria's got herself some important friends. She's a good kid, a real good kid."

"You haven't answered my question," Ford said.

"I'm not trying to hide anything. I just saw her around Rosedale, and took her out for beers a few times. I was waiting her out, I'll be frank with you. I don't like making the first move. Some guys got to be pitching for it all the time, but I let 'em come to me." Buddy took a deep drag from his cigarette, and let the smoke drift slowly between his smiling lips. "I'm not blowing my own horn, but I'm not a bad good-looking guy. I say that, not bragging, but just as a fact. I don't have a big job, or dough or anything, but I'm young, Mr. Jackson, real young, and that makes waiting easy. I got time—time for 'em all."

"If your relationship was so casual, I wonder why she's interested in you now," Ford said.

"She was kind of gone on me, I figure," Buddy said and smiled complacently. "You ever been to her room?"

"Where was that?"

"In that house in Rosedale at the grade crossing. They used to be a shoemaker worked in the basement. They rent rooms now. That's where she was staying when I met her. I went there a couple of afternoons. When it was raining, well, we bought some pizzas and went there and listened to a little radio she had. I kind of guessed she was sort of gone on me, a guy can tell, you know. She'd lie on the sofa looking at the ceiling and smoking, not looking at me, and I knew it was

92

just a matter of time." Buddy blew on the ash of his cigarette until it was glowing vividly, and then he grinned at Ford over the fiery tip. "She's a good-looking kid. Lots of Mex girls have legs like fence posts. But not Maria. If she'd shave them they'd be even better, don't you think?"

"If your fine is paid, and you're released, what are your plans?"

"I don't know—hunt around for a job, I guess."

"Where?"

Buddy looked surprised. "Around here. It's nice country."

"What kind of work do you do?"

"Mushroom houses for as long as I could stand it. Then I pumped gas, but I'm no mechanic and that's what they want."

Ford stood and picked up his hat from the table.

"Hold on, Mr. Jackson," Buddy rose too, and wiped his hands anxiously on his gray denim trousers. "I thought I was getting out. I thought you was going to help me."

"I'll let you know if anything develops," Ford said.

"You don't know what it's like here." Buddy glanced nervously at the closed door. "He's mean! You know what happens if you get out of line? Ice-cold baths, in water up to your neck in an unheated room in the basement. Four hours, five, he don't care. It's a nice safe way to half-kill a man. We can't say nothin'. He says we're dirty, need a scrubbing. The guards got scrubbing brushes with bristles two inches long like spikes. They can rub you raw. Don't just stand up and go, Mr. Jackson. Please give me a break."

"Maria asked me to find out what happened to you, that's all," Ford said. "I'll tell her you'll be out when you've served your time." He looked steadily at Buddy and the silence became charged and significant as their thoughts joined in complicity on the form of an invisible woman. Buddy swallowed slowly, and the sound of it was dry and painful in the silence. "Mr. Jackson, this really isn't a good place to look for work," he said. "This time of the year, it's all wrong. If I got out of jail, I'd pull out of this part of the country fast."

"Where would you go?"

"Upstate New York. I got cousins up there." He shifted his weight nervously. "Only thing, I'd need a little stake. Enough to get started on."

"How much?"

Buddy scratched his head. "The best thing would be if I could pick up a used car cheap. That'd save bus fair, and I could move around easier looking for work. In New York, I mean. All I'd need then would be a little to keep me going, you know, for meals and cigarettes and laundry until I got a job."

"Say three hundred for the car, another hundred to tide you over?"

"That would do it fine, just fine, Mr. Jackson."

Ford gave him one of his business cards. He was amazed at his own assurance; his voice and hands were steady as rocks. "When you're released stop at my office. My secretary will have the money."

"I surely appreciate this, Mr. Jackson. It's not the sort of kindness you expect from a stranger. I won't do anything to disappoint you, don't you worry." He smiled cheerfully. "You'll get your money's worth, don't worry."

"There's one thing," Ford said, and again he was amazed at the authority in his voice. "The assault and battery charges will remain open. You might be picked up on that again anytime." This wasn't true, of course, but Buddy nodded quickly and said: "I understand, Mr. Jackson. They won't find me around here. I had enough of Warden Thomas. You can depend on that."

"I hope I can," Ford said.

Ford drove slowly back to Cottersville. When he lit a cigarette, he saw that his hands were shaking and he could feel his heart pounding as if he had been running a race. What had come over him? Where had he pulled that performance from? he wondered uneasily. The cool eyes and hard voice, the ruthless treatment of a helpless youngster, who normally would have elicited nothing from him but sympathy and compassion. And what was he buying for his four hundred dollars? That's

94

what nagged at him; would he see her again? Yes, to explain what had happened to Buddy. He was committed to that. But then what? Would he stand with his hat in his hand and say good-by? Walk away from her trailer, mission accomplished, his legal duties discharged?

Later, after he had cashed a check for four hundred dollars, and put the money in an envelope with Buddy Tatnall's name on it, he went into the restaurant in the lobby of his office building for a cup of coffee. For reasons he didn't understand, the familiar sights of the city had brought him to a sad and weary decision, and, as he sipped his coffee and looked at himself in the mirror behind the counter, seeing well-cut clothes and a youthful face balanced by wings of gray hair at the temples, he knew that he wouldn't push this foolishness any further, that he wouldn't see Maria Ruiz again.

In the bank he had felt guilty; in the streets, nodding to friends and business acquaintances he had felt like a fool; now he simply felt as if he had earned a reprieve he didn't wholly welcome—it was like being cut from a football squad and knowing that the bumps and bruises were over but so was the hope of glory; or scratching a horse and escaping the possibility of a broken shoulder but losing forever the chance of driving home a length or two ahead of that particular field.

Ford didn't understand why he had risked as much as he already had, but he knew he would make no further gambles. He thought of the coldness of her trailer, and her wary, defiant eyes and he sighed as heavily as if he were saying good-by to something that was very familiar and important to him. Paying his check, he looked up the number of the Esso station in Rosedale and dialed it. A man answered and he gave him a message for Maria Ruiz, saying simply that Buddy Tatnall would be released from the county workhouse tomorrow morning.

"O.K.," the man said. "That all?"

"That's all, thank you," Ford said deliberately, and replaced the receiver. He sat in the booth a moment, giving himself time to accept the finality of this decision, and then he sighed once more and went upstairs to his office.

He gave Mrs. Simpson the four hundred dollars he had promised Buddy Tatnall, and he said to her: "There'll be a young man in for this tomorrow. And I'd like you to call Joe Kelly and tell him we'll take care of Clarence Tatnall's fine."

"Yes, Mr. Jackson." She made a quick note of this on her calendar pad. Then she said, "Mr. Delucca's waiting in your office. He didn't have an appointment, but you don't have anyone else this morning so I told him to wait."

"Delucca? George Delucca?"

"Yes." She looked concerned as she saw the frown on his face. "That was all right, wasn't it?"

"What? Oh yes. Quite all right. But I've got to step over to the courthouse for a moment. Tell him that, please. If I'm delayed, I'll call you." He smiled pointlessly at her, and walked quickly out of his office. In the street he turned right and strode briskly toward the center of town, passing familiar shops and buildings without seeing them, and exchanging mechanical smiles or greetings with people he encountered on the sidewalk. He knew Cottersville by heart, the baroque and soot-stained bank, the ponderous old courthouse, the rows of brown-brick office buildings, the garish red front of the department store, the luncheonettes and record shops, the elegant canopied entrance of the Ashley Hotel, and the bleak gray growth of the colored section which formed a crust over the edge of the city where the Belt Line railroad tracks came over the bridge from the switching yards.

He knew all this very well, and practically everyone in town was familiar with his tall figure, his conservative clothes, his friendly and youthful face. Seeing him, Ford knew, people would assume he was on his way to a board meeting at the bank, or hurrying to keep an appointment at the courthouse. But the truth was he didn't know where he was going, or why he had turned tail on George Delucca. Goddamn Wiley Poston, he thought, as he waited for the light to change on Church Street. He must have blabbed the story of the Henderson deal all over the county.

Ford walked around the block, passing the courthouse

(where his father's name stood out on the bronze plaque beside the entrance), and the Darby County Historical Society, and the red-brick bulk of the Cottersville library. He strode along briskly, one hand holding the brim of his Homburg against the gusts of cold wind, but he knew his air of purpose was fraudulent; he had nowhere to go, and behind a façade of confident industry he was sick with worry and guilt.

It was ludicrous and pointless, he knew, to be delaying the meeting with Delucca. He was simply postponing the inevitable, like a schoolboy taking the longest way across the campus to put off for a few minutes an interview with a stern Head.

This thought so irritated him that he stopped abruptly in the middle of the block, turned around, and walked back to his office.

CHAPTER 6

GEORGE Delucca was sitting in the black leather chair beside the roll-top desk smoking a cigar. He stood casually when Ford came in, and smiled as he removed the cigar from his mouth.

"Hello, Mr. Jackson. I hope you'll excuse me dropping in unexpectedly."

"That's perfectly O.K.," Ford said. "How've you been, George?"

"Fine, just fine. And you and the family?"

"We're all well, thanks. Recovering slowly but surely from Christmas."

Delucca made no move to shake hands, but there was nothing unfriendly in his manner; he stood smiling at Ford, one hand thrust casually into the pocket of his tweed jacket, the other holding the cigar a few inches from his lips. "I'm glad I'm not interrupting your schedule," he said.

"Not at all." Ford glanced at his wrist watch as he sat down at his desk. "Just give me a minute to check these letters, O.K.?"

"Of course. I could drop back later, if you're busy."

"No, I'll be with you in a minute. Sit down, please."

"Thanks." Delucca stretched his legs comfortably as he glanced about the office. After a moment he nodded appreciatively and said: "You've got a nice tone here, a nice balance. It's serious, which is right, but it's also got warmth. I like it."

"It wasn't planned that way," Ford said. "It's early hodge-podge, I'm afraid, with bits and pieces added when Mrs.

Simpson or I thought of it."

As he shuffled through the routine mail, Ford watched Delucca from the corner of his eye, but he learned very little from his manner or expression. Delucca seemed to be in a comfortable mood, puffing on his cigar while his eyes roved casually about the office.

Ford's composure returned with an abruptness that in itself was pleasantly reassuring. He felt sustained by the pleasant and familiar shabbiness of his office, and encouraged by Delucca's respectful appraisal of its appointments. Delucca would have, he suspected, a peasant's awareness of the mechanics of snobbery; he would be at home with, or contemptuous of, mahogany desks and heavy carpeting, and elaborate intercom systems, knowing exactly how one acquired these things, but the old black leather chairs, the roll-top desk and Princeton class pictures, they were something else again altogether, these gentle reminders of caste and tradition and privilege.

Delucca must be about forty, he thought, although he looked younger than that, with his tall, powerful body, thick black hair, and a complexion still smoothly tanned from the summer's sun. He had quite a local reputation as an athlete and sportsman, and there were rumors—inevitably, since he was a widower—of his interest in women. Ford considered these items carefully while pretending to look through his mail. He was studying Delucca as carefully as he would a witness in court, regarding him frankly as an opponent, taking his measure, and analyzing his probable strengths and weaknesses. Delucca was a fine bowler, with a one-ninety average in the Sons of Italy League, and he played handball well enough to have advanced, one year, to the quarterfinals of the State Championships. He hunted pheasant and deer, and on New Year's Day hosted a party for hundreds of friends and business acquaintances at the White Hackle, serving bowls of champagne punch and platters of ring-necks and venison from the stocks in the freezers of his restaurant. Ford had heard that he drank sparingly but choicely, vintage wines and fine old brandies, and that he was nearly as good a cook as the White

Hackle's chef. But what did all this add up to? Ford wondered. What was the essential contradiction about the man—why, in short, did all his activity seem somehow incongruous and irrelevant?

It was just the look of him, Ford decided, the warm but calculating eyes, the bold and swarthy face, the strong, curved nose which arched above his full red lips like a scimitar, and gave his features a permanent expression of almost sinister confidence. It was a face charged with contradictions; you could imagine Delucca as both meek and arrogant, shrewd and credulous, tender and violent. It was a face, Ford thought finally, that didn't seem to have much relationship to a world of P.T.A. meetings, humdrum business affairs, and other such gentle concerns. Even the clothes he was wearing—a gray tweed jacket, dark flannel slacks, tasseled alligator moccasins—seemed inappropriate to his broken nose and bold dark features.

Ford was convinced of one thing, and one thing only, from his appraisal of Delucca—you couldn't take him at face value. As he put aside his letters and smiled at Delucca, he decided he had better keep this fact in mind.

"Well, George, what is it? What did you want to see me about?"

"You may have heard, I tried to buy the Henderson place." Delucca smiled ironically. "In fact, I thought for a while the deal was set. Tom Moran took my check, I signed some papers, and I thought that was all there was to it." Delucca was still smiling, but there was a touch of bitterness in the curve of his lips. "You heard about this, by the way?"

Ford didn't intend to be drawn into a game of cat-and-mouse. "Yes, I heard about it," he said. "I gather there was some confusion on Tom Moran's part. The place had already been sold to Wiley Poston when he accepted your check, wasn't that it?"

"Yes, that was about it," Delucca said. "But I had to read Tom's letter about five times before I understood what he was trying to say. I'd like your opinion of it. Legally, that is."

"Sure. May I see it?"

"I'd better read it to you. It's handwritten, and Tom must have been nervous as the devil about something when he wrote it. But I've practically memorized it." Delucca took a letter from his inside breast pocket, and flipped it open with a precise, deliberate snap of his wrist. "It goes like this," he said, and began to read Tom Moran's letter in a flat, noncommittal voice: " 'Dear George: One of those terrible unexplainable things has happened, terrible because I've been guilty of a serious mistake, and unexplainable because I can't see even now how it could have happened.' " Delucca looked up at Ford. "You can tell how upset he is, I guess. I didn't know what it was all about, of course, even though my check for the Henderson place was clipped to the letter."

"I'm sure he feels badly about it," Ford said.

"Oh sure. He goes on apologizing for a couple of paragraphs, then he finally gets to the point." Delucca glanced at the letter, and began reading again, but now there was a hard, dry edge to his voice. " 'I am sure you will understand, George, that when I first broached the subject of the Henderson place to you, my mind was completely free from any thought that it was in any way unavailable at that time. But prior to our talk, and unbeknownst to me, Herb Randall in my office had instituted negotiations with Mr. Wiley Poston, whom I believe you know, and had reached a conclusive stage in these talks of which I was not aware. I had been out dating the flu bug for a couple of days, and wasn't on top of everything going on. Maybe, George, we'll wind up putting all the blame on that flu bug.' "

Delucca glanced at Ford with a faint smile. "That last part about the flu bug is in parentheses, from which I gather Tom thinks it's kind of a joke. And maybe it is. But then he winds up like this: 'So George, I can assure you the blame is solely mine, and I am heartily sorry for any and all disappointments the return of your check may bring you, but I give you my assurance I will not rest until I have found a property for you and yours that will more than compensate' "—Delucca paused and shook his head slowly—" 'for the disappointment about

101

the Henderson place, now the Poston place, which, for your sake, I am sorry to say.' "

For a moment Delucca stared in silence at the letter, and then he replaced it in his breast pocket and glanced at Ford with a quizzical little smile.

"You can see why I had to read it half a dozen times," he said.

"He's obviously embarrassed."

"Yes, he sure is. But there's a kind of frightened tone, too. Do you think he's afraid I'm going to sue him?"

"I couldn't say, George," Ford turned a bronze letter opener around in his hand, and the sunlight glinted on its ornately worked surfaces. "You know the answer to that. Do you plan to sue?"

"What sort of case would I have?"

"If you could establish that Moran's mistake cost you money, you'd have the basis of a suit. If you bought furniture, retained an architect, broke your present lease—if you're out of pocket in any such instances, then you might recover from Moran."

"Yeah, but supposing the loss is just personal? You know, the disappointment at missing out on a nice little farm. How about that?"

"It's a much more tenuous area," Ford said carefully. "I wouldn't attempt to anticipate the court's reaction. A judge might be inclined to the view that Moran's embarrassment over an honest business mistake was sufficient retribution in this case. You both lost, in a sense, and those losses—it might be argued—cancel each other out."

"Well then, there's my children's disappointment," Delucca said thoughtfully. "There might be something in that. I have two daughters, eight and twelve, and they're pretty emotional and excitable at that age, you know, full of plans and day-dreams. They've taken this pretty hard. They'd been out to the farm, picked out their bedrooms, decided what stalls they'd put their ponies in, and they even named their ponies, you know how kids will do a thing like that. Pancake and Gypsy. Funny names, eh? But funnier still is that they didn't

102

even have ponies then. But they knew they'd have them when we moved out to the Henderson place, because I'd promised them, and naturally they believed me. So all this is a shock to them. They don't understand the legal angles—all they know is that I didn't deliver what I said I would. And of course they've talked about our plans to all their friends at school, and that makes it even tougher to take. They feel—well, who knows how kids feel?—like they were caught lying, you know what I mean? You understand?"

Ford wanted a cigarette badly, but instead he continued to turn the bronze letter opener slowly about in his fingers. "I don't think it's possible to interpret their disappointment in legal terms," he said evenly.

"I forgot the legal side of it for a minute. I was just curious to know if you understood their disappointment."

"Of course I understand that," Ford said, and then he reached for a cigarette, for he had the sudden nervous suspicion that he had been deliberately maneuvered into this casual and friendly discussion of Delucca's problem. He shouldn't have said a damn thing, he knew; given no opinion, offered no analysis. He had been smugly and stupidly careless, taking Delucca at face value, confident that an old roll-top desk and a few class pictures would keep him frozen in an attitude of smiling deference. Delucca was here to set a trap; and he was blundering into it like a fool.

But Delucca's manner was still mild and thoughtful, as he nodded and studied the firm white ash on the tip of his cigar. "I see what you mean," he said slowly. "You feel their disappointment is a pretty tenuous argument to hang a trial on, eh?" Delucca's expression changed subtly as he was talking, Ford saw; he still sat comfortably relaxed in the deep chair, but his eyes had narrowed slightly, and there were dull spots of color at his cheekbones. "You think I'd better forget the whole thing, eh? Tell my daughters that's life? Let them cry themselves to sleep a few more nights?"

"I wasn't aware that you were asking me to suggest a course of action," Ford said evenly. "I've given you a general opinion.

What you do is your affair."

"Meaning, I'm not a client of yours?"

"That's right," Ford said, in the same even tone. This should have been his position from the start, he knew, a simple refusal to discuss the problem professionally.

Delucca grinned at him. "Don't worry, I'm not asking you to take me on as a client. I realize that could be embarrassing. Supposing Wiley Poston and I showed up in your office at the same time? That would put you in an awkward spot, eh? 'Conflict of interest,' isn't that what they call it?"

The words shook Ford from his position of ethical detachment. "What do you mean?" he said, trying to keep his voice level.

"You understand, all right." Delucca came to his feet suddenly in one powerful movement, and there was a cold, ugly look about his eyes. "When I got Tom's letter, I figured it was just tough luck. I believed him. But then I heard a very funny story going the rounds. It seems—"

"I don't think I have time—"

"You better find time," Delucca said, in a voice trembling with anger. "It's a story about a lottery that took place in your home, two weeks ago. Wiley Poston's not just a thief, he's a blabbermouth. It's a bad combination if he's going to make a career out of it. He told the whole story to the locker room at the Cedars last week. He told it to a pal sitting at my bar a few nights ago. It was too good to keep. All about how you'd screwed the dago bastard who had the gall to buy himself a home on the Downs."

"I'm to accept your account of what he said?"

"Go on, deny it! Deny the whole thing. You're thieves, why should lying bother you? You think this is guesswork? Scraps of gossip I overheard?" Delucca put his big hands on the top of Ford's desk, and leaned forward slowly, the cold, ugly smile tightening on his face. "It was Tony Marshall, Harvey Shires, and Wiley Poston who met in your house that night. The one item on the agenda was how to screw me out of the Henderson place. You put pieces of paper in an ash-

104

tray, and Wiley Poston drew the one with the X on it. He went to Tom Moran that same night and threatened to smash him unless he took his check and returned mine. Now let me hear you sit there and deny it."

"You have most of the facts correctly," Ford said, shrugging, but his attempt at composure was pointless, for the words were like lye on his tongue. "There was a drawing at my home. I didn't take part in it. I suggested we offer you a price for the Henderson place that would give you a profit on the transaction."

"You went to the lynching, but you come up roses because you didn't tie the rope around my neck or larrup the horse across the ass. Is that the plea you're copping?"

"The decision wasn't made without considering the moral issue," Ford said. The words made no sense at all, he realized, they were simply weird noise floating from his mouth, but he couldn't sit silent and helpless under the heat and weight of Delucca's anger. "My friends believed that they had a right to that property even though you had paid down earnest money. They felt their prior, though unstated, right had been violated by Moran."

" 'Prior unstated right'!" Delucca laughed scornfully. "Would you like to go into court with that story? You could rape my daughters with that argument. You've got a prior unstated right to any goddamn thing you want. Is that it, Mr. Jackson?"

Ford stood slowly, and he felt a tremor in his legs, a dryness in his mouth. Delucca's words had struck him like blows, and the blood was pumping heavily and angrily through his body, but he knew the anger was defensive and fraudulent, an instinctive reaction to shame; it had no validity or relevance to the facts. "I told you I didn't take part in the drawing," he said heavily. "I was opposed to it. But your present attitude and language makes me wonder if my friends weren't right."

"Oh, I'm vulgar all right," Delucca said bitterly. "If I'd whipped off my cap and said, 'Thanks for the shafting, gents!' everything would be just dandy. Of course, I'd still be screwed out of the property. I suppose you expect me to understand how impossible it would be for a dago restaurant owner to buy a house that's almost, not quite, but almost in sight of Tony Marshall's. I don't belong to the Cedars. I belong to Peaceful Pines, which you call Pizza Pie. And my kids go to St. Patrick's, not Miss Crane's. There's no place in the Downs for them. Full of superstitions, fanatics ready to gun down the Protestant heretics. And you believe it!" Delucca brought his fist down with a crash on Ford's desk.

"You believe it! You believe in your prior unstated rights! What did you do in the war? You flew a desk, didn't you? Tony Marshall was an Admiral's aide! Shires was in Public Relations. And Wiley Poston, that big sonofabitch with his hairy chest and Purdy shotguns, he was in Army Procurement. Even in a war that prior unstated right keeps working for you. None of you heard a shot fired in anger, while I got the job of ram-rodding an infantry platoon through Europe. You grab what you want, you always have, and justify it with bullshit about tradition and values and prior unstated rights. You're so blind that one of these days you're going to walk straight into a buzzsaw. And the guy you hear laughing will be your old dago buddy, George Delucca. Sleep tight, Mr. Jackson, you'll never know what hit you."

Afterward, while the crash of the door was still echoing in the office, Mrs. Simpson came in and looked anxiously at Ford.

"I didn't know whether to interrupt or not," she said. "They must have heard him shouting clear down to the street."

"He's had some business losses—he's upset."

"They are emotional, of course." She watched him curiously. "Are you all right, Mr. Jackson?"

"Yes—yes, of course."

"I'm going down for coffee. Would you like some?"

"No, thank you."

When she had gone, Ford sat down at his desk and put his head on his arms. Delucca's presence seemed to fill the room; his anger still throbbed in the air, as palpable as the heat from a blast furnace. But the heat was in his own cheeks, Ford

106

knew; he was ashamed of himself, and, in some way he didn't understand, he was ashamed of Delucca. They were partners in that; bound together in a complicity of shame. If Delucca had only been angry, it would be different, Ford thought wearily. But Delucca was hurt and humiliated, stung and resentful because he had been excluded from the company of people he claimed to have nothing but contempt for.

Ford raised his head and turned to look out the window behind his desk. He could see the corner of the courthouse, the red bricks looking almost black on this dreary day. The pigeons with their dirty, blue-white colorings were like brush marks against the background of a low gray sky. Ford found the view distasteful; it was familiar, that was its special curse, and he felt a desperate urge to separate himself from everything that was known and familiar to him, to disengage himself from this fixed and predictable collection of instincts and impulses which the world knew as Ford Jackson.

He called his home, and told Catherine he wouldn't be home for dinner.

"Well, Mrs. Jackson already phoned she's staying in Philadelphia to have dinner with the Quillings. Neither of you be here, then."

"Yes, that's right. Thank you, Catherine."

At seven-thirty that night Ford walked down the muddy pathway to Maria Ruiz's trailer. He had spent half of the afternoon driving aimlessly through the countryside, and the rest of it in a small bar on the main road between Cottersville and Rosedale. He had sat sipping Scotch while the afternoon faded away, and the headlights of homeward bound traffic flashed by outside in thick noise formations. There were young men in jeans and sweaters playing darts, and hillbilly ballads poured from the jukebox with belligerent reverence. Ford's thoughts had circled a dozen subjects: Wiley Poston, his brother Clay, Alicia, Janet. Where was his son? Ginny was flunking French!

And he had realized at last that he was deliberately keeping his thoughts focused on these legitimate concerns. It was obvious he didn't want to think about himself, about why he hadn't gone home, or why he wanted to see Maria Ruiz.

The dogs snarled at his heels as he walked unsteadily through the darkness to Maria Ruiz's trailer. She must have heard them, for the door opened before he could knock, and he saw her standing a few feet above him, with the light from the trailer shining on her white skirt and bare legs.

He put one foot on the first step and a hand against the trailer to steady himself, and she leaned forward and said anxiously, "You better come in. What's wrong?"

"Thank you," he said slowly and distinctly.

In the trailer he sat carefully on the edge of the studio couch while she put his hat and coat in the closet. The wood stove was glowing and the draft made a soft roaring noise in the trailer. He hadn't eaten since breakfast, and the warm air made his head feel light. She sat on the arm of the big chair, and looked at him with a puzzled but good-humored smile. He had the feeling she was resisting a temptation to giggle at him. He fingered the knot of his tie and pushed a strand of hair back from his forehead.

"Would you mind if I had a drink?" he said with dignity.

"No, please, if you want. But there's nothing here."

"I brought my flask. No rule against that, eh? No rules here at all. Every man's trailer his castle. Do what one pleases. Or what pleases one." He smiled brightly, but his face felt as stiff as cold leather.

"You want a glass?"

"Yes, please. With a little water."

He took the leather-bound flask from the pocket of his jacket and removed the aluminum top with care, feeling for some reason it was important to do this job efficiently and precisely. She brought him a clean glass half-filled with water, and stood watching him expectantly, with a good-humored little smile on her lips. Now what did she expect? he thought. That I'll spill it down my vest? The glass was thick and decorated with blue and red polka dots, and he thought, it's a peanut butter jar, without a doubt it's a peanut butter jar. I might point out that this is pretty funny, too, he thought, using a peanut butter jar for twelve-year-old bourbon. Pretty damned funny if we must have something to giggle at.

"You're sure you won't join me?"

"No, I can't drink it. But—I drink beer?"

"Very well, have a beer then."

"There's no beer."

"That settles that, eh? How old are you, Maria? Do you mind telling me?"

"No, I have—I am twenty-two."

"Isn't that a coincidence. I'm also twenty-two. I look older, of course. Go ahead, tell me the truth. I look older, don't I? But I've been through a war, and that has a certain aging effect on men." Something twisted in his mind, like a flash of remembered pain. Delucca's voice seemed to be hammering at the inside of his skull. *"You flew a desk, didn't you? Thief! Thief!"* "It wasn't much of a war, Maria," Ford said heavily. "Nothing much happened. It was a war on paper. Through a certain prior, though unstated right, I elected to spend the war keeping an account of various orders relating to the naval operations in the port of New York. There were occasions when I was forced to make the dangerous journey to Washington in the line of duty, but for the weary veteran, there were dances at the Mayflower, and a lobby full of young women who felt—well, how shall I put it, considering our tender years?— they felt, let us say, that all of those young desk pilots needed a last patriotic sexual experience in the event, however unlikely, that they might be sent to sea to engage the enemy. So it was war, after all, Maria. I commanded an armada of fitness reports, a flotilla of paper clips and rubber bands." Ford stared at the glass in his hand. It was odd, he thought, he was not speaking now but he could hear his voice going on and on, mouthing wry defenses inside his head.

Maria was watching with a puzzled smile.

"You don't understand, do you?" he said to her.

"I don't know—you're sad?"

"That's fairly accurate, I guess." He saw with surprise that his glass was empty; he had no recollection of drinking the whisky. "Could I have some more water? No objection to my having another drink, eh?"

"No, I will bring it."

While she was away he tried to remember why he had come here, and tried to figure out why he was behaving so preposterously. Awash with self-pity, the scuppers sloshing with maudlin tears. Well, why? But he couldn't think straight, and it wasn't just the whisky, he knew. It was a fear of where his thoughts would take him. Somehow Maria Ruiz and George Delucca were linked together in his mind, coiling and twisting about the same problem. But how did Maria fit into this?

Vaguely, he knew; there might be forgetfulness here, if not salvation. Two wrongs did not make a right, and one sin did not cancel out another, but shame could be erased with a deeper shame.

In his confusion, it seemed to Ford that he had accidentally stumbled on a profound truth. In the human condition, atonement was always readily at hand, for penance was only a matter of self-degradation and the opportunities for self-degradation were, of course, boundless. To be mean, squalid, ignoble, that was no trick at all, he thought; the areas of potential deceit and betrayal stretched about all mankind like a vast, suppurating swamp. I have it now, he thought, one truth, anyway.

When she came back from the kitchen with his glass, half-filled with water, he added whisky to it and sipped the drink slowly. The rationalizations he had constructed so laboriously were already falling apart in his mind, but the effort of trying to think seemed to have cleared his head.

"Did you get my message today?" he asked her.

"At the gas station? Yes. What's he going to do?"

"You mean Buddy?"

"Yes."

Ford paused and sipped a little whisky. He couldn't tell anything from her expression or inflection; she was still smiling at him, but politely now, like a child waiting for an adult to finish a serious story. She seemed younger tonight, he thought, with her hair free and falling like smooth black wings to her shoulders. The angles of her face seemed less harsh, and there was a gentleness and tolerance in her expression that softened the wariness of her eyes. Maybe it's just because the trailer is warmer, he thought. She was wearing only a short-sleeved cotton dress and black loafers, but seemed quite comfortable as she settled back in the chair and locked her hands around her knees. Her arms were very thin, and he saw the slim sharp ridge of her collarbones curving away from the column of her throat. The orange reflections from the stove gave a rosy tone to her bare arms and legs, and touched warm points of light in her eyes. She looks happy, he thought, smiling that way, she looks young and happy. It's because I'm here with the news about Buddy, he realized wearily.

"Buddy's going away," he said. "He's going to New York."

She looked puzzled then. "Going away?"

"That bothers you?"

"How can he go away? He has no money."

"I gave him enough to buy a car and live on until he finds a job."

"But why? He isn't your friend."

"I know, he's your friend. Was he important to you?"

"Important? I don't know. When you have no friends, anyone is important, maybe."

"You have no friends?"

She shook her head quickly. "No, there are Roby and Martha here. And the Clarks. They own this trailer. And Buddy. They are the only people I meet—met since I came from California."

Ford emptied his glass. "This is truly the land of opportunity," he said. "You haven't done badly. Buddy told me you liked him. Is that right?"

"I didn't know him well. I was worried about him, because it was my fault he got in trouble." She looked at him with a new expression; the puzzled smile was gone, and her eyes were alert and wary. "Why do you care? Why are you asking me about it?"

Ford stood and held himself erect with an effort. "I'm sorry, it's none of my business," he said. "If you'll get my coat and hat I'll go. I paid Buddy to clear out of here. Tomorrow I'll tell him to forget about it."

"You pay—paid him to go?"

"That was the condition on which I arranged for his release. I was eliminating competition. I wanted you, and I decided to buy you. But I'm not quite the simpleton that makes me sound. Not quite." Ford's voice was thick and fuzzy in his ears, and the lights in the trailer were flickering weirdly against his eyes. "I'm just out of practice, that's all. I forgot about sending flowers. I forgot that my hair is getting gray at the temples, and that you're twenty-two." Ford swayed as he turned toward the door, and he would have fallen if she hadn't caught his arm. "Thank you, thank you very much." He had never felt so miserable in his life. He was drunk and helpless and disgusted with himself; if he could have apologized to her, or explained himself in any way at all, he would have tried, but he knew he was too sodden to articulate his feelings.

She turned him around, pushing at him gently, and he suddenly found himself sitting on the couch. "I'm sorry, I'm very sorry," he said. "I'm making a nuisance of myself."

"I'll get you coffee. You shouldn't drink any more whisky."

"Yes, I know. I'm sorry."

"It's all right."

He was dimly aware of the slim motion of her body as she hurried into the kitchen. There was an impression of quickness and grace, light flashing on her brown arms and legs, the soft cadence of her moccasins on the linoleum floor, and then —later, he knew, because he was lying on his back—the clatter of a cup and saucer as she leaned over him, frowning faintly, a strand of silky black hair touching her smooth cheek.

"Can you drink some?"

"I'm terribly sorry. I'll go in a minute."

"It's all right. You were drinking too much."

The last thing he remembered was her worried little frown,

112

and the strand of black hair against her cheek. He dreamed that he was in his own home. There was an argument going on, with voices rising like the yelpings of excited dogs, and a woman with sad, injured eyes was shifting unhappily from chair to chair, because someone was throwing darts at her face, tiny darts with suction cups, which struck her flesh with popping little noises before dropping off to the floor. He didn't know who she was but he felt terribly sorry for her. And there was nothing he could do for her.

When he opened his eyes again, his first sensation was weary gratitude for the silence in the trailer. There wasn't a sound. It seemed incredibly quiet. There was no draft roaring up the stovepipe, and he realized that it was cold in the trailer. There was a warm, slight weight against his hip, and when he turned his head he saw that Maria was sitting beside him with her arms folded over her breasts. He saw a reflection of the lamp light in her eyes.

"The coffee got cold," she said. "I can heat it."

"No, don't, Maria. You know why I came here tonight?"

She nodded slowly and he saw the soft swaying motion of her long hair and the flash of light in her eyes.

"There's nothing here but me," she said, and her hands, when she put them against his face, were small and hard, and cold as ice.

CHAPTER 7

THE turning of a doorknob awakened him, and he opened his eyes quickly, blinking them against sunlight, not yet sure where he was, but already feeling the warmth of guilty memories starting up in his body.

Janet came briskly to the side of his bed with a tray of orange juice and coffee.

"Well, you're the night owl, I must say. I went up at eleven, and it seemed ages before I heard you come in. You were noisier than Peter, actually, banging about and showering."

Ford raised himself cautiously on one elbow and looked at his bedside clock. It was ten, and the room—his peaceful familiar room—was bright with sun and fragrant with coffee.

Janet was dressed for the city in a brown tweed suit and yellow blouse. Sitting on the side of his bed, with her long legs crossed and the sunlight heightening the blond streaks in her hair, she looked cleanly and matter-of-factly attractive.

"I had *the* most boring time in Philadelphia last night," she said. "With the Quillings. John is simply reveling in middle age. He's given up sailing. 'At my age, it's become a chore,' *that's* his attitude. He makes dreary jokes about sex being a thing of the past, and he just roared when Evvy and I were talking about Metrecal. What difference does it make how we look? That was his attitude. Where were you last night, by the way?"

Ford drank the fresh orange juice, poured himself a cup of coffee, and tried to collect his splintered thoughts. "We've run into a little snag on the library," he said. "Until the present

114

there's been fairly general agreement that the new site would be about a mile outside Cottersville, in that wooded area near Tinicum that Tony Marshall owns. He's contributing the land, you know. But suddenly the locals are up in arms. They feel their children won't have easy access to it, and they're holding out for a site in the city. Or even more idiotically, they want the funds spent in remodeling and expanding the present building."

"Were you at Tony's?"

"No—but his feeling, and mine, is that spending money on the old library is just damn foolishness." Ford knew Janet had no interest in business matters; already she was looking critically at her nails. He sipped his coffee and went on: "We'll have the same problem again in five or six years, and we wouldn't be able to realize more than fifty per cent of our investment in the present site. There's damn little market for obsolete libraries, but that's a fact of fiscal reality the locals are choosing to ignore."

"It must be tiresome," Janet sighed crisply, commiserating with him but putting the matter at rest. "I've got news! Mother called this morning. Poor thing, she's forgot all about *la crise* of the holidays. She says it was the sweetest time. I think she's being a bit tricky though, because she obviously wants to make up for *something*. You know how obliquely she apologizes! Now she wants us to open the place in Palm Beach for her. She suggested we go down right away and absorb some sun, and she'll join us next month. It's the one thing she thinks she can do for us obviously. I must say, though now *I* sound like John Quilling, I'm getting weary of winter. Wouldn't you like a month of sun and golf?"

"It's a pleasant prospect," Ford said, and sipped the last of his coffee.

"Shall I tell her yes?"

"I'm afraid I can't take the time now," Ford said, and his voice was so unexpectedly firm that she looked at him with one of her girlish grimaces of alarm.

"Heavens! You poor man! What's so urgent here?"

115

Ford poured himself another cup of coffee, and tried to think of a reasonable answer. His mood was a strange one, confused and determined at once, but there was something oddly exciting in the tension caused by contradictory emotions. He felt irritable and impatient and restless, but at the same time quite pleased with himself, and these irreconcilable attitudes seemed to be tightening his nerves and sharpening his senses to a point of almost painful awareness. He felt that he was seeing everything with peculiar clarity, and his skin was so alive and receptive to sensation that the smooth weight of the linen sheet on his flanks was as gratifying as the flesh of a woman.

Last night had been so natural and uncomplicated and—he thought for a word—innocent, that was it, so innocent that he could think about it in his wife's presence without remorse or shame. Somehow it had anesthetized the pain of Delucca's scalding words, and it had left him feeling more confident and cheerful than he had in years. Leaving her trailer in the darkness he had felt like shouting at the faint cold stars, and his mood had been as exultant as a schoolboy's on the first miraculous release from the burdens of virginity.

She had wanted to please him simply and honestly and completely, and he wondered if it had been that flattering submission and attention to his needs which had given a sense of freshness and innocence to his passion, or whether there had been anything else, some tenderness or grace that had made their chance union significant and sustaining.

He didn't know; and he would never know probably, for last night could never happen again. That much he did know; he wouldn't see Maria again. The taboos of his environment were restrictions he not only accepted, but had helped to establish; they stood about him like sturdy columns, and he had no intention of smashing them by rebelliously gratifying the needs of his body.

That he was convinced of, without doubts or reservations. He was certain he would not repeat last night's erratic adventure. But with all this certainty and conviction, there was still

116

an area of confusion in his thoughts. Why was he so stubbornly determined not to go away?

"I simply can't take the time now," he said again to Janet. "There's work at the office, this library thing, and so forth."

"Oh dear! Mother will be crushed. She tries so hard to make the right gesture every now and then."

"Why don't you go down?" Ford was hardly conscious of speaking; the words sounded suddenly in the air, charged with their own life, their own significance.

"Oh, I'd hate to leave you all alone in the frozen north," Janet said, but he knew from her excited little smile that he had given her what she seemed to want most in life, which was the opportunity to submit to and to please her mother.

"It's worth considering," Ford said. "Your mother will be happier if you went, I imagine."

"Could you get down for the odd weekend?"

"Yes, of course."

"All right then, I'll call her." Janet clapped her hands in excitement. "I'll call Peter first, he's at the Thompsons', and then Mother. Ginny's going to Stowe tonight, and then back to school so that's no problem. Oh Ford, are you sure you don't mind?"

"I'll be mildly envious, that's all."

"You are a dear. I've got to rush. Will you be here for supper?"

"Absolutely." His tone was firm. "You can count on it."

After breakfast Ford drove across the Downs to Wiley Poston's place. The snow was gone from the ground, except for irregular patches in the meadows and cornfields, but it looked to him as if more of it was waiting behind the dark clouds moving silently across the sky. And the air was cold and humid, and heavy with the mists rising from soggy leaves and damp earth.

Wiley Poston was shooting trap in the meadow behind his sprawling old home.

"Hold everything," he called, when he saw Ford. "I got forty-six now, and you better not bet I don't get fifty. Pull!"

he yelled to the colored boy who stood behind him, and the boy threw his weight against the lever which sprung the trap twenty-five feet in front of Wiley. From the earthen revetment a clay saucer sailed across the sky, and Wiley swung onto it, the shotgun locked so smoothly and tightly into his shoulder that it seemed like an extension of his heavy body. The gun banged, and echoes rolled down the meadow, and the saucer flew into bits.

"Forty-seven!" Wiley cried happily. In spite of the cold wind there were drops of sweat on his forehead, and his big broad face was flushed with exertion. He waited tensely until the trap was reloaded, and then shouted: "Pull!" Swinging fast on the saucer, he fired and missed, and swore in disgust. "Like I never had a gun in my hand before," he said.

"That's too bad," the colored boy said, smiling at him. "That's too bad, Mr. Poston. But forty-seven, that's good, that's very good."

"I ain't really kicking, Bunny," Wiley said, grinning down at the dark, friendly little face. He pulled the boy close to him and rubbed his back with rough affection. "No sir, I'm not complaining a bit."

From the revetment a dark head appeared. "You through shootin', Mr. Poston?"

"That's enough, I guess. Now you and Bunny clean things up good, you hear? Pick up these cartridge cases and rake up them busted pigeons. Ford, let's go into the box and have ourselves a beer."

The "box" was a small timbered house which Wiley used as a gun and trophy room, and occasionally for beefsteak parties after stag shooting matches. From the inside of the box there was a fine view of the trap, the meadows beyond it, and distant woods standing neatly and formally against the gray sky. Wiley went behind the bar and opened two bottles of beer.

"You know, they're good kids," he said, nodding toward the colored boys policing up the cartridges and broken pigeons around the trap. "John Collins' grandsons. He worked for my daddy till the day he died." Wiley grinned and took a pull

118

from his bottle of beer. "You see that little one, Bunny? He can handle that sixteen-gauge of mine damn near as good as I can. I was working him on my four-ten, but that didn't satisfy him at all. I was afraid it might knock him on his tail, but he kept pestering me so I put a rubber cushion on the butt plate and told him to try his luck." Wiley began to laugh. "Ford, it was funny, that little kid no bigger'n a minute swinging on those birds. I pulled for him all one morning and I was ready to quit before he was. He's going to be a fine shot, you watch."

There was a look of smiling affection and interest on Wiley's face as he looked out at the two boys working around the trap, and it suddenly occurred to Ford how ironical it was that men were so often judged solely by their reactions to crisis; it was the shattering, nerve-wrenching, once-in-a-million threat or debacle that a man had to face heroically, or else be branded forever as a cheat or a coward or a liar.

Men didn't get enough credit, it seemed to him, for years of casual decency, for a friendly and efficient attention to the normal demands of their environment. Comforting aging and difficult parents, tolerating the impatient mistakes of youngsters, tipping a hat to custom and convention, easing the frictions of everyday living with tact and good manners—none of this counted if a man was caught with his hand in the till, or with a friend's wife, or running the wrong way from artillery fire. The world pitied mothers who sobbed that their sons were good boys, the best God ever let live, while those same sons were being tried for rape or murder, but mixed with that pity there was always a certain complacent humor, it seemed to Ford, for the world apparently enjoyed the illogic of people begging to be pardoned for failing the big tests because they had passed certain little ones.

Ford wondered at the direction of his thoughts. He had come here to talk to Wiley about Delucca. Wiley had failed a test there, and so had he, though Wiley wouldn't see it that way. They weren't going to get caught, and that made the big difference. But he also realized that in coming here to warn

Wiley, he was compensating in a way for what he had done last night. He was returning to his own camp.

"Wiley, I stopped by to give you some information," he said. "George Delucca knows what happened with the Henderson place. He knows about the drawing that took place in my home. He knows that you drew the marked ballot, and that you put the pressure on Tom Moran."

"How did you find all this out?"

"He came to my office yesterday. The drawing was held in my home, so he probably thought I was the logical one to talk to."

Wiley was grinning sheepishly. "Old big-mouth, that's me. I get a little tanked up and I kind of run on and on." He shrugged, and finished his beer. Then he said: "So he knows about it. What difference does that make?"

"Unless he goes to court, it probably won't make any difference. But as I said that night, I don't like this business, I don't like it at all. Since it's over and done with, I'd advise you to stop talking about it."

"Hell, you didn't do anything, Ford."

"Neutrality is a commitment, of course," Ford said.

"Now look, why did he go to you? I'm the villain in the piece." Wiley was grinning, but his eyes had narrowed and color was rising in his face.

"I told you, since the drawing was held at my place he assumed I was responsible."

"Let him assume what the hell he wants," Wiley said, and went around the bar to open another bottle of beer. "And let me tell you one thing right now. It's Moran who gave him the shafting. That's right, his buddy, Tom Moran, who kneels down with Delucca every Sunday of the year at St. Patrick's." Wiley pointed a blunt finger at Ford. "Moran could have told me to go to hell. Right?"

"It might have cost him his business," Ford said.

"Never mind about that. He could have said no deal. But all he did was look the situation over very carefully and when he saw what side his bread was buttered on, that's all there

120

was to it. The words 'right' and 'wrong' never got into the conversation. Moran didn't give a damn about the ethics of it. The money mattered, nothing else, so down the drain went his good old pal, George Delucca."

Wiley had a point, Ford realized; Moran might have stood his ground and taken the consequences. Instead he had buckled to pressure and betrayed his friend. The verdict on Moran, if the facts were assayed in court, would be that he was a liar and a fraud, and no one would excuse him because he was an amiable companion in a card game, escorted his old mother to church on Sundays, and denied himself certain pleasures to keep his two daughters in a refined Catholic boarding school. All of this was pleasant but irrelevant; they were the small tests and challenges of life; Moran had failed the big one.

"Let me say one more thing then," Ford said. "Delucca may not take this business to court. It's all hearsay and gossip, there's nothing on paper. But we've made an enemy, and that's something to consider."

"You always take things too seriously," Wiley said, and something about him, the look of him, the hairy forearms, the beefy, smiling face and glinting little eyes, suddenly irritated Ford.

"Delucca knows a good deal about us," he said. "The White Hackle's a handy listening post. People drink and talk. Delucca just listens, I think. That's worth remembering."

"So what the hell does he know?"

"That I was in Naval Administration, for instance. That Tony was on Admiral Finchley's staff."

"Hell, that's no secret. It's in the local paper every time either of you make a contribution, or a speech, or pee into the wind, for that matter."

"He knows you were in Army Procurement," Ford said.

Wiley looked thoughtful. "How'd all this come up?"

"He thinks we picked nice cozy spots for ourselves in the war. To prove it, he's got a little list. And you're down for Army Procurement."

Wiley was staring at him from behind the bar, one big hand clamped about a beer bottle. For a moment he was silent, but a line of tension was appearing about his mouth, and his eyes had become ugly. "So what was he? Some big hero?" he said at last.

"He was a platoon sergeant in the infantry."

"About all the sonofabitch would have the brains for." Wiley looked thoughtfully at Ford. "And you figure it's odd he knows about me? The Army Procurement thing?"

"It's worth thinking about," Ford said.

"Yeah, I guess it is," Wiley said, and drummed his fingers restlessly on the top of the bar.

What was troubling Wiley now—as Ford had known it would—was that only a handful of his close friends knew that he had been in Army Procurement. He had been assigned to the Manhattan Project, not in an important capacity, simply as a purchasing agent, but because every detail of the work was classified, he had been given a cover commission, and cover functions, in the Coast Artillery; and this, even after all the years, was the way most people thought Wiley had spent the war. Delucca's information was disturbing, for it indicated he had a reliable pipeline to Wiley's background, but it was hardly grave enough, Ford thought, to account for the growing anger and suspicion in Wiley's expression.

"So that's what you came here to tell me, eh?" Wiley said in a deceptively gentle voice.

"No, I came here to tell you he knows about the Henderson place."

"Well, I got to believe that," Wiley said slowly. "I don't figure you're trying to tell me anything in a roundabout way. Not your style, I know that."

Ford suddenly remembered, and cursed himself for forgetting, that there had once been some mild gossip about Ellie Poston and George Delucca, and just as suddenly he understood Wiley's anger, and the direction of his thoughts. Wiley would have to wonder now if Delucca's information had come from Ellie. There had been nothing between Delucca and Ellie, no one believed that for a moment. A trivial accident had fanned the rumor, an incident so commonplace that it

122

wouldn't have caused a stir at all if it hadn't involved Ellie Poston. She'd had a flat tire at the White Hackle one night when Wiley was off hunting or fishing somewhere. The night was bad, the road service truck broke down on the way, and Ellie had waited until dawn for it to arrive. Delucca had stayed, too, and they had sat in his office and had a few drinks. When the tire was finally changed, Ellie drove on home. That was all there was to it, but some people wondered why Delucca hadn't changed the tire himself, or had one of his waiters do it, and why had they waited in his office, which was equipped with a couch, as everyone knew, and so forth and so on.

Questions had buzzed about for a week or so, sent flying by Ellie's friends chiefly, but she was too confident, and too attractive, to inspire loyalty; and her friends had taken a harpy's delight in inflating the incident out of all sense and proportion.

Wiley was still frowning thoughtfully at Ford. "Well, thanks for the friendly tip, old pal." He raised his beer bottle in an ironical salute. "I'll study on it. Indeed I will."

Ford drove his wife to the station in Wilmington after the weekend. It was a surprisingly mild day and Janet was in a cheerful mood as she inspected her drawing room. It looked cozy and expensive, with books and magazines in a chair and Ford's roses filling the air with fragrance. "Now don't linger, quoth she," Janet said, and gave him a quick hug. "I'll miss you, so do try to get down soon. Promise?" She drew back from him and smiled brightly into his eyes.

"Yes," he said. "Yes, of course."

That night he had dinner at the country club. After coffee, he lit a cigar and walked out on the terrace to enjoy the soft air. For this time of the year it was freakish weather, as gentle and promising as the first days of spring. There was the smell of damp earth on the wind, a musky, fertile aroma that rose like steam from the muddy bases of the boxwoods that bordered the terrace. The sky was dark and there were faint, lonely stars on the horizon.

From where he stood he could see the flag on the eighteenth green fluttering in a bar of light from the dining room. The fairway stretched away like a huge black tunnel, and even the sand traps were lost in the darkness. The course would be playing well, he thought; and tomorrow he might try the back nine. He could imagine his cleats digging into the spongy earth, the fabric of a flannel shirt smooth against his skin, and the air fresh on his cheeks. It would be very pleasant to spend the whole afternoon here, and then to shower luxuriously and have one or two good Martinis before dinner.

And then what? he thought. To drive away with the car humming powerfully under his hands—driving to what? He realized nervously that all of his thoughts were sensual, and that the name of Maria Ruiz was shining in his mind like a a star. He was appalled to realize how firmly she was fixed in his thoughts. Was it because he was temporarily free from all other responsibilities? Was it just opportunity, luck, good timing? Was that why his hands were suddenly cold, and his heart was beating faster?

No, he knew better. There was no choice for him now but release or frustration, for he had discovered that he still carried within himself the potential of passion. How long had it been lying dormant? Or had it ever really been alive?

A door opened behind him and he heard the click of high heels on the terrace. He turned and saw Ellie Poston coming briskly toward him, a smile lighting her clever, confident face. She wasn't beautiful, or even pretty, but there was an aura of brilliance about her which radiated from a vivid good health and athletically high spirits; as she walked quickly across the terrace, bright yellow hair and glistening teeth shining in the soft illumination, there was a suggestion of challenging strength in the coil of her firm hips and the swing of her long, muscular legs. Her mink was slung like a cape about her shoulders, and there was a gentle glow of pearls at her throat.

"I thought I saw you slip out here," she said, putting a hand lightly on his arm. "What's the matter? Poor boy miss his little Janet already?"

124

"Why naturally," Ford said.

"You're just striking the proper, husbandly attitude. You can't be hunting, so soon. Your glands, or whatever makes men miss girls, they don't work that fast, do they?"

Ellie had a need to make men uncomfortable, Ford thought, as he watched her bold eyes searching his face for reactions. In her arsenal of harassments were long, intent stares, confidences given in breathless whispers, meaningful smiles, and a playful fingering attack on the persons of her male victims. She was forever losing a shoe, a glove, or a wrap, and begging men to retrieve them for her, and she was always alert for situations which held an opportunity for innocent but intimate physical contact; she was a compulsive adjuster of men's ties, a lap-sitter, a shoulder-leaner and knee-nudger, and despite her impeccable grooming, she usually needed a male hand to refasten a bracelet, or a male eye to judge if her slip were showing or her stocking seams were straight.

Ford tossed his cigar over the terrace railing and took out cigarettes to free his arm from the light pressure of her finger-tips.

"Where's Wiley?" he asked, and offered her a cigarette.

"Thanks, I'd love one." She held his hand to guide the flame of his lighter to her mouth. "Wiley, the dear boy, is at the bar getting fried. It's one of his determined nights." She looked serious for a moment. "You saw him this morning. Was he in a foul mood then?"

"He seemed all right."

Ellie sighed. "He's been beating on me all day, for some reason. I don't know what I did. From the way he's acting you'd think I used one of his golf trophies as a chamber pot."

It wasn't that, Ford realized; it was the thought of wearing horns working on Wiley.

"How long will Janet be gone?"

"Six weeks or so, I imagine."

"We can't let you languish all that time. We'll get you a girl. Now what kind would you like?"

"I get a choice, do I? Hellcats from Port Said, great blond

125

Valkyries from the frozen north?"

"Don't worry, this will be strictly platonic. I'm not going to have Janet accusing me of seducing you by proxy. But just for fun, what sort of girl would you want?" She brushed a bit of cigarette ash from his shoulder with a flick of a finger. "Janet's blond and high-strung. Is that what appeals to you? You know, I've often wondered what she's like in bed (if you'll pardon my dirty little mind). Is she all squeals and abandon? Or cool and avant-garde-ish?"

"I think I'll take the Fifth on that."

She laughed. "Ford, I'm embarrassing you."

"I'm merely standing on my constitutional rights."

"Afraid of incriminating yourself? Let me tell you a secret, Ford." She was standing so close to him that he could see the reflections of the terrace lights in her eyes. "The girls think Janet's pretty damned lucky. You're good-looking, you stayed thin, and you kept your hair. You don't drink like Wiley, and you don't bore the bejesus out of everybody the way Harvey Shires does, and you don't run off to New York for fun and games like your brother Clay." She sighed. "I know Janet's a dear, but supposing you had the whole county to choose from, what sort of a girl would make you start pawing the ground?" She tilted her head to one side. "Would she be anything like me, do you imagine?"

"Well, I don't know, Ellie." He tried to strike a tone that was both light and thoughtful, in deference to propriety and also to her feelings, but he was entertained by the odd notion that his experience with Maria Ruiz might have marked him in a way that would alert other women to the fact that he was now at stud. Was he exuding some subtle scent? Or was there a look in his eye, a curve to his lips, that would warn a woman a tomcat was stalking by?

"You don't know?" Ellie smiled ruefully. "There's a flattering reaction."

"It's realistic, at least. I'd have to think of you as if Janet and Wiley didn't exist. And that's impossible."

Someone fumbled at the terrace doors, and Ellie stepped

126

back from Ford as Wiley Poston lurched into sight and stared about like an angry, befuddled bull. Standing with his feet braced to support his weaving body, he shook his head back and forth, ponderously and deliberately. "Goddamn, goddamn," he muttered, in a thick confused voice. "Oh, goddamn."

"Eat something, dear," Ellie said lightly.

"Oh shut up, you bitch."

"That doesn't sound like you, sweetie."

"Who's that? Hi, Ford, old pal. Good old Ford. The tipster. She making a pass at you?"

"I was trying to talk her into going to a motel, but she's not buying it. Very prudish wife you've got, Wiley."

Wiley grinned at him, but there was an ugly, worried glint in the depths of his muddy eyes. "Sure she is, sure she is," he said very slowly and emphatically, as if he were driving home the conclusive point in an argument. "Come on, let's go get a drink."

Ellie took his arm companionably. "I don't want to shock you, dear, but may I mention that dirty, four-letter word called food? It's something people eat. Shall we try some? Just to make it an even once?"

"I don't want to short-circuit this glow. Come on, leave Ford alone. Let's get a drink?"

They went inside together, but at the door Ellie turned and gave Ford a fleeting, intimate smile, and then rolled her eyes despairingly to the heavens.

Ford threw his cigarette away and walked purposefully through the men's lounge to the cloakroom, where old Peter McGuire, the attendant, put aside a copy of the *Saturday Evening Post,* and stood up smiling.

"The Wolters and Colonel Meggs are in the cardroom, Mr. Jackson. They were looking for a fourth a while ago."

"I don't think I'll play bridge tonight, Peter."

Ford spent that night with Maria Ruiz. He woke early in the morning, before there was a sign of light against the windows, and lit a cigarette. The match flared vividly in the darkness. She was lying in the curve of his arm, her dark hair shining and free on his shoulder, and this seemed strange and miraculous to him, as miraculous and mysterious as the fact that she had been waiting for him to come to her last night. The trailer was cold, but her body was warm against him, and he could feel the soft swell of her breasts as they rose and fell with her breathing.

Ford thought she was asleep, but when he moved his arm to tap the ash from his cigarette, she stirred against him, and said: "Do you want anything?"

"No, Maria. Go to sleep, please."

"I can make some coffee."

"No, please."

"I don't want to sleep."

"All right." He felt subdued, and overcome with the weight of his responsibility to her. "Listen to me then. You're a child. I'm a married man twice your age." Ford sighed as he spoke the banal, tiresome words, for they seemed to color the situation with their own drabness and despair. What came next? *We can't go on like this* . . . "Do you want me to come here again?" he asked her.

"Do you want to?"

"Yes, it's all I want. But listen to me, please. Do you know what it will be like? Do you understand? I can't take you anywhere. Not for a walk, or a drive, anything. Do you realize that?"

She sighed sleepily. "You can come here."

"Not always," he said, but she didn't answer him, and he knew from the soft steady rhythm of her breathing that she had fallen asleep. He pulled her close to him, holding her as tenderly as he would a child, and watched with a certain resignation, and a certain apprehension, the first light of the new day shining on the windows.

Later, when he thought back to that first week, to those nighttimes of nearly violent love, he realized that it had been the least significant period in their relationship. They hardly spoke to each other that first week; they had no confidence in

128

words. Their greetings were strained, and the time they spent together over a drink or a cigarette was awkward and difficult. When the dogs yelped around the trailer it was almost a relief, for their ludicrous yelpings at least broke the uneasy silences that stretched between them. Their only communion was sexual; only that basic act was strong enough to bridge the lonely distance that separated them. But later, when he thought of that week, it was always with a tragic sense of loss. For he had hardly talked to her, or looked at her, and he had been relieved when she turned the lights off and there was no longer a need to pretend that their relationship was anything but physical. Then, locked against her slender, straining body, he could forget who he was and where he was, and lose himself in the selfish gratification of his needs.

He had no idea of what she was thinking or feeling, in fact he had no curiosity about her at all, and it came as a blunt surprise when she told him one morning that she couldn't see him that night.

"But why?"

"It's Saturday. I am going to confession. For communion tomorrow."

"Oh, I see. You'll tell the priest, and he'll forgive you?"

"I think so."

At first he had been amused; he could imagine her whispering her indiscretions against the latticework of the confessional, and a weary father of the church waving her sins away, welcoming her back to grace. She was such a little simpleton, he thought, such perfect material for a religion of mumbo jumbo, and black-and-white absolutes. But as he thought about it further, his mood changed from good-humored indulgence to one of sharp irritation. What right did she have to discuss their relationship with anyone else? And then he saw a trap opening at his feet. Supposing the priest asked her with whom she was sleeping? Would Maria tell him? He didn't know if this was part of the ritual or not. But what bothered him most, he realized at last, was that she thought of their relationship as sinful. This was oddly deflating. He had been guilty

about seeing her, for it violated the standards of his background and training, but it came as an unpleasant surprise to realize that she had felt the same way.

Ford stayed home Saturday night, and he was so irritated with her he decided to stay home Sunday night, too. The weekend, however, dragged on endlessly. He went to devotions Sunday at St. James Episcopal, where Canon Smathers, resplendent in a snowy surplice, preached a homely sermon on the evil effects of television on children. "An hour spent viewing a series of tasteless dramatic situations is truly a double waste of time, for in addition to squandering one's attention on an illuminated box of mediocrities, one has also lost the chance to employ that time more profitably—even if only whacking a ball about under God's cheerful sky, if not in more pointedly cerebral pursuits."

Ford rode in the afternoon, taking the Blackbird over a half-dozen miles of rough hunting country, and when he came home the big mare was blowing hard, but he was alert and stimulated, his cheeks stinging from the cold winds, and his body lightened and freshened by the exercise. Catherine was happy that he was staying in.

"You going out every night, Mrs. Jackson think I'm neglecting you."

Ford soaked himself for half an hour in a hot tub, letting the pleasant tiredness flow from his body, and then he got into an old tweed suit and went down to the living room. He made a Martini and stretched out in the deep chair before the fire, feeing quite drowsy as he sipped his drink and watched the flames leaping up from the oak logs. The house was so still that he could hear the soft ticking of the grandfather's clock in the foyer, and when Catherine called him for dinner he sat up with a start, for in the comfortable silence with the heat and light of the fire on his face, he had drifted into a peaceful half-awake state that was as anesthetic as the deepest sleep.

But after dinner this benign torpor deserted him. Pacing restlessly, and smoking one cigarette after another, he attempted to analyze the specific reasons for his sudden impa-

130

tience. She would be at the trailer now, he thought irritably. Soul glowing with purity. God, it was absurd! The ugly smirches of their carnal explosions cleaned away by a magical wave of the priest's hand. Was that what she really believed?

At least, he thought, she must believe that she had committed a sin by going to bed with him, and this was what angered him. Why drag him into it? He was a stranger to her cult, he wanted no part of its intricate morasses of guilt and fear, he didn't want to be involved in any way at all, either as a partner in crime or the innocent instrument of her defections. His own guilt was more rational than hers. He was certain of that. He knew precisely what laws he was breaking, what taboos he was violating, while her fear stemmed from a blend of black magic and pagan superstitions.

On a sudden impulse he strode down to his study and looked up the Roman Catholic Church in the encyclopedia. There was a great deal about it, a great deal more than he wanted to know, he thought irritably. Origin, History, Orders—it was endless. With a cigarette cocked upward in his mouth, he flipped through the pages of small print, looking hopefully for a heading which might conceivably relate to his problem. But the quest was futile, because he didn't know what his problem was. He wasn't interested in the morality of their relationship. His exasperation with her was rooted in physical needs; he was too honest to diagnose his torment as a spiritual ache.

He was angry because her church had cheated him out of a night with her, and because his own stubbornness had cheated him out of still another. All he could think of was the feel of her body, the tense muscles in her thighs, the curve of her breast, the silky down on her slender legs. He didn't give a damn whether she thought their pleasure was sinful. Something he hadn't known he possessed was now possessing him: the full and powerful capacity for passion. All of his nerves seemed laid bare for a stroke of pleasure, and his whole body was awake and alert to sensual stimulus. The warmth of the room, the leaping flames, the heavy softness of the rug, the smooth chamois shirt on his back, they all made him think of the trailer, the girl, the relief waiting for him there.

He made up his mind to go to her, but as he was pulling on his overcoat, the phone in the study began to ring. He hesitated a second, tempted to ignore it, but he realized that Catherine would take it in the kitchen, and run after him to the parking lot whether the message was important or not, so he turned into the study and picked up the receiver.

It was his sister-in-law, Alicia, but her voice was so odd and high that he couldn't make out what she was saying.

"Hey, hold on," he said. "What's the matter?"

"Please, Ford, could you come here right away? For God's sake, please! I think Clay's gone completely out of his mind."

"Now take it easy," he said. "What's he been up to?"

"Please, I'm frightened," she cried, and her voice was so soft and desperate that it sent a chill down his spine.

"All right, Alicia. I'll be right over. Just take it easy."

CHAPTER 8

THERE was no traffic on the Downs, and he was at Clay's home in less than five minutes. Lights streamed from both floors, and shadows moved sluggishly across the driveway, as the trees bordering it twisted under a rising wind. Alicia must have been listening for his car, for she pulled open the front door of the house as he hurried up the walk from the parking circle. When he came into the foyer, she said, "I'm sorry I had to call you, Ford, but there wasn't anybody else."

"Never mind that. What's the trouble? What's he done?"

"I don't know what's wrong with him. He's upstairs in his room now—he either fell asleep or passed out. I couldn't manage him before. I was afraid he'd hurt himself." She was speaking quite calmly, in a clinical voice, as if she were discussing the symptoms of a stranger, but Ford saw the way her hands were clenched at her sides, and he knew she was making a desperate attempt to keep herself under control.

He patted her shoulder gently. "Come on, let's relax. While he's sleeping we can talk things over peacefully. What sort of foolishness was he up to?"

"I understand the zeal of temperance workers a bit better now," she said, as they walked down the corridor to the glass-walled living room, and it wasn't a flippant comment, Ford realized; she was in dead earnest. "If I had an ax I might go looking for some saloons to hack up. You'll think I started at home, from the look of things. But this is Clay's work—or therapy, I don't know which."

Ford stopped in the archway of the glass-walled wing, dismayed by the appearance of the room. The place looked as if it had been struck by a storm; two sofas were tipped upside down, their stiff legs pointing at the ceiling like those of dead animals, and most of the pictures had been torn from the walls and piled in a heap in the middle of the floor. Some of the canvases were ripped and shredded in a way that clearly suggested a fist or foot had done the damage, and their frames had been smashed into grotesque, crazily angled patterns. The fire tongs were lying under the coffee table, and there was a Daliesque design of empty bottles and broken glasses tangled up with a bunch of fresh roses in the seat of a leather chair.

"For God's sake, did he do this?"

"Yes, it's his way of releasing inhibitions." She sounded tired, and almost bored, now. "Children have tantrums and throw rattles. But he's got a whole big house to rip apart."

Ford felt as guilty and embarrassed as if he had been the one who had torn the room to pieces. He straightened the sofa and fire tongs, but when he began to pick up the broken glass, Alicia sighed and said impatiently: "Don't bother, Ford. I'll take care of it later." She sat down in the deep chair beside the fireplace, stretched out her legs, and put her head back wearily. "It just doesn't matter. He doesn't give one sweet damn. Why should I?"

Ford was troubled by her listlessness. He would have felt less worried if she were furious or disgusted or contemptuous. But her resignation lent an ominous finality to the situation. Normally she was so alert and spirited, so competent in conversations or arguments, that it gave a pleasantly provocative tone to her personality; but now she looked as if all capacity for feeling or caring had been squeezed from her slight body. As she settled deeper into the chair, with her legs crossed and her eyes focused indifferently on the ceiling, Ford wondered suddenly if Clay had any notion of what he was doing to her. Didn't he have eyes? Or didn't he care? He was grinding her down to nothing, destroying her confidence, her capacity to feel or care about anything. Was he too callous or too stupid to realize that? It seemed incredible. Everyone who knew them envied Clay; particularly the men. They all realized he had picked himself something from the very top drawer. Even now, Ford thought, with her face still, and her eyes looking wearily at nothing, there was something challenging in her very indifference; with the firelight touching her neat ankles, and glowing softly about her smooth hair and quiet face, there was a wistfulness about her that was oddly disturbing; she was like a little girl who had missed the biggest party of all, he thought, a little girl who had planned to go as naturally as she planned to draw her next breath, but who nevertheless was sitting home along with golden bracelets as heavy as fetters on her wrists, too stunned to cry, to hurt to feel anything anymore.

He sat down and lit two cigarettes. "Now when did this thing start?"

"It seems pointless to talk about it," she said, but as she took the cigarette she gave him a sudden, wry smile. "That sounds stupid, of course. I called you like a keening spinster, so I must have wanted to talk. Well, let's see." She nodded about the room. "This started about an hour ago. Before that, there was a leisurely build-up. And much of it was quite pleasant. What I mean is, the day started fine. He played badminton this afternoon and came home about four in a very sweet and sunny mood. The maids are out and he decided to make a production of dinner. Steak broiled over apple logs in the fireplace, salad with black olives and tomatoes and Parmesan, baked Idahoes with sour cream and chives. Oh, it was going to be the biggest, fattest dinner served in the whole state of Pennsylvania tonight. But first we must have two, mind you, just two, very cold, and oh-so-dry Martinis." Alicia looked down at the backs of her hands. "I said fine. I'm tired of sounding like his den mother. But two Martinis didn't do the job.

"He made a long funny speech about how the human liver is a masochist, and unless you punish it with liquor it's apt to sulk. And then he sneaked a drink while he was stirring up

135

the second batch, and he drank most of that himself, and by then the evening wasn't looking so cheerful." Alicia frowned faintly. "You know, it's like throwing a switch. Suddenly, between one breath and the next, he's out of reach—absolutely gone. One second he was talking a lot of cheerful nonsense, and the next thing he was yelling at me as if I were God's greatest slut. He can't mean everything he says, but the words stick to me like ticks or maggots. I wake at night and think of them, and it makes me want to vomit."

"I think he's got to see a psychiatrist," Ford said. "Have you ever suggested that?"

"Yes, I have. But when he sobers up he's very boyish and contrite, but also very stubborn. He claims he doesn't remember what he said or did, and he can't bear to discuss it. He feels badly enough, he insists, without getting the chapter and verse read to him, and he swears he's turning over a new leaf and won't touch so much as a drop of wine in the future, and so on."

She stopped speaking and glanced up nervously. From the second floor there was the sound of a door clicking shut; then footsteps moved above them. "Don't tell him I called you," she whispered quickly.

"Alicia?" It was Clay's voice, cheerful and thick, but Ford sensed a thread of suspicion coiling under its bright surface.

"Yes, Clay. Come on down. Ford's here."

"Well, he picked a bad time to drop in, unless he's got a dump truck to clear up the debris."

He came quickly down the stairs; they could hear the brisk, graceful rhythm of his footsteps. Ford got up as Clay came into the room.

"Now no lectures, no recriminations," Clay said, shaking his head like a groggy fighter. "Can't stand it just now. But I will answer all reasonable questions." With a comically stern gesture, he pointed at the torn canvases and broken frames heaped on the floor. "They offended me! I got sick of their whimsy-whamsy impressionistic gloom, so I put them out of their misery. Next question? I tipped over the furniture

136

for the same reason that mountains get climbed—because they were there! Of the broken glasses and bottles, I have no knowledge. My suspicion is that they're the work of mercenaries sent out by the Steuben Glass people." Turning then, he smiled at Alicia, but through the smile Ford could see a look of helpless anguish about his eyes. "So shall we consider the subject closed now? Forget our childish pranks, and concentrate on having a nice drink all around? Ford? What would you like?"

"I don't think I care for anything just now."

"Very well. Then Alicia and I will have to drink alone. That's what's happened to us, you know. We sit on the floor with a bottle of sticky peppermint schnapps between us, and we drink from tiny glasses and giggle like naughty children. Fine thing, eh?"

Clay's eyes were clear, Ford saw, and except for a few strands of hair falling over his forehead, he seemed in good shape. In tweeds and a red flannel shirt, he looked the picture of a proper young country gentleman, calmly sure of himself, calmly ready to enjoy the pleasures of his home on a winter's evening. But it was impossible to judge his condition from his appearance; Clay could erase the effects of a weekend of drinking with a few hours' sleep, and no matter what strains he put on his lean hard body, it always snapped back into shape as if it were constructed of leather and whalebone. But Clay's nerves betrayed him; he couldn't relax after he had been drinking heavily, and now he was pacing about, smiling obliquely at Alicia and fiddling with the buttons of his coat.

His seemingly aimless pacings brought him to the bar. "So Alicia?" he asked her. "What's it going to be?"

"Nothing, thanks."

Clay turned and looked at Ford. "You mind if I help myself?"

"For what it's worth, I think you've had enough."

"Do you now? I'm glad to have your solemn views on the subject." Clay dropped ice cubes into a tall glass, added two jiggers of whisky and a splash of water. "I'll file them with

Dad's advice about not playing cards with strangers."

"Will you listen to me a minute?" Ford said quietly. "Just put down that glass and listen?"

"No thank you." Clay grinned and saluted him with the glass. "Thanks all to hell, but no thanks. I don't intend to put the drink down. And I don't intend to hear any sermons."

"I didn't drop by here casually," Ford said, but he regretted the remark at once, for Alicia shook her head quickly at him, and he realized that Clay had noticed her reactions.

"Now what's all this?" Clay said slowly. "Just what in hell do you mean, Ford?"

"It won't help," Alicia said, looking steadily at the growing anger in Clay's face. "Never mind, Ford. It doesn't matter."

Clay retreated a step, and then another, until his back was flat against the wall. He tried to smile, but the effort twisted his features into a grimace of pain. "She called you, eh?" he said to Ford. "Is that it?"

Ford was wrenched by the shame and humiliation in his brother's expression. Every line in his face seemed to have been etched there by guilt and pain; he had pressed himself against the wall, and turned his head sharply away from them, and his twisted body and corded neck suggested a man in chains and fetters, naked and vulnerable under the eyes of his persecutors.

Ford knew there was nothing he could say or do that would ease his brother's misery. Clay had to help himself; this was all his fault, but Ford loved him in spite of that, and he almost hated Alicia for being here and seeing him this way, for knowing what she did about him, and for being connected in any way at all with his torment. "I'm not going to bore you with lectures and sermons," he said gently. "Alicia called me because she was worried about you, afraid you might hurt yourself. I don't blame her, Clay. And you won't either, when you get hold of yourself."

"She called you, goddamn it," Clay said, his voice rising hoarsely. "She called you!" He pointed a trembling finger at Alicia. "You want everyone to know! You want pity! Dear

138

Alicia! Poor Alicia! Saddled with a drunk. But so brave and uncomplaining!" Clay began to laugh, but the sound was like a sob. "And who else did you call? Your father? Your friends? The *New York Times?*"

"Oh dear God, stop it," Alicia said wearily.

"Now you appeal to me! Now you want me to take you off the hook. 'Dear God, stop it!'" He mimicked her accents with savage accuracy. "You love the first round, don't you? Then you cry for help."

"Hold on," Ford said sharply. "She called me because you were behaving like a madman. You should be grateful to her for giving a damn one way or the other."

"Ah yes, I expect I should be grateful," Clay said, with a bright, mocking smile. "Sweet Alicia! Always considerate, always gentle. I drink to your charms." He emptied the glass with long deliberate swallows, and then hurled it violently against the wall. The sound was explosive; fragments of glass flew about the room like bright hysterical insects, and then scattered onto the floor with a noise that was like the splintering of thin ice.

In the silence that followed there was only the sound of Clay's ragged breathing.

"Now you're behaving like a spoiled child," Ford said coldly.

"Which is precisely what she wants you to believe," Clay said. "There's only one side to the story, and that's dear Alicia's. Look at her!" He crossed unsteadily to where she was sitting and shook a finger in her face. "There she sits! Pretty, eh? Fragile, eh? The delicate triumph of French governesses and fine schools and a father who thinks she's only slightly more heroic than Joan of Arc."

"Will you stop it?" Alicia said, in a dry, careful voice.

"But I'm merely complimenting you, my sweet? Isn't that what you want? Affection, tenderness, love—haven't I heard you begging for all that lately?"

"Perhaps," Alicia said, in the same dry and careful voice. "Does that make me unnatural?"

"Oh, you're natural enough, don't worry about that. You're

right in step with all the other bitches in the county. You want to run everything. You want your men jumping up and down like monkeys on a stick. You've got just one weapon, and that's your perfumed little bodies and your hatful of bedtime tricks. You use your sex like a lasso, jerking back any poor bastard who tries to bolt for it. You—"

"Stop it!" Alicia screamed, and leaned forward until her forehead touched her knees. "God, stop it," she cried faintly, and her desperate breathing was like that of someone who had been struck cruelly and unexpectedly in the pit of the stomach.

Ford caught Clay's shoulder, and pulled him around to face him. "Shut up now, shut up," he said. "I don't want another word from you."

Alicia stood and ran from the room, with the back of one hand pressed tightly against her mouth, and Clay looked after her with a faint, lopsided smile.

"Now Ford, don't be upset," he said. "You should be here when we pitch a real one. This just qualifies as a minor skirmish." He raised his eyes to the ceiling, but there was no sound of Alicia's footsteps on the stairway, or on the floor above their heads.

Ford walked to the archway of the room, and saw Alicia crossing the foyer with a fur coat slung about her shoulders, and one hand still pressed tightly against her mouth. There was something desperate and fearful in the sound of her high heels on the floor, and the straining sob that seemed to be trying to tear itself from her throat. She jerked the door open and the wind blew her hair into tangles. For an instant she hesitated, shaking her head hysterically, and then she stepped into the night and pulled the door shut behind her with a crash that echoed noisily through the house.

Clay turned uncertainly toward the sound, an expression of alarm spreading over his flushed face, as slowly as ripples moving on the surface of a sluggish pond.

"She go out?" he said, in a thick puzzled voice.

"Yes, she's gone," Ford said.

140

"Stop her," Clay said weakly. "Oh, please stop her, Ford. Please stop her."

They heard a car start up in the driveway, and Clay sat down heavily on the arm of a chair and put his hands over his face.

"Please stop her, please," he said, but by then the sound of the motor was already fading in the night.

"She's got good reasons for leaving," Ford said. "Why should I stop her?"

"I know, I know," Clay said in an anguished voice. "But help me, Ford. I'd die if she left me."

"I don't think there's anything funny about this, but that's a funny comment, if you'll forgive my saying so. You chased her out, don't you realize that? Are you too drunk to remember what you said?"

"I didn't mean any of it. I don't mean to act like this. I love her, Ford. Help me, please help me!"

"O.K., I'll help you," Ford said. "I'll tell you what a hundred-dollar-an-hour psychiatrist would tell you. Stop drinking. Will you do that?"

"Yes, I swear it, Ford. Please believe me."

"O.K., I'll help you up to bed. You need some rest, and a few weeks on the wagon, before you can think this thing out clearly."

"Will you wait here till she comes back? Please, Ford." Clay's voice had become so thick and tired that words blurred together in a nearly incoherent croon. "Tell her I'm going to try. Tell her I love her. God, don't let me lose her! Please, Ford."

"Sure, sure," Ford said gently, and pushed a strand of hair away from Clay's eyes. "Don't worry. I'll wait and talk to her."

Clay was as docile as a repentant child, and Ford had no trouble in giving him aspirin, and getting his clothes off, and finally rolling him into bed. After snapping out the lights, he went downstairs and tidied up the mess in the living room. He made himself a mild drink then, and looked through the Sunday papers, but after a while he put them aside and stared into the dying fire. He could not help wondering if this pain and bitterness was some kind of visitation on him, a tribute exacted by God or fate for the affair he had begun with Maria Ruiz. But he was too logical, and too comfortably agnostic, he realized, to accept that; Clay's problems were Clay's: they couldn't be the result of a divine lottery based on the turn of mystical wheels of compensation.

The night moved slowly, prodded by the mournful quarters struck from the clock in the foyer. At twelve-thirty Ford was yawning, and he knew there was little point in waiting any longer for Alicia. She must have stopped at one of her friends for the night.

There was nothing more he could do now, but he was reluctant to leave, for he knew something was wrong here, something he couldn't analyze or understand, and it frightened him.

He shuddered uncomfortably when he went outside, for the cold winds and slowly moving shadows raised a prickly goose flesh on his body, and the sensation reminded him of a fear he had known in his childhood, when he had been swimming at night at the shore, and had felt a sudden movement near him in the water, and then cold eddies swirling about his legs.

You knew something had crossed your wake then, something alien and possibly dangerous, but you couldn't see it, and you had no desire to feel around for it, so you headed back to the beach as fast as possible, hoping that whatever it had been wasn't circling through the darkness to make another run across your course.

That was his mood driving home that night, but the next morning, after calling Clay, his world seemed to fall back into safe and orderly focus. Clay was Clay, after all, plainly indifferent to normal restraints and conventions, but hearing his cheerfully rueful voice on a clear sunny morning made this seem much less ominous than it had last night.

"I obviously broke all records for knotheaded behavior," Clay said lightly. "Do you think maybe there's a future for me in horror movies? Seriously, Ford, I'm grateful to you, and fried as I was, I remember what you said about drinking. And

142

from now on, I'm going to be the dryest-worthiest, nondrink-ingest burgher in the whole community."

"That's the spirit." He paused, and then said: "How's Alicia?"

"Well, the climate is cool, but I see faint signs of better weather on the horizon. I know I was a sorry mess last night, and so does she, so we've got that much in common. But things will work out. I guarantee you that."

"I'm sure they will. But watch the drinking."

"Like a hawk." Clay laughed softly. "And how many drunken hawks do you remember seeing around these parts?"

Ford drove off to his office in a good humor. The day was brilliant, and an optimist could sense the presence of spring waiting in the wings on a morning like this; the sky was blue, the sun was bright as a golden plate, and where it splashed through the bare limbs of the red maples it was easy to im-agine that the color was caused by new buds flowering into leaf in tones of amber and bronze.

That afternoon he bought a portable television set, and that night he drove to Maria Ruiz's trailer. He knew she would be waiting for him; there was no reason for this conviction, none at all, but a certainty stemmed intuitively from the sing-ing excitement in his blood.

She was wearing an imitation flower in her hair, but her eyes were solemn and anxious.

"Last night—" she said, and made a nervous little gesture with her hands instead of finishing the sentence.

"I couldn't, Maria. I wanted to be with you, but I couldn't."

"I thought you were mad about me going to church."

"No, it wasn't that. Please believe me."

She saw the television set then, and the solemn look disap-peared magically from her face. It touched Ford to see the child take possession of the woman so instantly.

"Can we plug it in here? Can we watch it?" She pressed her hands to her cheeks in a gesture of wonder and excitement. "Could it work here?"

"Sure it will. That's why I brought it. It's for you, Maria."

She studied his face anxiously. "For me? Won't you watch it, too?"

"Yes, we'll both watch it."

"What shows do you like to watch?"

He couldn't help smiling at her attempt to include him in this good fortune. "I'll watch whatever you like."

"We'll watch together. Can I plug it in now?"

"Yes, sure."

Ford sat on the studio couch, and watched as she knelt quickly to plug in the set behind the lamp table, and as he studied the curve of her spine and the flex of muscles in her slim arms and legs, he had the sudden and uneasy feeling that he was in the presence of a stranger. She seemed to fill the air with the radiant excitement of youth. All the light in the trailer was drawn to her quick, slender body. He was dazzled by her energy and animation, but he felt oddly depressed and worried, for this childishly eager creature seemed to have no connection with the awkward and uncommunicative girl he had slept with the week before, and on whose body he had spent his passion in self-engrossed frenzies.

But when she stood after plugging in the set, the illusion of strangeness vanished. She seemed to sense his distress then, and the child and woman became one as she took his face in her hands and smiled tentatively at him.

"What's the matter? You look so sad."

"No, nothing's wrong."

"Why couldn't you come here last night? Is it because of any trouble?"

"Yes, but it doesn't concern us."

"Is it about money?"

"No, but a friend of mine needs help."

"You shouldn't think about him here. I mean, you shouldn't worry here. O.K.?"

She sounded so crisp and maternal then that Ford couldn't help laughing at her, but she seemed so hurt and baffled by this that he took her in his arms and held her until she was smiling again. Then she scrambled up and turned on the television.

He learned more about her in the next week, but the picture he was able to put together with the bits and pieces of information she gave him remained tantalizingly streaked and incomplete. She never talked about herself unless he asked her a direct question, and then in such a rambling fashion, and with such little emotional emphasis and chronological order, that it was like listening to a cheerful but distracted child chattering in his ear. She had been in the States for about eighteen months, and had spent most of that time in Florida and California. Her home was outside San Germán, Puerto Rico, where her father and two of her brothers worked as farm laborers. The third brother was a clerk in a leather goods shop in San Juan. She had been to the United States once before with her mother. She had been five then, and wasn't sure whether they had gone to Florida or New York. She had a remarkable capacity for living in the present, it seemed to Ford, for her past apparently held no claims on her, and when she talked of sugar mills or cane fields or streams she knew, it was as if she were discussing things she might have seen or read about long ago in a child's picture book.

But when he attempted, clumsily and ineptly, to establish some sort of financial relationship with her, he discovered a strange layer of sensitivity beneath the passively cheerful surface of her personality. By that time, they had settled into a routine, without discussion or deliberation. He came to the trailer at night around seven, with things for supper: steaks, chops, delicatessen cole slaw and potato salad. She was a serious, determined, but quite bad cook, and while she fussed around in the small kitchen, punctuating each crisis with shrill wails of distress, Ford made himself a drink and watched the news on television. He did not attempt to analyze or understand their relationship. For him this was a moment of peace in a vacuum. There had been cheerful notes from Janet, Peter,

145

and Ginny, things seemed to be going well with Clay and Alicia, and there were few demands on his time other than casual dinner invitations from friends who assumed he was living a quiet bachelor's life. These he had put off with one excuse or another, and he had allayed Catherine's gloomy concerns about him by packing her off for a two-week visit to relatives in Lynchburg.

When he was with Maria he was content, and he thought of nothing else. He enjoyed eating with her, for he was amused by her childish appreciation of food, and he enjoyed postponing the hours of darkness, for when he was ready to leave in the morning it always seemed that the night had slipped by him somehow, the time telescoped into mere fragments of intensity and excitement.

He knew she had no money, and he decided to do something about it. But he found himself reluctant to bring the matter up. A man with more dash or experience, he thought, wouldn't shilly-shally around this way. But he was afraid of offending her, or of startling her, and he was also afraid—he admitted honestly—of securing their relationship with what might be firm contractual bonds. When it was over, when he had to leave her, what then? If he gave her an income, she might, reasonably enough, expect the rights of any other employee. Two weeks' notice, severance pay, letters of recommendation!

But now his responsibility was minimal; he owed her nothing, he had made her no promises, he hadn't changed her way of life, or spoiled her with gifts or money. But he despised himself for these cautious rationalizations. The fact was, he did owe her something, and he was responsible for her; he couldn't take what she offered so generously, and then hurry off with his coat collar turned up like some middle-aged lecher bolting in shame from a whorehouse.

He put off the issue another week, meanwhile rehearsing speeches which usually began, "Since I've more experience than you, my dear—" or "My judgment is sounder than yours, believe me—" but these were such obviously debatable points that his legal faculties rejected everything he added to them.

146

Finally he became so embarrassed and exasperated that he plunged into the subject without any preamble.

"Maria, you don't have any money, do you?"

She was sitting cross-legged on the studio couch facing the glowing square of the television screen. She was watching the Three Stooges. One was trapped in a wooden box and the other two were attempting to extricate him with chain saws.

"Maria!" he said.

"Oh look at them," she said. "Look at them." She was giggling helplessly. "Watch them!"

At this point, to his relief, there was a commercial and Maria let herself fall backward on the couch, still laughing helplessly. "Oh, they are so crazy, so crazy," she said.

"I want to talk to you a minute."

"All right. But I'm going to have hiccups."

"You don't have any money, do you?"

"Just a little." She was breathing hard from laughing so much, and her slight chest rose and fell rapidly. For a moment she was silent, and he couldn't guess at her expression; in the glow of the television screen her face was only a small pale blur. She lay perfectly flat on the couch as motionless as a slim white statue except for the shallow rise and fall of her breasts. "Why?" she said at last. "Why do you want to know?"

"I didn't mean to upset you," he said. "It's just that I know you don't have any money, and I'd like to do something about it."

"I don't want you to."

"But listen, you're not working."

"That's all right."

"We'll call it a loan, if you like. Couldn't you agree to that?"

"No, I don't want you to give me any money. I've got a job anyway. At the Esso Station. Copying accounts in a book."

"Supposing the people who own this trailer come back? You'd have nowhere to go."

"That's all right."

"It's not all right," he said irritably. "How many free trailers do you think there around here? Roby and Martha live in the first one. Who's in the middle?"

"An old man. Luis. He works in a mushroom place."

"Very well. Where would you go then?"

"Somewhere else. It's all right."

"Stop saying everything's all right, over and over again, like a little fool. Everything's not all right, and I want to do something about it."

"You can shout, but I won't take any money."

"I'm sorry, Maria." He suddenly felt quite helpless; he could sense her antagonism and it made him uneasy. "No, listen, please," he said quickly, and when he stood to snap on a lamp, and turn off the chattering television set, he realized his hands were trembling slightly. "I just wanted to help you. If you don't want me to, we won't talk about it anymore. But I don't understand your attitude."

"Maybe I don't either," she said, but he knew she wasn't telling him the truth, for in the lamplight he could see a sad little frown shadowing her eyes.

The thin white dress she wore was molded to the curves of her slight figure, and it gleamed like ivory against her bare brown arms and legs. And as he looked down on her, seeing the thick hair spread like a loose dark frame about her small face, he was suddenly swept with a frightening premonition of loss. He sat down beside her quickly, but when he put his hands on her shoulders, driven by an urgent need to touch her, to satisfy himself of her physical presence, he felt her body stiffen slightly. "What's the matter?" he said helplessly. "Please tell me what's the matter."

"Let me go," she said, her thin shoulder twisting against the pressure of his hands.

He moved away from her, confused and hurt by her reaction, but after she sat up and pulled her skirt down, she confused him still more by putting her head on his shoulder, and rubbing her cheek gently against the hard fabric of his jacket. "You don't understand," she said, in a low voice. "You don't understand at all."

"No I don't, dear," he said, but there was no comfort in the

148

admission; he simply felt very weary and very unhappy. But when he took her in his arms, she clung to him with fierce strength, her fingers digging painfully into his upper arms. "What is it?" he asked her helplessly. "What have I done to you? Do you think I was trying to buy and pay for you, like something over a counter?"

"No, please." She drew back from him until he could see the light shining in her eyes. "You don't have to come here," she said as gently and tenderly as if she were speaking to a troubled child. "I don't have to wait here. That's what I want. Just to have it like this. Don't you understand?"

"No, no I don't," he said, almost angrily, as if the very force of the words could sweep away the implication of hers; but he knew in his suddenly tired and lonely heart that he was lying to her, lying to himself; he understood clearly now. She wanted no ties, no claims on her, she wanted to be free to say good-by to him with an easy conscience. The irony of it was beautiful, as fitting and inevitable as an elegant equation in pure mathematics.

The trailer was warm, and the draft made a soft steady roar in the silence. In the lamplight he could see all the details of her cleanly angled features, and watch her strange, defiant eyes as they moved slowly to study his face.

"You're angry now?" she said, and touched his cheek with her thin cool fingers.

"No, not angry. Not that."

He had known it would end, of course; he had known that this was only a brief reprieve from frustration, a temporary release from passions he had hardly known he possessed; and, in a clinical fashion, he had imagined how it all would be, the last words, the smiles, the wave from a doorway, the tears even —he had thought of these things carefully, knowing they were inevitable, knowing with complete certainty that he would never risk his position, his family, who he was and what he was, to continue seeing this girl; but he had never guessed it would end at her decision, abruptly, unexpectedly, between one sentence and the next, and leave him with a feeling of loss and loneliness that was close to terror.

"Nothing's different," she said, watching his face and eyes. "You shouldn't be sad here."

"I know. I'm not."

"Can I make some coffee? Do you want some?"

"No, I don't think so." He took her hands and kissed them. "Do you?"

She smiled and shook her head, and the lights in the trailer shone in her thick black hair.

In the night she told him about her job; it was part-time work, two hours a day, three days a week, posting credit bills in a master ledger. Her handwriting was excellent, she told him with serious pride, and they were paying her ten dollars each week.

It was a significant amount, he thought wearily; it was enough to keep her free.

CHAPTER 9

FORD spent a miserable day in his office. The routine was exasperatingly dull, and the demands on his time and attention seemed endless. He couldn't concentrate on anything but Maria. If he could take her away, he thought, find her an apartment somewhere, in Philadelphia, or New York or Baltimore, then perhaps he could see her on a permanent basis. He had known of men who had done this sort of thing, organized their lives around two homes, juggling propriety and passion with the aid of intricate timetables, fast cars, last-minute train connections, plus, he thought wearily, the knack of lying like a trooper, and making damn sure that the appropriate personality, reactions, nicknames, and all the rest of it, stayed securely locked up in their proper compartments. It was perfect work for a certified schizophrenic, he decided hopelessly. Not for him. . . .

In the afternoon Harvey Shires called him about the spring race that was held every year to raise funds for Miss Crane's School.

"Ford, I've put everything aside to get the point-to-point rolling smoothly. I'll need help, of course, that's why I'm calling you. My feeling is, get the jump on this sort of thing early, wrap it up in one neat package before it gets out of hand." He laughed briskly and efficiently, almost as if he feared some shrewd rationing agency was keeping a careful account of these humorous punctuations. "Now: you're a two-bird-with-one-stone man, right?"

"What's that?" Ford was still wincing from Harvey's carefully expended bursts of laughter.

"The point is, and here's what I meant by getting a jump on things, Betty Cattlett plans to talk to the directors of Miss Crane's this month about fund raising and the state of the exchequer, which I wouldn't be surprised is woeful indeed."

As Harvey cashed and spent two more chuckles, Ford wrote Betty Cattlett's name in a tight scrawl on a piece of scratch paper. She was headmistress of Miss Crane's.

"Here's my suggestion," Harvey went on. "The directors of Miss Crane's are the same people we'll need for the point-to-point. So it struck me to combine the two operations. We'll all be at the school board meeting anyway, so we might as well take that occasion to thresh out the point-to-point. What I mean is, Betty can make her report, and you and I can find time to work on the race—the same night, I mean."

"Yes, I understand," Ford said.

"Fine. The meeting's at our place. Cocktails, dinner, board meeting, and point-to-point. One neat package. How does it strike you?"

It all struck Ford about as temptingly as a flounder across the face, but he said: "It sounds fine, Harvey." He drew a circle around Betty Cattlett's name. "What's the date?"

"The twenty-third. Say sevenish at Chez Shires?"

"Fine, I'll be there."

"Good!" Harvey laughed again, but this time his hoarded merriment didn't come from the big vault; now it was a small and discreet, as if he were fishing it out of a change purse. "You've been a hard man to corral since Janet went down south, I gather. Ellie Poston tells me she's tried half-a-dozen times to get you for supper."

"It's been a good chance to catch up on some back work."

"Man doesn't live by bread alone, old man. We all need a fling. You know what I do when I find myself getting stale? I take an afternoon off and play squash until I'm absolutely bushed. That, plus a good steak and about ten hours of sleep, brings me right back up to par."

"Squash, eh?" Ford said. "Well, I'll remember that."

He hung up and tried to make his thoughts run in orderly channels. There was some work to do yet, a few calls to return, but when he tried to concentrate on these simple, mechanical chores, his thoughts skittered off in a dozen irrelevant directions. He realized guiltily that he hadn't written Janet since she had gone to Florida, while her letters, full of chatter and gossip, came in three times a week. He decided he had better write to her now. She was a good woman, he thought, gloomily and virtuously. What had her letters been about? The weather was fine, the course was playing well (except the fourth and tenth greens were burned), the Fayes and the Wilsons were down (and Cynthia was a blonde again)—there were three exclamation points after that information, he recalled, as he swung his typewriter into place.

The letter was a chore. "The fourth gets a baking all afternoon, but I don't see why the tenth should be in trouble. Say hello to the Wilsons for me." He tried to think of something that might interest her. "Catherine and Anna are doing their usual excellent job of running things with maximum efficiency and maximum emotional strain. I thought, with you away, it was a good time to pack Catherine off to her sister's place for a couple of weeks. She does need the rest. Don't worry about me, I'll survive."

He sat back and lit a cigarette. The sky was gray beyond his windows, and there were dirty streaks of snow on the roof of the courthouse. The weather was like this when he had first seen Maria—cold, heavy, lifeless. He remembered his curious feeling about her, as she had walked away from him that day in Rosedale, with chapped hands thrust in the pockets of a red jacket, and her blue jeans so frayed from wear and launderings that the fabric showed thin and white at her knees and hips . . . wild birds wheeling against low gray skies, a single hawk in a tall tree scanning the meadows for a furtive stir of life. . . . He had seen the loneliness, the defiance, but not the fear of traps.

He made an effort to finish the letter. "Saw Ellie and Wiley at the club the other night, living it up, of course. Had a

pleasant drink with Clay and Alicia a couple of Sundays back."
Somehow he finished it.

As the afternoon wore on, he became worried and restless.
She might be gone by now, he thought despairingly. Pacing
his office, he smoked one cigarette after another, as the lights
of Cottersville winked on below him, and threw flickering
reflections at the shadows pressing against his windows. She
wanted nothing from him, neither his money, his protection,
nor his love. He had no hope that she would be waiting for
him tonight. With perfect clarity, he could imagine the dark
empty trailer, the cold stove with its heap of dry ashes, the
closets stripped of her few clothes—the shirts and jeans, the
white cotton dresses, the black moccasins, the scuffed sandals.

He waited for darkness like someone awaiting his own ex-
ecution, and when Mrs. Simpson opened his door to say good
night, he almost started at her pleasant, familiar face. When
she had gone, he began pacing again, wondering why in God's
name he had chosen to involve himself in such a hopeless,
impossible affair. Even if she were at the trailer tonight, it
would only be a respite; it would happen another night then,
that was all, and he would be left behind, pathetic and weary,
with no one to share the burden of his love and passion. That
was the damnable thought now; that he was earthbound, tied
to responsibility, while she was free as a wild bird. It was a
miserably unfair arrangement; he was expected to accept her
terms without argument, abide by all her rules and decisions,
while she apparently wanted to answer to no one, and to follow only the call of her childish, capricious heart.

It was ridiculous. He was suddenly furious with her, and
with himself, for he knew he was behaving like a fool. He had
surrendered all control and authority without a murmur, listening numbly and helplessly while a semi-illiterate child
half his age called the tune. Why should he pay any attention
to her at all? She hardly knew what she was saying most of the
time. Hopping from one subject to the next without relevance
or continuity, giggling at the idiocies on television, cutting at
her steak like a little savage, she hadn't a brain in her head.

154

But he was letting her establish the boundaries of their relationship, deferring to her as if she were a Supreme Court judge. Maybe I've been too gentle, he thought. She was probably used to waking up with a black eye and a drunken lout yelling at her to bring him a can of beer. That could be arranged then, if that's what she wanted. And, as he drove to her trailer that night, he realized that he was savoring the excitement of his anger, relishing the intensity of his feelings. Every muscle in his body seemed to be straining against the pull of exhilarating tensions. The sudden exposure to the emotional extremes of fear and anger, of despair and hope, made him feel wonderfully alert and mettlesome; it was as if a cold clean wind were blowing through compartments of his body that had been sealed off for years. The pendulumlike swings of emotion struck remote, dead nerve ends, and caused them to vibrate and sing with the anticipation of keener sensations.

He couldn't wait to get to her; his anger sustained him through the drive through the dark countryside, charging him with elation and confidence. But when he turned into Beech Road and saw the lights of her trailer shining through the trees, the hard, aggressive belligerence went out of him like the air from a punctured balloon.

He felt weak with relief, limp with gratitude. For in his heart he had been almost certain she was gone. . . .

To add to his confusion—and the shaky feeling that he had been saved by a miraculous, shoestring catch—she was in an exuberantly happy mood. The night before might never have happened; there was no reserve in her greeting, no appraisal of speculation in eyes. She hugged him so tightly that they both laughed and let out their breath with gasps, and then she took his coat and made him sit down while she fixed a drink. She chattered at him from the kitchen like a child about to burst with excitement. "You know Luis? He lives in the trailer between me and Roby and Martha? It's his Saint's Day next week."

Ford lit a cigarette, and listened gratefully to her voice. He didn't follow what she was saying; he simply absorbed the sweet sound of it, letting it soak into him like sunshine on a cool day. The stove was drawing well and the trailer was warm and clean. There were plates and napkins on the coffee table, and seeing them, he remembered that he hadn't brought anything for dinner. He interrupted her to tell her this. "You forgot?" she said, looking around the door of the kitchen at him. "Well, there's cans of everything. And cold steak and pickles. Is that all right?"

"That's perfect," he said. It sounded better than any food he could imagine. "Absolutely perfect."

She brought him a whisky with water and ice, and sat on the arm of his chair while he sipped it.

"It's all right?"

"Yes, just right."

She slipped down onto his lap and snuggled close to him. She put both arms around his neck and let her head rest on his shoulder. Then she sighed comfortably, and he felt the slow soft swell of her breasts against his body. "Oh, you always say everything is all right," she said.

She lay curled in his arms like a contented child. She was wearing a dress he hadn't seen before, a pale blue dress with short sleeves, and frayed white stitching about the collar. It had been laundered until it felt as thin as paper, but it looked beautiful on her, perfectly right with the ribbon in her hair and the white socks turned back neatly at her ankles. There was a feeling of trust in the relaxed warmth of her body against his, and an innocence in the clean, soapy smell of her hair. For a moment, as he held her tightly to him, he was overcome with an emotion that was so sad and powerful that it nearly brought tears to his eyes.

"Did you hear what I said about Luis?" she asked him suddenly.

"Only that he's having his Saint's Day."

"Oh, you didn't listen." She sat up and looked at him reproachfully. "You didn't hear what he's doing."

"I'm sorry. Tell me again."

"He's having his Saint's Day, and he's giving everybody a

156

party next week." She twisted around to face him squarely, smiling now with excitement. "He's roasting two pigs outside over a fire. He told me about it. Inside the pigs he puts onions and mushrooms and apples and outside he covers them with peppers and tomatoes and olive oil. He wants everyone to come, and Roby is going to play his guitar."

"He wants me to come, too?"

"Yes, he asked me about it." She watched him curiously. "You don't want to?"

"When is it?"

"At night," she said slowly. "It's all right."

"I didn't mean that. Yes, I'd love to come. Tell him, will you? Can I bring anything?"

"No, he's got everything. He's going to be happy." She sighed and looked serious. "He has a very hard time. He's old and his work is hard. And he can't read or write English. Once some of the men he works with wrote things on a piece of paper for the grocery store. You understand? But the words were all dirty ones, and the man in the grocery store was mad. He thought it was a joke of his, of Luis's, I mean. Do you understand? Luis was unhappy." She looked at him uncertainly. "Maybe it's funny. Do you think it's funny?"

"No, I don't think it was funny. It was stupid and cruel."

She seemed relieved. "That's how I think too." But then she looked at him and giggled. "But it's a little bit funny. A little bit. Don't you think so?"

"O.K., it's a little bit funny." He couldn't help smiling at the animation in her face.

"Can I make dinner now? Do you want another drink?"

"All right, one more. Then I'll sit here and watch you."

"That's crazy. Turn the television on."

There were many things about that night he never forgot; but above all he remembered how she looked in the blue dress with the ribbons in her hair; and the trusting warmth of her body, and the feeling he had experienced, then, so preposterous in a man of his age and limitations, that he still had tears to shed for himself.

CHAPTER 10

L UIS'S party was on the twenty-third of that month; but it didn't occur to Ford until it was too late to do anything about it that he was expected at Harvey Shires's that same night. The notation on his desk calendar was not to be argued with: Harvey's—7 P.M. There was a suggestion of reproof in the precision of his handwriting; it reflected a man of serious responsible habits, who couldn't possibly be involved in the choice between a pig roast or a school board meeting. Goddamn it, he thought. It was now three o'clock; he couldn't get a message to her, and he didn't like driving out to her trailer in broad daylight.

The meeting might be brief, of course; and Betty Cattlett's report might not provoke any long-winded recapitulations from board members; and he just might get the point-to-point business settled quickly with Harvey.

If it worked out that way, he should make it back to Maria's by nine or nine-thirty. But his hopes faded when he arrived at the Shires' that night. There were twenty-five or thirty persons in the long living room, and by the time Ford was served a drink the number had grown to forty-odd. No one seemed in a hurry; they stood about laughing and talking, lighting cigarettes, freshening their drinks. Dinner was a long way off. Harvey Shires was in his element, for he knew that any meeting contained the potential of crisis, and he gave the impression that he alone understood the weighty problems facing them. As he welcomed his guests, smiling at the women and giving the men bracing whacks on the shoulder, it was as if he were assuring them all of his rocklike support in this hour of trouble.

The large room soon became warm and stuffy. The Shires were dog people, and there were dozens of small ones snarling around under the chairs, or licking placidly at empty cheese or fish trays. Ford avoided a flirtatious sparring match with Ellie Poston by retreating into a corner, and buttressing his position with old John Cotterwell's bulk. John Cotterwell, in addition to being as wide as a barn door, had no interests in life but the market and fox hunting, and Ford was protected not only by his size, but by the sturdy wall of clichés with which the old man sealed off their corner of the room.

"Saturday's meet was most interesting," he said to Ford, and his rumbling voice was like a roll of cannon fire warning off attackers. "I've seen Lowry's covert drawn a thousand times, I suppose, but I can't recall an occasion when hounds were held into the wind as far as the stock fence without coming on the line again. It was most curious. The huntsman assumed, I imagine, that the fox had turned three-quarters, so he jumped the fence, held the hounds still further into the wind, and made his next cast on a line you might call AB, if you take A for the stone bridge and B for the northeast point of the covert. Now the odd thing there will be apparent to you. I imagine. Can you guess where the hounds checked?"

Dinner was served at eight. Afterward Dora Shires led the women away, and the men sat at the table over cigars and coffee and brandy. It was nine-thirty before the sexes were socially coupled in the living room, and by then Ford realized wearily that he couldn't see Maria that night.

After everyone was seated, on chairs or on the floor, Betty Cattlett rose to deliver her report. "First, I think we must offer our mutual thanks to Harvey and Dora for giving over their lovely home to what, I fear, may be a dry recital of facts and figures."

Harvey, who sat cross-legged on the floor with a pipe jutting from his square face, dismissed her thanks with a graceful wave of his hand.

Miss Cattlett continued: "I might say at the outset that Miss Crane's reflects a certain national pattern, in that costs are rising while income shows a tendency to run—perhaps *flee* is the more accurate word—in the opposite direction." There was a general laugh at this, and Betty Cattlett turned pink at the success of her joke. She was a slim, earnest soul, a model of spinster graces; she reminded Ford of a fading rose, somehow gently and sweetly sad. In a strengthened voice, to indicate that the fun was over, Miss Cattlett plunged into the present state of the school's finances.

Ford was at one end of the long room, and Miss Cattlett stood near the other, facing the group; at that distance he could barely hear her low, musical voice. But he knew what she was saying; he had heard it all before, many times. Maintenance costs were rising; graduation was scheduled for the second Wednesday in June; the gym needed a new wing, or the girls' showers were inadequate, or the pipes in the science lab had to be torn out and replaced; it would be a source of gratification to parents and board members to know that 82 per cent of the senior class had already been accepted in colleges of their choice, among which—another source of gratification, certainly—would be Smith, Vassar, Bryn Mawr, Sweet Briar, and Bennington.

Ford glanced at his watch. It was ten o'clock but things seemed to be moving along smoothly. Hope stirred again; he might make Maria's by ten-thirty. He and Harvey could skip the post-mortem on Betty's report, and get at the point-to-point. The race wasn't until the first week of April, so tonight's session was only a ground-breaking operation. He could make sure it was brief, by promising to write out some reports and recommendations. That would do it; anything written with a substantial number of subheadings and parenthetical alternatives was absolute catnip to Harvey. Ford knew he could handle the whole affair himself with half a dozen phone calls. They would need fifteen or sixteen patrol judges; two clerks of scales; two paddock judges; a blacksmith; an ambulance; a doctor and a vet. Programs, ribbons, refreshments. The Poplin volunteer fire company was a pillar of strength; it had ambulances, jeeps, tentage, and its ladies Auxiliary would do the hot dogs, hamburgers, soup, and coffee. The Cottersville *Examiner and Recorder* would handle the printing. Parking by the Boy Scouts.

The race was approximately three miles over fair hunting country, and at least three horses would go down somewhere on the course. One year, Ford remembered, not even half of the starting field finished; three horses came in riderless, two stayed down after hitting fences, and four or five cut flags and disappeared into the woods surrounding the course. That was when Wiley Poston broke his shoulder, and Sam Harris cracked three transverse processes in his back. Ford had won the point-to-point that year, on a calm, well-made chestnut gelding named Caravan. Ten years ago; when he was still riding races.

John Cotterwell's voice fell like a heavy weight across his thoughts.

"What's that you said, Betty? I'm not sure I understand."

Ford glanced up and saw that Betty's face was flushed; she seemed quite nervous. "I mentioned—because it's something the board may wish to act on—that we have an application from a Negro. She's sixteen, and her father is an Army major stationed at the Northrup base."

John Cotterwell nodded his large, bald head, and closed his eyes once more. Everyone else in the room, however, stirred about restlessly; it was as if a window had been opened and an unpleasant draft was blowing in. Lighters snapped and tiny flames leaped at the tips of fresh cigarettes. Then there was a curious silence. Tony Marshall crossed his long legs and looked at the backs of his hands. Wiley Poston went quietly to the bar, and Sam Harris, bulky and hot in a tweed hacking jacket, stared vacantly at the design in the carpet. Most of the women were smiling neutrally into space, but Ford knew from Ellie Poston's mouth that she was suppressing a burst of laughter.

Finally Tony Marshall turned his narrow, silvered head and

looked at Betty Cattlett, who stood in the middle of the room as if she were in the dock.

"That's interesting," he said pleasantly. "I think we'd like more details, however."

"Yes, of course, Mr. Marshall. Major Green called me last week. He's not too happy about the school at the base, and . . ."

"Now ain't dat a shame," Wiley said, in a soft chuckling voice. "Gotta teach dem chilluns to count good. They gonna be havin' babies in five or six months, 'stead of nine, les' you 'struct 'em good."

Everyone seemed to have been waiting for some such remark, for it was followed by a burst of relieved laughter; it was as if Wiley had taken a potentially fatiguing problem, and turned it around so that everyone could see it was a pretty good joke, if you just looked at it from the right angle.

Miss Cattlett waited for the laughter, and the whispered elaborations on Wiley's theme to subside, before she said: "Well, in a way, Mr. Poston, Major Green's concern is understandable. Sarah Green's an unusual child. They've lived in Paris for the last three years, and she's had the advantage of excellent schooling. All of her work indicates not only superior intelligence, but orderly and responsible habits."

"One minute now," Tony Marshall said. "You've talked to her?"

"Yes." Miss Cattlett seemed to be having trouble finding a comfortable place for her hands; she put them at her sides, then locked them together at her waist, and finally let them flutter in front of her, like small pale birds tethered to her narrow wrists.

"I'm sorry, I didn't understand that," Tony Marshall said. "Let's start at the beginning. I'd like this step by step."

"Blow by blow, you mean," Wiley said.

"Very well. Major Green called me last week, as I explained. He'd made applications at Rondelay and Towhill, but they'd given him little encouragement. He called us as a last hope, I imagine."

162

The stubby pipe came slowly from Harvey Shires' clamped jaw. "One point here," he said thoughtfully. "On the phone, did he say he was a Negro?"

"Yes, of course. He asked me if I would talk to his daughter, and I said yes. I saw no harm in it. That's where the matter rests."

There was a long awkward silence then, and Ford glanced about trying to analyze the mood of his friends. Standing at the far end of the room, he had a good point of observation; the group spread from him in a ragged semicircle, which enclosed Miss Cattlett's slight figure like a large hook.

The predominant reaction seemed to be one of embarrassment, he thought; it was as if everyone wished, for Miss Cattlett's sake, that she hadn't got herself into this situation. They were pained for her, and they rather hoped she'd have the good sense to change the subject, or dismiss it firmly and forever, instead of standing there twisting her hands together and waiting for them to excuse, or ignore, or extenuate this social gaffe.

This seemed to be the general emotional response, save for Wiley's; he had gulped down his drink, and was at the bar once more splashing whisky into his glass. Ford knew he was stoking the fires of the renowned Poston temper, flexing and hardening his emotional muscles. But when he turned away from the bar, with a full glass in his hand, he was smiling pleasantly. "I don't see why anybody thinks this is a problem," he said. "We have an application from a colored girl. I don't see why Miss Cattlett talked to the girl's father. That just raised her hopes unnecessarily, it seems to me. Anyway, it's beside the point. The point is, we don't want this application. What's there to do but send it back and get on to the next order of business?" Wiley glanced around the room inquiringly, but his pleasant smile and reasonable manner were traps laid for the unwary, Ford knew; he was spoiling for a brawl, fidgeting to jerk the trigger on his temper.

"Well, I don't know," Harvey Shires said, taking the pipe from his jaw with a steady hand. He frowned and shook his head slowly. "I don't know if we've looked into this with sufficent care. My colonel once said something—"

"Oh hell, Harvey," Wiley said. "Are you going to talk about your war experiences, or about our problems?"

Dora Shires looked at him angrily. "You're the one who said it wasn't a problem, remember"

"The colonel's point concerned booby traps," Harvey said, after taking three meditative puffs on his pipe.

"Well, we're concerned with boogie traps," Wiley said shortly. "Let's forget your old colonel, eh?"

Harvey made no further effort to press his point—whatever it had been. He sat like a tweedy, prosperous Buddha, thoughtful, impassive, and seemingly untouched by the scraps of argument and discussion floating above his large head. He did not appear to be hurt, or put out; he had simply withdrawn his counsel from the group, thus condemning it—one could infer from his faint smile—to rudderless voyages on the seas of folly and unreason.

Ford felt Harvey had shown good sense in not tangling with Wiley's rock-hard antagonism. What difference would it make? The issue was already decided. More accurately, there was no issue here in the first place. But, as the talk went on he found himself thinking about the girl named Sarah Green. Three years in Paris, Betty had said. Twelve full seasons. The city was probably not a glittering spectacle to her; it would be as familiar and comfortable as her home town. In the winter there would be glass-walled sidewalk cafés, with pumping stoves and frosted windows, and hot chocolate alongside a stack of schoolbooks. Spring would be the Bois de Boulogne neighborhood circuses, the women selling violets, priests pedaling along with loaves of bread beneath their arms, fishermen on the Seine. She would go away in the summer, everyone did, to a village in the south, a resort town in Provence, some place like that. And autumn would be chestnuts roasting, chestnut trees turning to gold, and cats blinking comfortably beside the cashiers in the little restaurants.

Ford realized he was making up lists from books he'd read;

he didn't know Paris at all. And then, with complete irrelevance, he thought of old Luis, who, Maria had told him, didn't know how to read, but knew a strange and interesting way to roast a pig. Ford sat apart from the group and its tensions, thinking of Maria.

Wiley had found someone to argue with, for his voice was rolling around the room with sensual belligerence, and Ford's thoughts switched to the little colored boy Wiley was teaching to handle his shotgun. That was an odd thing; that was about the last thing you'd expect Wiley to teach him. How to shoot. . . .

"Now I'll tell you something funny," Wiley was saying to the group in general. "We've heard the usual talk about how exceptional this girl is. Speaks French, high IQ, daughter of an army officer, and so forth. But what's that got to do with it? Ever notice how quick the pinkos are to start talking about Ralph Bunche and that old professor at Tuskegee every time the subject of colored people comes up? It's a damn thin argument. About like saying if you cut the scent glands out of one skunk, that'll make the rest of them smell like violets. If you accept this one girl, smart as she may be, you might as well throw open the doors to every pickaninny in the county."

There didn't seem to be any disagreement with Wiley's comments, Ford thought, although some of the women seemed gracefully pained by the bluntness of his language. But he was surprised at his own reactions; as a lawyer he knew the folly of indulging his emotions, but despite that, he was savoring a cold bright anger that seemed to be straining inside him like some ferocious but calculating animal.

Laddy Thornburg had leaped up to add something to what Wiley had said, and Ford's anger twisted almost painfully, as Laddy cried: "Hear! Hear!" and smiled cheerfully about the room. Laddy Thornburg was in his middle thirties. He had been expelled from eight or ten prep schools, for drinking and brawling his family insisted loyally, but they were simply putting the best possible face on the matter, for everyone knew Laddy had an embarrassing tendency to run about campuses at night in his underwear, and this, plus the fact that he hadn't learned to read until he was eleven, made the odds against his staying in any imaginable school preposterously long. He was passionately fond of horses, and over the years had come to resemble these creatures of his affection; his teeth were long, his face was bony, and whenever he became excited—clotheslines of flapping garments were one specific cantharis—he had a habit of tossing his head about in a mettlesome rhythm, which, in turn, caused his stringy blond hair to flap across his forehead and eyes like a mane.

"Just one thing to add," he cried now, in his high, whinnying voice, and, under the emotional strain of articulating his thoughts (and of not disrobing, Ford thought disgustedly) Laddy's head began its curious, equine thrusting and tossing, and his hair was instantly thrown into a consequent flagellant frenzy. "One thing more, people try to get their children into good schools so that they can meet the parents. Parents of other children, that is. They can get into our houses that way, get to know us."

"Well, you're safe till you get married and have some kids," Sam Harris said irritably, and Ford realized then that the feeling in the room wasn't quite as unanimous as he had thought; some of the people present were afraid of Wiley's temper, and still more were eager to stay on Tony Marshall's side in any argument, but Laddy's comments, taken with his appearance and reputation, had suddenly made the notion of discrimination mildly farcical. Bill and Mollie Simpson, he saw, were exchanging smiles, and Walter Duville, who was a vestryman of the Cottersville Methodist Church, seemed disturbed as he turned to say something in a low voice to the Cullinans.

Ford didn't know the Cullinans well. They were new in the area, a young and attractive couple with two small children. Cullinan was in public relations at Inter-Allied Chemical. His wife, Sally, was an attractive girl who had worked in fashions, or something like that, before her marriage. She had silky blond hair, and didn't ride. The Cullinans were poor, but

166

very well liked; they were considered engaging and pleasantly off-beat. They invited odd, stimulating people down for weekends, designers, newspapermen, and so forth. They were both amiable and well informed, and Ford remembered that Clay was very fond of them. But Sally didn't look very amiable just now, and Walter Duville was smiling sympathetically as he talked to her, apparently attempting to provide her with an ameliorating explanation of Wiley's and Laddy's attitudes. But these people didn't count, Ford knew quite well; the Cullinans, the Simpsons, Walter Duville, Sam Harris—they wouldn't affect the issue at all. For they wouldn't speak out, from either fear or uncertainty, and even if they did their words would carry no weight.

The issue would be decided by those whose words did carry weight, and when Tony Marshall cleared his throat quietly, it became very evident where a respectable measure of that weight lay; for the talk died away quickly then, and the room became alertly attentive.

"Now one thing occurred to me," Tony Marshall said, running both hands over his smooth silvery hair. "Bear with me if I put in some detail. Presently certain of us make up the annual shortages in the school's budget. The fact that we operate at a deficit is no reflection on the management of the school. We're not interested in making a paying proposition out of Miss Crane's. But—" And here Tony Marshall sighed and put the tips of his fingers together so they formed a neat cage.

"There's no point in not being realistic. Who knows what may happen in the next five or ten years? Or next year, for that matter. Costs might skyrocket. Our personal circumstances could change. The school, in short, might become an impossible burden for us to support as individuals. In that event we'd have to look around for some relief. The likeliest source would be one of the foundations. I can think of several offhand we might approach. But here we run into a troublesome chain of circumstances. The foundations operate under tax-exempt charters, and the government is looking into their situation pretty closely, as most of you know. Here's the point: if a tax-exempt foundation aids a school which excludes certain citizens—follow this closely now—it could be argued that federal funds, in the form of tax-free money, were being used in a project which isn't available to all taxpayers."

Tony Marshall smiled sympathetically at the frowns on some of the women's faces. "I know, I sound like a Philadelphia lawyer, but it can't be helped. I'm trying to be as explicit as possible. The foundation—name any one you like—might be justified in regarding us as a very hot potato indeed. In effect we're asking for federal aid, and we can't qualify for it unless our doors are open to all citizens, regardless of that neat trilogy of tolerance, race, creed, or color. Mind you, this is only my view of things. Perhaps we need a legal opinion. Ford, what do you think?"

Ford hadn't followed Tony's arguments too closely, but he nodded anyway, and said: "I imagine you're right, Tony. There's no precedent that I know of, but perhaps we might set one." Ford's thoughts had been roaming in confusing areas. He was wondering what his relation to this problem was, what the *I* of his personality had to do with it. These people here were his friends, the solidly human warp and woof of his existence. Their opinion of him gave him his identity; he didn't live in a vacuum, he existed, in a fundamental sense, in them. The core of his being, even his knowledge of himself, wasn't centrally located; it was centered outside of himself. He had no special worth or value, except as his actions and attitudes had gained the love or respect of those who knew him. But this parceling out of himself, if that's what it was, was surely accidental, a tithe paid to birth and terrain. To define himself more deliberately, he would have to seek his identity in other mirrors. He wished he knew where to look for them.

"Precedent?" Tony Marshall said, with a good-humored smile. "No, I have no crusader's zeal, Ford. We're not aiming to push back any legal frontiers. Our attitude is one of vulgar self-interest. Now." He glanced about the room, and rubbed his hands together. "We have an application from a young colored girl. She's clever, responsible, and so forth. Supposing we act favorably on that application. Where would that leave us?" There was a sudden, surprised stir in the room, and Tony Marshall raised both hands in a placating gesture. Wiley was staring at him incredulously, a glass arrested halfway to his mouth.

"I said supposing, remember," Tony Marshall went on. "All right, supposing we take her in. What's the situation then? There are obvious disadvantages; we're in agreement on that. But there's a definite advantage in being eligible for a foundation grant, if that ever becomes necessary. I'm not pleading either side of this issue. But I want you to look at all the angles. If we accept this girl, we need never accept another. We can't be accused of discrimination—we can point to a colored girl on the campus. We can say, in effect, there she is, Exhibit A for the defense. We've admitted her because she met our standards. There was no outside pressure from any individual or group. Therefore it's obvious we have nothing against Negroes, per se, and no barriers to keep them out of Miss Crane's. With that position established—through one status Negro— we can turn down all other applicants on any grounds we choose."

"But Mr. Marshall, wouldn't that be a shocking thing to do to this child?" It was Sally Cullinan who said this, and Ford was surprised at the anger in her voice, and so, quite obviously, was Tony Marshall, for he turned and looked at her with a cautious smile.

"I'm afraid I don't understand."

"She'd feel like—well, what did you say? Exhibit A for the defense. She's obviously a perceptive child, and she'd realize very quickly that she was simply on display—like something in a cage. I think it would be kinder to turn her down flatly, than to do this to her."

"I see your point, my dear," Tony Marshall said, but his eyes drifted past her to her husband, and it was obvious he was adding a note to whatever file he might have on John Cullinan. They both worked for the same company in a sense,

169

the difference being that Tony Marshall largely owned it. And Tony Marshall held the notion that a woman's contribution to men's affairs should be kept to a graceful minimum. And he would be wondering now, Ford thought, why Cullinan didn't keep this pretty wife of his on a shorter leash. But his voice and smile were good-humored, as he said, "Sally, what you say is true. But it's only one consideration in a problem with dozens of angles to it. We can't give any one area top priority—not even this child's feelings."

John Cullinan took his wife's hand. "It's a complicated business, honey. Tax angles, all the rest of it."

"I know." She looked at him steadily. "I was oversimplifying, as usual."

Tony Marshall smiled indulgently. "That's a charming trait. I wouldn't worry about it. But this is one of those tiresome things we can't take the risk of oversimplifying—much as we'd all like to."

"Hell, she's not oversimplifying," Sam Harris said unexpectedly. "She's just making noises like a human being. What's so god-awful about considering this kid's application on its merits?"

"Christ!" Wiley said explosively. "Do we have to spell it out for you?"

"Now that's enough, Wiley," Tony Marshall said. "Sam, Miss Crane's is a school, first and foremost. But it's also a large parcel of real estate set on two hundred prime acres of ground. If we depreciate the school, we stand the chance of depreciating land values. Don't you realize that?"

"I thought we were talking about something else, Tony."

"You'd understand what we're talking about if you were called on to put the same money into the school that some others of us do."

"Maybe. And thanks for reminding me I'm poor." Sam Harris grinned at him. "But if you're pulling rank, I could remind you your grandfather was plowing fields for mine a hundred-odd years ago."

Tony Marshall stared at him for an instant, and then he

smiled faintly and glanced up at Betty Cattlett. "I'm sorry, we got off on a tangent. But I think you know our feelings in the matter. I've pointed out one dubious advantage of an affirmative decision, but that is outweighed by other considerations."

"Amen, amen," Wiley said.

"Now hold on a minute," Ford said, and there was a surprised stir in the room as he stood and made his way slowly to Betty Cattlett's side. He glanced down at Tony Marshall and said, "You're forgetting one thing, we don't have any authority in this matter at all. It's Betty's responsibility as headmistress to make the decision. If you'll read the charter, you'll find that's clear enough. Of course, if she does her job in a way we don't approve of, we can fire her. But until that possibility develops, I suggests we leave this matter in her hands."

"I'm not forgetting the charter, and so forth," Tony Marshall said casually. "I'm aware of Betty's area of responsibility. But I don't think we're encroaching on that. We simply expect her decisions to reflect our interest. Correct?"

"Well, let's see about that," Ford said. He turned to Betty Cattlett and smiled reassuringly at her, but this took a considerable effort, for he was nearly lightheaded with confusion and anger. She looked uneasily at him, but he saw a light of hope in her eyes, and he realized that all she had wanted from the start was someone to buttress her against the money and anger in the room.

At least, he hoped that was what she wanted.

He said: "Now, Betty, this girl, Sarah Green. She's qualified to do the work at Miss Crane's?"

"Yes, Mr. Jackson. There's no doubt about it."

"And how about other areas? Manners, work habits, and so forth. Do they seem adequate to your standards?"

As Betty Cattlett hesitated, the silence deepened; there was a hard, metallic tension running through the smoky room, as if wires of emotion were being drawn slowly out to a predictable breaking point. Then she said: "Yes, they're quite adequate, Mr. Jackson."

"Well, what's your feeling then?"

"I—I'm not sure."

"You're inclined to accept her? Or not."

"Yes." She whispered the word. Then she said passionately: "Of course I want to take her. I know the problems. I haven't been teaching school for twenty-six years with my eyes shut. But to deny this child the education she needs would be worse than starving her."

"Then I think the matter's settled," Ford said, and at that, the straining silence cracked and broke into a thousand pieces. Everyone began talking at once. In the sudden clamor there were notes of irritation, surprise, exasperation, and even some humor, but above it all Wiley Poston's voice soared violently and frantically like a foghorn, bleating hoarsely of unseen dangers. "Goddamn it, Ford, nothing's settled. You're not railroading this through me, I can promise you that."

"There's nothing you can do about it," Ford said. "It's Betty's decision; you and I have nothing to say in the matter."

"What in God's name is wrong with you, Ford?" Wiley stared at him incredulously. "You ready to wreck the school for this one darky?"

"As Tony pointed out earlier, Miss Crane's is a large parcel of real estate situated on two hundred choice acres of land. I don't think any child, whether she's black, blue, or technicolored, is likely to destroy it. The wrecking job, if it's done, will be done right in this room. You can swing the first pick, if you want, by moving we fire Miss Cattlett."

To Ford's astonishment, he realized that he had about half the room on his side; he had expected emotional storms to rage about his head but, except for Wiley, the reactions of dissent were confined to anxious cluckings and head-shakings, while the rest of the group—the Simpsons, the Duvilles, the Cullinans, and to his great surprise, Harvey and Dora Shires—were smiling, cheerfully or philosophically according to their degree of enthusiasm at the turn of events. And he realized then that he had carried the issue, not with logic or eloquence, not by rallying them in support of a principle, but simply because he couldn't be bullied or threatened by anyone in the room. They might smile tolerantly at Sally Cullinan's distress, and ignore Sam Harris's disapproval, but there was no one present who was willing to risk a showdown with him on this matter. It was very simple; he had money and position and influence behind him, and was too formidable to attack; he could stand on principle, do the decent thing, at no cost at all. If he were in the right, fine; but supposing he were wrong?

Tony Marshall said thoughtfully, "You're being stubborn about this, which isn't like you, Ford. But just to test the fiber of your resolution, supposing I tell you here and now that if this girl is admitted to Miss Crane's, I'm going to withdraw my contribution to this year's deficit." He cocked an eye at Ford, as if trying to bring him into clearer focus. "What do you say to that?"

Ford smiled. "Tony, I've been buying G.E. and G.M. just as long as you have. Don't worry about the contribution. We'll manage."

"You're serious then?" Tony Marshall frowned at the backs of his hands a moment, but when he looked up at Ford there was the suggestion of a smile about his mouth and eyes. "All right, I'll go along with you, Ford. We may regret this step. Then again, we may not. Now I suggest we get on to the next item of business."

"Without me, goddamn it, without me," Wiley Poston said. "Ellie, get your coat. Harvey, thanks for your whisky. And since you're bubbling and grinning like a fool at what Ford's done, that's the last drop you're going to buy for me."

Old John Cotterwell woke with a start, and blinked like a fiercely complacent owl at Wiley's wide, retreating back. "They have bloody awful tempers, those Postons," he said, shaking his huge bald head in solemn disapproval. "They aggravate it with whisky, of course, and young Wiley's father was no exception in that respect. I remember a most unusual meet— twenty-five years ago, I shouldn't wonder—when he got into a disgraceful row with the Whip after the hounds had checked near the McIntyre line. The facts were most curious. The first cast had obviously been made in desperation, since the scent had been lost in a field of onion grass."

The evening wore on; tensions eased, and the atmosphere was almost normal by the time the meeting came to an end and Dora Shires brought in a tray of sandwiches and a pitcher of cold cider. But by then it was far too late to see Maria.

. . . She refused to accept his excuses. She sat stiffly on the edge of the studio couch, deliberately avoiding his eyes. There was a cold reproach in the line of her straight back, the sharp turn of her head. He saw her in profile, his impression composed of details: black hair lying with sexual grace along her cheek, slim tendons ridged against the smooth skin of her throat.

"Maria, look at me," he said. "I couldn't get here, I wanted to, but I couldn't. I had a business meeting. I made that date long before I knew of Luis's party. There was no way to let you know."

"You didn't plan to come. You told me yes, but you didn't mean it. You didn't care about Luis. I waited until nine. Roby and Martha were sorry for me. So was Luis. Because they know I'm a fool."

Ford was ashamed of himself; her angry eyes and hurt mouth made him feel quite cheerful. "Very well, let's go see Luis now," he said.

"What do you mean? What for?"

"I couldn't get to his party. The least I can do is tell him I'm sorry."

"You didn't want to come."

"I just got the two dates mixed up, that's all. Are you coming with me?"

"Where?"

"To Luis's, of course."

"You don't know him, he'll think you're crazy."

"I'll introduce myself, don't worry. Should I bring a bottle of whisky? Does he like to drink?"

"I don't know," she said miserably.

"I'll take something just in case," he said. "You wait here.

I'll try not to be long."

"Why can't I come?"

"Men sitting around over drinks, that's no place for a girl. You wait here."

She looked at him for the first time that night, and he saw the unhappiness in her eyes. "Don't be like this with me, please," she said. "Don't be hard and make fun of me."

"I'm sorry," he said. "Believe me." He took her arms and raised her to her feet. "Come with me," he said. "I think I should tell him I'm sorry. Will you come with me, please?"

She sighed and touched his chest with the tip of her finger. "All right. But don't be that way with me anymore, please."

Luis was a tall, nearly bald man, with bright blue eyes in a bony brown face. He wore clean new overalls and a black sweater. When he realized why Ford and Maria had come to see him, he became solemn and uneasy, but after a small glass of whisky it was as if an electric light bulb had been switched on inside him. His eyes glowed in his thin bony face, and he began to chatter excitedly of other birthdays and other fiestas, and the rushing words made brilliant, streaked pictures of villages and mountains, of flushed women and tireless dancers, of freshly baked bread, and beans cooked with hot sausages, and the colors of wine in the sun. He broke off in mid-sentence, shocked and appalled that he had forgot to offer them food. The remainder of the barbecued pig was cold and white, and each slice was surrounded by a thick crust of fat. In the fat, which was sharp with tomatoes and garlic and olive oil, there were grains of coarse black pepper which exploded like tiny embers on Ford's tongue.

When they were leaving, he said: "May I leave the bottle of whisky? As a gift on your Saint's Day?"

Luis refused it twice, the first time sternly, the second time wistfully, and then he took it in his hands and nodded quickly and enthusiastically, while a smile so large spread over his face that even the crown of his bald head seemed to glow with pleasure. As he waved good-by to them from his cold, clean trailer, he hugged the bottle in his arms, and called something

175

after them in Spanish.

"What did he say?" Ford asked Maria.

"That it's all right about last night. He knows you wanted to come."

Sometime during the night Ford opened his eyes. The trailer was dark, although faint bars of moonlight were twisting about the walls and ceiling. Outside the wind seemed to be rising frantically, and the tossing of trees caused the light to flicker around the trailer. Maria stirred in his arms, and rubbed her cheek against his shoulder.

"Listen to me," he said.

"All right." She sighed deeply.

She was so warm and sleepy that he hated to disturb her, but he couldn't forget the curious dream which had waked him.

"Listen! Are you asleep?"

"Yes," she said, moving her cheek slowly against him.

He twisted around and raised himself on one elbow. The blankets slipped away from her bare shoulders. "Oh, cover me up," she said with childish irritation. "Oh, please." The movement of his body disturbed her position and she turned on her back with a weary sigh.

"Can't you go to sleep?"

"No." He put his hand on her bare stomach and shook her gently. "Wake up. Listen."

"All right."

He shook her again, harder this time, and she squirmed protestingly under his hand. "Don't do that," she said. "Please, I'm awake."

"Let's go away somewhere," he said. "I had a dream about it. We were near the sea, and it was quiet."

"What were we doing?"

"I don't know. We were just there. Would you like to go away for a few days?"

"Where?"

"It doesn't matter. To a place by the ocean. Or just drive somewhere."

"Oh yes," she said, and sighed comfortably and burrowed

176

her face in the pillow. "That's very nice."

"Wouldn't you like to go away?"

But she was already sound asleep.

He didn't mention it again that week; but as the rains began in February, freezing and coating the limbs of the trees with glittering ice, the notion of going away with her became an obsession; he thought of nothing else. He spent all his time dreaming of places he might take her, and each new background, each new framework he placed her in, heightened his need for her, and made the hours he was forced to spend in his office intolerably dreary. He imagined her in the compartments of trains roaring across the country; at the race track wearing a cool slim dress and white gloves; on ships, in hotel rooms, beside pools with her arms and legs shining like honey in warm sunlight.

But she only laughed when he talked to her about it.

"No, I don't want to," she said.

"It's for me, it's selfish. I want to do something for you."

"Isn't it all right now? We can go and visit with Luis. Or Roby and Martha. Why do you want to go away?"

He wasn't sure. He wanted to amuse her, to spend money on her, but more than that he was driven by a vague but powerful need to seek new sensations and stronger stimulants; he was desperately eager to enlarge his capacity for feeling, to explore and savor the limits and reaches of his passion. He wanted to test and extend himself, to add stress on stress, and challenge on challenge, until he knew for certain that each of his senses, and every nerve in his body, had rendered up a final tribute to his demands. He had a frantic conviction that his body contained layers of sensitivity and response which had never been touched or sounded; rich, unworked veins of feeling which would repay any effort it might require to reach them.

And so strong was this belief of his, that eventually he wore down her smiling refusals. She gave in with a sighing, timeless plaint: "I don't have anything to wear. . . ."

He went to Philadelphia early the next morning to shop for

her. The experience was an act of creation; he found himself playing God in what seemed the most innocent possible fashion. He discovered he could transform her into just about anything he wanted to. A spectator at a Hunt Meet in tweeds. Something lovely and modest in a short black evening dress with a skirt that swung like a bell over pink petticoats. She was one thing in this, another in that, and he was delighted by his power to mold and change and transform her, with just a smile or a nod to the salesgirls.

He made a reservation that afternoon for a suite at the Château d'Or in Harbor City. Someone or other had told him it was the finest on the beach, resplendent and grossly expensive. He wasn't worried about seeing anyone he knew there. He couldn't imagine anyone he knew spending a night in such a place.

He lunched on snapper soup and shad roe at the market near Reading Station. This place, with its hanging sausages and cheeses, and the cold sharp smell of fish soaking in brine barrels, had been a favorite of his crowd years ago. They had come here after the theater for oysters and ale, with girls who lived in Bryn Mawr or Paoli, Rose Valley or Villanova. He remembered *The Philadelphia Story* with Katharine Hepburn. Was the calla lily thing in that? And Alexander Woollcott in *The Man Who Came to Dinner*. The war play, what was it? *Idiot's Delight?* Yes.

The counterman recommended the cheesecake, but Ford didn't want dessert.

"You training for something?" the counterman asked him. "Live a little, man." He had sparse gray hair, and red blotches on his face that looked as if they would be sore to the touch. He was smiling.

"No thanks," Ford said.

The girls with the shining hair, and the football games, and the ale and oysters after the theater, that was all fine and dandy, he thought, but his most vivid memories of that time were the voices of Raymond Gram Swing and Elmer Davis, speaking in accents of doom about the news from Europe.

178

They knew war was coming, everybody knew it. Their lives would be tossed up for grabs. No one knew how it was going to work out. After all the tennis and riding and golf lessons, all the worries about school, the squeaking through trig, the debates over taking or not taking Latin and Greek, the long, meditative conferences with faculty advisors at college—all the time and preparation meant very little in the end, for things had turned out a good bit differently from what parents and educators thought they would. He and his friends talked only of training courses and flight programs—V-7, V-5, ninety-day wonders, various deals and deferments that might be latched onto if you spoke fluent German or could do graduate work in math.

Their speech was interlarded with service slang long before they got into uniforms. They knew you requested permission to "go ashore" even if you were stationed on the twentieth floor of an office building in Chicago. And you didn't say twentieth floor, you said "twentieth deck," and you didn't take the elevator, you "went below." There were jokes about saluting. "If it moves, salute it." And tales of a hoary old Chief at Great Lakes with nine gold hash marks who refused to salute anything but Regular Navy. And Rodger Dodger old codger, I'm a commander too. But that one came later, along with the jokes about combat flyers and VD and rock-happy Marines, and young navigators plotting battleships on courses through Colorado and Wyoming.

But none of them seemed to realize they were living in historic and fateful times, Churchill's finest hour to the contrary. The present always seemed to be whored by the past, he thought, and he wondered if this was true of everyone.

From where he sat he had a view of the sky through a streaked window, and the sky was as gray as dead ashes, and a thin, miserable rain was falling on the city. The counterman followed his gaze, and grinned and said: "Nice weather, eh? Real nice weather—for ducks." And Ford recognized him then, with a sudden unpleasant start, as the alert, wisecracking youth who had served oysters and ale to him and the various girls from Paoli and Bryn Mawr almost twenty-five years ago.

"Yes, it's bad," Ford said.

"Well, I look at it like this," the counterman said, with a winking, confidential smile, as he swiped his cloth around Ford's section of the counter. "You used to be able to say it's good for the farmers. But now they get paid for not planting things, so who's it good for, eh? Just the ducks, right?"

Ford smiled at him but his cheeks felt as stiff as old leather. He would be goddamned, he thought, if he'd be whored again by his past. It wasn't worth it; nobody's was.

"Hey, didn't you used to come in here a long time ago?" the counterman asked him curiously.

"No," Ford said.

He hurried to the parking lot where he had left his car, holding the brim of his hat and leaning into the rain and wind, and hurrying, hurrying, as if time were a hound at his heels.

CHAPTER 11

TEN minutes after they were shown into their suite at the Château d'Or—by a bellboy whose politely neutral expression exactly matched that of the desk clerks and elevator operator —Ford knew the whole idea had been a miserable mistake.

Maria sat nervously on the edge of the wide bed, as if reluctant to disturb the brocade coverlet, and looked about with cautious, defiant eyes. The suite was three time the size of her trailer, he realized, and even the bathroom could probably sleep six at a pinch. It was a caricature of the plumber's craft, with a bidet, a glass-walled shower, a six-foot tub, double hand basins, and dozens of foamy white towels and virgin cakes of finely milled soap. There were shaving mirrors, full-length mirrors, and magnifying mirrors and a control board studded with switches that operated sun lamps, exhaust fans, air-conditioning ducts, and glowing tubes of fluorescent lighting.

Why in God's name had he brought her here?

He drew the draperies across the windows and lit a cigarette. It was eight o'clock, and he wondered if they should go down for dinner or have something sent up. She was probably hungry. They had stopped for coffee and sandwiches several hours ago, at a diner outside of Camden, New Jersey.

"Well now," he said briskly. "How about dinner?"

"I don't care."

"Would you like a drink first? Or tea or coffee?"

"No, please."

"We're here to enjoy ourselves, you know." He sounded sickeningly hearty, he knew.

181

"It's very big," she said, and nodded quickly and matter-of-factly about the room as if it had long been understood that they both approved of size.

"I have an idea," he said. "Supposing we send down for a drink before we change. O.K.?"

"Yes, all right."

She was wearing the gray tweed suit with brown pumps, and looked very simple and proper, with her hair in a bun and a pale blue scarf at her throat. On the drive over from Pennsylvania, he had held a match to her cigarette at a stoplight and her hands, cupped briefly about his, were like those of a child, thin and brown and clean, with rosy, unpainted fingernails. But to his distress, she had seemed pensive and withdrawn, and there had been no sense of adventure to their excursion, no spark of excitement. He had found himself making conversation, explaining the gray belts of industrial growth they were driving through, and discussing their significance in the accents of a father imparting useful information to an indifferent child.

He could think of nothing to say that would interest her, or make her burst out laughing spontaneously, and turn to him with expectant grateful eyes. She stared at the heavy darkness that was settling over the necklace of lights formed by cracking mills, and he had no idea at all of what she might be thinking about; everything about her was strange and unfamiliar, the apathy, the polite, incurious responses, even the unaccustomed sheen of nylon on her slender legs—this was all alien to his concepts of her, and in the long silences that stretched between them it seemed as if they were sitting on opposites sides of a high, impassable wall.

He wondered again why he had brought her here. And he thought with moody nostalgia of the trailer where—if they were there this minute—she would be chattering happily in his ear, or making something to eat or drink, or lying on her stomach on the couch giggling at the foolishness on television. And where, he thought, they would eventually switch off the lights and go to bed without reserve or embarrassment, and

182

where he would take her to him as naturally as he would a glass of cool water on a hot summer day.

Everything was wrong that night. From the overly elaborate food which was wheeled in on a bulky steam table, preposterous with its sputtering alcohol burners and intricate warming compartments, right on to the quick and almost furtive kiss she gave him before moving far to her side of the big bed and going to sleep.

But she wasn't sleeping, he knew; occasionally she would forget to regulate her breathing, and he could hear her sigh then, like a lonely, irritable child. He lay awake smoking a tasteless cigarette and marveling at his own stupidity. It was late before he managed to fall asleep.

But in the morning, after one sleepy, startled look around the room, her spirits soared magically. Springing up in bed, she knelt beside him, and her knees dug sharply into his back as she shook his shoulder with both hands. "Oh, it's so wonderful," she said. "Oh, get up, look at it." Ford turned over and put his arm behind her and rubbed a hand slowly over the backs of her slim legs. He was breathless with need for her, as he looked up into her bright laughing eyes, and saw the long black hair streaming down her bare shoulders. She smelled of sleep, and a faint cologne, and the muscles in his stomach became cold and taut as he felt the find down of her legs against the palm of his hand. "Maria," he said, and turned to put his other arm about her, but she slipped away and sprang to the floor on the opposite side of the bed.

As she ran into the sitting room, calling excitedly over her shoulder for him to join her, he realized with regret that rousing him had been the farthest thing from her mind. Like a child she just wanted company, a witness to all this fun and novelty. It was better than last night, at least, he thought. At least she was happy. Considering the way she'd left him, he felt in a commendably philosophical mood as he picked up the telephone and ordered their breakfast.

He had no notion what had revived her spirits so miraculously. After a bath she wandered barefoot through their rooms, hair piled up on her head, and a huge towel wrapped around her body. She seemed delighted with everything, the white telephones, the thick carpetings, the lavish bathroom, and the view of the smooth, gray waves charging endlessly at the white beaches.

"Now you like it," Ford said. "What was wrong last night?"

"I don't know. It just seemed big then. I didn't know it was so beautiful."

He sensed she wasn't telling him the truth, but he didn't press the point.

They went swimming that afternoon. At first, she was startled at the suggestion. She sat on the edge of the bed, one bare foot resting on the other, and shook her head obstinately.

"No. I don't—I can't swim."

"That doesn't matter. There's a shallow end. You can just splash around."

"No. Isn't it cold?"

"Of course not. It's a heated pool."

"No, I don't want to. I don't have a bathing suit. We used to walk in a little stream when I was little, but I didn't like it. The stones were sharp."

"There are hardly any stones at all in this pool. You can get a suit in the locker room. They rent them. There's an attendant there, a woman, who'll show you where to put your clothes."

"Can you swim?"

"Fairly well."

She sighed. "Is it fun?"

"Well, yes."

"You want to?" She regarded him with a comical little smile. "Swim?"

They hadn't been out of bed since breakfast. He smiled back at her, and said: "Yes, I want to swim. Come on."

She sighed. "All right."

The surface of the pool was pale green, and smooth as a pond on a still summer day. Music floated eerily through the warm, humid, faintly medicinal air, and echoed with ringing, buoyant sounds from the heavy mass of calm water. The wicker chairs and lounges at the sides of the pool were empty, but a white-jacketed waiter wearing a yachting cap stood languidly behind a small bar which was decorated with crossed tridents, and mermaids whose tails twitched and flickered in an exotic neon frenzy. Ford swam two slow lengths of the pool waiting for Maria. When she came out of the women's locker room, wearing a tight black bathing suit and holding a rubber cap uneasily in her hands, she looked so shy and nervous, so painfully thin and delicate, that he felt a gentle stir of compassion for her; but when she smiled and came tenatively to the edge of the pool, his heart did a slow, heavy flip-flop inside his chest, for there was a poignant appeal in her tentative smile, and she moved with the lovely awkward grace of a young heron.

He had to coax her to come into the water, but when she slipped into the shallow end of the pool a little shriek of surprise and delight burst from her lips.

"Oh, it's so warm." She jumped up and down and the water sparkled like cut glass on her hair and eyelashes. He had an impulse to take her in his arms, to comfort and reassure her, for it suddenly seemed tragic to him that she should be worried and concerned about the vulgar trappings of this hotel. He wanted her to see them for what they were, to enjoy them or laugh at them, whichever she wished. But the thought troubled him for it wasn't rooted in passion; it was kinder than that, and it reflected a consideration and responsibility that had no relation to his physical needs.

They walked on the cold empty beaches the rest of that afternoon, until the last sunlight faded and blurred into the gray colors of the sea. The wind was stingingly cold on their cheeks, and the sand was so hard and packed that their footprints stretched out behind them as cleanly and precisely as if they had been made in frozen snow. They collected pocketsful of seashells and counted the ships cutting along the gray horizon. When it was nearly dark, Ford bought containers of

185

coffee from a drugstore on the boardwalk and they settled down on a ledge of smooth rock in the lee of wooden pilings that supported a pier. The breeze blew her hair back from her forehead, and when they tried to drink the coffee they found that their hands were too stiff with cold to manage the cardboard containers efficiently. Gulls were wheeling and screeching above their heads. Maria looked up at them, staring straight up, so that the tendons in her throat were in clean relief against her skin. She stared at them for a long time, and he said: "Now what are you thinking about? What do you see?"

She smiled at him and put her head against his knee. "I don't know. I was playing a game. I was trying to see it so well that I could remember all of it. Not just as one thing, but all the little things too."

She didn't want to go down to the dining room that night.

"Can't we eat right here?" she asked him wistfully.

"Sure. Whatever you like. But I thought it might be fun to get dressed up, and listen to some music. But I'll call room service."

"No." She sighed humorously. "You want me to go?"

"I think you'll enjoy it."

"All right. If you want me to."

He smiled at her. "I want you to."

Ford showered and put on a dark suit, and made himself a drink in the living room while she was dressing. He could hear her light quick footsteps, the soft rush of water in the tub, the rustle of fabrics, and every sound struck his nerves with an almost painful flick of excitement. He looked out at the darkness where he could sense the limitless motion of the sea, and smoked a cigarette and sipped his drink. Trying to sort out his memories of the day, he thought of the pool, their walk along the beach, her strange, childish excitement that morning, but the details blurred into a general sense of contentment and what isolated itself finally was the moment they had rested on the rocks in the lee of the pier, and she had stared up through the gathering darkness at the gulls. Why that seemed especially important he didn't know, but it seemed for some reason to embrace the essence of the whole day.

The door opened, and he turned as Maria came into the room. She smiled and made an awkward gesture with her hands. "Is it—am I all right?"

"You look lovely," he said. "Lovely, Maria."

She was wearing the short black evening dress and the warm lights of the room gleamed on her bare shoulders and arms. The flaring skirt, with a shine of pink petticoats about the hem, swung neatly and precisely about her slim brown legs. Her long dark hair was braided and coiled in a single glistening knot at the back of her head. She smiled tentatively at him. "Are you sure?"

He could only sigh at her question. She was beautiful. There was strength and grace in every line of her body, and a lovely excitement and hope shining in her eyes. He was touched by her need for his approval and reassurance; and he was saddened by all the things she didn't know, for one day she would probably know them all too well. "Yes, I'm sure," he said. "Very sure."

Ford asked for a corner table in the dining room, which was nearly empty. A string quartet played gently and apologetically, as if reluctant to disturb the candlelight atmosphere and cathedral silence of the vast room.

"How would you like a shrimp cocktail and a sirloin steak?" he asked her.

"Oh wonderful. With catsup?"

"Of course." Ford glanced up at the waiter just in time to see the tail of a tolerant smile disappearing around the corner of his mouth. "That will be for two," he said shortly. "The shrimp cocktail and the sirloin with catsup. You can save the sauce Béarnaise and the sauce Bordelaise for Rotary."

"Why, yes, of course, sir. Of course."

"The steak medium rare. And with that we'll have the baked potato, asparagus, and some good fresh celery if you've got it, instead of a salad."

187

"Yes sir. I'll see that everything's just as you wish it. And would you care for something to drink first?"

"Yes. One Scotch mist and one bottle of beer."

"Very good, sir."

Maria looked at Ford when the waiter went away with the menus. "You were—angry with him?"

He didn't want to talk about the waiter. "No, I was just hungry. Aren't you?"

"Oh yes. Walking on the beach in the wind was so much fun."

In the candlelight there were warm shadows at the base of her throat, and in the gentle hollows formed by the thin ridge of her collarbones. He could see the reflections of the candles shining in the depth of her startlingly clear brown eyes, and she looked so lovely then, with her shoulders bare, and the dark hair swept back from the clean lines of her face, that he knew he might say something foolish and extravagant if he so much as touched her hand.

"Please talk to me," she said.

"All right. What shall I talk about?"

"That was silly. Talk about anything. I just like to listen."

He thought of telling her of the school board meeting, and the colored girl named Sarah Green. That would make him look nice and worthy. She would approve of the picture he could draw of himself standing tall and righteous against the unfairness and stupidity of his friends. But he was too honest to try to buy approval for that ambiguous performance. The incident still troubled him, and he didn't take any comfort from the credit he had gained in some areas, or the irritation he had created in others. Clay had called him the morning after the meeting, bubbling with good-humored congratulations. He despised all formality and convention, and so he had assessed Ford's performance as a blow struck in behalf of his own convictions. And Sally Cullinan, when they were leaving the Shires' that night, had squeezed his arm unexpectedly, and had given him a quick, grateful smile. "I'd just about resigned from the human race," she'd whispered to him.

188

"Thanks for letting me keep my membership card."

Which was all pleasant enough, except that Ford knew he hadn't earned this approval at all, for what he'd done hadn't cost him a damn thing. He had simply exercised the privilege of authority, as he'd exercised it tonight over the trifling matter of catsup. He had put Sarah Green in Miss Crane's with no more effort than it had taken to remove a supercilious smile from the waiter's face. And in his heart he wondered if he really gave a damn whether or not Sarah Green got into Miss Crane's. If it had cost something, would he have paid?

He saw that Maria was frowning faintly. "I'm sorry, I was supposed to be talking to you," he said. "I forgot."

"It doesn't matter. I'm happy."

"You're sure?"

"Oh, yes."

But she was still frowning, and her eyes seemed sad. He wondered what was wrong. It was as if a switch had been thrown inside her; shadows had replaced the light in her face.

"What's the matter?"

"It's really just nothing. But everything is right, and it's what I was afraid of. Do you know what I mean?"

He had no notion of what she was getting at. "That doesn't make sense," he said. "If everything's all right, why worry?"

"You wouldn't be able to understand," she said.

"I can understand anything you tell me," he said. He picked up her hand and pressed it gently between his. "I want you to believe that. I'll understand anything you say."

"How do you know? How are you so sure?"

Ford had an answer to this question, a kind and sensible and reassuring one, but he startled himself completely by not using it; instead he tightened his grip on her hand, and said: "Because I'm in love with you. Anything you feel, anything you're afraid of, I'm sure I can understand. . . ."

He told her this again in their room, and again as they lay together in bed, but he couldn't make her believe him, for each time she shook her head stubbornly and said, in a helpless, worried voice: "You don't know anything, so it doesn't make any sense. You don't know why I'm afraid, you can't understand." She went on this way for another few minutes, repeating the same words over and over again, and making halfhearted but irritable efforts to pull herself free from his arms. Finally she lay quietly against him, and Ford said: "All right, I don't understand. Do you feel better now? Is that what you wanted me to say?"

"Oh, I don't know. It's no good to talk." She snuggled close to him and put her head on his shoulder. "Can we go walking on the beach in the morning? That's all I want to do. . . ."

Sometime later the phone began to ring. He raised himself on one elbow and fumbled around for the receiver. Pressing it against his ear, he said: "Yes, hello?" Maria stirred beside him, but then turned on her side without altering the slow steady rhythm of her breathing. The room was dark and he could see the green hands and numerals of his travel clock shining on the night table. It was three-thirty.

"Yes?" he said again, for he could hear nothing but music and faint laughter in his ear. "Hello? What room are you calling?"

"Ford you devil!" It was Wiley Poston's voice, charged with rich, drunken exuberance. "You're a devil, that's all you are."

"Where are you?" Ford came fully awake then, as alert as if a lightning bolt had exploded in the room.

"Just down the hall a piece." Wiley's voice suddenly soared into a whoop of laughter. "I'd of sworn you didn't have it in you. Where'd you find her? My eyes clicked together like a pair of bowling balls when I saw you there in the dining room. You try to get *her* into Miss Crane's, and we won't have nothing to squabble about. Damn, how'd you meet her? She got any sisters?"

"What are you doing over here?"

"Trying to buy a hunter from Arny Goldman. He uses this can house for an office. Now you go on to sleep. Don't worry, I ain't seen nothing. But Ford, give her a good-night kiss for old Uncle Wiley, hey?" With a last choking burst of laughter, Wiley hung up.

190

"Who was that?" Maria asked him sleepily.

"The room clerk. Don't worry, go to sleep."

"Are we leaving tomorrow? Going back?"

"Yes, early, I think. Please go to sleep."

When her breathing settled into a gentle even rhythm, Ford sighed and put out a hand for a cigarette.

But they didn't go back the next morning. He was troubled by Wiley's call, and Maria seemed to sense that something was wrong. Ford didn't want their trip to end this way, so he turned his car south and drove down the coastal highway through Avalon and Stone Harbor and Wildwood, and stopped for the night at a motel outside of Cape Way.

He wasn't worried about Wiley's talking. Wiley had certain inflexible standards which stood like props under his notions of gentlemanly conduct. You didn't bet cinch hands in friendly poker games, you didn't make passes at your friends' wives, you didn't reproach pals for what they said or did while drinking, and you never spread news of a buddy's extramural sexual activities. So that wasn't it. Ford didn't feel embarrassed or guilty, but he did know that the heedless innocent phase of his relationship with Maria was over. The vacuum enclosing his happiness had been split wide open. From now on he would have to be clever and careful, and in an area of lies and maneuverings he knew there were seeds of shame and self-disgust. They were already sprouting, he realized unhappily, for Wiley's call had made him think of Janet. Her last few letters had been short and querulous. She couldn't understand what was keeping him from joining her. Was everything all right? When was he coming down? She wanted a definite date. And so forth and so on. Her mother had joined her, and that wasn't helping matters, Ford knew.

They saw gulls and wild ducks on the way down to Cape Way, and heard them calling in the marshes formed by flat, icy sheets of water seeping inland from the ocean. The air was streaked with fog, and the sun was a feeble glare under the low gray sky. But some of the scrub bushes were already turning green and the dark hard earth was soft where the frosts were melting. It was lonely, empty country, and the bars and motels shone like neon oases through the thick, salty mists.

They played darts and drank beer in the lounge of the motel, and the next day they drove to Lewes Beach and ate king crabs at a tiny restaurant with a glassed-in terrace. They talked and laughed in a comfortable fashion and she seemed very much at ease with him; but the shy and tentative awareness of a fuller communion which they had known briefly at the hotel was gone. Thinking of those moments of sweet, natural intimacy made him feel irritable and depressed. He had never know the languishing sickness of self-pity before, and he was dismayed at his bitter resentment of the vague "they" which threatened his happiness. It seemed to him that he had got very little out of life. He looked into his past and saw himself moving about precisely and formally in a dance without meaning. And when there was a chance to charge his life with significance and fulfillment, "they" stood ready with a thousand hysterical arguments to oppose and destroy it.

This moment now was fine, with salt air all around them, and beer in beaded mugs and platters of sweet red crabs on the table, but Ford wanted more than this. He didn't know how to go about getting it, though. And he didn't know how much he would have to pay for it.

CHAPTER 12

CATHERINE had returned while Ford was away. She was waiting for him when he came up from the parking lot, and he knew from the solemn look on her dark face that something was wrong.

"Well, did you have a nice trip?" he asked her.

"Yes sir, Mr. Jackson. And my sister sends her regards to you and Mrs. Jackson. But your brother been here three or four times this weekend looking for you. And he don't seem right at all. He always talk funny, but now it seems like he talking crazy."

"When was this? When was he here, I mean?"

"He came first Saturday afternoon. Then he came back after dinner. Next time was Sunday in the morning. Then he called yesterday, two or three times. So far I haven't heard nothing from him today."

"I'll get in touch with him, Catherine."

"You better do that. And Mrs. Jackson called last night. She and her mother both expect you down there for some sun."

"Was my brother drinking?"

Catherine stiffened loyally. Clay had always been her favorite, and she seemed to interpret Ford's question as a reflection on her judgment. " 'Course he was drinking some," she said. "He always do. And it never bothers him. Just makes him jokative. Not like some others I know. But he worried about something. And it ain't drinking, that's not what bothering him anymore." Like most Negroes in the County, she used "anymore" for "now." "You had your breakfast, Mr. Jackson?"

193

she asked him then, with a glint of suspicion in her narrowing eyes; her tone and manner indicated that only a ferocious, unsteadying hunger could be responsible for his disloyalty to Clay.

"Yes, I have," he said, smiling in spite of the worries nagging at him. "But I'd like some coffee, please."

Ford walked down to his study and threw his overcoat over the arm of a chair. The house and its pressures seemed to settle on him with a smothering weight, as he dialed Clay's number. But Clay wasn't home; the maid said he'd gone out and hadn't said when he'd be back. Alicia wasn't there either. Ford called the Cedars and talked with the locker-room attendant, a courtly old Scotsman he had known for years.

"Why yes, Mr. Jackson, Mr. Clay was here for a bit Saturday afternoon."

"Barney, I'd appreciate it if you'd be honest with me. What shape was he in?"

"Well, sir, if a gentleman can't be a bit free and easy in his own club, that's not a good thing, is it?"

"Was he drunk?"

"I believe you might say so, sir. You know how amusing he can be. But this seemed a bit different. I tried to get him to have some coffee and take a nice rubdown, but I couldn't manage it."

"What time did he leave?"

"About five, I think."

"Thanks, Barney. Thanks very much."

Ford tried the Cottersville Trapshooters, and a half-a-dozen friends, without getting a line on his brother. But from the overly casual manner of some of the people he talked with, he surmised that Clay's behavior must have been fairly erratic. When he went into the office later, Mrs. Simpson confirmed this guess. Clay had called her at home Sunday night.

"I'm not exactly sure what he wanted," Mrs. Simpson said with a nervous little laugh. "What I mean, I wasn't sure he was serious. He told me he'd been arrested for staging a cockfight in the basement of the Episcopal Church. That was a joke, of course, but then he asked me to come and get him, and he became—well, quite emotional. I tried to find out where he was, but I couldn't understand a word he was saying."

"Try his home, please. If he's not there, keep ringing every ten minutes or so. And try to find out where Alicia is."

But there was no news of Clay until late in the afternoon. And then it came from Catherine.

"He here now, Mr. Jackson," she said, in a low, rapid voice. "Better get on home."

"What shape's he in?"

"He wandering around like he don't know where he's at."

"You keep him there. Get Jones to help if necessary."

"I'll mind Mr. Clay. I don't need Jones messing with him."

"Thank you. I'll be right there."

Clay was lying in the study, stretched out on the long couch with a glass and a bottle of Scotch on the floor beside his trailing hand. He was wearing a dinner jacket, but his black tie was pulled down from the collar of a soiled shirt, and streaks of blond hair were matted against his damp forehead. He smiled brightly at Ford, but his eyes remained hard and wary, like cold tiny flames gleaming in the wastes of his sullen face.

"You may mount the pulpit," he said, in a thick, sonorous voice. "We all is waitin' on you, Preacher Jackson."

"I thought you were going to quit drinking for a while."

"Why so I was, so I was." Clay heaved himself to a sitting position and fumbled around shakily for his glass. "But it seemed kind of pointless. I mean, temperance is for the intemperate, and so forth. I simply can't qualify for A.A. I was blackballed, as a matter of fact. For holding my booze like a gentleman. For always being polite, gracious, and well-groomed." He rubbed his unshaven jaw, and smiled with secret amusement into his glass. "It's not that I'm too stoned to handle a razor, old man. No indeed! I'm growing a beard. Then I shall put myself into a bottle, an aging beatnik to be washed up on the shores of some distant Bohemia."

"Why did you start drinking again?"

"I told you. Since I handle it so elegantly, it seemed point-less not to."

"I heard about some of your elegant drinking over the weekend."

"My dear pals couldn't wait to slip the knives in, eh? Did they whisper all the scandalous details into your large, quiver-ing ear?"

"I have no details, and I don't want any. I'd just like to know why you're beating yourself stupid with a whisky bottle."

"Oh, you've got to have details! That's the most amusing part of my sodden saga." Clay picked up the bottle of Scotch and began filling his glass with a surprisingly steady hand. "Notice that?" he said, smiling approvingly at the even flow of liquor. "Nerves like a frigging mongoose. Saturday afternoon there was one nice, gamy detail. Tony Marshall said to me, and I quote: 'If you can't handle liquor, then I suggest you leave it alone.' And I said to him, and again I quote: 'If you can't contribute anything fresher than that to the discussion, I suggest you keep your big fat mouth shut.'"

"I'll take your word you behaved like a fool."

"Be a pal, and hear the details. At dinner in my shiny little evening suit, I got into two seedy brawls. One with our fat-headed club manager, who had an absurd notion I'd had enough to drink. The second was with Harvey Shires, who had an equally absurd notion I was paying court to Dora just because I'd jabbed her bottom a few times with a swizzle stick."

"That was Saturday night. Where were you Sunday?"

"I drove about the countryside at high speeds. I'm not sure of Sunday's details. Let's see. I was at the Colloways' briefly. They were having a party. I pepped things up, since it was all very dull, and then went on my merry way."

"When were you home last?"

"I'm not sure, old man."

"Don't you give a damn about Alicia? Have you called her?"

A spasm of pain twisted Clay's features. He got up un-steadily, and put a fist tightly against his mouth. "Stop grilling me, for Christ's sake," he said. "Have a drink or something.

Don't sit there staring at me like God Almighty."

"I don't feel that way," Ford said. "I'd help you if I knew how. But there's no point in having a drink. What good will that do?"

"Who knows? Can't we pretend I'm just a garden-variety lush who's stopped by his brother's home for a little hair of the dog, and a little sympathy? Do you have to act like I'm a frigging neurotic who ought to be in a straitjacket?" Clay sat down slowly, and his breathing was like a weary old man's in the silence. "I'm sorry," he said. "I didn't mean to sound like a whining fool." He poured more whisky into his glass and slumped against the arm of the couch, folds of flesh bulging over his collar and cummerbund. The rate of his physical deterioration shocked Ford; his face was gray except for a vivid, unnatural flare of color at the points of his cheekbones, and when he raised his glass to his lips he had to hold it tightly in both hands to keep the liquor from spilling down his chin. The hard, curving lines of his body had been thickened and coarsened in just a few weeks; the normally resilient tone of his flesh was dead and gross. He must have been on this binge for days, Ford thought.

"Alicia's walked out on me," Clay said, and finished his drink in a convulsive swallow. He made a face, and rubbed a hand over his slack lips. "I took it like a sport. Good show, bite the bullet, far, far better thing I do now, and all the rest of that crap." He held the empty glass to his forehead, and began to laugh in a high, choking voice. "I just don't give a damn, you see." The strength seemed to be draining from his pathetically huddled body; his laughter subsided into spasmodic gasps and his head rolled erratically on his shoulders, as if he were trying to evade a stinging flurry of invisible blows.

Ford closed the door of the study, and sat beside him.

"When did this happen? Where did she go?"

"Go? Where did she go? Oh, she's still in residence." Clay laughed weakly. "Models of togetherness, that's us. Only she spends her nights somewhere else. I'm available for morning coffee, that's all. The nights are for loving communion with

197

the chap who succeeds to my—well, my nighttime rights."

"Do you want to tell me who it is?"

"God, why should I be mysterious about it? It's George Delucca."

"I don't believe that for a minute. You're drunk, you don't know what you're saying."

Clay shook his head helplessly, and when he turned to Ford there were tears glinting in his eyes. "You know what's ghastly? I admire the sonofabitch. You'd think I'd want to put a gun to his head. But no! I wish him all the best. What kind of a freak does that make me? For Christ's sake, tell me!"

Clay's voice had risen to a shout. He tried to struggle to his feet, but the effort exhausted him, and he slumped back with a groan, his arms and legs sprawling helplessly on the couch. Broken words sounded in his throat, but his mouth was pressed so tightly against the arm of the couch that Ford couldn't understand what he was trying to say; he heard only choking cries of pain. Clay's fist beat weakly against the couch, and this exertion seemed to drain the last of his strength, for his voice faded into a petulant croon that was as senseless and terrible as the spent weeping of a child.

Ford straightened his arms and legs, and put a pillow under his head. He waited until Clay was asleep, then went to Janet's bathroom and took three sleeping tablets from her medicine cabinet. He crushed and stirred them into a mild whisky and water, and placed the glass on a table in the study, within reach of Clay's hand. Then he put the Scotch bottle away, pulled on his overcoat and went into the kitchen, where Catherine was sitting with her hands locked in her lap, and an expression of dramatic suffering on her dark shining face.

"He's sleeping now," Ford said. "I want you to sit with him until I get back. If he wakes, give him the drink on the table. Don't let him leave here under any circumstances. No matter what he tells you, make him stay, if you have to sit on him."

"I'll take care of Mr. Clay. He'll do like I tell him. But why's he acting this way, Mr. Jackson?"

"I don't know. I just don't know, Catherine."

The night was as turbulent as his thoughts. Winds shook the winter-black trees and the frozen limbs clanged together like iron bars. A sudden lash of rain struck his windshield like a flail. In the yellow tunnels of his headlights he saw that the black asphalt road was running with water. He thought of Clay's anguished, ravaged face, and the choking cries tearing from his throat. And he thought of George Delucca and Alicia, and then—as a streak of vivid lightning cracked across the sky—he remembered guiltily that Maria was afraid of thunderstorms, and that he had promised to see her tonight. Each of his responsibilities was like a magnet pulling him toward danger; each face that blazed in his mind seemed to be crying to him for help.

As he swung into Clay's driveway he saw that Alicia's convertible was parked in the graveled turnaround in front of the house. He had been hoping she wouldn't be home, he realized; if she were out, he could have swung the car around and gone to Maria.

He knew his responsibilities could destroy the delicate fabric of his happiness; and he had longed for a reprieve on any terms.

The maid took his coat and told him Mrs. Jackson was changing.

"I believe she's going out, sir."

"Picked a miserable night for it, didn't she? I'll wait in the living room. Tell her I'm here, please."

The draperies were drawn across the glass walls in the summer living room, and cedar logs burned in the hanging fireplace. The flames danced and flickered over the red tile flooring. Ford warmed his hands and frowned as he looked about the room. He remembered the last time he'd been here, the furniture overturned, the pictures ripped from the wall, and the mess of broken glasses and flowers tangled in the seat of a chair. He had been afraid that night, for Alicia and Clay. Now he was afraid for himself and Maria.

He turned from the fireplace as he heard Alicia's footsteps.

"I'm sorry to barge in this way," he said, as she came into

199

the room.

"Don't be ridiculous. I've got time for a drink, if you have. Do you mind bartending?"

"Of course not. What would you like?"

"A Martini, I think. But not one of the deadly thousand-to-one jobs."

She was wearing a snug, red-wool dress, with deceptively simple lines. Ford had always appreciated women's clothes, and this particular dress struck him as something very special and festive. The tawny colors of the room were a perfect background for her shining brown hair and delicate complexion, and, as she picked up a cigarette and lighter, the firelight flashed on her gold bracelets and earrings, and ran in brilliant streaks about the sheer nylons on her graceful legs.

Ford filled a shaker with ice, and added two long splashes of gin and a sprinkling of vermouth. While the Martinis were chilling he sliced curling peels of skin from a plump lemon and rubbed them about the rims of two long-stemmed cocktail glasses. He dropped the lemon peels into the shaker, and began to stir the drinks. "You going out?" he asked her.

"Yes. I've got a date."

"A date?" He smiled at her. "Who's the lucky guy?"

She sat by the fire and crossed her legs. "It's nice of you to put it that way." She looked up at him then, and met his eyes directly and steadily. "It's George Delucca," she said.

"I didn't believe Clay. I thought he was working his way through the D.T.'s."

"You've talked to him? Where is he?"

"At my place. In pretty bad shape. But he's sleeping now." Ford filled the cocktail glasses with the cold pale blend of gin and vermouth. "Try this for size," he said, and put the glass down on the table beside her.

"Perfect," she said, after sipping it.

So it was true, he thought. And how beautifully civilized they were being about it. Sipping their drinks judiciously, smiling at one another as casually as if they were discussing the weather, rather than the fact that she had walked out on

Clay and was now rolling in the hay on a one-night-stand basis with George Delucca. The cool little charade revolted him; if they were going to talk about her affair with Delucca, they should use language blunt and ugly enough to fit the facts. Instead of which they were chatting and smiling as if she were waiting for some crew-cut youngster to take her off to the Senior Dinner Dance.

He remembered Clay and Alicia's wedding and the golden aura of promise and privilege that had sparkled about the heads of those fairy-tale lovers. The bridal party had filled a floor of the largest hotel in Wilmington. Girls from Sweet Briar and Bryn Mawr and Swarthmore, young men from Ivy colleges, all glowing with youth and confidence, all stimulated by the glamour and perfection of the wedding. Pigskin luggage and camel's-hair coats and leather-wrapped flasks flung about on sofas and chairs. White gloves and alligator pumps and bottles of Chanel decorating suites with profuse lovely elegance. Tickets for the Sugar Bowl, reservations at Stowe, cars lined up to whisk groups off to Pine Valley or Piping Rock or Aiken. Clay and Alicia were like bright stars at the center of a glittering pinwheel, and when they rushed away after the reception, the wheel flew apart and scattered happy groups of their friends in all directions.

There could hardly have been a more auspicious start for two young people, he thought helplessly. The bridegroom was as handsome and proud as a tall golden lance, and the girl smiling happily and gracefully at his side was an ultimate distillate of good breeding, old money, sound values, and elegant cultivation. Gifts had been showered benignly upon them: trusts, endowments, new silver, old silver, a hunting box, diamond earrings, English saddles, a pair of Virginia hams— these last bizarre items had been presented by Wiley Poston, Ford remembered, and had caused some elderly eyebrows to rise in mild disapproval.

And this is how it's ending, he thought; with Clay drunk and bloated and helpless, and the ultimate distillate of good breeding and sound values coupling with a muscular tomcat named George Delucca.

"You're angry, aren't you?" Alicia said. She had been watching his face.

He couldn't frame a temperate answer. "I think it's a damn shame," he said shortly. "I think it's a disgusting business any way you look at it. And I can't believe you've thought very carefully about the consequences of what you're doing."

"I think I'd better mention one thing before you go on," she said carefully, and while her voice was clear and level, a touch of color was rising in her pale cheeks. "I don't intend to listen to any talk of shame and guilt and betrayal. Those words don't mean anything to me."

"Well, how fortunate."

"That I'm so insensitive, you mean?"

"Alicia, please! I'm Clay's brother and I'm worried about him. But I've been your friend too, for a long time. I'm desperately concerned about your happiness. I think you've made a reckless decision. You've had provocation, I know all about that. But what you've started with Delucca can smash you and Clay to pieces. I think you need help as much as he does."

"Perhaps you can help Clay. I can't."

"You're certain of that?"

"I'm not very certain of anything. I know I've tried to help him. And I know I've stopped trying. That's all I'm sure of, Ford."

"Would you mind telling me why you're so cold and final about this?"

"Do you remember the night I called and begged you to come over? Because I was frightened of the way he was acting?"

"Yes, of course."

"When I left here that night I didn't know what in God's name to do. But I knew if I stayed I'd become hysterical. So I drove around, not knowing or caring where I was going, until I came to the White Hackle. I stopped for a brandy. George Delucca came by and said hello to me. I said 'Hi, neighbor' or something like that, because I'd heard he'd bought the Henderson place. He explained what had happened, what you

202

and Wiley and Tony Marshall had done to keep our countryside pure and uncontaminated. You did a very surgical job, I gather."

Ford was stung by her expression; she looked both puzzled and disappointed, as if some valuable and stable object had suddenly twisted itself out of shape before her eyes. He wanted to tell her how the Henderson deal had come about; to explain that he had no part in it; but the ground beneath his position was too shifting and uncertain to support either conviction or anger. But because her attitude placed him on the defensive, he said irritably: "Well, is that why you went to bed with him? Because he's a victim? Because he needs a woman's gentle hand to wipe away his tears?"

She looked away from him quickly, but not before he saw that her lips were trembling. "We may not ever talk about this again, Ford," she said. "For your sake—since you're concerned about Clay—I wish you could listen without being sarcastic."

"I'm sorry," he said. Ford suddenly felt weary and helpless. "I tried to hurt you because I'm ashamed of the way we handled the Henderson deal. It's irrelevant now, but I tried to persuade Tony and Wiley to go about it differently. I've always respected your approval, and I'm sorry I've forfeited it. But that aside, I hope it wasn't Delucca's disappointment over a piece of real estate that prompted you to start this affair with him."

"No, that wasn't it, of course," she said. "I didn't feel sorry for him. And I'm not blaming Clay, or pretending I was driven into this. That night at the White Hackle we talked for a long time. Two or three hours anyway. I told him what happened. You may think that's curious, but he seemed kind and wise, and I didn't have anybody else to tell. His advice was about the same as yours a few weeks ago. Give the poor guy a chance, roll with the punch, these things work themselves out. Et cetera, et cetera. When it was time to leave, I didn't want to go home. I didn't suggest we go to a motel—but I think I made it clear I wouldn't object if he suggested it."

"You were drinking brandy all this time?"

"I wasn't drunk, if that's what you mean."

"Is that how it started?" Ford tried to keep his tone neutral, but the bitterness he felt gave it an unexpectedly sharp edge. "You indicated you were available, and he said fine?"

"If that's what happened I wouldn't consider it any of your business. I'm telling you because you're worried about Clay. George wasn't one damn bit interested in what you call my 'availability.' When he sensed I might be, he was as shocked as you are now. He signed my bar check, and told me to get my coat. He insisted on taking me home in his car, but one of his waiters came along behind in mine, so we were a nice respectable convoy. Believe me, the last thing on his mind was light dalliance with a shaky young matron. I'm very grateful to him now. But at the time I felt like it was just one more goose egg to chalk up for my side."

"You're grateful to him? Why?"

"Because he didn't take advantage of the fact that I was so bruised and damaged that I might have bawled like a baby if anyone had so much as patted my hand. When you've been humiliated enough, and kicked enough, you find yourself grabbing at a smile or a gentle word the way a starving dog grabs at a bone. He could have had an effortless little conquest. Nothing was stopping him, certainly not me. He just couldn't stand the notion that I'd be so grateful I might lick his hand. I think it was generous of him."

"He behaved decently, I'll grant that. But it hardly calls for canonization."

"Aren't you just a bit surprised that he behaved as he did?"

"Frankly, yes. I've heard he's got quite a reputation with the ladies."

"I thought you'd miss the point," Alicia said coolly. "It was surprising, but for reasons you can't see. After you'd treated him like dirt, after you'd made it brutally clear that you didn't want him or his daughters breathing the oh-so-pure air of the Downs, after all that, he still wouldn't take advantage of an opportunity to treat me as a common slut. That's what I thought was generous. Not making war on your enemy's women—isn't that a quaint, old-fashioned notion?"

"Well, I gather he eventually overcame that quaint old-fashioned notion," Ford said.

"With my help. And Clay's."

"I thought you said Clay had nothing to do with this."

"He didn't affect my decision. He affected George's. We got home that night about two o'clock. Clay was waiting for us, and he behaved so contemptibly that I wished—I mean this literally—that he would just die, stop breathing, collapse, and never move again."

"Please, Alicia," Ford said gently. "That doesn't sound like you. I don't think you mean it. But let me get this straight. I left here that night around midnight. Before leaving I had a talk with Clay. He was terrified because you'd gone. And ashamed of the way he'd acted. He told me he couldn't bear the thought of losing you. I wasn't very sympathetic, believe me. I told him he'd behaved like a fool, and that I saw no hope for him unless he quit drinking cold. He promised me he would. I gave him some aspirin and got him into bed. He was sleeping soundly when I left."

"He was awake when we got here," she said.

"Let me finish. I called him the next morning, but he said nothing about seeing you and Delucca. He sounded remorseful, and so forth, but he told me—I remember his words—that he knew he'd been a mess the night before, and so did you, so you had that much in common."

"He's lying. Either that, or he blacked out and doesn't remember. You wonder why I seem so cold and final about this? Clay didn't play the haughty squire or the suspicious husband. Oh no! He was delighted to see George." Alicia rubbed her arms with a quick, convulsive gesture; a violent shudder had shaken her body. "Yes, so pleased," she said, in a low, trembling voice. "He simpered around him pretending he was pimping for me. He described me in clinically sexual terms, defining my charms like a circus barker. But like an honest merchant, pointing out various hidden blemishes too. He explained what I was good at, and what I wasn't good at. What I

205

liked, what I disliked." Alicia's voice was rising slowly and steadily, and she spat the words out as if they were filth on her tongue. "Do you understand? He wasn't making things up. He was telling the exact truth about me, as only he could know it."

Alicia suddenly shook her head and pressed the tips of her fingers against her temples. "We left—I don't remember it—we just left. He tried to hit George, I think. I don't know. I just prayed for it to be over, for him to die, to choke, anything that would stop it."

Ford watched helplessly as she tried to get herself under control. She brushed a tear from her cheek, lit a cigarette with shaky hands, and picked up her drink.

"Do you intend to divorce him?" he asked her then.

"I don't know—yes, I suppose so. I've talked to him about it. He knows I'm seeing George, but he refuses to believe I'm serious. He's playing his familiar roles—the tragic clown, the penitent little boy, the defiant rakehell. So far he's been too elusive, and I've been too shaky, to get anything at all settled."

"If you do get it settled—get a divorce, that is—then you'd marry Delucca?"

She looked down at her tightly locked hands. "Perhaps, I don't know. He's a Catholic, and that seems to raise all sorts of problems."

"Are you telling me in all seriousness he won't marry you because you're not a Catholic?"

"It complicates things, at least," she said with a wan smile.

Ford was suddenly swept with irritation. "Damn it, who's he trying to fool? At present he's sleeping with a married woman which, according to his religion, is a sin punishable by eternal damnation. He takes that chance cheerfully enough, I presume, but balks at marrying you—which isn't a sin at all, but simply a matter of social inconvenience. Does that make sense to you?"

"Frankly, not much. But it does to him. He's concerned about exposing his two young daughters to what he calls a 'mixed marriage.' They do mean a great deal to him. So does

206

his religion. Those things do make sense to me. If you believe in God at all, it seems absurd not to take the whole bit seriously. Our friends believe in their church. They regard God—I don't know—like some wealthy and socially impeccable broker who drops in on Sunday mornings to give them tips on the big market in the sky."

"Couldn't you simplify things a bit by becoming a Catholic? Or would he find something wrong with that, too?"

"I could become a Catholic, sure. But I'd rather not have to pretend I believe in things I don't."

"But you'll continue seeing him? Whether or not you're— well, what should I say?—spiritually acceptable to him and his daughters?"

She smiled faintly. "That's what seems to bother you. That he's cheeky enough to think I'm not good enough for him. You know, Ford, I've discovered that there are some taboos in life which weren't established solely by the good gray folk on the Downs. Maybe that's the way things balance out. You didn't find him acceptable as a neighbor; he can't find me acceptable as a wife."

She spoke lightly, the gentle smile still playing about her lips, but under her bland, whimsical tone, he sensed an unmistakable blaze of conviction; it wasn't just sympathy for the underdog, or anger at injustice, or indignation at the trials of an impersonal victim which had caused this serenely challenging light to glow in her face and eyes; in her manner he recognized the strength and confidence of a woman in love.

He felt stirred by a weary compassion for her then. It made him feel clumsy and helpless. For there was no way he could put this into words. She was vulnerable and exposed and the consequences of what she had plunged into would slash her to pieces. But she didn't know that now, and she wouldn't listen to him if he tried to tell her.

She had ventured like a reckless child beyond the walls of a strong fortress, and while she took a heedless pleasure in chasing one strange delight after another, she ran the risk of losing herself forever in a trackless no-man's land.

She was standing. "I really must go, Ford."

"Yes, of course." He rose too. "Is there anything you want me to tell Clay?"

"No, there's nothing, Ford."

Clay had waked while Ford was out. Catherine had made him drink two bowls of soup, and he had responded quite amazingly to this nourishment. And also, Ford guessed, to Catherine's loving, bullying attentions, and her fierce grumbling resentment at whatever it might be that was troubling and badgering him so unfairly. He was back in the warm, secure embrace of violently partisan approval; he had been called incorrigible, naughty, reckless, and impossible—in gentle, chuckling tones, while food was spooned into him, and his bruises were allowed to heal under the warmth of fondly protective eyes.

Ford closed the study door. Clay glanced at him with a wary, little smile; he had sobered up enough to gauge Ford's expression accurately.

"You talked to Alicia, I guess," he said.

"Yes. Do you want her back?"

Clay winced and rubbed his forehead. "If I were a decent character, if I had any kindness in me, I'd say no—regardless of what I felt. The nicest present I could give her would be to get the hell out of her life."

"Do you want her back?"

"Yes. With all my heart and soul. Do you believe me?"

"I'm not sure. You apparently drove her to Delucca. She told me what happened the night he brought her home."

"Please, for God's sake. Don't you think I feel rotten enough about that? I can't bear to think of it. I was drunk, I was trying to strike a light note—I was joking. But it all went wrong."

"I'm going to try to break up this thing with Delucca. For Alicia's sake. There's nothing for her with him. So you're getting a last chance. But first I'm going to tell you something; if you continue drinking, and if you ever—just once, goddamn

208

it—throw this Delucca thing up to her, I'll handle her divorce so fast it will be over before you sober up. Now do you understand that clearly?"

"Yes, yes," Clay said. He couldn't seem to meet Ford's eyes; his gaze wandered desperately about the room, as if seeking some place where there might be a refuge or solace for his misery. "I understand, yes," he said thickly. "I don't deserve it. I don't deserve her, I've ruined everything with this brainless boozing. But I want a chance. You don't blame me, do you, Ford? Please say I've got a right to this last chance."

"I don't know about rights. You're getting a chance, anyway. It's up to you from now on."

"What can you do, Ford? It's too late, it's just too late."

"Maybe," Ford said. "If it's too late, it's too late."

Clay turned his head away. "Please help me," he said in a frantic little voice.

"All right. I'm going to try. Do you feel up to making the stairs? Or do you want to sleep down here?"

"This is all right."

"I'll leave the light on, if you want."

"No." Clay smiled wearily. "Turn it out. Mother always left one on in my room. Do you remember: It wasn't that I was afraid of the dark. Oh, no! I was just too imaginative, too sensitive. I'd stay awake all night making up fantastic stories about the furniture if the room was dark. Do you remember all that?"

Upstairs in his bedroom, Ford paced the floor restlessly and smoked a cigarette. Finally he turned off the lights and lay down in the darkness. He was trying not to think of Maria. He couldn't see her tonight; he couldn't see her again until he had done what he had to do for Clay and Alicia. They were important; they had to be saved, because they were part of him, because they represented the continuity and sanity of his existence. But he bitterly resented their demands on him. They admitted weakness, they confessed inadequacy, they cried out for help. But he couldn't do that. Although he was no stronger

209

than they were.

The weight of his passion was a lonely, frightening burden; it seemed to press down on him as finally and as terrifyingly as a gravestone. And he, too, longed to cry out to someone for help.

CHAPTER 13

AT ten the next morning Ford pulled into the parking lot behind the White Hackle. It had been raining all night, and the tall oaks and maples that lined the driveway were black and dripping with water. The restaurant had been remodeled on the frame of a stately old home, and now it oozed a blandly spurious Deep South charm, with white-columned porches and delicate fretworks of wrought-iron balconies girding the second-floor windows.

There were four dining rooms on the first floor; three were small and intimate, but the fourth extended the entire width of the house, and its windows looked out on superb views of meadows sparkling with tiny ponds.

Ford stopped in the broad hallway that led to the main dining room. The beige carpeting was like foam rubber under his shoes, and through the gloom of the gray morning, he could see the glint of chandeliers ahead of him, tables heaped with plates and silver, and the orchestra stand with its empty chairs and music racks. He had never been here at this hour before, and the quiet seemed incongruous. Then footsteps sounded crisply, and a slim woman with gray hair appeared in the arched entrance to the dining room. She was Maggie Donovan, who, Ford knew, ranked just below Delucca in the echelons of the White Hackle.

"Hello, Mr. Jackson. I thought I heard someone come in."

"Good morning, Maggie. I stopped by to see George. I hope he's got a free minute."

"There's someone with him now. But I don't imagine he'll

be long. Would you like to come up to his office?"

Ford followed her up the broad curving stairway to the second floor, where there were offices, powder rooms, and—for a clique of Delucca's friends—a barber shop and a small, compact gymnasium with steam cabinets, sun lamps, and showers. Maggie took him into the reception room off Delucca's office. The wallpaper was a soft yellow, and the old pine furniture had been rubbed down until it shone like warm honey. She gave him the morning paper, but as he opened it he became aware of voices rising behind the door of Delucca's office.

Maggie frowned faintly, as if assaying the content and the significance of the conversation that poured clearly through the open transom above the door.

"He won't be long," she said then, coolly and judiciously. "He's talking to one of the waiters."

"No hurry," Ford said, but he couldn't concentrate on the newspaper.

"Okay, go on, Sulkowski," Delucca was saying, in a coldly deliberate voice. "The customers got under your skin, did they?"

"That's right, Mr. Delucca. They couldn't make up their minds about anything. Kept changing their orders around like I was some IBM machine."

Sulkowski, Ford thought—that would be Ed Sulkowski, a tidy, middle-aged man with thinning gray hair and small undistinguished features. He was a good waiter, in Ford's opinion, unobtrusively swift, as obedient as a trained monkey.

"You had table six," Delucca said. "The Morrisons, the Gottshalks, and the Whitheads. And they couldn't make up their minds, eh? So go on."

"Well, I want you to understand I didn't blow up all of a sudden. It was going on all through dinner—first they didn't want this, then they didn't want that. I was running back and forth from the kitchen like I was bucking for a coronary. I swear that's the truth, Mr. Delucca. It was after dessert, after coffee, that I got fed up right to here. They wanted four brandies, two green mints. So I bring 'em. Then they want

212

three green mints. Mrs. Morrison, she's changed her mind. So back to the bar I go. It still ain't right. Mr. Gottshalk, he don't want the brandy. He wants a coffee with white rum. Back to the bar again. Now Mrs. Morrison changes her mind again. 'I don't care for the brandy,' she says, without looking at me or saying what she *does* want. So I stand there waiting while she's talking about her kids at school with Mrs. Whithead. Finally she tells me she wants a beer, so I take the brandy back and bring her a beer. Right away, Mr. Morrison decides he wants a beer too. He could of told me when I was getting Mrs. Morrison's, right? So I said to him—and this is all I said —I said, 'You don't care how you work my ankle, do you?' Honest to God, that's all I said! And he blows up like a volcano, goes yelling to Miss Maggie. I ain't proud of what I did. But I'm a human being, not a dog. And no job on earth is worth being treated like a dog for."

"I see," Delucca said. "You want to quit, eh?"

"Well—no. I didn't say that."

"You want me to fire you then?"

"No, Mr. Delucca. That ain't what I want."

There was the sound of a fist slammed heavily onto a desk top. Delucca's voice rose angrily. "Get this through your head, Sulkowski! Morrison picked up a tab for sixty-eight bucks here last night. For that he expects and deserves service, and by the sweet Jesus Christ he's going to get it. You hired out as a waiter. You asked for the job! I didn't come looking for you. Now all of a sudden, you got temperament! What the hell do you think you are? A violin player? A movie star? Or a union organizer maybe? You want to climb on a table and make speeches about the rights of man?"

"Mr. Delucca, please. I just meant—"

"You meant shit! You work here, you'll do the job right all the time, perfect, correct, attentive, and not just when you feel like it and your feet don't hurt."

Maggie Donovan had crossed her arms and was listening with a thoughtful, appraising frown to Delucca's tirade. She nodded occasionally, in a grimly judicious manner. There was no doubt whose side she was on, for when Sulkowski attempted to defend himself, she sighed impatiently, as if this were an impertinent digression from the issues under consideration.

"You can't just fire me, Mr. Delucca," Sulkowski said desperately. "I had provocation. Our local's had cases like this before. If the provocation's sufficient, it ain't the waiter's fault, Mr. O'Brien told us."

"You're whistling for the union cops, eh?" Delucca's voice was softer, but now his anger and disgust seemed much more genuine. "You're the one who yapped off to Morrison. Your bad manners could cost me five grand a year. But you don't care because you can yell for your business agent. You had provocation! Your sensitive Polack feelings were hurt because a customer asked for a bottle of beer. Christ!" They heard Delucca's feet hit the floor with a crash, and then the rapid clicks of a spinning telephone dial. "O.K., Sulkowski, you just listen!" There was a pause; then Delucca said sharply: "Local 180. This is Delucca. Is Babe O'Brien around?"

"Please, you don't have to call him," Sulkowski said.

"You brought his name up, not me. So listen! Babe? Delucca. How's the kid? Great! Now look, I got a waiter here who insulted a customer last night. You're damn right— a good customer. What did he do? What do I care? Maybe he jabbed him in the ass with a serving fork. Hell no, I'm not serious. It's Ed Sulkowski. Yeah, he's been O.K. till now. What I want to know is, are you going to give me trouble if I fire him?" There was a long pause and then Delucca said grimly: "Yeah, and I'm worth thirty-nine jobs to your local, just remember that too." After another pause, Delucca said: O.K., O.K., Babe. How about some handball next week?"

Seconds later, the phone was put down with a soft click.

"There was the American labor movement speaking in its authentic voice," Delucca said bitterly. "You know what he told me, Ed? Can you guess? 'Fire the bastard!' That's what you pay dues for. If it's any consolation, I feel as lousy as you do now."

"Well, if I'm fired, I'm fired," Sulkowski said in a feeble

little voice.

"You're not fired," Delucca said sharply, and Maggie Donovan pursed her lips in disapproval. "I wouldn't fire you now if you set fire to Sam Morrison. But, goddamn it, let's be realistic. You and I know Sam Morrison is a flannel-mouth jerk." Ford had to suppress an inclination to laugh; he had never heard a better description of Sam Morrison. "I'm supposed to sweat whether he has a good time in my joint," Delucca went on, but now there was a dry and weary thread of humor running through his voice. "He complains to Miss Maggie about something, and I've got to go downstairs and listen while he tells me the Chablis he ordered isn't quite as flinty and well-bred as something or other he got from a tap in France while he was over there on his honeymoon back before the First World War. He's got a palate like a wool mitten. He knows Burgundy comes in bottles with hips, and Bordeaux in bottles with shoulders, and that's all he does know. But I listen to him, and I pay attention to him, because that's the business I'm in. Our job is to give Mr. Morrison what he wants for his dough. Now you think you can remember that, Ed?"

"Yes sir, I'll remember it."

"O.K., then let's forget this. Take a pheasant from the freezer and give your wife a treat over the weekend. And be nice to the trade from now on, Ed, or so help me, things'll be different next time."

Ed Sulkowski came out of Delucca's office with a shine of perspiration on his small red face. He walked past Ford with quick, jerky steps, as if his central motors were whirling about at desperately erratic speeds.

Maggie Donovan slipped from her desk and went into Delucca's office. "Mr. Jackson's here to see you," she said.

"All right, send him in."

Delucca sat with his cordovan brogues propped up on his desk. He wore a camel's-hair sports jacket, dark brown slacks, and a white shirt with a red wool-knit tie. There was no trace of the interview with Sulkowski in his expression or manner; he didn't rise, he didn't take his feet from his desk, and the look he gave Ford was one of casual inquiry.

"I'd like to talk to you privately," Ford said, and glanced up at the open transom.

"O.K. Let's go down to the bar."

In the empty lounge off the foyer, the small black tables were set for cocktails. Delucca seemed to be checking the appointments of the room as he waved Ford to a table. He glanced critically at bowls of nuts, ashtrays, and books of matches emblazoned with spurred cocks, before turning to the bar where orange slices and shavings of lemon peel were arranged in silver saucers and a plump bartender in a white jacket was solemnly spooning cherries from a jar into a glass bowl.

"Tony, go have some coffee," Delucca said, as he sat down and began to strip the cellophane from a cigar. "So what can I do for you?" he asked Ford. He lit his cigar, staring steadily at him, and the spurting flame from the lighter flared brightly across his hard, tanned face and glossy black hair.

Ford waited for the bartender to leave. Then he said: "It would be pointless to say I hope we can keep this friendly. Let's try to be functional at least. For what it's worth to you, I'm not taking sides. I'm not making any judgments."

"Anybody as neutral as that can't be concerned one way or the other."

"You're wrong. The fact that you're seeing my sister-in-law concerns me deeply."

"Ah, so that's it. I thought you might be here to complain about an overcooked steak or something."

"Obviously you're the one who isn't concerned," Ford said quietly. "It's the only inference I can draw from this whimsical attitude of yours."

Delucca drew a deep breath and let it out slowly. "Alicia told you about us?"

"My brother did. I talked to her last night. She admitted it."

"I can see how impartial you are. Admitted it! Like she was caught rolling in the hay with one of your grooms.

"All right, I'll withdraw the word. I'm not here to quibble

216

about shades of meaning. I'm here to ask you to stop seeing her."

"Well, I figured that. You don't look like you're about to apply for the job as best man. One thing I'd like to ask you! How come you're carrying the ball? Where's your brother?"

"He's not well."

"He's drunk. Isn't that what you mean?"

Ford realized that Delucca was trying to make him lose his temper and this gave him confidence; for he knew from his legal experience that people in the wrong were usually reluctant to discuss their problems calmly and reasonably. They always hoped, unconsciously at least, to obscure their guilt with smoke screens of emotion.

"All right, if you prefer the word drunk, we'll refer to him as a drunk," Ford said.

"And you still want Alicia to stick with him? In spite of that?"

"Yes, I do. They have the same backgrounds, the same friends, the same interests. Over the long run, their best chance of happiness lies in staying together."

"You think she's happy with him now?"

"Obviously she's not. There are ups and downs in all marriages. But let me say this: those ups and downs are even bumpier in the arrangements you're providing for her. She tells me you won't marry her because of some religious conviction or other. Do you feel there's any hope in that situation? One-night stands, weekends in New York, the odd afternoon in a cheap motel? Do you imagine she'll thrive on that schedule?"

There was a suggestion of mild derision in the twist of Delucca's lips, but when he pulled slowly on his cigar the glowing tip illuminated the anger in his narrowing eyes. He studied Ford thoughtfully. "Maybe that wouldn't bother me," he said. "Life's a series of one-night stands, isn't it? I got a steady run, with matinees Wednesdays and Saturdays. Why should I want to change things?"

"Why did you want to buy a home on the Downs?"

217

Delucca stared evenly at Ford. "You really got nerve," he said. Color was rising in his darkly tanned face. "Maybe gall's the word."

"You wanted to change things. You wanted a horse barn and ponies, a pleasant country life for your daughters. But it didn't work out, did it, George?"

"I got a roof over my head, don't worry about me."

"Not the one you wanted. Are you afraid of my question? Why did you try to buy a home on the Downs?"

"I needed a secluded place for a floating crap game," Delucca said very softly. "That barn on the Henderson place looked just right. And the kids were going to grow marijuana in the greenhouse. For pin money, so they could pay for their own abortions."

"Forgive me, but I don't find that funny."

"It's a matter of viewpoint, Mr. Jackson."

"Well, I intend to be serious. I hope you won't find it a strain. You wanted those things for your daughters. Horses, good schools, a pleasant way of life in the best section of the county. Isn't that right?"

"Supposing I did. What do you want for yours? Outhouses? A shack beside some dump? A room over a garage? I've got the same right you have to try to be a good father. Maybe that will strike you funny."

Ford lit a cigarette, and said, "Of course it doesn't. Let's assume you had bought the Henderson place. How old are your daughters?"

"Eight and twelve."

"They'd have a good deal of fun, of course. Ponies, open fields, and so forth. But they wouldn't belong to the crowd that shows horses, and fox hunts. They wouldn't take tennis and golf lessons at the Cedars, or go on sleighing and skating parties with the youngsters from Miss Crane's. But they'd know all of that was going on, and eventually they'd realize that what you'd bought for them was standing room on the sidewalk outside a candy store. They could press their noses against the windows forever, but they could never get inside."

218

"Maybe they might have turned into outlaws," Delucca said, smiling oddly at the glowing tip of his cigar. "They've watched lots of television. They'd raise hell on the range, cuttin' 'em off at the pass, bushwhacking foxhunters in the gulch. The dago kids, twirling spaghetti instead of lassos." He drew a slow deep breath, as if he couldn't get quite enough air into his lungs. "All right, it didn't work out," he said, staring down at his big hands. "You're here about something else. Get the hell on with it."

"It could have worked out pleasantly, though," Ford said. "It still might."

"What do you mean by that?"

"I think you understand. But if you want me to spell it out, I will. I want you to stop seeing Alicia. You want a home, and certain other things, on the Downs. Somewhere between those two goals, there's an area of accommodation, the makings of a bargain, I think."

"Keep spelling," Delucca said. "I want to see all the fine print."

Ford suddenly felt a bitter contempt for himself, and for what he was doing; but balancing that was an equal contempt for Delucca, who was watching with a speculative smile on his full lips, and tiny lights of interest shining from his lidded eyes. He was figuring the angles, Ford knew, checking the various strengths and weaknesses of his position, and estimating with complacent shrewdness the profits to be gained in the haggle over a woman's body. Delucca would know that acts of contrition and expiation and love were also acts of commerce, and that fear and guilt and passion were tangible, measurable factors to be used like counters to manipulate the affairs of men. But Ford wasn't intimidated by this, for he could imagine how meaningless Delucca's goals were. Delucca would drive a shrewd, savage bargain, of course, but, like any other savage, he'd trade what was priceless for a handful of beads and tinsel.

"Here's what I propose," he said. "I own several properties on the Downs. The houses would need remodeling, but the

219

situations are just as good, I think, as the Henderson place. You could have whichever one suits you best. We'll work out a comfortable mortgage arrangement. If you care to join the Cedars, I'd put you up and make it my business to see that your application is acted on favorably. As far as your children are concerned, if you'd like them to go Miss Crane's, I'll do everything I can for them."

"I hear you shoehorned a colored kid in there," Delucca said. "After that, a pair of wops should be a cinch." He grinned faintly. "Well, are you through? Is that the package?"

"Did I forget anything?"

"No, you touched all bases, I guess. Home, club, school, something for everybody. And I wind up a proper gentleman. Is that the shiny ring I can grab from this merry-go-round? A country squire chasing foxes in a red coat?" Delucca rolled the cigar slowly between his lips, his eyes crinkling with amusement. "I assume I get to ride with the Darby Hounds?"

"You still think this is a joke?"

"That's just a peasant reflex, Mr. Jackson. Instead of choking up with gratitude, I hide behind grins and wisecracks. But I'll be serious, if you want. You'll do all this for me on one condition. Which is that I kindly stop sleeping with your sister-in-law, right?"

Ford held his temper with an effort. "If it amuses you to refer to her like that, go ahead."

"I'm being serious, that's all. I want to call the shots accurately. So we understand this deal." Delucca rubbed his hands together briskly. "You know, we need a drink. Nothing like a sociable drink to pep up a business conference. What'll you have?"

"Nothing, thank you."

"Come on, don't be like that. Let's lubricate the wheels of commerce, eh?" He smiled over his shoulder at Ford as he walked to the bar. "And you might need a drink before we're through." He collected a bottle and two shot glasses and returned to the table with the mincing, elaborately precise steps of an obsequious waiter. His dark features were twisted into

220

a caricature of smiling conciliation. "This is eighteen-year-old bourbon, Mr. Jackson, sippin' whisky we call it, with pardonable pride. I think we can dispense with water or soda." He placed the glasses on the table with a gesture that suggested a nimble subservience, and filled them to the brim with a practiced turn of his wrist. "Just try that. I'm sure you'll enjoy it."

"I told you I didn't want a drink."

Delucca shrugged indifferently and downed his drink with a quick flip of his hand. Then he put the glass on the table and looked at Ford with a cold smile. "O.K., let's cut all the crap," he said, in a voice that was suddenly bitter with anger. "You've been talking about good schools and clubs, about areas of accommodation, about gentlemanly bargains. None of it sweetens the stinking fact that you're here pimping for your brother, trying to buy his woman back with cash on the line. That's the filth you brought here with you, so let's start calling it by its right name. You're a pimp. And you're offering me a chance to play your game, to grovel in the dirt with you!"

Delucca swore in a choking, inarticulate voice, and swept the glasses and bottle from the table top with a furious swing of his arm. "You think you've got me figured out, eh?" he shouted over the splintering crash of glass. "And what are you going to offer the next guy who comes along? You thought of that? Supposing he's a caddy or a groom? You going to buy him a home on the Downs, and a membership in the Cedars, too? Because I won't be the last one! What she can't get from that drunken brother of yours, she'll get somewhere else." He began to laugh then, harshly and bitterly, and his eyes were shining with a strange brilliance in the straining frame of his face.

"You'll change the whole tone of the community. Go out to play golf and you'll find stable boys in your foursome. There'll be milkmen and plumbers living all over the Downs. Just because they had a roll in the hay with little Alicia Jackson. The word will spread. Christ, how it will spread." Delucca put a clenched fist against his forehead. "Anybody who wants

221

to make it big here, will have to make it with her first. They'll be swarming around the place picking out their estates in advance. They'll be comparing notes—" His voice broke suddenly, and he moved his fist from his forehead and ground it slowly and brutally against his lips.

The bartender appeared in the doorway of the lounge, his eyes switching anxiously from Delucca to the shattered glass on the floor. "Anything wrong, Mr. Delucca?"   .

"Get out of here," Delucca said hoarsely. Sweat had formed like blisters on his forehead, and he was still grinding his fist against his mouth. He stared at the table, breathing slowly and heavily. "You too," he said to Ford. "Get out."

"If you want, all right. But I know you didn't mean any of that."

"What do you know. You don't know a damned thing."

Ford was sickened by the pain in Delucca's face. Or by his own grossness and ignorance, he didn't know which. Christ forgive me, he thought, wearily.

"It couldn't work with us," Delucca said in a cold, empty voice; he hardly seemed aware of Ford's presence. He sat with his shoulders slumped and his hands hanging at his sides. "If she left her husband while he's sick and needs her, she'd never be happy about it. And if she wasn't happy, I couldn't stand it. There are two strikes against us everywhere we look. She can't see it, but I can."

"What are you going to do?"

"Do?" Delucca stood and began pacing the floor, the broken glass crunching under his heavy brogues. He pressed both hands tightly to his temples. "Do? It's done. It's all over. I told her last night. Finished. Kaput. Over. Save your place on the Downs, and your goddamn clubs and schools. It's yours for nothing. You got it all free. Bighearted George! Stitching up her self-respect, propping up her ego, making everything all right. And I get hooked in the process, so hooked I'd need a knife to cut it out of me."

"You're in love with her?"

"It's over, you want it in writing?" Delucca said bitterly.

"I can understand how you feel. I'm sorry."

"I told you once, you don't know anything about it."

"Perhaps," Ford said quietly. He looked out the windows and saw the limbs of a maple tree moving like black arms against the sky. And he thought of Maria then. "You'd like to be at peace with her," he said slowly. "To talk to her without thinking of all the things you can't say. You wish you could be the first man she ever met, and that everything between you was fresh and clear and honest. Instead of going to her with a sack of fears and pressures and worries on your back. And I'll tell you what's worst of it all. You make complete sense to each other. And not one damn bit to the world. Isn't that right, George?"

Delucca had stopped pacing. He was looking at Ford curiously. "You sound like it's a town you might have played," he said. "When was it? Lately?"

"Yes," Ford said.

"Maybe I should sympathize with you," Delucca said dryly. "Funny, but I don't."

Ford stood up slowly and collected his hat and gloves. "You were right about the drink," he said. "I could have used it."

Delucca nodded indifferently toward the bar. "Take one."

"No thanks, I'll be going."

"Just one thing. Don't ever tell her you were here. She might think I didn't make up my own mind. That would make it rougher."

"Is there anything else I can do?"

"Just leave, I guess. I'm sick of you, and I'm sick of myself right now."

"You know, I can't blame you," Ford said.

At his office Ford told Mrs. Simpson to try to get him a reservation on the afternoon flight to Palm Beach.

"Yes, of course." She smiled warmly. "Shall I wire Mrs. Jackson you're coming down?"

"If the reservation's confirmed, yes."

"She'll be pleased to get you away from this miserable winter of ours. And I think you could use some sunshine, Mr. Jackson."

He could use something, Ford thought. But what? He longed to go to Maria, to take her away somewhere, but until he knew what he was going to do with his life, he couldn't do that again.

Mrs. Simpson was still standing in the doorway. "There's something I've been meaning to ask you about," she said. "Do you remember a while back—around Christmas, I think—you gave me four hundred dollars in cash?"

"Why, yes," Ford said, and felt his heart shift with a sudden, uneven stroke.

"You said a young man would be by for it?"

"Yes, that's right. His name was—Tatnall, right?"

"Yes. You wrote it on the envelope. Well, he hasn't picked it up, Mr. Jackson, and I don't like the idea of keeping that much cash in my desk. Shall I hold on to it? Or deposit it in our office account?"

"He didn't come by for it? You're sure?" He knew his voice sounded strained and anxious. "Well, that's odd," he said, and cleared his throat.

"Yes, I thought so too. I called Sheriff Thomas and he told me Tatnall had been released the day after you'd talked with him at the workhouse."

"I see." Ford drummed his fingers on his desk top, aware of Mrs. Simpson's curious eyes. "I think you'd better deposit the money. It's nothing important. Just a small claim I'd handled for him."

"Well, I hope he shows up for it," Mrs. Simpson said.

"I'm sure he will," he said slowly.

Ford spent ten days in Palm Beach with Janet and her mother. Mrs. Marsten's home, which was two blocks from Worth Avenue, was one of the few things in life which seemed to satisfy her completely. It had been bought for a song by Mr. Marsten during the depression, and it stood now as a symbol of his sound business instincts and, more importantly,

224

as tangible evidence of his affectionate concern for the comfort of his wife's declining years. "He knew he wouldn't live to enjoy it," Mrs. Marsten frequently remarked through heavy sighs. "But he didn't want me staying in hotels. He always said, 'Old girl, when I'm not around, I'd rather you didn't have to depend on room clerks and bellboys.' But he would have loved it so. The golf and the swimming! He was such an old silly about keeping fit."

But as hard as she tried to sound distressed about all this, her attempt usually failed; she couldn't soften an edge of satisfaction in her voice when she spoke of poor Mr. Marsten, and she seemed too complacently aware of her own stoutly pumping heart, and the proprietary press of her buttocks against the cushions of her favorite wicker lounge.

Janet had spent the winter cultivating a tan. With a non-typical fixity of purpose, she had devoted all her time and energy to the task, and had succeeded in baking her flesh to the shade of a strong cigar. She breakfasted in a bikini on a wide plastic sofa in the garden, after oiling and basting her arms and legs and shoulders as if they were joints being readied for the oven. The contrast of deeply browned skin with her blue eyes and gray-blond hair was not unattractive, but she seemed to feel there was still room for improvement, for she lay spread-eagled the morning through under the full glare of the sun, protected only by cotton eyepads and the token bits of cloth at loins and breasts.

In the afternoon they went to the Bath and Tennis Club, or played golf at the Everglades. In the evenings they sat about the screened porch, with the living room air conditioner pumping its damp exhausts into the night, and sipped cold drinks and listened to the insects droning about the garden.

Ford was smothered by the atmosphere. Everything Mrs. Marsten said irritated him. He knew this was unfair, but he could not help it. She was on a self-improvement binge, and was querulous because Janet wouldn't join her. She baked bits of colored clay in the kitchen and gave names like Mood and Stillborn to the results. She belonged to a study group, and reported its quarrels every night at dinner, in such a manner that it nearly drove Ford from the table.

He was strangled by feelings of guilt and anxiety, and thinking of Maria only added to his gloom. Where was she now? Had she called him at his office? Or did she give a damn that he had gone away? And Buddy Tatnall. . . . Where was he?

Janet affected a flirtatious pique at the fact that he hadn't written oftener. "Three teeny, measly letters," she said, removing one oil-soaked cotton patch to peer toward where he was sitting with his morning coffee. "Just three! I did hope you'd at least tell me how cold and miserable it was back home." She replaced the eye patch and consigned her body to its customary posture of immolation under the lambent heat of the sun. "What were you doing, for heaven's sake? You didn't see the Postons, I know. Ellie wrote me. You must have been an absolute hermit."

"I tidied up some odds and ends of work," he said, from behind his newspaper.

They talked a good deal about the children. Peter and Ginny had both been writing regularly to Janet. Ginny had become serious about school this term, apparently perceiving at last the relationship between work and grades. She was aiming at a B-plus average, but seemed to feel her math instructor was trying to frustrate her ambitions. "He's very poor, and hates everybody but the scholarship kids," she had written. "They sigh about detergent rash and chipped nails, and he acts like they're hiking barefoot through Siberia. If he knows you ride or sail you'd have to be an Einstein to get a decent mark. So keep my dark, dark secret!"

Peter hadn't decided about his Army service. He could enlist now for two years, and then return to Princeton for his degree. But he was thinking about the Marines, it seemed.

"Did he say anything about that Catholic business?" Ford asked Janet.

"No, thank heavens. And please don't mention it when mother's around. I haven't told her. It seems to have blown over, anyway. I guess it's like communism or marijuana, something young people just have to *flirt* with at one time or another."

The night before he left, Ford suggested they all have dinner at the Everglades. Mrs. Marsten looked unhappy. Her study group was discussing the Algerian problem that evening. In French. She had talked of nothing else for the last few days. She was eager to join Ford and Janet, obviously; but after poring over dictionaries and phrase books for hours every night, and beleaguering Ford for help in translating words like "unfair" and "ungrateful" and "plastic explosives," she could find no graceful way to change her plans. So chewing her lip bravely, she went off alone.

Ford and Janet had a pleasant time. She drank three strong Martinis at home with deliberate relish, and when they got to the club her mood was one of holiday extravagance. She remembered something about the night Ginny was born and it started her giggling helplessly. They had been at a dance at the Cedars and Ford was wearing a white linen suit. When it suddenly became imperative to leave for the hospital, several friends had accompanied them. Someone began calling Ford "Dr. Jackson" on the way because of his white jacket, and the joke had spread all over the hospital. What had made Janet giggle almost hysterically was the memory of the young doctor who had delivered Ginny. He had been called in at the last minute, because Janet's obstetrician, old Dr. Radcliff, had gone off to a medical meeting in New York, certain the baby wouldn't be along for another few weeks.

The earnest young substitute, whose name they couldn't even recall now, had been taken in by the joke about Ford's being a doctor and had discussed Ginny's delivery and Janet's postnatal condition with him in the gravest of technical terms, until Ford had interrupted him by saying, "Well, I gather it's a girl, and that everybody's doing fine," and the young doctor had said admiringly: "You older men cut right to the meat of things, don't you?" And this line had been a favorite with their crowd for years afterward. Appended to any situation or comment, it always provoked howls of laughter.

It had been a pleasant evening, Ford thought, as he was getting ready for bed. He and Janet still shared some worthwhile memories after all these years. And it had been good to see her cheerfully giddy with Martinis, and free from the deflating pressures of her mother's frowns and sighs. But the words he was forced to use to frame these thoughts depressed him. Good, pleasant, worthwhile . . . they were accurate enough, of course; precisely right; pale, temperate, unexciting. To describe their life together, now, or in any conceivable future, Ford knew he would probably never have to look for words with any more color or voltage.

When he came out of the shower with a towel around his waist, Janet murmured a drowsy good night to him, and fell asleep almost immediately.

Ford had dinner with Clay and Alicia the night he got home from Palm Beach. It was an uncomfortable evening. Clay tried too hard to be amusing. He seemed nervous and uncertain, as if something had smashed the mainspring of his hard, irreverent confidence. But he looked better, at least, Ford thought; the sagging lines were gone from his face, and his eyes were clear and alert. He took nothing but a token sip of wine at dinner.

While he was off in the den rummaging around for a new recording, Alicia poured Ford's coffee and said quietly, "You needn't worry about us anymore. As you can plainly see, we're back together sharing bed and board with feelings only a few miles short of pure ecstasy."

"I'm glad, Alicia. Honestly, I am."

"I'm not very much interested in your gladness, Ford. Everybody's got what they wanted out of this but me. You have little brother living with his devoted wife again. Little brother's got me, which is what he apparently wants. Even George is happy with his altruistic pose. So that leaves me? What do I get, Ford? You're a lawyer. Who can we sue?"

They sat facing one another across the coffee table in the

228

summer living room. She was wearing a brown jersey dress with a wide black ribbon in her hair. The severity of her clothes might have been chosen to match the bitter expression about her eyes and mouth.

And Delucca loved her, he thought. Was torn and twisted with his need for her. And he still did this to her. Because of something that was more important to him. Ford couldn't suppress the sudden, almost traitorous thought that Delucca had chosen stupidly.

"I'm sorry, Alicia," he said. "I hope you'll believe me."

"Nice girls belong in their nice legal beds," she said coldly. "There's another cliché for you. Courtesy of George Delucca."

"It's all over then?"

"Definitely and completely. Courtesy of George Delucca once again." She turned her head and stared down at the fire. "I accepted his decision—his brush-off—with exquisite breeding and manners. 'So sorry, my dear. Understand perfectly. Best all around. Cheerio! Pip! Pip!'" She drew in her breath with a sharp gasp, as if a brutal and totally unexpected pain had suddenly shot through her body.

"Oh yes I did!" she said, in a voice trembling with the pressure of tears. "I begged him to let me stay with him. On his terms. On any terms. Live abroad, live in California, or in a tent on the Cottersville Pike. I didn't give a damn. I'd leave Clay, divorce Clay, hire somebody to dump him in the lake strapped to a barrel of whisky. But wise old George wouldn't buy any of it. Not a penny's worth."

Clay came hurrying into the room with a touchingly triumphant smile on his face. "I found it, Alicia," he said. "Wait until you hear this character! Ford, he does a routine about a guy from Brooklyn on his first trip to the country. He sees a farmer milking a cow, and he thinks—but you've got to hear it!" He stood smiling at Alicia, tentatively and anxiously, like a nervous child desperately attempting to assure himself of his mother's approval and affection. . . .

It was midnight when Ford got home, but he knew there was no point in trying to sleep.

He walked in the garden beside the house for almost an hour, smoking one cigarette after another, and feeling with a sense of restless excitement the soft, moist earth settling springily under his shoes. The night was mild for March and the moon was riding high in a clear sky. Soon the maples would be blazing, he realized, their hard red buds glowing like a warm feathery fire in the stands of timber. And bright green spears of skunk cabbage would be thrusting up through the swamps, and all the lawns would be delicately colored with crocuses and blue squills. Ice would melt, and water would stand in pools in the meadow, and run swiftly alongside the back country roads, rippling and shining with impatient noise and movement.

Ford felt a sudden excitement sweeping through him as he walked up and down the dark, damp-smelling garden. It was as if an intolerable burden had been lifted from his back. He had kept his bargain with Clay, and with himself. His brother's house was in order; and Alicia would eventually know that was for the best. In time, in time . . .

Now he was free.

The lie didn't bother him, for he was hardly aware that he was lying; all he knew was the cold strength of his need for Maria.

He looked at his watch and he went inside; it was Sunday morning.

CHAPTER 14

THE Catholic church in Rosedale was crowded for nine-o'clock Mass. Ford found a seat in one of the back pews, edging himself in with Dr. McIntyre, and Tom Pyle, who worked in Simon's Hardware Store. They made way for him with quick, surprised smiles.

The air was heavy with flowers and incense. Candles flickered in candelabra on each side of the tabernacle, their soft golden lights playing over the waxy sprays of Easter lilies on the altar. There were many Puerto Ricans in the congregation, small scrubbed men, and dutifully solemn-looking women.

Everyone stood when the priest and altar boys entered the sacristy, and through this sudden shifting and stirring, Ford saw Maria in one of the pews facing the altar railing. She was wearing the gray tweed suit he had bought for her, and a white scarf in place of a hat. Her shining black hair was pulled into a soft knot at the base of her neck.

The congregation knelt as the priest prayed at the foot of the altar. Ford lost sight of Maria then, but by moving sideways slightly he found her white scarf and—when a man turned his head to cough—he saw the smooth slim line of her throat. Her hands were clasped together, and her head was bent low, so that her fingertips almost touched her chin.

The ritual of the Mass seemed as strange and unreal to him as underwater fantasy; the stocky priest and his alert acolytes seemed to float through a haze of incense and sunlight, and the glossy trappings of the ceremony—the golden chalice, the brass candelabra, the muted rose and purple of the priest's vestments, which flared like a bullfighter's cape as he made his precise wheels and turns—all these threw off splintered, dazzling reflections from the cold sun pouring through the windows above the altar.

Ford was lulled into a trancelike state by the narcotic blendings of tedium and ritual. It seemed to him that something important was going on at the altar, but there was more sensibility than sense in his judgment, more feeling than thought; the effect of mystery and significance was created by crude theatrical techniques, he knew, cabalistic garments and incantations, by softly chiming bells, and fragrances that invoked racial memories of ancient splendors and pageantry. But there was no criticism in this appraisal; he felt an odd need to be accepted here, if not with approval, then with tolerance, and so he stood and knelt in unison with the congregation, and raised and lowered his head on cues from Dr. McIntyre and Tom Pyle, and tried to adjust himself inconspicuously to the crowd's practiced responses to the priest's gestures, and to the chimes which sounded at varying intervals from the altar.

When the Mass came to an end, and the priest left the altar, Ford allowed Dr. McIntyre and Tom Pyle to precede him into the aisle. As he waited for Maria to make her way to the rear of the church, his smile felt as stiff and dry as something made of wax.

When she saw him waiting in the last pew she hesitated and looked quickly over her shoulder, as if she were searching desperately for an escape through the crowd; but the heavy press of bodies pushed her along relentlessly.

He joined her when she reached his pew, and they moved with the crowd through the foyer with its dully gleaming holy-water font, and down to the sun-splashed sidewalk in front of the church.

Under a light fair sky, the spell created by the chimes and incense was broken. Men lighted cigarettes, women clung to the hands of restless children, and the air was noisy with the rush of traffic on the highway, and cheerful scraps of

232

talk about the weather, and bowling and business.

They stood facing one another in a vacuum created by their own tensions, and Ford knew that several groups of people were watching him discreetly.

"Let me take you home," he said.

"No, I can't."

"I want to talk to you."

She looked embarrassed. "I can't go with you."

"All right, we can talk here."

She smiled uneasily and pushed a strand of hair from her forehead. "They're watching you," she said.

"They don't have much taste. They should be watching you."

"Let's go, please," she said nervously.

They walked away from the church. Ford nodded to people who smiled and said hello to him, but Maria stared straight ahead, her hands locked tightly about a small purse. Tall buttonwood trees lined the streets, their rough trunks marked with gray and white patches like the hides of old animals, but the upper branches were full of thin sunlight, which splashed down and dotted the lawns and sidewalks in bright patterns of copper and gold. The church crowd was well behind them, but Maria was hurrying so that her high heels sounded in staccato bursts on the old paving stones. Ford caught her arm, "What's the matter? Why don't you want me to take you home?"

"Roby and Martha, they're coming for dinner."

"You mean lunch, I imagine."

"They say dinner in the middle of the day. Does it make any difference?"

"And who else is coming?" Ford said, watching her face. "Buddy?"

She looked at him curiously. "Buddy? Where is he? Do you know?"

"I thought you might."

"I never seen him—I *have* never seen him," she said, shaking her head irritably. "It was before Christmas that I—" she hesitated before saying tentatively: "that I saw him? Is that right?"

"How the devil would I know?" he asked her irritably. "You saw him, or you didn't. Which was it?"

She looked confused. "I think it's saw. Is seen better?"

When the sense of her question dawned on him, he felt almost weak with relief. "Saw is correct," he said. "Perfectly correct. It was before Christmas that you saw him."

"Yes, that's what I told you."

"I know." The muscles in his face felt queer, and he realized that he was resisting an impulse to burst out laughing.

"What's the matter?" she said, looking at him anxiously.

"Nothing's the matter. What are you having for dinner?"

"Potato salad, it's already made." For an instant her air of reserve dissolved; she sighed irritably. "But it's no good. I made it with onions and mayonnaise and it's bitter. But there's bologna and bread and pickles."

They came to his car, and she stopped uncertainly. Ford put his hands on her shoulders, and turned her to face him.

"I'm sorry I didn't tell you I was going away," he said. "I had to think about things, to make up my mind. Now I must talk to you."

She rubbed her cheek with the back of her hand, in a childish gesture of embarrassment. "All right. But I told you about the potato salad. It's not good at all."

As they drove out of Rosedale, Ford thought of what he wanted to tell her. He had lain awake most of the night thinking about it. Somehow, he had to arrange to continue seeing her. On a permanent basis, a peaceful and honorable basis. Regardless of the consequences. It had been blazingly clear in the night, with every consideration subjugated to his longing for Maria. He had reduced his problem to its only important essence; passion had cauterized the wounds he might inflict on Janet and the children. But in the daylight, with sun and air around him, and the hum of traffic in his ears, it was all different somehow. . . .

"What did you want to tell me?" Maria asked him.

234

"It can wait until after lunch."

Fortunately she seemed happy to sit and watch the country-side sliding by her window. But the evasion exasperated Ford. He knew precisely what he wanted to say, but he found it difficult to put it into clear and simple words. When they got to the trailer, he decided to talk to her before Roby and Martha arrived, but the chance was gone by then, for she changed into slacks and a white shirt, and plunged anxiously into preparations for lunch.

Ford turned on the television. He felt awkward and in the way. She fussed about the kitchen, murmuring breathless injunctions to herself and yelping with distress over one crisis or another, while he smoked a cigarette and stared without interest at a news program.

There were jars of wood violets and snowdrops arranged neatly on the window sills, and the card table was set with very shiny knives and forks. In the middle of the table was a bowl of fresh spring leaves. Cigarettes were standing in a pair of egg cups.

She had done all this for Roby and Martha. She hadn't been waiting in despair for him. She had her own interests, her own friends to keep her happy. He was here as a supplicant, a nearly middle-aged man, to give him all the best of it, with graying temples and pointlessly fine clothes, warming himself gratefully in the presence of her glowing youth. The plans he had made and the dreams he had dreamed last night suddenly seemed preposterous. To take her away! To Spain or South America, where he would find her an apartment or villa, and where she would be comfortable with her own language about her. And there, in a villa on the sea, or an apartment in a splendid city, she would wait dutifully for him, trying on clothes, listening to the radio, sipping a drink at a sidewalk café, eating her meals alone. . . . Oh yes she would! Killing months of her life while waiting for that magical moment when his plane landed, his key turned in the lock. . . .

"Aiee!" she cried suddenly. There was a look of comical guilt on her face. She pressed both hands over her mouth in

235

a childish gesture of alarm. "I forgot the beer," she said. "I told Roby I would get it last night. He even gave me money. Oh, I was sure I wouldn't forget."

Ford sighed wearily. "Don't you have anything else?"

"But he likes beer. And he drinks it only Sundays. It's too hot in the mushroom houses to drink in the week. Oh, he'll think I'm a fool."

"I might possibly avert this disaster."

"What?"

"I can get some beer."

"No, everything's closed. It's Sunday."

"I'll find some. Don't worry. What kind does he like? A nippy American brand? Or a full-bodied, creamy lager from Germany?"

"What's the matter? You sound funny? Are you mad about something?"

He was spared the ignominy of a truthful answer or the childishness of a sarcastic one by the arrival of Roby and Martha, who knocked twice, ritualistically, then pushed the door open and crowded into the trailer.

Ford had met them a half-dozen times during the winter, and they grinned at him now, quickly and shyly, as if they weren't quite sure of their welcome.

Ford hadn't seen Roby in the daylight before, and he felt a stab of compassion now as he saw, in bright sunlight, the hideous blue birthmark on his left cheek, the grooved and corroded patch of flesh as big as a man's hand, which glistened on his face from his hairline down to the firm edge of his jaw. But the disfigurement, once his eye had attested it, had said, in effect, "Yes, it's real, it exists!" seemed only to emphasize the cheerful light in Roby's eyes, and the graceful proportions of his massive frame. He wore freshly laundered jeans and a white shirt, and his chest and shoulders rose like an inverted anvil from a waistline that looked as flat and springy as something made of bone and leather. Like many big and powerful men, his manner was shy, almost apologetic, as if he were embarrassed at towering over the group, and was eager to re-

236

assure everyone that he had nothing but peaceful thoughts in his heart.

His wife, Martha, was small and chattery, with pert blue eyes and blond bangs. She lisped slightly, but seemed to know this was an attractive defect, for she grinned cheerfully over her sibilant difficulties. She wore slacks and sneakers, and a little pink sweater with rhinestones around the collar, and her openly adoring attitude toward Roby made Ford feel embarrassed and irritable.

Before lunch, Ford drove over to the Cedars with Roby and brought back a case of cold beer. Roby seemed cheerfully awed by the smooth graveled parking lots, the tall pine trees, and the broad sweeping expanse of the first fairway, and Maria and Martha both were impressed when the men returned to the trailer with Roby carrying the wooden case of beer in one hand as effortlessly as he might an extra glove. But Ford's mood was subdued by then, for driving back Roby had said casually: "You know a fellow named Buddy? Buddy Tatnall?"

"Yes. Why?"

"Well, he came around the other night. Late. He didn't see her. She don't know anything about this. He had an idea, I think, there was some money in it for him, because he knows Maria. And I guess he meant there was something in it for me, too, but I ain't sure. Because I told him to go and mind his own business before he got through with what he was saying."

"And? What did he do?"

Roby's smile was puzzled. "Do? Well, he went off, naturally. I don't tell a man that just to use up breath. He won't be back. Because I told him wandering around in the dark like he was, something just might fall on him by mistake. But I thought you'd like to know."

"Yes. I'm grateful, Roby."

"She's a good kid, a real good kid. You know, some of them act wild because they think it'll make it easier to get along. I guess it's like the immigrants a long time back, raising Cain with their kids for speaking whatever language it was they did

237

in the old country. Like it was a mark on them. Some of these Mex and Puerto Rican kids act that way. They wouldn't at home, their old man would wallop 'em. But here they figure unless they drink and cut up it'll look like they don't belong." He sighed cheerfully. "Or some damn thing. But not her. Not that Maria. She's got some sense, I tell you. You don't never need to worry about her. . . ."

After lunch Martha implored Roby to get his guitar. They drank beer and listened as he sang half-a-dozen songs in a pleasantly mournful voice. "The Wabash Cannonball" . . . "The Streets of Laredo" . . . "The Wreck of the Old Number Nine" . . . "Snowball" . . . Martha beamed proudly while he slapped and plunked his guitar, and crooned of roundups and lost loves, and headlights rushing at one another through the night on the same track . . .

"Why are you sad?" Maria asked him, when they had gone. She rubbed his cheeks with the back of her hand, as a mother might to gain a child's attention. "Come on, what's wrong?"

For a moment he didn't answer her; he was thinking of something else. In trying to understand his own confusion and fears, he had suddenly gained an insight into hers. "What was wrong at the hotel?" he asked finally.

She sighed. "Because it seemed like it could work, that's all. In the dining room, in the black dress, it didn't seem impossible. For a minute, it seemed that way."

"And that frightened you?"

"Yes," she said.

He understood her then. Sadly and helplessly, he realized that she was afraid of the same thing he was. The thought of it working. . . . And the problems that would come with facing that. . . . If they made plans, talked of divorce, settlements, leases, trusts, the children, visiting schedules, if they jabbed buttons that would start the cold, impersonal machinery of the law clanking and chewing at their needs and problems, then this secretive, innocent, almost childish pleasure would be destroyed forever. As long as everything was preposterously impossible, then it made a kind of sense. . . .

238

"Is there any whisky left?"

"You want a drink?"

"Yes, I'd like a big one, please."

She brought him a whisky with water, and smiled tentatively at him as he sipped it. "What did you want to tell me? To talk about?"

"Oh hell, there's no use in talking," he said wearily. "It doesn't help." He took her wrist gently and drew her down into his lap. "Is that O.K. with you? That we skip the talk?"

She nodded gravely, as if she understood exactly what he meant, and then she sighed and put her arms around his neck, and her head down on his shoulder.

But Ford didn't really understand what he was afraid of. Or why he had resigned himself so suddenly to the thought of losing her. Because he still wanted her desperately, and he saw her every night. His days dragged interminably. He made no calls, returned none, and saw no one if he could help it. He was blind to the changes in the country around him. The earth was softening, the wind stirred with a mild promise, and the first wild flowers were spreading across the meadows. He found himself checking his watch a dozen times an hour, attacking trifles of work to kill a bit of the day. Time seemed to be trapped, frozen, immobile; it was like crossing a desert to go from breakfast to lunch, and his afternoons were further wastes of tedium and frustration. But when he was with her at night, hours passed in a finger snap, and their first embrace seemed to blend smoothly into their last, with no sense of time between them, as if they were only fragments of the same dream.

He tried to understand himself. He searched restlessly for meaning in his life. When he met friends by chance, he stared at them in wonder; those familiar healthy faces suddenly seemed alien and absurd to him. They existed in apparent contentment, entertaining one another, looking after their business interests, worrying about bomb shelters and the state of the world in a puzzled fashion, putting sons and daughters through school, and obviously accepting their place on the human treadmill without anger or joy, or even very much interest.

Ford's mood had become desperate; he felt ignorant and uninformed, as if he were the butt of some monstrous, sniggering joke. This instant in his life should be critical and conclusive in some way, he knew; but charting a course and finding lights to steer by, this was beyond him; he felt as if he were sailing through life under permanently sealed orders.

Words such as "learn," "know," "aware," leaped out at him from the pages of magazines and newspapers. He found himself putting questions to himself and to strangers—waitresses, delivery boys, elevator operators. Yes, the weather's fine; so what do we do about it? Does it make any difference? Everyone he talked to struck him as complacently half-awake; with out-to-lunch signs lettered permanently on their foreheads.

One night in Maria's trailer, Roby made a remark about the war that caught Ford's attention. "I just got one thing out of it," Roby said, "but that put sense in my life, I tell you."

Ford sat forward eagerly. "What was that? What was the one thing?" The television was chattering, and he gestured impatiently to Maria. "Would you turn that down, please? Go on, Roby!"

"I'll make some coffee," Maria said, switching off the set.

"No, bring me a drink," Ford said. "Roby?"

"The coffee would be fine," he said.

"Well, go on," Ford said. "What was it?"

"Oh! Well, it was after the war, really." Roby leaned back in his chair and stretched out his legs. In the shadows he bulked formidably in the small trailer, with only a small patch of his raw birthmark shining in the soft lamplight.

"We were stacked up in camps in France waiting for Libertys to take us home. It was like the first days in basic training. There was some drinking and helling around, but not too much, because everybody had his ear glued to the loudspeakers. They went all day and all night, telling you when your outfit was going, and what dock you was sailing from and everything. And nobody had much faith in guys he'd known for just a few days. I mean, you go into some little town figuring on

240

getting drunk, and right away you'd wonder if the guys you were with would take care of you if you passed out, or got into trouble. It wasn't like being in a regular outfit. So it was kind of quiet."

Maria came in from the kitchen with a tray. Ford took his drink, and she gave Roby a cup of coffee.

"Thank you," Roby said. "Thank you, Maria."

"Is it strong enough?"

"Too hot to tell. But it smells just right."

"So? What happened?" Ford said impatiently.

"Oh. Well, one regular outfit come in then. A couple of companies of paratroopers from the Seventeenth. They hadn't done much in the war, got over too late, but they were full of all that glory crap that had been pounded into 'em, and they were in a real hairy mood. Everybody kept away from 'em, because you get in a battle with one paratrooper and soon you'll be fighting a whole damned platoon. One night they got a small-scale riot going in the Red Cross." Roby paused and sipped his coffee. Then, after an appreciative smile at Maria, he went on: "I was sergeant of the guard that night and I was playing solitaire in the CQ's office. One of my guards came busting in to tell me about it. A company of paratroopers were raising hell in the Red Cross, and the woman that ran it, a real nice French lady, had got on them to stop it or get out. One of the paratroopers hit her. Didn't shove her, or slap her, he really hit her, with his fist, and she went sliding over the floor like a bean bag, really busted up. So some GI's yelled for the MP's. Guards, that is. But them paratroopers weren't about to let anybody lock up one of their buddies, no matter what he done. Particularly with everybody waiting to catch a boat home.

"So the first guard shows up gets knocked on his tail. Then the corporal of the guard came busting in. They's a hundred and twenty paratroopers surrounding the guy who hit the French lady, but the corporal goes in to try and take him. Well, they took off his MP brassard and damn near made him eat it. They jerked the carbine out of his hands, and threw

241

him out on the sidewalk on his head."

Roby grinned faintly and sipped his coffee. "That's the story my guard tells me. A hundred and twenty paratroopers saying frig you to the whole guard mount. We just had eight privates on each shift, and three corporals, and me and the lieutenant. Sixteen men were off duty now, in the sack. I told the guard to fall 'em out. Then I went into the company commander's office where the lieutenant was sleeping. He was a dumpy little guy with sandy hair and a red face. He looked crabby all the time. I didn't know him, he was just another casual on the way home. But I'd seen some First Division shoulder patches when he was getting a razor out of his foot locker, so I thought he must have been around.

"That was a good outfit, the First. So I woke him up. Well, he won't even listen until he's drunk some coffee from the top of the stove, and then he blinks at me and rubs his face all over with his hand, and he tells me to fall out the guard. That's done by then, so he puts on his jacket and goes outside where the guard is lined up. He don't call 'em to attention. He just tells 'em they're going down to the Red Cross for a prisoner. Then he gives an order none of us heard since we were playing at being soldiers in training camps. He says, 'Fix bayonets!' in a way that makes it sound like he was asking them to button up their flies or something. Hell, none of them men knew *how* to fix bayonets. They unhooked 'em from their cartridge belts, and turned 'em around this way and that, like a gang of recruits, before they finally got 'em fixed on their rifles. Then the lieutenant says, 'All right, let's go!' And he takes off without another word, still sleepy and crabby, heading straight for the Red Cross. He didn't turn around to see if anybody was following him. Some joker sounds off: 'Hey, Lieutenant, how many of them jump boys we supposed to kill?' And the Lieutenant says, 'Well, you kill all you have to.'

"When we get to the Red Cross, the lieutenant pushes through the doors and looks down to where there's over a hundred paratroopers standing in a solid bunch around their buddy. He tells me, 'Come on, Sergeant, let's get him,' and then he walks into that bunch of paratroopers pushing 'em aside like they was sheep, and grabs the guy who hit the French lady, by the collar.

"We took that boy out of there, and marched him right to the guardhouse and locked him up. And the lieutenant went back to his office and settled down in the sack to sleep. But I wouldn't let him. I figured it was one of the strangest things I'd ever seen. That lieutenant, he *knew* those soldiers were ready to come and get him if there was trouble. Somehow, he'd made them ready to use them bayonets. Without talking at all. So I says to him, 'Lieutenant, those paratroopers, they're American troops too. You wouldn't stood by and watch 'em get killed, would you?' And he says, 'You bet your ass I would, sergeant.' And I said, 'How could you do that?' And know what he told me!"

Roby leaned forward and looked solemnly at Ford. "He said to me, 'Because I don't give a damn, sergeant.' And then he pulled the blanket up around his head and went off to sleep."

"And that's what made sense to you?" Ford asked him. "Just that? That he didn't give a damn?"

"Sure," Roby said. "And I think of it when I got problems. And I tell myself the same thing. That I just don't give a damn." Roby seemed embarrassed by Ford's bewilderment. "You try it, it works," he said.

"You'd have to mean it, of course."

"Why, naturally. Like the lieutenant did."

Ford smiled at Roby. He suspected that this big, gentle man had never used the lieutenant's philosophy in his life. Unless it had been to make up his mind about having another beer, or keeping someone honest in a poker game.

"Would it help anything?" Maria asked him when Roby had gone. "Just not to give a damn?"

"I don't know. I don't think so." Ford pulled her close to him and rubbed her shoulder. "The lieutenant was one of the lucky ones maybe. He was probably born not giving a damn."

CHAPTER 15

THE following morning Ellie Poston rang him at his office. "Do you know the latest guessing game in our parts?" she said, in a cheerful, teasing voice.

"No, what's that?"

"Where you've been hiding out. Some people claim you're running a still. Others think you've got a fancy woman over in Philadelphie."

The raillery in her tone made him uncomfortable. "It's nothing so glamorous, I'm afraid. I've been working."

"At night, obviously. I've tried you at home half-a-dozen times."

"Why didn't you call me here?"

She laughed huskily, and he felt a stir of exasperation as he imagined the merrily sadistic expression on her clever face. "Ford, I didn't want to talk to you while you're surrounded by molting old law books. I wanted to catch you in front of a fire, sipping brandy and feeling sorry for yourself."

"I haven't had much time for that."

"Oh, you men are so damn deflating. Janet's off in Florida imagining you're miserable. Every time I go away I'm sure poor old Wiley will get drunk and miss me terribly. Instead he ties flies and oils his guns and doesn't even know I'm gone. Now look: *don't* say you're busy. I want you to come to a party to-night. It's our anniversary, and I'm trying to scoop up a group for dinner at the White Hackle. Clay said he'd come if you would. What's the matter with him lately? He's acting so dreary and proper. You think Alicia has finally got a ring through his nose? You think she's actually wearing him down?"

"Now how would I know?" he said, feeling an uncomfortable anger flowing through him; and it quickened as she laughed and said: "Ford, you sound shocked! That's interesting. You're always so cool and contained."

"What time is your party?"

"Good, you'll come! Seven-thirty here for drinks, and then dinner when we can pry the Martinis out of Wiley's hot little hands."

"O.K., fine." If there were no complications, he could get away by ten or ten-thirty. . . .

"I hope I'm not interfering with something more interesting," she said with another teasing little laugh. " 'By now."

The evening started off well. With Ford they were seven in all: Clay and Alicia, the Postons, Sam and Sara Harris. A fire was burning in Wiley's study, and the room had a comfortable, cluttered look to it, with its hodgepodge of guns and trophies and hunting prints, and the numerous photographs of Wiley squatting beside dead game, or staring out solemnly from the ranks of various teams he had played on in college.

Wiley was in a sentimental mood. His eyes became damp as the toasts were proposed to him and Ellie, but, inevitably, he took on too large a load to carry with good will, and by the time they left for the White Hackle his spirits were sour. He insisted that the married couples split up for the drive to the restaurant. He wanted to take Alicia, but she shook her head without looking at him and got in quickly with Sam Harris. Clay and Ellie went off together, which left Wiley with Sara Harris, who started at him severely, and said: "You're already drunk enough, so you mind the road, Wiley." And from the thrust of her jaw, and the determination showing in her plain, no-nonsense face, it was fairly obvious that she would embellish and amplify the injunction right to the door of the White Hackle.

Wiley was disgusted at the way things had worked out. "So little Alicia's above it all," Ford heard him murmuring as he climbed into his car. He sounded as petulant as a child deprived of a treat, and Ford realized that he must have been looking forward to a bit of sociable knee squeezings and rump pinchings on the way to dinner. But why Alicia? he thought. And then he wondered if Wiley could have heard some talk about Delucca and Alicia. If so, he would consider her fair game for anyone. This would stem from his odd notions on poaching; he considered the first man to poach a field a bastard, but that anyone who followed him was just shrewdly taking advantage of a good thing. . . .

At the White Hackle Ford was seated between Alicia and Ellie Poston. The restaurant was jammed as usual, with couples standing three-deep in the lounge bar. Wiley wanted a drink but the Harrises, who were eaters not drinkers, collared a waiter and menus immediately, and, after exchanging alert questioning glances with one another—and apparently reaching agreement by some sort of gustatory telepathy—Sam instructed the waiter to bring them shrimp cocktails, sirloins with baked potatoes, and tossed salads with Roquefort dressing. They then commenced to nibble on rolls and bread sticks and radishes.

Wiley looked at them in disgust. Ford ordered a Martini he didn't want, to prevent Wiley from blundering into a morass of self-pity at having to drink alone on his wedding anniversary. He hoped to get dinner over quickly, and he knew that arguing with Wiley would only prolong it.

With a full glass in front of him, Wiley's humor improved. He grinned about the table, his eyes small and bright in his flushed face; he reminded Ford of a mischievous chimpanzee just then, as he ducked his head and scratched his chin, and finally concentrated his sharp, drunken malice on Clay and Alicia.

"Clay, boy, what's with you?" he said, with a prodding and insistent joviality. "You want a drink, don't you? Come on!" He laughed softly and swung his big, round head toward Alicia, affecting a comical truculence with the thrust of his jaw and shoulders. "What's the matter? You got other plans

246

for him tonight? Want him all bright-eyed and bushy-tailed?"

"Now that's hardly any of your business," Ellie said archly, but her attempt to elaborate on Wiley's innuendo merely deflected his anger.

"For Christ's sake, let's don't start this evening by telling me what is and what isn't my business," he said, picking up his drink. "O.K.? That's a little tiny quirk of mine, remember? I like to decide that by myself, baby."

Ellie put her hand on Ford's arm. "You wouldn't believe it, but he can be crabby at times."

Dinner progressed slowly and sporadically, delayed and checked by Wiley's querulous complaints to the waiter, and sarcastic swipes at Ellie. The Harrises ignored the tension at the table; they ate heartily, in a steady, efficient fashion, as if they were stoking up their bodies for a trial of strength and endurance. Occasionally they nodded at one another, full-mouthed and approvingly.

The large room was warm and fragrant, and the crystal chandeliers in the high ceiling cast a soft, flattering glow on the diners. The string quartet was playing something Ford guessed was Mozart; the melody was refreshingly sweet and graceful and if it had a color it would be that of peppermint candies.

"Do you have a cigarette?" Alicia asked him then.

"Yes, of course." As he lit it for her, he noticed that she hadn't touched her food. She was wearing a dark dress with pearls, and her face seemed drawn and pale. "Not hungry?"

"No. When's Janet coming back?"

"In a few weeks, I imagine."

They chatted perfunctorily for a moment or so, and Clay leaned forward to listen to them. His smile was touchingly anxious; he had seemed concerned at her silence, and was obviously relieved that she and Ford had found something to talk about. But she didn't answer a question Ford asked her a bit later, and when he turned to repeat it, he saw that she was staring over Clay's head with a nervous frown shadowing her eyes. She had stiffened slightly, and as she clumsily shook

247

ash from her cigarette, he realized that her hand was trembling. Glancing up, Ford saw that George Delucca was crossing the dining room to a corner table. He was with his two young daughters, and a stocky, white-haired woman, who gripped his arm tightly while staring about with sharp excited eyes. Two smiling waiters led the group across the floor.

"What's the big attraction?" Wiley said irritably. He was staring at Ellie, who had also been watching Delucca. But at his question she turned to him and said lightly: "Nothing— I just thought that was Debby Collett sitting over there with the Rileys."

Ford felt embarrassed by the tension he could sense in Alicia and Ellie; it was as palpable as an electric current.

Wiley twisted in his chair and stared around the room. "So the star of the show has arrived, eh?" he said in a thick, amused voice. "Big George-a-Deluc'." He chuckled softly. "Nice family picture, isn't it? Cute kids, big proud daddy, and I suppose the old lady is mama mia. You know, I'll bet it's a birthday. Maybe we should send over a bottle of wine, or a cake or something." He was grinning at Alicia and Ellie. "You think that's a good idea? Treat big George to a little surprise? Show him there's still some good old neighborly spirit around these parts?"

"Come on now, eat something," Ellie said. "Everyone's ready for dessert but you. And then I think we should go back to our place for stingers. Doesn't that sound tempting?"

"Now don't be rushing things," Wiley said. "Clay, maybe you and me should go over and wish Delucca many happy returns. Give him all our best, eh? Though that might be kind of unnecessary. Anyway, we could compliment him on his taste —on clothes, eh? And what else? You got any ideas?"

Alicia turned to Clay. "I'd like to go," she said.

"Yes, of course." His face was white. "I'll bring the car around."

"Damn, this is an unsociable group," Wiley said. "No neighborly spirit at all. Well, that ain't how this little country boy was raised." He picked up his half-full highball glass and got

unsteadly to his feet. "I'll go wish him all the best by myself.
To hell with you people."

"Wiley, you'd better sit down," Ford said.

"Now don't be barking at this old nigger," Wiley said, looking at Ford with an ugly little smile. "I don't remember ever
buttin' into your business. And pretty cute business it was
at that. Now you all just sit here and talk about what an ornery
bastard I am. Ellie, she'll give you details."

"I don't think that's funny," she said coldly.

"I grieve all to hell about what you think," he said, and
turned away from the table. He stopped frequently on his pas-
sage across the floor, stepping aside with exaggerated bows
to let waiters pass, and occasionally thumping friends on the
back, and pausing to laugh and talk with them; but his erratic
course took him slowly but steadily toward Delucca's table in
the corner of the room.

Clay hadn't gone to get the car. He was staring with miserable, worried eyes at Alicia's profile. "Do you want to leave?"
he asked her.

"No, not now." She turned to Ford and gripped his arm with
surprising strength. "Will you stop him?" she said. "Please?"

"I'll try," he said.

She looked into his eyes, studying his expression carefully;
but she didn't release his arm. "You must do better than that,"
she said quietly. "I can't stand any pressure, I'm afraid. Do
you realize what I'm telling you?"

"Yes," he said. "I'll stop him."

Ford made his way rapidly across the crowded room, but by
then Wiley was standing at Delucca's table, his weight partially
supported by the hand which he had braced against the back
of the old woman's chair. "Now this is a wonderful sight,"
he was saying, in a thick, cheerful voice, as Ford came up behind him and took his arm. Wiley looked at him with a wide,
lopsided smile. "Decided to join me, eh? Neighborly old Ford."

"Let's go back to our table. Come on."

"Well, first you've got to pay your respects to this nice family."

"Yes, of course. Now let's be going."

"You sound like we got something more important to do than chat with this nice old lady." Wiley sighed humorously and shook off Ford's hand. "She's just come down from New York for a few days to visit her grandchildren. She's Delucca's mama, did you know that? The trouble with the world is that people just don't have time for good old-fashioned manners anymore. Mrs. Delucca, my name is Wiley Poston, and I consider it a privilege to meet you."

Delucca's mother did not seem embarrassed by Wiley's overtures; she looked up at him with lively interest. "I'm glad to meet you," she said, and when she smiled the candlelight glinted on a gold tooth in the middle of her mouth. "All my son's friends I'm pleased to meet." Delucca's daughters beamed at her; they were round-faced little beauties, with creamy olive complexions, and eyes as lustrous as black cherries. Delucca sat perfectly still at the head of the table; his body seemed as hard and immovable as a slab of rock, but Ford saw the wings of his nostrils flare whitely as he drew a deep slow breath.

"Let's go, Wiley," Ford said.

Wiley chuckled indulgently. "I'm not at what you'd call my best, Mama Delucca—I've been drinking with a very smart and sophisticated crowd over at my table. They're real smart, they think, but I would trade 'em all for one nice simple woman like you. This country needs people like you, I mean it. And you'd like it down here, I know. You ought to get that no-good son of yours to buy you a nice place out in the countryside."

Delucca's mother laughed and said, "Oh, no, I think I'd miss all the buses and cars where I live."

Ford saw that Delucca was ready to stand; he had shifted his position slightly, and placed his hands flat on the table, and there was something almost sensuous in that slight, crouching motion of his body. He had lifted his head to stare at Wiley, and the color burned darkly in his face as Wiley dropped a hand on his mother's shoulder in a comfortable, familiar manner.

"Now you come see us often," Wiley said to her. "We need your kind of people. Honest, decent folks, who believe in the old ideas about marriage and children, and one guy and one woman sticking together. Maybe next time you come down we can have a big spaghetti dinner, provided you'll honor us by doing the cooking. How does that sound?"

She looked uncertain and Ford realized she had sensed Wiley's sarcasm now; she was watching Delucca's face anxiously. "It's something to think about," she said, and put a hand gently on her son's arm.

Ford tightened his grip on Wiley's bicep and pulled him a few feet away from Delucca's table. "Ellie's ordered you a nightcap," he said. "Let's go."

"Well, to hell with her and to hell with you, pal," Wiley said thickly. "I seem to have brought my own booing section along tonight. Any move I make, there's six loyal and true buddies ready to tell me I'm a drunken sonofabitch."

"For Christ's sake, shut up!"

"Ford, don't say that to me." Wiley's little eyes searched Ford's face deliberately. "Don't ever tell me to shut up, hear? As a kind of favor to both of us, O.K.?"

"Do whatever you damn please then. You're behaving like a moron."

Wiley sighed and fingered the lapels of Ford's dinner jacket. "You're taking a lot of liberties tonight, old pal. I don't relish it much. So you just go on back where my wife and your sister-in-law are squirming in their chairs about Delucca, and I'll go on over to the bar and have a few quiet drinks. That suit you, pal?"

"Perfectly." Ford almost wished Wiley would hit him; he could hit him back, once at least. Twice with luck. . . . He was disturbed by his anger, for he considered physical violence stupid, but at the moment he was seriously tempted to punch Wiley straight in the face and take the consequences.

"Why don't you do yourself a favor and go on home?" he said.

"Oh frig you," Wiley said laughing, and walked with long

251

determined strides toward the lounge bar.

As he returned to his own table, Ford was aware of a series of casual and apparently uncoordinated movements among the staff of the White Hackle. First a waiter tagged along behind Wiley as he crossed to the bar, and then Delucca stood and walked quietly through the dining room, pausing briefly to say a word to the headwaiter who stood beside the velvet rope in the foyer. When Delucca walked on, pushing through the doors leading to the front steps of the restaurant, the headwaiter snapped his fingers to catch the eye of a bartender, and then shook his head quickly before turning to nod at Wiley, who was moving up impatiently to the bar. No one around Ford seemed aware of these small maneuverings, and when he reached his table Ellie looked at him gratefully, and said: "Well, bravo! But what's the forecast? Inflate life preservers? Prepare to ditch?"

"It could be," Ford said.

The Harrises were spooning vigorously from tall fluted glasses of parfait, and Clay and Alicia seemed hopelessly trapped in a moody, uneasy silence. Then Ellie touched Ford's arm, and said, "Oh God!" in a resigned voice. "Could you try to cope just one more time?"

Wiley was now having trouble at the bar. He was shaking a banana-sized finger in the bartender's face, and Ford saw that the roll of flesh bunched above his collar was a fiery red. They couldn't hear what he was saying, but it was easy to guess that it wasn't casual or whimsical, for people on either side of him were collecting their drinks and moving discreetly away from his immediate vicinity.

"If you could just get him to the car," Ellie whispered to Ford, and he sighed and said: "I'll give it one more try."

As he entered the lounge bar and came up behind Wiley, the bartender was saying smoothly but firmly: "I'm sorry, Mr. Poston, but I can't serve you any more to drink tonight."

"Look, buster, I'm not drunk," Wiley said. "I can walk a straight line, and do that Peter Piper pickled pepper bit till the cows come home. So just ladle out a little drinking whisky

252

like you're paid to."

"I have my orders from Mr. Delucca, sir."

"*He's* judge and jury, eh?" Wiley turned and looked across the room toward Delucca's table. "Where'd he go? What the hell does he mean, flagging me?"

Ford touched his arm. "Look, Wiley, Ellie sent me on a peace mission. She's got a double Jack Daniels waiting beside the lamp in the window."

But Wiley's temper was in full control now, and he turned to Ford and said, "Keep out of my business, damn it." Then he put his meaty hands flat on the bar and leaned toward the bartender. "You just get that cute grin off your face when you're talking to me. Or I'm going to come over this bar and wipe it off. This ain't funny. Friends of mine heard you refuse to serve me." He turned and stared angrily at the Calloways and the Swahnes, who were doing their best to escape his attention. "Right, John? Right, Nancy? You heard him brush me off like some wino begging for a thimbleful of dago red, right?"

John Calloway smiled diplomatically. "Well, I didn't hear the exact words—but I notice your area remains kind of dry."

"Refusing to serve a man who is sober is a slander, and it's legally actionable," Wiley said, jabbing his finger at the bartender.

Half the people in the dining room had turned their heads toward Wiley's wrathful voice; many were on their feet for a better view of the argument. The headwaiter came quickly to Wiley's side, and said pleasantly: "Mr. Delucca will be back in a moment, Mr. Poston. You might wait at your table, or in his office, if you prefer."

"Where the hell did he go?"

"He's gone out to the rear parking lot. One of the attendants had the bad luck to scrape someone's fender, and Mr. Delucca wants to inspect the damage." The headwaiter seemed to be trying to sooth Wiley's feelings, or deflect his antagonism, with a soft flutter of details. "It's his policy to look into such matters personally. The restaurant is perfectly liable, it isn't that at all. Mr. Delucca's concern is getting the matter adjusted as quickly as possible. In a pinch, we can do small repairs here while our client is enjoying his dinner, and that eliminates the bother of . . ."

"Damn, who wound you up!" Wiley said hoarsely, and pushed past him toward the front doors, moving with rapid, forceful strides, his large cannonball of a head tucked down between his outthrust shoulders.

The bartender and the headwaiter exchanged smiles that came and went on their lips as quickly as the light from a snapped-off electric bulb. Then the headwaiter shrugged ruefully and strolled back to his post beside the velvet rope.

Ford went outside and walked down a graveled path toward the rear parking lot, but within twenty feet two uniformed attendants came out from the shadows and stepped in front of him.

"We'll bring your car around, Mr. Jackson," one of them said, touching the peak of his cap with a forefinger. "You can just wait in the foyer where it's nice and comfortable."

"I don't want my car. I'm just out for some air."

"I understand, sir. Well, this path is pretty uneven. I'd suggest you try that walk in front of the restaurant."

"This suits me."

"Look, please don't put us in a spot, Mr. Jackson. Know what I mean?"

"Sure, I know what you mean. But I didn't see you, either of you. I couldn't have. I came around the other way."

The attendant looked at him shrewdly. "Through the lounge, eh? By the side entrance?"

"That's right," Ford said, and the two men stared at one another uncertainly, and then one shrugged and said: "O.K., I guess that's got to cover us," and stepped aside to allow Ford to continue down the path to the rear parking lot.

Wiley stood in the middle of the asphalt turnaround with the overhead lights shining on his bald head. "Delucca!" he shouted, with his hands about his mouth, so that his voice soared like a foghorn through the night. Ford stopped in the darkness as he saw a movement between two parked cars, and then the white patch of Delucca's dress shirt emerging from the shadows.

Wiley turned quickly toward the sound of his footsteps.

"I've been looking for you," he said, as Delucca walked onto the turnaround. "What the hell's the idea of telling your bartender not to give me a drink?"

"Because you're a pig," Delucca said slowly, and deliberately. "And I don't like pigs grunting around my place. Now you keep away from me and my family, you hear? You come near me again and I'm going to make you regret it."

Wiley grinned and moved slowly toward him, his weight balanced evenly, and his big solid jaw tucked in behind his left shoulder. "Oh I'm coming near you, dago," he said. "Near enough to unscrew your head." His left arm came out and up with surprising speed, and his fist jarred into Delucca's shoulder, jolting him off balance. "You got a real big mouth, dago," Wiley said, watching him carefully. "I'm wondering how you're going to sound when you're hurt a little."

Wiley's bulkiness was deceptive; it was muscle that bulged under his clothes, not fat, and his reflexes were not much slower than they had been when he had played all-conference football in college. And he loved to fight; he heartily enjoyed what he called "a little knuckle stuff" with any and all comers, and he was grinning expectantly as he moved in on Delucca again, stalking him now with a bobbing, feinting head, and poised fists. He suddenly charged in close, swinging short, chopping blows from the outside, and his breath came in loud, emphatic snorts each time his fists landed with solid thumping sounds against Delucca's arms and shoulders.

Ford knew very little about boxing, and it was difficult for him to judge how much damage Wiley was doing. Delucca fought in a buttoned-up style, with fists close to his head, and elbows tucked in against his body as if he were more intent on protecting himself than returning any of Wiley's blows. To Ford it seemed the fight could have only one outcome, for Wiley was landing frequently and heavily, while Delucca's occasional jabs were too smooth and short to have any real

255

force behind them. Wiley's technique was to brace himself solidly with his feet spread wide, and then swing his arms as deliberately and powerfully as if he were holding weights in his clenched fists, and when these blows struck Delucca's arms or sides the sound was like that of a flat paddle landing heavily against a padded punching bag.

But Delucca occasionally hit Wiley before these blows landed, and his short jabs usually found a target somewhere between cummerbund and the first pearl stud on his dress shirt. Their only effect, however, was to add to Wiley's fury; he cursed, or sucked in more air, and then erupted in wind-milling flurries of blows which forced Delucca to pull himself even more tightly into his defensive cocoon of fists, shoulders, and elbows. He was weaving and ducking more now, it seemed to Ford, and many of Wiley's longest punches were missing him completely, but Delucca still took no advantage of Wiley's occasional slips and lurches; instead he seemed deter-mined to remain on the defensive, and his attack, if it could be called that, was confined to those short, almost tentative punches, which appeared to be experimenting with their target, rather than making any attempt to destroy it. They made considerable noise, however.

Then Wiley missed a punch and almost went to his knees. He recovered himself and looked around desperately for Delucca, who stood behind him with his hands at his sides.

"You don't fight any better than you drink," Delucca said. "Shall we leave it like that?"

Wiley turned around slowly, the air whistling in and out of his loose lips. He was trying to speak, but couldn't; his chest rose and fell like that of a desperately spent swimmer. It seemed to take him a very long time to raise his fists.

"I'd advise you to leave it like this," Delucca said.

Wiley shook his head. "Not yet, dago," he said.

"You said that once too often now." Delucca walked straight into him, slapping two feeble punches aside with a gesture that suggested disgust more than anger, and then, as he jarred Wiley's chin up with the heel of his left hand, Wiley fell helplessly against him, and only the physical resistance provided by Delucca's weight prevented him from falling flat on his face.

Ford was frightened by the loose, disjointed look of Wiley's sprawling body, and he realized now that Delucca's smooth, well-timed blows must have been hitting him with the impact of a meat cleaver. He had learned something about fighting, he thought irrelevantly, as he left the shadows and walked into the lighted area of the parking lot. Wiley was game and powerful, but he had no more chance against Delucca than he would have had against a man with a .45 in his hand. He thought that if Delucca hit Wiley again he might easily kill him, and he was determined to prevent that even if he had to offer himself as a victim to Delucca; but that wasn't necessary, for as Delucca glanced around at the sound of footsteps, he was in the act of lowering Wiley carefully to the ground.

"Can I help?" Ford asked him.

"Let's get him to his car. He'll be better off coming around alone. He can figure out how he must have slipped on a banana peel or something."

"He was quite drunk. I presume you realize that."

"Yeah. And I presume you're remembering the time he dumped some college kid on his ass. Or slugged it out with a cabdriver in a couple feet of snow? Well, he should stay in that league."

"You can say that, I guess. You won."

"I should make him look good? Balls! These country club commandos would be better off at home clouting their wives."

They carried Wiley's loose body to his car, and with considerable difficulty, wedged him into the front beside the driver's seat where Wiley began to snore, deeply and comfortably, like a large exhausted baby.

"It never settles a damn thing," Delucca said, staring in disgust at the backs of his hands. He turned them around slowly, as if they were accidental and somewhat repulsive appendages to his thick, muscular wrists. "I decided a long time ago I'd never use them like this again. So much for New

257

Year's resolutions."

"Well, as Ed Sulkowski said in another reference—you had provocation."

Delucca looked at him uncomfortably. Then he grinned and struck Ford lightly on the arm with the edge of his hand. "You want a drink?"

"I'll take a raincheck, if I may. I've got to see someone."

"O.K. I'll tell Mrs. Poston her husband's sleeping out here. You going back inside?"

"Just for my coat."

"Still playing that town, eh?" He struck Ford's arm lightly again, in a gesture that was oddly personal in its suggestion of commiseration and friendliness. "You know what it's called, I hope. Nowhere."

Then he walked slowly across the parking lot, the lights shining on his thick black hair. He was rubbing his fist slowly across the back of his mouth.

Ford came home from Maria's at three o'clock in the morning. There was a light in the study, and two messages propped up on the coffee table, scrawled in Catherine's round, childish hand. Mrs. Poston had called twice, and wanted to talk to him, no matter how late he got in.

Ford tore up the notes and went up to bed. Ellie would be eager for a recap on the brawl between Wiley and Delucca, but he was in no mood for it. As he lay in bed smoking a last cigarette, he could not escape the unhappy realization that his time with Maria was being compressed into increasingly shorter and less satisfactory intervals. Or, to look at it another way, the demands of his own existence seemed to be growing more insistent. Maria's trailer was a haven for irrelevant concerns. He couldn't think of anything important there; only his own pleasure. He sighed and put out his cigarette. Tonight he had coached her on questions she would be asked in applying for a driver's license. Roby had been letting her practice in his car. Tomorrow she would take her test. . . . It seemed incredible to him now that her enthusiasm and excitement could have given him such pleasure. But what right did he have to squander his time so selfishly? That's what his world would want to know. And he felt like telling his world to go to hell. . . .

He experienced the same strong but illogical feeling the next day in his office. Of necessity there were things to do; things he had been avoiding for weeks. But he resented the telephone call, the questions put to him, the decisions and judgments he was expected to make. And when Mrs. Simpson came in to tell him that Mrs. Poston insisted on speaking to him, he picked up the receiver on his desk with a sense of total exasperation.

"Yes, Ellie. What is it?"

"And a gruff good day to you, sir. Didn't you get my message last night?"

"Yes, but it was quite late. What's up?"

"I've got to see you, Ford. It's serious."

"I'll be in all afternoon."

"So will I. What I mean by that cryptic comment is that I twisted the bejesus out of my ankle last night. Lugging my Führer into our castle, he sagged on me like I was a friendly lamppost, and that was a bit much in my three-inch heels. So—" She let out her breath softly. "Supposing you stop by here, Ford."

He felt like swearing. "I've got a very tight schedule, Ellie."

She laughed gently, with an insinuation he didn't like. "I'm sure it's tight, Ford. But this is serious. So how about sixish. It won't take long."

"All right. And how's Wiley?"

"Supposing we save that for cocktails."

Wiley's home reflected his personality; it sprawled across the slope on which it was situated in a casual manner, expensively but carelessly informal. The views were superb, and the winding approach had been thoughtfully planned and landscaped, but Wiley had marred these effects by putting up kennels and greenhouses and sheds for his fighting chickens wherever it struck his fancy, so that his large and impressive fieldstone home looked as if were under siege from a ring of squat, functional outbuildings.

It was dark when Ford arrived there, and the carriage lights glowed on the walk leading to the front porch. Ellie answered his ring.

"Maids' night out," she said. "When Wiley goes off like this, I let them go too. Because when he gets back I may need them for weeks on end. When they owe me time it's like having money in the bank. Here, give me your coat."

She was wearing a full, brown tweed suit, and a tailored white shirt tucked under a broad cordovan belt. Massive gold bracelets jangled on her wrists, their flickering colors matching the lights in her streaked blond hair.

"You've got to make drinks," she said. "I'm claiming invalid privileges. Let's go into the living room. The den's a mess. Wiley was in there throwing guns and things around this afternoon. He's gone shooting."

She was limping, he noticed, as he followed her into the living room. There was a white silk scarf knotted in a small neat roll about her left ankle, and she was wearing flat gold slippers. In the living room, the draperies were drawn, and logs blazed in the tall, fieldstone fireplace. It was a snug and pleasant room, with thick rich carpeting, creamy old wallpaper, and a few characteristic touches of Wiley's: notably the black leopard skin before the hearth, and the huge drums which were painted with Confederate flags and used in place of lamp and coffee tables.

As Ford made drinks, Ellie settled into a long sofa with a grateful sigh, and propped her injured ankle on a pillow. She wasn't wearing stockings, and the neatly rolled white scarf stood out in gleaming relief against her lightly tanned legs.

Ford gave her a drink, and she said, "Now this is cozy, isn't it?" in a mocking, half-teasing manner which somehow seemed to translate the potential intimacy of the situation into an established fact. "Much more comfortable than your office, I'm sure. And you look terribly tall and distinguished in front of the fireplace, with that gray in your temples"—she grinned and rubbed the edge of her glass across her lips—"and that thoroughly impatient frown on your face. I wonder what I'm keeping you from."

"Nothing but dinner," he said.

"We could stir up something here, of course. Would you like a nice filet, a green salad, and a bottle of wine?"

"Not tonight, I'm afraid. I can't, Ellie."

She laughed. "I'm not surprised. You're always on the wing these days. And these nights. Please don't frown like that. I'm being a bitch. But it makes you rather interesting. Not only interesting, but irritating. You know I always go mad over puzzles. Give me two things that are supposed to fit together and won't—or can't—and I become obsessed with them. You remember those nails that were twisted into loops that fitted together? And once you got them apart, you could never find out how to put them back again?"

"Yes, I remember," he said. "Where's Wiley off to?"

"Where's Wiley isn't as important as how's Wiley."

"O.K. How's Wiley?"

She looked thoughtful. "In a very bad mood. I'm used to his explosions and sulks, but this is different. He was cold as ice this morning. When he went out he told me he'd be at the bank if there were any calls. Tony Marshall called just after he'd left—Wiley had called him earlier. They had a date, apparently. Wiley got back after lunch, and there was still no change in the weather. It was still ice cold. He wouldn't even *swear* at me, let alone talk. He just collected some guns and drove off."

"Where to?"

"Probably down to Lancaster for pheasants. He only took some extra socks and the .12 gauges, so it can't be a full-dress safari." She extended her empty glass in a comically imperious manner. "Fix this, angel man. I can get tight tonight without feeling guilty about it. This is a medicinal binge. Seriously, my ankle feels as if it spent the night under an anvil or something."

Ford made her another drink. "What did you want to talk to me about, Ellie?"

261

"Can't you sit down, for heaven's sake? There's room on the sofa."

"I don't mind standing. It's a relief after a day in the office."

She raised her glass to him in an ironical salute. "Your health then, sir, sitting or standing. Now what was that fight about last night?"

"Wiley said a few things that Delucca objected to."

"What sort of things?"

"I believe it was how he said them that caused the trouble. A literal transcript of his remarks might sound harmless enough. But his tone made it evident he regarded Delucca's mother as a bewildered peasant just off the Ellis Island ferry. There was a needle in everything he said, not so much at her as at Delucca. If he was trying to irritate Delucca, you've got to give him top marks."

"Did you hear what they said outside?"

"Yes, most of it."

She was watching his face carefully. "Was there any mention of me?"

"No, there wasn't."

"They weren't fighting about me then?"

"I'm quite sure they weren't."

"Well, you remember the ridiculous story that went around last year about me and Delucca?"

"I don't believe that had anything to do with last night."

Ellie sipped her drink and ran her tongue slowly over her red lips. "It might have indirectly triggered Wiley, of course. He was looking for trouble last night. Not in his usual charming, democratic way. Specifically, he wanted trouble with Delucca."

"I'm no psychiatrist," Ford said. "After Wiley's had too many drinks, it's hard to guess why he says or does anything. The fact is, he butted into a private family party and behaved like a boor. Delucca objected to it. That's what the fight was about."

"I hope you're right. If they'd got into a fight over me, it would have been even sillier than those silly rumors. They *were* absurd, of course. But I never did anything to put a stop to them. I guess I enjoyed the notoriety." Ellie smiled up at him and settled herself more comfortably in the deep couch. "Would you like to hear the torrid details of the night I spent with George Delucca? You're fascinated, I can see," she said, in a mocking little voice. "Just breathless! Well, what happened is that I read through three copies of the *Saturday Evening Post* waiting for the repair truck to come over and fix my car. George, meanwhile, worked away at some papers on his desk. Occasionally, these were sultry exchanges. A cup of coffee? No, thank you. That light O.K.? Yes, it's fine." Ellie sighed and looked up at the ceiling. "It was sheer madness. Still, when my dear friends began wagging their pointed little tongues about it, I just smiled and let them wag away. It was rather flattering.

"And I got an unladylike kick out of Wiley's reaction. After years of competing with bird dogs for his attention, it was exciting to catch him peeking at my letters and hanging around doorways to hear who I was talking to on the phone. It was fun at first. Then it became a bore. Then it became sheer hell. I got just as much abuse from Wiley as if he'd caught me in bed with Delucca. So I wound up with the unpleasantness of an affair and none of the gratifications. Not very good planning, would you say?"

"It's probably better than the other way around."

"That's your dusty old judicial way of looking at things." She shifted her foot on the pillow and winced slightly. "Ford, could you be a dear and do something about this ankle of mine? It's suddenly giving me hell."

"Have you had it looked at?"

"I didn't think it was all that serious. Be a pal. You'd do as much for a lame hunter."

"I might do more harm than good. I'd suggest you grin and bear it until you can get in to Dr. Jackeson."

"You couldn't possible hurt anyone with those nice kind hands of yours. Don't hands tell a lot about character? Ever notice Wiley's? They look naked unless they're wrapped around a gun or a drink."

"Well then, let's take a look at it," Ford said, and sat down at the end of the sofa. This was in fact the quickest route to the front door, he knew; for he understood her mood quite well, and he knew that unless he gratified her need for a little mischievous intimacy, a bit of friendly, hearty titillation, she would smother him with petulant recriminations, block his exit with tedious, half-baked theorizings on his puritan inhibitions and fears. As he unwound the scarf from her ankle, he thought with some humor that at least he needn't worry about the propriety of the situation. Only discretion could compromise them; only silence would be damning. And he knew he could trust Ellie to blab this everywhere. "There we were, just the two of us, and I couldn't help thinking how it would look if someone barged in and found Ford, of all people, *ministering* to me like one of those gigolos-cum-masseurs—" And so the incident had an inevitable, built-in innocence. . . .

There was nothing at all wrong with her ankle. He rubbed it gently and moved her foot about in a slow circle, knowing that her nervous flinchings, and half-suppressed gasps of pain, were simply necessary testaments to the respectability of the situation. The slim bones in her ankle and instep were as hard and smooth as ivory under his hands, the tanned flesh as springy firm as foam rubber. She sighed gently, and settled deeper in the couch, so that her leg rested in his lap, and the hem of her tweed skirt moved up over her brown bare kneecap. "That's really quite marvelous," she said softly. "You could do this for a living, Ford."

"I don't think it's broken," he said, smiling at her.

"No, probably not." She moved her foot about in a slow but vigorous circle, and he could feel the muscles in her calf flexing insistently against his thighs.

"O.K.?" he said then. "I think it's all right."

"You do have nice kind hands," she said in a murmuring, drowsy voice. She pressed her arms across her breasts, and shivered pleasurably, as if her body were cold, and she were trying to wrap herself in the warmth of the room, draw the sensuous heat from the spurting logs about her, enclose and insulate her senses with the creamy glow of firelight, the heavy slumbering silence. "You mustn't rush right off," she said, and he heard another tone in her voice then, a ring of soft but deliberate challenge.

"I'm afraid so, Ellie. This looks like a perfectly good ankle to me, by the way."

"That's a medical opinion, I gather—not a romantic one."

"It's a good ankle, period. Good to walk on, good to look at."

"Don't go. I mean it Ford. I thought you'd understand what I told you about Delucca. I got nothing from him, and nothing but hell from Wiley. I think I'd like it the other way around. Like it very, very much."

Ford squeezed her ankle deliberately, and she laughed, and said, "Of course there's nothing wrong with it. I just wanted to enjoy the nice warm feel of your hands. Don't look solemn now. The house is cozy and quiet, and I'd like another drink, and a little talk with you. Do you mind so terribly?"

"No, but I think you've got me confused with one of our Saturday night Lotharios. You should know me better than that, Ellie. I'm one of the original Model A Fords." He hoped to make her laugh, to smile at least. "I'm still chugging along all right, but I'm not built for freeways and turnpikes."

"I haven't got you confused with anybody else at all," she said. "You know that, don't you." There was such a calm insistence in her voice, that he glanced at her thoughtfully; her eyes were half closed, and they looked dark and drugged in the shifting, uneven shadows that flickered across her face from the fireplace. She did not intend to speak until he did, he knew; there was a deliberateness in her silence, and a sense of challenge and superiority in the knowing smile curving her lips.

"What does that mean?" he asked her.

"Wiley told me about the girl you've been seeing," she said. "Oh, you mustn't blame him. He was tight, and he was humiliated by what had happened to him. I was surprised, of course." She grinned and shook her head slowly, so that the firelight sparkled in her streaked blond hair. "Please don't be angry," she said, as he moved her legs aside and got to his feet. "It's nothing I'd ever mention to a soul. But it did make me think you needn't go all the way over to Harbor City for fun and game." She stretched luxuriously and her full breasts arched themselves against the thin fabric of her shirt. "Is she so much younger than I am? So much prettier? What's the matter? I'm right next door, Ford. I'm within arm's length. It can't be moral qualms. What is it? Afraid of Wiley?"

"I'm afraid anything I say will sound pretty damn absurd," he said. "Will you spare me the chore of being obvious."

He didn't want another drink, he wanted only to leave, but he couldn't on this note, so he went to the bar, and added a small touch of whisky to his glass. When he turned around she was standing so close behind him that he nearly brushed against her, and when she laughed he could smell the liquor on her breath mingling with the perfume in her hair.

"I don't want to spare you anything," she said, staring up at him with an odd, intent smile. "If you'll go to bed with her, why not me? If we went up to the guest room and laid together in a nice, clean bed, would my kisses be so different from hers? Would my body make you long for hers? That's all I want to know. Be as obvious as you have to. Perform your distasteful chore—that was your word, wasn't it?"

"You're the wife of one of my oldest friends," he said. "I've had a hundred dinners in your home. Wiley taught my son to shoot. I was an usher at your wedding. That's how obvious I have to be. As far as I'm concerned I don't remember a word of this conversation. I think you might well do the same."

"Dear old friend," she said, and rubbed one hand lightly down his arm. She smiled and studied his face with half-closed eyes. "You thought I just wanted to play footsie, eh? Flirt a little? I'll tell you a secret, dear old friend, dear old wedding usher." She began to laugh. "I had a drink before you came. Quite a few! Wiley gets smashed, and runs off to purge his naughty guilt feelings by slaughtering birds and beasts. I sit home alone. Shall I ride? Play golf? Sometimes I do. Sometimes

I take a few drinks, all alone in my big, empty house. Wiley expects me to be waiting here when he gets back. But sometimes I wander through the big, empty house in shorts, listening for the sound of a window being forced, a door being jimmied. Praying for prowlers! Christ, I'd surprise them! They'd think they'd won the Irish Sweeps; they'd think it was Christmas all over the world."

She smiled shrewdly at him, her eyes shifting with the expressions in his face. "And what about her, dear old friend?" she said. "Isn't she someone's cherished daughter? Do you play golf with her father? Make out her brother's tax returns? Wiley told me she is dark and beautiful, but jailbait, Ford, prime jailbait. How do you ease your conscience about that? I'm too old! Isn't she too young?" Ellie drew a deep breath, and the tendons bulged darkly under the coarse skin of her throat. "But you Jacksons can do no wrong. You believe that, don't you. You stare down your nose at me for being honest, for offering you more excitement than you'd find with a hundred teen-age chippies. But it's different with her, isn't it? That's no chore, is it?"

Ford turned and walked from the room. He felt sickened by the raw shame and bitterness in her face. As he was pulling on his coat she came into the foyer and leaned against the front door, one foot crossed negligently over the other, and her arms hanging limply at her sides.

"You're going off to her now, I guess. Eager to get away from this tiresome old bitch."

"For Christ's sake, shut up," he said. "You don't know what you're doing to yourself."

"Sermons from the Mount, eh? Wisdom from the pure and worthy Jacksons. You're kind of ridiculous. I know all about you, Ford. And all about Clay."

"Just what does that mean?"

"I took one of the warriors home last night. Alicia took the other, that's what I mean. Delucca came over to our table to tell me Wiley was *hors de combat*, and Alicia stood and put her arms through his, and said, oh so tenderly, 'Take me with you now,' and Delucca thought it over, carefully and solemnly, and then he said, 'All right, let's go,' and away they went, leaving poor dear Clay sitting there all alone with a gentlemanly little smile on his face."

Ford stared at her; it was obvious she was telling the truth. "It gives you real pleasure to tell me this, doesn't it?" he asked her.

"No, Ford, no!" The tone of his voice seemed to strike her like a blow; the heavy slackness of passion disappeared from her face, as she put a hand up to her mouth in a childish gesture. "Oh God," she said weakly. It was as if she had just waked from a bad dream, and he was the first object she recognized; the drugged look faded from her eyes, leaving them clear and bright with panic. "What do you want?" she said. "Where's Janet? I didn't say anything. You know I didn't! Can't you pretend I didn't?" She was beginning to weep, softly and helplessly. "You know I didn't! Don't you, Ford?"

He patted her shoulder gently. Her body was trembling, and her breath made a ragged noise in the silent house. "You had me going, I'll admit," he said, forcing his lips into a smile. "It was a very neat leg pull."

"Say that to me again. Please, Ford."

"You should be on the stage, of course," he said, as she clung to him like a frightened child.

"I'm such a bitch, an ungrateful bitch. He'd die without me. You know how Wiley is."

"Just go easy on me when you tell your pals, O.K.? Say that while I was resisting your charms, I finally noticed that you were resisting an impulse to burst out laughing."

"I didn't mean any of it. I'm not lying. I know what I mean and what I don't mean. No one else could ever know."

He patted her shoulder again, stricken with a weary compassion for her fears. "I told you, you should be on the stage," he said.

She begged him to stay until she stopped crying, until she got herself under control; not for a drink, not even a cigarette, but just until she could stop crying. He knew she would always be grateful to him, and would always hate him, whether he stayed or not, so he smiled at her and patted her shoulder a last time, and hurried away from Wiley's house as if it were on fire.

CHAPTER 16

FORD stopped at his home before going to Maria's. He paced the floor of his study with a drink in one hand, and a cigarette in the other, trying to make up his mind what to do about Clay. He thought about Clay since that was his plain responsibility, but, even importantly, because it was a means of insulating himself from the lacerating memories of the scene with Ellie. He couldn't escape the guilty conviction that it had been his fault, that he was somehow responsible for her senseless, hideous humiliation. Everything that had happened to Clay and Alicia, to Delucca and Wiley and Ellie, now seemed related to him in an ominously logical fashion. He had been so proud of his new and invigorating capacity for passion that he had whizzed by all the signposts that might have warned him of danger. And Clay seemed to be the only anchor he could find to check his drifting fears.

What should he do? Call him, of course, to find out if Ellie was telling the truth. That was plain enough, but he didn't want to call his brother; he wanted no more guilty secrets and dreary responsibilities.

Occasionally he glanced nervously from his watch to the telephone as he paced the floor. There was a bond between the two instruments, a connection of causality, because he knew he couldn't go to Maria until he had talked to Clay. He seemed hung between the extremes of pain and pleasure. The minutes fled by, and he longed to fly with them, but he couldn't make himself lift the receiver and call his brother.

Chimes sounded faintly in the foyer then, and he heard

Catherine's heavy footsteps hurrying from the kitchen toward the front door. Somehow this unexpected caller jolted him into a decision. He dialed Clay's number quickly, knowing he had an excuse to interrupt their conversation. . . .

"Yes, hello?" Clay's voice rang sharply in his ear.

"Well, how're things? How's it going?"

"Ford! I'm surprised to hear from you. After last night I thought you might be over working the main event at Madison Square Garden."

"It was some evening, eh? And everything's O.K. with you?"

"Why of course. I'm aging gracefully and wisely, but what the hell? Aren't we all? At the moment I'm enjoying the firelight on the hearth, and the sight of my friends' homes shining reassuringly on the horizon. Within those snug, unmortgaged walls, the kiddies may be getting smashed on blackberry brandy, and daddy may be belting mommy across the chops, but from my view it looks like an ad for America the Beautiful." Clay laughed softly. "It's a time for reflection and nostalgia. With the wee folk creeping from the shadows to act out their ancient stories in the firelight of our dreams."

"You sound in fine shape," Ford said.

"I'm not drinking up a storm, if that's what you mean. I'm just having a mild Scotch."

Catherine opened the study door. "Mr. Landon's here. He's hoping you got a minute free before dinner."

"Excuse me, Clay. Thanks, Catherine, tell him I'll be along soon."

"And what about dinner?" she asked him.

"I'll be going out."

"It seems like you always going out anymore," Catherine said, and pulled the door shut with a resentful click.

"Am I keeping you from something?" Clay asked him.

"No. Tom Landon just stopped by."

"You impress me. Does the bank president deliver your monthly statements in person?"

"I don't know what he wants. But I'm glad everything's O.K. with you. Will you think I'm a stuffy bastard if I advise you not to let that mild Scotch turn into a half-dozen?"

"Please don't worry about me," Clay said. Then he sighed faintly. "I know you didn't call just to say hello. Your fears, if such they are, ring clearly through the ether. Alicia returned my fraternity pin last night, as you may have heard. After the brawl was over, after the break of day—" Clay laughed shortly. "I wonder if you're as sick of my collegiate cut-up role as I am? Ned, the fun-loving Rover. The campus clown! Christ, I can't even talk about the most significant thing in my life without sounding cute about it."

Then his voice became sharper. "Please listen to me, Ford. Alicia's tried, these last few weeks. And for a while it seemed to be working. There was more communication, more respect, even a little fun. But last night tore it. She says she loves Delucca. I'm not sure. What I do know it that I haven't given her any reason to cling to me. That's my job from now on—to see if I can change her mind. It's my job, do you hear? Don't think I'm not grateful for what you've done. You've argued my case with her, and with him, but I don't want you to do anything more. Let them alone. It's my job, and I've got to handle it. Do you understand?"

Ford was puzzled by his reaction to this conversation with Clay. As he walked down the hall to the living room, he realized that his paramount feeling was one of relief; he was out of it now, in the clear, at Clay's insistence. This was the best possible thing for everyone concerned, he told himself; and because he honestly believed this, he felt almost cheerful as he went in to shake hands with Tom Landon.

Landon said: "I hope I'm not interrupting your schedule, Ford. I just took a chance you might have a moment free before dinner."

"Don't worry about it. With Janet away, my schedule's pretty flexible. Would you like a drink?"

"Well, I've had dinner, but I could manage a bourbon and water, I think."

As Ford made their drinks at the bar, Landon looked about the room and nodded at the paintings and furniture with a suggestion of judicious appreciation. "You have a fine place here," he said. "These colors, and the old and new things, it's very interesting."

"I forgot you haven't seen it before."

"Well, no."

Landon was short and stockily built, with reddish gray hair, and a pale, square face from which his pleasant blue eyes stared out shrewdly but amiably on the world. Normally he projected a benign and healthy confidence, which, since he was a Midwesterner, was generally assumed to flow as much from the superior functioning of his stomach and bowels as it did from the reasonably high estimate he held of his own skills and competence. But Landon looked off his usual comfortable form, Ford thought, as he gave him a drink and suggested he take one of the chairs at the fireplace. He seemed tired, and there was a muscle pulling at the corner of his mouth.

"Well, what it is, Tom?" Ford asked him.

"I'll make it brief, don't worry," Landon said with a quick smile; he had noticed Ford's discreet glance at his wrist watch. "Wiley Poston and Mr. Marshall were in this morning. They want me to press George Delucca for immediate payment on his note with us. They're concerned about our liability there—at the White Hackle, that is—which is not only their right as board members of the bank, but their obligation. It's a perfectly legitimate concern, and I'm pleased they feel such a keen interest in these matters." Landon took a long swallow from his drink, and then rubbed the back of his hand fretfully over the tiny muscle quivering at the corner of his mouth. "The only disagreement, if that's not too strong a word, is whether their concern is valid or not."

"They think it's a bad loan. You disagree?"

"Well, that's oversimplifying it. But yes, I suppose you could put it that way. I think the loan is sound, although I'm aware these things are open to varying opinions, and I'm not just disregarding their interpretation completely." Landon finished his drink, and fumbled in the outside pocket of his

273

jacket for a package of cigarettes.

They must have given him a bad time, Ford thought, as he watched him draw a deep mouthful of smoke into his lungs. Landon was a paid employee of the bank's board of directors. And Wiley and Tony were members of that board—Wiley to satisfy some vague need for a façade of fiscal responsibility, and Tony to run things. Not surprisingly—considering the amount of their deposits and the weight of their positions— they tended to regard the Cottersville bank as modest extensions of their personal checkbooks.

"Well, differences of opinion make horse racing," Ford said, and looked deliberately at his watch. He wanted no part of the bank's hassle with Delucca. He knew what Wiley was up to, though he didn't understand how he had dragooned Tony Marshall into throwing his weight in with him. "So how did you settle things?" he asked Landon casually.

"Would you mind if I gave you just a bit of background on the situation?"

"Very well. But I think I'd better tell you in advance I don't intend to get involved in this matter. Fair enough?"

"Perhaps you'll be disposed to change your mind after I explain the situation to you."

"There's always that chance. But it's a long one, I'd say."

Landon smiled ruefully. "I'll have to take it, since there aren't any better odds around. You remember we discussed George Delucca on another occasion. There was no particular significance to what we said—or what I said rather—but it did stick in my mind. This was when we were working together on that fund raising for the library, sometime before Christmas, I think. It was at lunch, as I recall, and I mentioned to you that Delucca was the sort of person who gave a certain thrust to the business life of a community. That is to say, he's not content to stand still. He's ready to take reasonable risks to expand and grow. Do you remember that conversation?"

"Yes," Ford said, although his recollections of it were vague. He did remember, however, Landon's mildly malicious amusement at the fact that Delucca had bought a home on the

274

Downs and his implication that it was fairly comical for grown men to be concerned about it.

"Well, perhaps that's not important," Landon said quickly, and Ford realized that he had misinterpreted the frown on his face. Landon guessed that he was bored or restless, but the fact was Ford found the memory of his connection with Delucca and the Henderson place painfully disagreeable.

Landon began to explain the details of the bank's loan to Delucca. "The physical plant of the White Hackle restaurant is worth at least twice the face of our note, which is one hundred thousand dollars at six per cent interest. The interest payments have been made promptly, but there's been no reduction of the principal. It's a demand note, which is what Delucca wanted, and on an instrument of that nature we like to see reductions made on a quarterly basis. I talked about this to George a month or so ago, and he explained that he'd had several freakishly bad spells of weather over the winter. Snow that came on weekends and knocked down his expected gross. But he brought his books down, and he's still operating at a very good profit, despite the fact that he's put more than thirty-two thousand dollars in cash into further improvements on his property. That's in addition to our hundred thousand, you understand. Our money went for the remodeling of the main dining room and the new kitchens and meat lockers. George—on top of that—put in a new powder room, a new parking lot, and invested in a pension-insurance program for his staff, which isn't just a philanthropic gesture, but a way of giving him a stable labor supply over the years. These improvements of his just reinforce our loan.

"I'm perfectly content to wait until spring for the first reduction on principal. But Wiley and Mr. Marshall have a number of objections to this. They feel we're too deeply committed to the success of a retail business. They say—and they have a point—that if a few bad weekends could make a dent in his profits, then a disastrous winter could force him to close down. Of course, you could say the same thing about a farming or dairy operation—or a supermarket, for that matter.

275

If we based our lending policy on the possibility of twenty-foot drifts lasting from September to May, then I can't imagine who we'd consider a good risk. Snow removal people, perhaps.

"But I'm not being whimsical about their concern. They have other points, too. The tone of the White Hackle has been established by Delucca; it's his manner, his personality, his dedication, which has built its reputation. Now—Wiley and Mr. Marshall argue—supposing Delucca died? Or lost interest in the place? Our money rides too heavily on the character of one man. If he failed us, where would we find a replacement? And do we want to get into the restaurant business, in the first place?"

"Delucca wasn't present at this talk?"

"No—I suggested we call him. But they didn't think it was necessary."

"I see. Well, what's the decision?"

"It was their decision. As an employee of the bank, I'll have to implement it. They want me to ask for a one hundred per cent reduction of principal tomorrow morning. Our interests, they insist, require that we call in that loan immediately."

"He has a day or so to raise the money, I suppose. What if he doesn't?"

"We'll file a lien against his property with the sheriff's office. That means foreclosure; that means he's out of business."

"And the bank's got a restaurant on its hands. How do you recover your equity? Sell the place?"

"Presumably, that's what we'd have to do. But I don't want to pull the rug out from under Delucca this way. Looking at at it from the coldest business viewpoint, he's an asset to the community. We need men who give us impetus and charge. If we destroy them, we're the eventual losers."

"I'm not a member of the board of the bank," Ford said.

"I realize that, of course. But you have weight in the area. Your opinion's important. I think if you talked to Wiley and Mr. Marshall they'd listen to you. Do you mind if I say something frankly? I'm in the banking business to make things grow, not to destroy them. Money is like a serum. Inject it at the right time in the proper amounts and you can perform miracles. Withhold it, and the patient dies." Landon looked at him steadily. "I don't think a doctor should make medical decisions based on his estimate of the patient's moral character. With certain obvious exceptions, that should hold true of a banker. If a man wants to borrow money to put a new roof on his home, I can't call him a poor risk because he doesn't share my political views, or because I have some private reason for disliking him."

Ford walked over to the bar and added a token drop of whisky to his glass. He felt it was a contemptible business from any viewpoint, but this only strengthened his determination to keep out of it. Talking to Wiley wouldn't help, in any case. He was behaving like a spoiled and arrogant child, and criticism or opposition would only infuriate him. But even if he owed Delucca loyalty, Ford realized he couldn't help him without disregarding Clay's feelings.

"I'll think it over, Tom," he said. "At the moment I don't see what I can do."

"I'd appreciate it if you'd say you can't—or won't do anything at all. I'd know where I stand then."

"Let's keep our tempers, Tom. Do you feel you've done everything you can?"

"Yes. I've used every argument I can think of. I've made my position crystal clear."

"Did you tell them you'd resign if they went ahead with this deal?"

"No, I didn't do that," Landon said slowly.

"Have you told Delucca what's going on?"

"I couldn't—I simply couldn't. The conversation I had with Wiley and Mr. Poston was confidential."

"Well, don't assume I'm being critical. There are steps I could take, I imagine. And steps you might take. The point is, will we? As I said, I'll have to think it over. Supposing I call you in the morning?"

"I'd appreciate it if you would, Ford."

After Landon had said good night and gone out to his car,

Ford spent a moment trying to guess what he had really wanted from him. Maybe there wasn't anything puzzling about it. Perhaps he simply objected to what Wiley and Tony were proposing, and was hoping to block them. But, coincidentally or not, he had come for help to a man he must have known had little reason to help George Delucca. Perhaps he had looked for support only where he was sure it would be refused, thus salving his conscience and giving him the green light to execute Wiley's orders. But Ford didn't really believe this. He didn't think Landon was that devious. Landon was probably like everyone else. He cared about the ethics of the banking business. And he cared about hurting George Delucca. But not enough to risk much for them. Ford didn't blame him.

At Maria's, he relaxed with a drink while she made dinner. But he couldn't stop thinking about Landon, and the curious problems of morality his visit had raised in his mind. It was easy enough to stand on principles in clear weather with well-shod boots. But how much could a man be expected to pay for what he believed in? And if there were price tags on convictions, what was the actual worth of those that were too expensive? Logically, nothing at all. But he knew he wasn't thinking of convictions or principles, only social habits and conventions. There were no absolutes in his life; nothing to give a martyr's loyalty to.

Maria sat in his lap after dinner and put her arms around his neck. "You can talk about it," she said. "It's all right."

"Now what's this?" He smiled at her.

"I thought you weren't saying anything because of—embarrassing me." She sighed. "You didn't remember it."

"I guess not." He was still smiling at her. "What's the matter?"

"The driver's test today. I didn't do it right."

"Damn, that's a shame. What happened? Was it the driving or the questions?"

"The driving was all right, I think. I stopped when he told

278

me, and made all the turns, and watched the traffic signs carefully."

"It was the questions then?" He smiled and shook his head. "Poor Maria. After all your work."

"Yes," she said.

"Well, you can take another test in two weeks."

"No," she said.

"Why not?"

"I don't want to." She got up from his knee and sat on the edge of the couch. She wasn't wearing make-up and her face was dominated by the sudden flare of anger and defiance in her eyes.

"Hey now. What's wrong?" He studied her stubborn mouth. "What did he say to you?" he asked her quietly.

"He asked me questions. That's his job. What to do if I had an accident. I know that. Then about speed limits, and how far I should stay behind other cars. It was two questions together, and I got mixed up. I told him I knew, but I had to think. I remembered what you said about the tens and hundreds—a hundred feet behind for each ten miles of speed. Then, while I was telling him, he made me stop. He laughed, not a real laugh, and asked me how far a hundred feet was. And two hundred. And three hundred." She looked steadily at Ford, the pain in her eyes passive and contained, like that of an animal in a trap.

"He told me the best way was to think how far I had to walk to get an unemployment check."

"Come here, Maria," he said.

"I don't want to."

"Please come here."

"Why are you mad?"

"I'm not mad. But please come here."

She stood up awkwardly, as if confused by the insistence in his tone, and he took her wrist and drew her down onto his lap. He rubbed her bare arms, and said, "I don't want you to worry about what he said to you, do you understand? But I

279

want you to tell me about it."

"It wasn't anything bad. It just made me feel ashamed. Like when I was little. Sometimes cars came to our village at home, and we would run to look at the people. They had good clothes, and boxes with things to eat and drink. It made me ashamed to have them see us, because we were little and dirty. But we always ran where they could see us. I don't know why."

"What did he say to you?"

"He told me I didn't answer the questions right. And then he said there was one question I must think about. He said if I was driving very fast with an open whisky bottle in my hand, what would I do? I told him I wouldn't do that—but it didn't make any difference, because he was smiling at me like he was before, not a real smile, I mean. And he said that was the most important question for all of us. We needed to know that more than anything else. Because if we got to drive a car that's what we always did."

Ford was confused by his anger; its intensity frightened him. "And then?" he asked her. "Then what, Maria?"

"He told me I couldn't get a license. He said to come back in two or three years, maybe."

"Can you tell me what he looked like, Maria? You know—please understand this—that he had no right to ask you those questions, or to talk to you like that. He has no right to ask you any question that isn't in the driver's manual issued by the state of Pennsylvania."

"He can ask me anything he wants. You know that."

"Goddamn it, don't say that."

"You know I'm right. Roby said I was right."

"What the hell does he know about it?" Ford held her close to him, he could feel the heavy stroke of his heart beating against the slight pressure of her body. "Will you try to forget it for tonight, Maria?" It was an effort to speak softly and gently to her; he felt like striking something with his fist.

"Why are you so mad? It doesn't matter, does it? That he made me feel—well, little again?"

"Let's don't talk about it anymore now."

280

She sighed and put her head down on his shoulder.

"All right?" he asked her.

"Yes, all right."

He held her close in his arms, and thought of the trooper. He was discovering hatred as he had discovered love; and he realized that both emotions were characterized by a sense of violence and frustration.

CHAPTER 17

IT was the beginning of a bad day; the morning was dark with heavy rain, and the west wind blew steadily and drearily through the winter-black trees. And that miserable morning began for Ford in the warm, tobacco-fragrant office of Lieutenant John Powell, who commanded the detachment of state troopers assigned to the testing of applicants for driving licenses in the state of Pennsylvania.

It was a day Ford would remember all his life. And later, when his thoughts returned to it, and he examined it minute by minute and hour by hour, he always wondered if anything he might have said or done could have changed the sequence of that day's events. He would never know, of course; the wheels of time were spinning, the hands of fate and chance were in motion, and it seemed to him that all the things he was and had been were fixed, immutable factors in the blueprint of that day. The words he had spoken, the decisions he had made, the turns he had taken at all the various crossroads of his life, were as impersonally significant as data fed into a machine; circumstances seemed to have shed their normal, whimsical natures; now they were ready to move in conspiracies of willful decision.

Lieutenant John Powell was stocky and gray-haired, with hard, alert blue eyes. It was difficult to imagine him in an environment which didn't include sharply pressed uniforms, Sam Browne belts, cleanly oiled hand guns, and subordinates who came to easy attention when they addressed him. Ford had known him for a good many years. In the normal intercourse of a small town they met regularly on official and semiofficial business; committee work, fund-raising drives, and so forth; but the stoutest bond between them was that the lieutenant, a dedicated and careful gunner, was one of the few men Ford allowed unrestricted use of his woods and fields during hunting season. And in an area where open country was constantly and remorselessly being encroached on by highways and building developments, this was a privilege the lieutenant held dearly.

He was in a smilingly reminiscent mood now, as he stood and added a touch of coffee to Ford's cup. "You know, Mr. Jackson, there's an old cock bird on your place, I think he squats back of your pond most of the time, that I'm going to get and mount for you one of these days. He's big as a turkey. His spurs looks about four inches long. But he's smart. I bet if I could catch him and teach him to talk, he'd tell me more about gunning than I've learned for myself these last thirty years. That coffee hot enough for you?"

"Yes, it's fine." Ford smiled a bit ruefully, as if he regretted having to digress from this talk of birds and shooting. "I don't want to tie up your whole morning, John. The reason I called, is that a girl Mrs. Jackson's thinking of hiring had a little trouble here yesterday with her driving test. She needs a license, or she won't be much good to us, of course."

Lieutenant Powell smiled sympathetically. "She didn't make it, eh? Well, that happens, you know. What was the matter?"

"I think she drives well enough. It was the oral examination that got her confused."

"Well, she might have been worried, mixed up, something like that. How old is she?"

"Twenty-two or twenty-three. She's a Puerto Rican, and she may have had difficulty understanding the questions."

"That could be it." Lieutenant Powell put a hand on his telephone. "We'll talk to the trooper, find out what she had trouble with." He winked at Ford as he picked up the receiver. "Maybe if she does a little homework between now and tomorrow, she'll get by O.K. What's her name?"

283

"Maria Ruiz."

Lieutenant Powell nodded and spoke into the receiver: "Danny. Yesterday, an applicant named Maria Ruiz. Get the trooper who tested her. Send him in. Right."

The trooper who entered a few minutes later had his gray, wide-brimmed hat tucked formally in the crook of his left arm. He stood at easy attention, and said: "You wanted to see me, Lieutenant?"

"Yes. Mr. Jackson, this is Trooper Joe Sadowski."

Trooper Sadowski smiled briefly at Ford. He was in his early or middle thirties, a big broad man with legs so thick that the muscles in his calves caused his black puttees to flare like funnels. His eyebrows came together like fat black worms above the bridge of a flat nose, and the short hair standing up from his skull looked as thick and smooth as if it had been applied with a spray gun. But his eyes seemed intelligent, Ford thought; in fact their alert appraisal of him and the lieutenant seemed incongruous within the square frame of his impassive features. Ford sensed a faint amusement flickering behind Sadowski's deliberately expressionless manner; it was too elusive to identify with assurance, but there seemed a suggestion of mockery in the politely inquiring tilt of his head, the rigid posture of his powerful arms and shoulders. He probably suspects why he's here, Ford thought; and he's not a bit worried about it. And he can't help letting us know that.

We will see, Ford thought. As a lawyer, he was always pleased to encounter the guardhouse variety. A man who could quote the Articles of War in his defense was usually frustrated if he wasn't allowed to; and to demonstrate the strength of his position he generally had to advertise its weaknesses.

Lieutenant Powell said: "Joe, you gave a test to a girl named Maria Ruiz yesterday, I understand. Right?"

"Yes, sir. I remember her quite well."

On the offensive from the first gun, Ford thought; a less confident man would have reflected on that opening question, frowned a bit, rubbed his jaw, put on a little act to indicate that his memory of the girl was casual and innocent, that her name was one of hundreds to pass under his scrutiny each week.

Ford studied Sadowski's heavy impassive face, remembering Maria's distress and humiliation, and thinking with cold relish about what he might do to this stupid, arrogant bully.

"We know she failed the test," the lieutenant said. "What was wrong?"

"Let's see, sir. Her driving was all right. She was a little nervous. She came over here in a beat-up old Chevvy, driven by a character with a godawful birthmark on his face. That probably didn't help much."

"Which do you mean?" Ford asked him.

"I don't understand, sir."

"I was just curious. Was it the beat-up Chevvy that made her nervous? Or the man with the birthmark?"

"Could be either, sir. Or neither. I just mentioned she was a little nervous driving. But she got through it all right. I couldn't fault her there. Driving won't be her trouble," Sadowski said judiciously, and a faint smile touched his lips.

Ford smiled too; he suspected they would soon be reaching fruitful ground.

"It was the oral, eh?" the lieutenant said. "The thing is, Mr. Jackson's got a job for this girl providing she can qualify for a driver's license. If she handles a car adequately, then the oral's just a question of more study."

"Generally speaking, that's true, sir. But some of them get more confused the more they study. She may be an exception. I don't know."

"Be that as it may. What questions did you ask her?"

"First, I asked her what she's required to do if she collides with an unoccupied vehicle. She got that O.K. Next I asked her about the speed limits in the state, and about the ratio of safe distances she should maintain behind other cars."

"Now that's two questions, Joe," the lieutenant said. "You asked them one at a time, you mean?"

"Yes sir," Sadowski raised his chin slightly; his small dark eyes became fixed on a point about a foot above the lieutenant's head. "May the trooper ask the lieutenant a question, sir?"

"Sure, go ahead, Joe."

"Has this girl made some complaint about anything I did or said?"

"No, what gave you that idea?"

"The lieutenant's line of inquiry, sir. It was a routine driver's test, so far as I know. But I know Mr. Jackson's an attorney, and I thought he might be here to represent her in a legal sense."

"Well, you thought a little quick and a little wrong, both," the lieutenant said quietly. "There wasn't anything in my questions to give you that notion."

"Sir, they usually have an excuse when they fail a test. I've seen that happen with them, on more than one occasion."

"Now let's get something straight," the lieutenant said. "When you say *them*, what do you mean? Puerto Ricans?"

"Oh, no sir." There was a touch of casual superiority in Sadowski's dismissal of the lieutenant's question. "All I meant to say was that people who aren't equipped to drive a car, generally don't have the fairness and judgment to realize that it's their own fault. So they blame us, naturally."

It was about then that Ford realized—or guessed—that Sadowski didn't like Lieutenant Powell. Either he was afraid of him, or didn't respect him. The former was more likely. But whatever the reasons, Ford knew that his place was on Sadowski's side. This was strategy as old as the law itself. The lieutenant was the judge here, and witnesses usually feared the judge, because he was paid a tithe of hinged knees and uncovered heads, and sat above the court in grimly splendid robes.

Ford said: "Lieutenant, perhaps I'm just wasting your time. I don't want you to be putting one of your men on the spot for me."

The lieutenant looked at him with a surprised frown. Then his mouth hardened a bit. "Mr. Jackson, I don't really believe you mean that. You know I wouldn't put a man of mine on the spot for you—or anyone else. I'm sorry you got that idea. Because it's quite inaccurate."

"Yes, of course," Ford said, and was gratified to notice that Sadowski was watching him with a faint smile, which seemed to be blended of both contempt and sympathy. "But it seems to me that it was the girl who made the mistakes. We can't blame the trooper for that, can we?"

"We aren't blaming the trooper. Please get that straight."

"Exactly," Ford said, emphatically. "I think he's got an imaginative approach to his job. I think he's to be commended for not allowing his judgment to become dulled by routine. You'll be glad to hear—and so will the trooper—that the girl is grateful to him. She was very nervous. But the trooper did his best to calm her down, make her relax. She was scared stiff, to put it bluntly. And he told her some jokes, and made some humorous comments, that should have put her in a more confident mood. Unfortunately, they did not; but I think the trooper deserves a plus mark for effort."

The lieutenant looked up at Sadowski. "Now that's very nice," he said. "Just what sort of jokes did you tell her, Trooper?"

Sadowski shrugged his big shoulders. "Well, it's like Mr. Jackson told you. I realized she was nervous, and I thought— well, that if she weren't so serious about it, like it was the end of the world, that some of the answers might come back to her."

"But your friendly manner didn't help matters?"

"No sir. She was too flustered."

"Now one minute, Sadowski. She passed the driving test. I assume she wasn't flustered then."

"No sir." Sadowski stiffened to a more respectful position, for there had been a significant change in the lieutenant's manner; he was leaning back in his chair and rubbing a large hand over his jaw, but his eyes had become thoughtful and cold.

"Well now," the lieutenant said. "She passed the driving test. Then she answered the first question of the oral. I gather she wasn't flustered then either."

"No sir." Sadowski gave Ford a look of tentative appeal. Ford nodded encouragingly.

The lieutenant said: "It was after your jokes that she became upset. Is that right, Trooper?"

"Sir, she was quite nervous all the time. Mr. Jackson mentioned that, sir. Didn't you, sir?"

"What's that?" Ford said innocently.

"You said she was nervous, sir."

"Yes, that's right. But I didn't suggest you were the cause of it."

"I know, sir." Sadowski looked confused. "I only want to make the lieutenant see that I was trying—well, to cheer her up. You said she appreciated that, sir, that she was grateful."

"I want to know what you told her," the lieutenant said, looking at him steadily. "If you're dispensing good cheer around here, I could use some of it, Trooper."

"I don't remember just what I said, sir. You know how it is, you make up a joke and don't think about it afterward." Sadowski fingered one of the buttons on his tunic. "I might have said, well, 'Take it easy'—or something like that."

"Now that's a very funny comment," the lieutenant said.

"It would be how I said it, sir, not the actual words."

"I see. But you don't remember what you said?"

"That's right, sir."

"I consider that curious. You remembered her name. You remembered that she came over here in an old Chevvy, with a man with a birthmark on his face. You remembered the exact sequence of the questions you asked her. But you draw a blank on the jokes you made that apparently upset her. Are you trying to make me guess?"

"No sir, I am not. But if I can say something, sir, I'd like to say you can't win on this job. I tried to give her a break, as Mr. Jackson's told you. I tried to cheer her up, but this is the thanks I get. If I treated them by the book, I suppose I'd hear about that, too."

Ford stood up decisively. "John, I'm sorry for causing this trouble. This business isn't worth it. The girl was amused and puzzled by whatever the trooper did say to her, and that's all there is to it. But I can imagine why he's reluctant to tell

288

you what he said. And I see no point in making a federal case out of it." Ford smiled at Sadowski. "We're men of the world, I assume. And what man of the world doesn't know the quickest way to cheer up a woman? A little flattery, a few kind words, right? I would guess the trooper told her she had nice eyes or good-looking legs, or something of that sort—to demonstrate he was a human being, and not just a cold, heartless machine."

"Was that it?" the lieutenant said quietly. "Is Mr. Jackson's guess a good one, Sadowski?"

Sadowski looked uncertainly from the lieutenant to Ford. It was as if he had heard the slow creaking of a trap, and knew any move he made might be dangerous. Color was rising in his broad dark face. "No, that's not a good guess," he said. "Not by a damn sight."

"Maybe you dispensed with the moonlight and roses," the lieutenant said. "Maybe you pinched her bottom to demonstrate you weren't just a heartless machine."

"I have the right to remind the lieutenant that he's making an accusation based on Mr. Jackson's guesses." Sadowski stared bitterly at Ford. "I'm a married man, I've been married to the same decent woman for sixteen years, and I don't have to take insults from anybody about that."

"Damn it, everything I say just seems to muddy the water," Ford said. "I'm sure you've got a wonderful wife, and I'm genuinely sorry if you feel I've cast any reflection on her. As a matter of fact, if you don't mind my saying so, I assumed that you're good-humored, and your friendly handling of this girl must have stemmed from your own happily married experiences."

"Let's cut out the double talk," Sadowski said. He placed his fists on his wide hips and looked grimly from Ford to Lieutenant Powell. "I ain't going to be shoved around just for fun." He pointed a finger at Ford. "I get the picture now. She told you I made a pass at her, right? That's her story! That I copped a feel, and flunked her because she didn't like it." He was nearly shouting; his eyes had narrowed to ugly little slits, and his face was flushed with anger. "That's the lie she's dreamed up, eh? I ain't surprised! These spics haven't any more morals than cats."

"No, she didn't tell me that," Ford said mildly. "She told me about the whisky bottle."

"And you didn't believe her! You wouldn't know the truth if it bit you in the mouth. You had to sniff around for another story, something fancy and filthy that would suit your opinion of a meatheaded Polack." Sadowski swung around to the lieutenant, his eyes blazing triumphantly. "Did you hear him? He had the truth from the start. She told him the truth! But he didn't believe her! He'd rather make me into a pervert, grabbing girls—" Sadowski's full, angry voice broke then, as if powerful fingers had been clamped suddenly around his throat. Then, as the lieutenant placed his big hands deliberately on his desk, the color faded from Sadowski's face and his lips began to twist and jerk into the semblance of a smile.

"I was a little excited there, sir," he said. "What I told you was by way—well, of example." He waved a hand nervously in the air, as if the memory of his words was buzzing around his head like wasps. The only sound in the office was that of his laboring lungs.

"Well, your memory's improving anyway," the lieutenant said, at last. "The joke was about a whisky bottle, eh? Now supposing you just settle down, Sadowski, and do some more remembering. And you can start by remembering I'm your commanding officer, and I don't want to hear you raise your voice in my office again, ever. You got that?"

"Yes sir. I'm sorry, sir." Sadowski looked quite different now; it was as if his body had been swollen and thickened and sustained by anger. Without it, he seemed to be shrinking inside his uniform.

Ford stared out the window at the large rain-swept area of concrete which was used for the driving examinations. It was marked with yellow lines, and posted with traffic signs. A car was going carefully around the course now, with a trooper in the front seat to note the operator's judgments and reactions.

Rising behind the wire-fenced examination course was the rain-blackened bulk of a public school. Ford's thoughts were as ugly as the view.

Lieutenant Powell was questioning Sadowski closely now, and Sadowski had belatedly retreated into the comparative safety of yes and no answers. He was lying, of course, and Ford knew he could turn and blow his evasions away with one or two bursts of theatrical anger. But he had no stomach for it. Did Sadowski deserve it? Maybe. He had humiliated Maria, used the power given him in trust to intimidate and humiliate her; he had behaved like an arrogant bully, but would probably go to his grave denying it, because he was a pure, white, 100 per cent American, and Maria's skin was a shade darker than his. In fact, it wasn't; but Sadowski's myopic hatred probably turned it coal black. Maybe he thought he'd done a good day's work in seeing she didn't get a license. He must reason in his thick, knotted head that if she could drive she would come over to his home and throw garbage on his lawn. Somehow, he was convinced she could hurt him. And so he had got in the first blow. And because he had hurt Maria, Ford had the right to hurt him. It seemed a cruel and tiresome circle. George Delucca had hurt Wiley. So Wiley Poston would smash Delucca. . . . They were all jealous of their right to hate. . . .

The world as he saw it that dismal morning seemed a preposterous exercise in the witless use of power. The motives and techniques were constant; the only variable factor seemed to be the amount of damage done. From concentration camps and Siberian mines, down—or up—to restricted clubs, discomfort was only a matter of degree; and in all areas the victims protested, if they could, and the ruling cliques thought up reasons to justify the inevitability and rectitude of their position on top of the human heap. The arguments advanced for bias and cruelty and the prolongation of torture were always comfortably and shrewdly thought out, and only slightly insane, like the conversations of gentlemen in a very superior lunatic asylum. Everything was relative: *this* pain related to *that* pleasure, *this* humiliation to *that* vindication—without one you couldn't have the other. No one—in the asylum anyway—seemed to doubt that there was a necessary and causal bond between these relationships.

The click of the door surprised him. He turned and saw that Sadowski had gone.

"Does this girl want to make a complaint?" the lieutenant asked him.

Ford shook his head slowly.

"You pressing it?"

Ford shook his head again. "I'm sorry I made a production out of it. I should have just given you the facts."

"You wouldn't have the truth that way."

"Maybe. But I don't know what good it does." He frowned faintly, trying to find the core of meaning in his drifting thoughts. He found himself longing for an absolute; a word, a position, a belief, that didn't shatter into bits at the first glancing blow from the smooth iron of compromise. "I may be wrong, John," he said at last. "Maybe it does some good after all. Do you mind if I use your phone?"

"No, go ahead," the lieutenant said. "If you're satisfied with this matter, O.K. All I can do is tack a reprimand to his file. Meanwhile I'll go out and see if he's stamping swastikas on applications."

When the door closed, Ford dialed the Cottersville Bank and asked for Tom Landon. He was put through after a short wait.

"Tom, this is Ford Jackson."

"Yes, Ford. I called your home earlier. And your office. No one knew where you'd gone."

"I'm sorry. I should have got in touch with you. But something came up. About that matter we discussed last night— what can I do?"

"You'd like to help Delucca? Is that what you mean?"

"Yes."

Landon sighed wearily. "I wish I'd got hold of you earlier. I'm afraid it's too late now. I talked with Delucca an hour or

292

so ago, and told him the board's decision on his loan. He said he could raise the full amount in two or three months; and I had to tell him that wasn't good enough. It wasn't a very friendly chat after that. Not that I blame him."

"You've filed the lien?"

"Yes. He'll be presented with a demand for the loan, plus interest, today or tomorrow. Shortly after that, we'll be in the restaurant business, I imagine."

"Now just a minute, Tom." Ford frowned faintly. The wall clock ticked against the silence. He watched the second hand draw its endless circle about the face of the clock. One minute. . . . He had made up his mind what he was going to do, but he gave himself that minute to think about why he was doing it. He wanted peace and reassurance. His decision was significant, because he had learned something this morning, through Maria. He told himself that, as he watched the second hand turning; but he didn't believe it. The decision was simply another exercise of power.

"Tom, I want you to make out a cashier's check to George Delucca for one hundred thousand dollars and send it over to him by messenger. Now what sort of collateral do you want?"

"Can you give me a check for that amount?"

"No. I haven't that much cash."

"O.K. We can make it a note."

"Fix it up anyway you like. But I want him to have the money this afternoon."

"Fine. Stop by in an hour or so. I'll have the papers ready."

As Ford broke the connection, he realized that Landon was chuckling in a cheerful, though somewhat breathless, manner.

Ford called the White Hackle Inn and asked for Delucca. He knew he should talk to him in person, but he justified his reluctance to do so with the argument that time mattered more than the amenities just now.

When the connection was made, he heard Delucca talking faintly but clearly to someone else. "Yes, that's what I mean, pal," Delucca was saying. He laughed and said, "O.K., watch it," and then his voice became sharp and distinct in Ford's ear. "Hello? Who's this?"

"Ford Jackson."

"Well, I'll be damned." Delucca's tone was elaborately ironical. "What can I do for you, Mr. Jackson? A nice corner table for tonight?"

"Listen to me, please. I talked to Tom Landon a few minutes ago. I told him to send you a check for a hundred thousand dollars this afternoon. You can tear it up if you like. Or shove it down Wiley Poston's throat. There are no strings to it."

"You're a little confused about the role you want to play. Shylock or fairy godmother. Make up your mind, for Christ's sake."

"Does that matter so long as the check's on the way?"

"You better try another shop if you want a nose bob done on your conscience. I'm not in that racket—I don't need your money."

"Well, I'm glad to hear that." Ford was shaken by Delucca's bitterness. "Your problems are straightened out then?"

"Do you think she'd let me go down the drain?"

"You mean Alicia?" That hadn't occurred to him; it was inevitable, of course, and somehow choicely appropriate, but it hadn't even crossed his mind.

"Sure. She wants to pawn her jewelry, sell lemonade on the highway, weave baskets for rich old ladies. Anything at all. That surprise you?"

"No, I guess it doesn't. I just hadn't thought of it."

"Well, this may, then. I don't want her money either. No one's getting their spiritual kicks bailing me out. This isn't a rehabilitation center."

"Do you mind if I ask what you plan to do?"

"I'm not doing one damn thing. The bank can have the joint. But I'll tell them where to find a buyer, and what price tag to hang on the front door. They can get their equity out in two weeks. I get the balance. And it's a sweet one."

"You're leaving here then?"

"Right, Mr. Jackson. In a Cadillac, the way I came. I'm

294

way beyond my pollution tolerance. I'm surprised anybody can live here without a gas mask."

The phone clicked sharply in Ford's ear. He stood motionless for an instant, the dead receiver hanging limply in his hand. And this particular moment was the one his thoughts always returned to first, whenever he searched for the reasons and meanings behind what happened that day. For his reaction at that moment was one of relief and deliverance. The tensions that had involved him so insistently and unfairly were over and done with; he was free from them all, it seemed then, released from every commitment and responsibility. There was nothing he had to do, nothing at all. But these conclusions, which seemed so apparent and comforting at that pivotal moment, were the ones he always looked back on with a sense of remorse and guilt.

In his own office, he asked Mrs. Simpson to order a sandwich and pot of tea for his lunch. He told her he wouldn't take any calls that afternoon. In the distracting involvement of work, he felt safe and secure from the world beyond the streaked, glistening windows of his office.

It rained throughout the afternoon. The wind pressed against the windows with mournful sighing sounds, and the shaded lamp on his desk cast gloomy shadows into the corners of the room. But he liked the feeling of being enclosed and enfolded within the ring of darkness drawn by the cone of light from his lamp; it gave him a comfortable sense of isolation and privacy. He realized that he had been painfully exposed and vulnerable lately, and it was pleasant to be locked away from the world, and minding his own business in the security and seclusion of familiar surroundings.

Mrs. Simpson interrupted him once to tell him Tom Landon had called several times.

"It's not anything important," Ford said. "If he calls again, just tell him the arrangement we discussed isn't necessary now. He'll understand."

In the middle of the afternoon Mrs. Simpson looked in on him once again. "I'm sorry, Mr. Jackson, but your brother's wife has been trying to get you since about one o'clock. She's called three or four times, at least."

"I've simply got to get these papers in order," Ford said. He felt then as if sullen and dangerous pressures were building up around his defenses. "Tell her I'm not in."

"Yes, of course."

"Wait a second. Is she at home?"

"Yes."

"Then tell her I'll stop by on my way home from the office. Around five-thirty. But I don't want to talk to her now. Make some excuse."

"Yes, Mr. Jackson."

Alicia was sitting in the summer living room before the fireplace. She stood up when he came in. She was wearing a slim black dress which seemed to draw all the color from her face. And she sounded tired, as she said: "Well, you must have had a busy day."

"Yes, there were people in and out on some things that wouldn't keep. Where's Clay?"

"That's always the essential question, isn't it? Where's Clay? How's Clay? What can we do to make him happy?"

"Now hold on. What's the matter?" He realized he had misinterpreted the tone of greeting; what he had thought was weariness was something very different. She was standing with her back to the leaping fire, and the reflections of the flames in her blond hair made a glowing ring around the bitterness and anger in her face.

"You don't know?" she asked him. "You don't know what's the matter? How damn convenient for you, Ford."

"You sound like you could use a drink."

"That's another important consideration around here. Have a drink! Get smashed! Forget everything else. Laugh and scratch; pretend life's a big happy joke!"

"It's Clay, I suppose," he said. "What's he up to? Where is he?"

"I don't know. Nor do I give a damn." She turned away

296

suddenly, and put the back of her hand against her forehead. "God, how could you do it? How does your mind work? You, and that drunken boor, Wiley Poston, and that pious, pretentious bastard, Tony Marshall, you ganged up on him like three thugs in an alley with knives and clubs. But that's not right, is it? You wouldn't do it in person, even at those odds."

"I think you'd better try to calm down," he said. "You might also try to get your facts straight."

"I've got them straight. I made that my business. You used the bank as your private firing squad. George knows the timetable of your little coup. You're not the only people with contacts and cozy secrets." She was pacing in a restless, compulsive manner, her high-heeled pumps ringing on the brick flooring, and every line of her slight body strung tight with tension. "That was the safe, shrewd way to go about it, wasn't it?" she said scornfully. "Let your trained monkey, Tom Landon, do the job."

"Alicia, we won't accomplish anything if you go on this way. I called Delucca this morning and offered to lend him enough cash to meet his obligations. I'd already told Tom Landon to make out the check. He was delighted to do it, by the way. So he's not the hatchet man you assume. Delucca turned me down flatly. I don't recall that he even said thanks. But that's neither here or there. The thing is, I offered to help him. But he didn't want it."

"God, God, you talk as if you'd behaved heroically! You don't recall that he even said thanks." She mimicked the judicious, neutral tone he had been using, savagely and accurately. "What about last night? When Tom Landon offered you the chance to stand up for a principle? The issue wasn't personal, it had nothing to do with George. The issue was what Ford Jackson, stout pillar of the community, would do to prevent a man from being cheated out of his business. And you did nothing! You waited until you could put it on a personal basis. Until you thought you had George in exactly the bind you wanted him. Then—and only then—you offered him a deal."

"You're completely wrong," he said. "And if this omniscient attitude of yours is something you've acquired from Delucca, let me say I don't find it very attractive. Now you listen to me," he said sharply, as she began pacing again, with a suggestion of impatience and exasperation in the set of her shoulders. "Landon came to see me last night with a vague proposal that I talk to Wiley and Tony. I don't think he had a clue what good that would do. Frankly, I think he simply wanted to share his problems with me. But in the first place, I'm not on the board of his bank. Secondly, talking to Wiley and Tony would not have accomplished anything, despite Landon's notions about my weight in the community. But the important thing was that I'd spoken to Clay earlier, and he asked me—implored is a better word—to stay out of his affairs. And Delucca is very much Clay's business. And yours, of course. He's not mine. I couldn't interfere at all without breaking my word to Clay. It seemed to me I had to stay neutral."

"And why did you change your mind?"

"It was a change of heart, not a change of mind," he said. "I realized what Wiley and Tony were doing was contemptible. There's no lack of precedent for it, of course. Some of the most respectable money around here stems directly from carefully timed foreclosures. But I wanted to stop them. There were no strings on my offer to Delucca. It had nothing to do with you or Clay. I want you to believe that."

"And what of your other offers? The home on the Downs? Membership in the Cedars? Good schools for his daughters? Was that all without strings, too?"

"He asked me not to mention our conversation to you," Ford said slowly. "I gather he wanted the satisfaction of telling you about it himself."

"That's a curious implication." She stared at him thoughtfully. "He's not what you'd call a gentleman, I suppose. So why act surprised when he doesn't behave like one? But aren't you forgetting that you made the proposition? That you put the cash on the barrel head to buy me back for Clay?"

"I guess there's no point trying to explain my reasons," he

said wearily. "The issue seems to be all settled. You're leaving Clay?"

"Yes."

"Would you consider trying a separation first? You feel strongly right now, I know. But it wouldn't hurt to put off the final step for a while."

"I'm sure of how and what I feel. I want to get away from this place."

"Are you suggesting things might have been different elsewhere?"

"Thanks for that, Ford." The anger had gone from her eyes and face; her expression was one of mild distaste. "You mean I'd have climbed out the windows of my locked room, no matter where we lived? Picked the lock of my chastity belt with hot little hands?"

"Please, Alicia. I meant nothing of the sort."

"Then what did you mean? I think you've blundered into something that frightens you. Because, perhaps it would have been different somewhere else. Different and better. The people we know, the people here on the Downs, have been taught it's wrong to love and respect certain classes of people. And we all have a childish kind of logic that either rebels against that, or twists it into something even uglier. If you aren't allowed to love them, then it's all right to hate them. And if it's right to hate one class, then it's got to be right to hate all classes." She was pacing restlessly, flinging out the words with scornful anger.

"Don't you see it's the right to hate that destroys people? Let them hate if they can't help themselves, but not righteously, for God's sake. Not as if they'd done their good deed for the day."

Ford was suddenly afraid that he might have bought his hours of peace that day too dearly; he couldn't explain or analyze this fear, but he was conscious of the helpless and dismaying conviction that while he was running from responsibility, time had been running out on him. . . .

"Alicia, I want you to help me understand your attitude,"

he said slowly. "I'm asking that as a favor. Because I feel quite stupid and inadequate just now. But I thought I was acting for the best. I thought saving you and Clay—your marriage, I mean—was the most important consideration."

"I understand that, for God's sake. I think I'll go mad if I hear any more talk about who's best and what's best. We're the best—that's all you mean."

The fire guttered fitfully; a tiny puff ball of smoke floated up suddenly from the burning logs.

"You put Clay on one side of the scales, George on the other," she said bitterly. "There was only one result. George Delucca was worthless. Without value, significance, importance. You could do what you wanted to him, because you've been trained to think of certain types of people as less than human. You wanted to save Clay! Is that your definition of the best? An irresponsible drunk?"

The fire leaped brightly under a draft of air, and Ford felt a coldness about his ankles.

"Please, Alicia," he said, frowning at the fireplace.

"Clay's twisted and broken, and all his charm can't hide it. You wanted us to stay together to fill out a pretty family picture. You didn't care what that would cost me." He made a gesture for her to be silent, but she shook her head desperately, and said: "No, you didn't give one damn. No one did. The only concern was protecting Clay. Shoring up his ego. Trying to make a man out of him. God, he's not half a man. He hasn't as much strength in him as George has in one of his hands."

"Please," he said, softly and insistently. The muscles in his back were hard with tension, but when he turned there was no one behind him; the cold wind, so appropriate now for some reason, was the only alien presence in the room.

He stared at Alicia. "Would you like a drink?" he said.

"No, I don't think so. But you go ahead." She rubbed her bare arms. "What's the matter? What's wrong with the fire?"

Ford held up a hand warningly; then he turned and walked slowly down the hallway to the foyer. The front door stood open, and a cold, gusting wind was sweeping the house. In his present nervous mood, the skittering shadows in the foyer seemed to be leaping away from the wind, as if in fear of its arrogant intrusion.

Inside the door, shining dully on the red brick floor, were the imprints of damp footsteps.

As he stared at them, he heard Alicia's footsteps clicking sharply in the hallway. Then he heard the sound of heavier footsteps over his head. As he raised his eyes to the ceiling, Alicia stopped beside him and put her hand on his arm. They stood together, staring toward the sounds above their heads.

Alicia swallowed. The sound was dry and clear against the silence which seemed to be tensing and stretching itself throughout the house. Then Ford's ear rang under the impact of an explosion. The whole house seemed to tremble; pictures shook on the wall as waves of sound leaped through the torn and scattered silence.

Ford ran toward the stairs, conscious of nothing but the absurd and pathetic noise Alicia's fingernails had made as he jerked his arm free from her hand. On the second-floor landing a maid stood staring down at him with frightened eyes. She seemed unable to move. He had to shove her aside, and then he ran down the wide hallway and pushed open the door of Clay's darkened bedroom.

There was an acrid stench of smoke in the air. Light filtered over his shoulder from the hallway, and he saw then, through this smoke-streaked illumination, that his brother, Clay, was lying on the floor grinning at him.

That's what he thought as he knelt beside him—that was his preposterous, frantic thought as he put a hand on his shoulder; but the lights blazed in the room then, and he saw the shotgun lying beside his brother, and he realized there was nothing left of Clay's face to grin with.

He turned blindly from the ghastly trick the light had played on him. He didn't want to see that blond head again, in this life or in his nightmare. And he said, in a thick, straining voice: "Get that light off. Don't come in here, anybody."

But it was too late for that. She had followed him into the room, and had snapped on the lights to see what was lying there on the floor. He heard her say, in a small, choking voice, "Oh, no! No! Ford, look at his shoes. They're soaking wet." And he never knew what she meant by that, although he guessed it was related in some hysterical way to the fact that Clay had never liked rain.

And so the day Ford would never forget came to an end.

CHAPTER 18

"YOU'LL see that his investments were all quite conservative. He had no interest in speculation. Practically everything is in blue chips and mutual funds. We differed on this, as a policy, but Clay preferred arrangements which didn't require his personal attention.

"I've listed his holdings in alphabetical order for your convenience. I think it would be helpful if we ran through them quickly. You'll see—on Schedule A—American Airlines, A.T.&T., American Viscose, Atlantic Refinery Preferred, and so forth. The amounts he owned, and the dividends, are in those right-hand columns.

"The mutual funds are in that next folder. Chase, Dreyfuss, Mass. Growth, Sterling, and one or two others."

Ford's voice was dry and precise, as emotionless as the names of the companies he had been reading off. Alicia sat in front of his desk in a straight-backed chair. She wore a black suit and held a bulky sheaf of papers in her gloved hands.

The morning was clear, and the office was bright with sunshine. Ford's voice fell clearly and quietly through the soft, early spring air, and the only other sound was the faint rustle of papers as he and Alicia made their way through the neatly stapled records of Clay's investments.

"About these mutual funds. I imagine your broker might suggest converting them to something more flexible. In any case—"

"Ford, please. I'm sorry. I can't follow all this just now. But I know everything's all right."

303

"Yes, it's tidy and sound, though, as I've said, on the conservative side. You can go through it all with your attorney whenever it's convenient. But I do want to point out one other thing: Clay left orders with his broker to transfer sixty thousand dollars a year to the Cottersville bank, in quarterly installments. That arrangement is still in effect. It might be a good idea to leave it like that for the time being, because you'll have some normal running expenses at home, and at the dairy. But actually there's nothing you need worry about. Everything is set up to run along quite efficiently."

"You think I killed him, don't you?"

Ford removed his glasses and rubbed a hand over his eyes. "I almost wish I believed that," he said. "It would answer the questions I keep asking myself. But I don't believe it. And I don't want you to say it again. Or even to think it."

"He stood there listening to me talking about him. I know that. It's not a simple matter to stop thinking about. He heard the hate in my voice. I didn't mean it, I tell myself, but that's no good. He heard me. We'd failed each other, and I was sorry for him, but that wasn't what he heard standing there in the foyer."

"We don't know that he heard anything at all. If he did, perhaps he knew that you were upset and angry. It's quite pointless to be worrying about it, Alicia."

So sadly and terribly pointless, he thought. The golden head and slender body were hidden from sight forever in the rich earth of the Episcopal cemetery. Clay had been dead now for two weeks, and there was nothing left of him in the living world but the rumors and stories that buzzed about the manner of his death, and the reasons behind it.

In this ferment of speculation, certain other news had gone practically unnoticed. Tony Marshall had bought Delucca's White Hackle Inn. It seemed he had wanted the land there for quite some time, which explained, to Ford anyway, why he had added his pressure to Wiley's in foreclosing it. But he hadn't driven a very sharp bargain. The Mussmano brothers and Clarence Turnbull, who were friends of Delucca's, had bid the property up to the sky to fatten Delucca's share of the sale. This was the story going around at any rate; whether it was true or not Ford didn't know.

Like many other things which happened at that time, it wasn't important enough to compete with the excitement surrounding Clay's death. The coroner decided it had been an accident, and this added to the gossip. There was talk of pressure and politics, which was nonsense. Coroner Davis had known and liked Clay for years, but, given the facts, would have returned the same verdict on any laborer or farmhand in the county. To Ford he had said in private: "Now, this is something we'll have to go into at the hearing. Was there any reason for him to have a loaded shotgun in his bedroom? Any reason for him to go up and get it that night?" And: "Could you say, well, that things were normal at his house that night?" The coroner had his misgivings, obviously. Ford didn't have the heart to lie to him, to throw up smoke screens to obscure his presently clear view of the matter. But help had come from Janet. When she arrived home, she was able to show Coroner Davis several postcards Clay had written her in the last two or three weeks. They were gay and cheerful, full of Clay's usual nonsense, and he had been favorably impressed with them.

But it was Wiley Poston who had saved what little there was left to be saved, by lying to Davis, flatly and belligerently. "Clay and I planned to go gunning the next day," he said, and his manner was so resolute and staunch that it was possible he had convinced himself that this was the literal truth. "I told the poor guy to check his gun, and to show it to Ford if he got the chance. The cartridge selector on that model was tricky. He didn't know a whole lot about guns. I knew Ford could tell him if it was working all right." And so a sad but respectable story had taken shape; Clay, seeing Ford's car in the driveway, must have gone up to get the shotgun to have Ford take a look at it. And then Alicia and Ford's account of the footsteps they had heard fitted smoothly into the picture. Clay had obviously been hurrying across the floor with the loaded gun. Innocently and tragically, he must have collided with a chair in the darkness. . . .

Ford hadn't seen or heard from Maria since Clay's death. He had written her a note, and had sent it to the post office in Rosedale. He had had no word from her. He had no way of knowing if she had connected him with the newspapers accounts of Clay's death. He had never talked to her about Clay, and he regretted that.

His memories of her seemed sadly faint and distant; her trailer was like some nostalgic, half-imaginary refuge of his childhood—no more permanent or realizable than the landing at the top of the attic stairs where he and Clay had played on rainy afternoons, or the old root cellar in the basement with its smooth stone walls and narrow ventilation shaft through which the sunlight threaded the air with shining, dancing lights. . . .

"I sent some of his things over to your place this morning," Alicia said. "Books and snapshots, school things mostly. I—didn't know him then. I thought you might like to look through them."

Ford went with her to the door of the outer office. "You'll call me if anything comes up? If you need anything?"

"Yes, of course, Ford. And thank you."

They shook hands, and looked directly at one another for the first time that morning. Then she turned and walked quickly toward the ancient, bird-cage elevators, her shoulders held back, and her footsteps sounding in neat, precise rhythms on the old hardwood flooring.

She was a lovely and wealthy widow, whose slim, well-bred legs were taking her off to George Delucca with all possible speed, and if it were possible to hate someone just a little, he thought, that was how he hated her as she stepped into the waiting elevator, after giving him a last tentative smile, and a childish wave of her hand. Just a little. . . .

When he got home that evening, Janet told him a package had come over from Alicia's.

"Yes, it's some things of Clay's she thought I might want."

"She wouldn't, obviously."

He had stopped in the study to make himself a drink, without bothering to take off his overcoat. Janet snapped on the lamps before settling down on the sofa. She was wearing an oatmeal-colored tweed suit that made her tanned arms and legs look almost black.

"Honestly, Ford, I know what you've been through, and I don't want to start hashing everything to pieces. But why didn't you tell me about Alicia and George Delucca when you were in Florida? It was obviously about as discreet as a stag party by then—that's what Ellie says, at any rate. You knew, didn't you?"

"Yes."

She frowned at him, and her pale-blue eyes blinked like shiny small mirrors against the cocoa-brown color of her skin. "Why in heaven's name didn't you do something about it? Were you just hoping for the best, or something?"

"I suppose I was," he said, without irony.

"Well, I gather you've been awfully busy," she said. She drew a fingernail slowly across her nylon-smooth kneecap. It made a sound like the tentative but challenging scratch of a small animal. "Hardly anyone saw you all winter, it seems." She raised her head and smiled brightly at him. "Anyone I know, at any rate."

He had been expecting this, sooner or later. Since she had got back from Florida, she had been spending most of her time with Ellie. He finished his drink, and said, "Where did you put Clay's things?"

"In your room. But it's about time for dinner." She was still smiling brightly, but he saw that her fingernails were leaving deep white grooves across her brown kneecap. "Please, Ford, don't start messing through them now."

"I'll just take a look."

There was a leather valise and a wicker crate on the floor at the foot of his bed, and he remembered them both with a painful and depressing wrench of nostalgia. The cracked and shapeless valise had been Clay's overnight bag when he was at the Hill School, and he had used it for years afterward on golfing or sailing weekends. It was stuffed now with clean T shirts, sneakers, heavy wool sweat socks. Tucked away between layers of clothing, Ford found the monogram which Clay had won in track in his senior year. The wicker basket was the size of an army foot locker, with a lid secured by wooden pegs. It was probably as old as Clay, he thought; it had traveled with them to picnics and beach parties when they were children, and it had ended its service with a kind of raffish smartness as a carryall for sandwiches and cocktail shakers at football games. It must have stood on the tailgates of a dozen station wagons at least, and it bore the scars of that rugged autumn duty; the lid was seared from cigarette burns, and he could still see where Wiley Poston had pulled off a long sliver of wood to use for stirring drinks.

When he opened the crate it seemed to sigh gratefully; a faint exhalation of dust rose gently from the clutter of books and papers, photographs and theater programs.

Ford spent a gloomy few minutes sifting through them. There were several volumes from the set of Shakespeare their father had given them one Christmas. Ford had most of the others downstairs in his library. He found some short stories Clay must have written at the Hill, but he didn't have the heart to read them. On a plain white calling card was a name he didn't know: John Cosgrove. He tried to remember; it seemed to him there were some Cosgroves over in Cape May. No, that was Costerly, or Cargrave, something like that. There were beer coasters, newspaper clippings, dozens of curling snapshots. He looked at a dusty scorecard from the Cedars. From the date he could imagine how the course had been playing, and he smiled as he saw that Clay had got a birdie on the long, par-five fifteenth. In December, that meant two fantastic wood shots. Which was probably why he had saved it. On a menu from a restaurant in New York called The Steak Box, someone had scrawled: "All beauty is a lack." And below that, in Clay's distinctive back-slanted handwriting, was the comment: "So sayeth John Paul Sartre, World Renowned Fartre."

It was near the bottom of the crate that he came on a neat stack of letters held together with a rubber band. They seemed out of place in this pile of yellowing clutter. The envelopes were stiff and white, and the postmarks were recent; the letters, six in all, had been mailed from New York within the past three or four months. The return address was on St. Luke's Place, which he knew was down in the Village, and the sender's name was Jaye Fisher.

He almost tossed them back into the basket. But he didn't; he opened one and read it. Then he read all the others. By the time he had finished, his fingers were trembling slightly.

But it wasn't guilt or embarrassment that had caused this reaction; it was an overwhelming sense of being close to Clay, significantly and intimately.

What he had read were love letters to his brother, nakedly intense, and nakedly revealing. An image of Clay he had never known was reflected in them; the marring streaks of cynicism and mockery were smoothed away, and behind them he saw truer values of humor and tenderness and passion.

The feeling of intimacy was so intense that he found himself staring in despair about the empty room. He was swept with the sad and hopeless feeling that he had missed the chance to say a final word with him.

This was what Clay had wanted of life. He tried to imagine her from the letters. He had an impression of someone vivid and tense, dark perhaps, with fierce intelligent loyalties. Fisher? Was that Jewish? An artist possibly, a designer, someone clever and bright like Clay?

There was comfort in thinking of her, for the simple fact of her existence seemed to make Clay's death less final and brutal; he still lived through her, and her existence would always be a proof of his. . . . There was no telephone listed under Jaye Fisher's name at the St. Luke's Place address. Ford thanked the operator and put the receiver down slowly. He had acted on an emotional impulse; he was hardly conscious of having crossed the room and picked up the phone. It would be better, kinder, to write, he thought. He was grateful to her, and he simply wanted to say that. And then he decided not to wait. There was no point to it. If he could help, he wanted to, right now. He picked up the phone and sent a wire to her at the address that was written on the envelopes.

At breakfast Janet looked at him with a strange, fixed smile when he told her he had to go over to New York that afternoon.

He caught the three o'clock Congressional in Wilmington, and arrived at Pennsylvania Station in New York at the top of the rush hour. It took him fifteen minutes to find a cab, and another twenty minutes to reach St. Luke's Place. The traffic was heavy, and a light snow was falling. As it melted, the streets turned black and slick under the yellow headlights.

St. Luke's Place faced a small park. It was a quiet and pretty street, with tall brownstone houses, and small sugar maples planted along the sidewalks.

Ford went up steep stone steps flanked by brass hand railings, and found Jaye Fisher's name on a card in a damp entrance hall. As he pressed the button beside her name, a buzzer began to click rhythmically in the lock of the inner door, and he realized she must have been watching for him from the window. The thought cheered him. On the train he had begun to wonder if what he was doing were wise. But the immediate answer to his ring eased his doubts; it indicated, at least, that he was expected.

A door on the first-floor landing was opened by a man of about thirty in a loose brown tweed suit. There was a smudge of cigarette ash on his cheek, and the black wool tie he wore was pulled down an inch or so from the collar of his white shirt. In the light falling through the open door behind him, Ford saw that he had thinning brown hair, and smooth pleasant features. He seemed tired or harried at the moment, Ford couldn't decide which; but when he smiled suddenly, a warm and engaging light sparkled in his clear blue eyes. There was something about his manner, Ford thought, which seemed to suggest that growing up had come as a mild surprise to him; but that he would play along with this little joke if that's what was wanted of him.

"I'm looking for Jaye Fisher," Ford said.

"You're Ford Jackson, of course," the young man said. "I think I might have recognized you even if I hadn't been expecting you. Come in, please. I can't tell you how pleased and surprised I was to get your wire."

Ford had extended his hand at the young man's first words; and now he felt his arm stiffening in front of him, like an independent extension of his body; it seemed as hard and wooden as a fence post.

The young man took his hand in a warm grip. "But I guess I shouldn't have been surprised," he said. "From what Clay told me about you, I might have expected it."

Still holding his hand tightly, Jaye Fisher drew Ford through the open door into a small, brightly lighted sitting room which smelled of coffee and cigarettes.

CHAPTER 19

"I wanted to go down to the funeral, of course. I thought he'd have wanted that. We always talk with assurance of what the dead would want, which is just damn selfishness, I suppose. But not knowing his friends or family, well, I decided against it."

Jaye Fisher stood at a card table on which there were bottles and glasses. He was making drinks. Ford sat in a straight-backed, wrought-iron chair with his hat and gloves on his knee. He studied the furnishings of the room deliberately and carefully, identifying and cataloguing them, saying to himself: "Yes, that's a chair; that's a sofa; that's a picture," in an effort to compose himself and anesthetize his reactions.

There was an orange and green painting of a woman with an irregular face and long hair and square eyes. There was a design or an abstraction, or something of that sort, which was constructed of angles drawn in ink on white paper. The two studio couches were covered in a coarse beige fabric, and there were several white metal chairs which looked as if they had been borrowed from ice-cream parlors. Books were heaped in big copper tubs under a bay window, and a small fireplace was filled with green leaves. The record player was long and shiny, and the shelves above it were crowded with albums.

"I must say I've been feeling better since I got your wire," Jaye Fisher said, as he handed Ford a drink. "We don't have to talk at all, if you'd rather not. Just the fact that you stopped by makes a great difference."

Ford had nothing to say; nothing at all. This emptiness,

this deflation, should have made him feel hollow and weight-less, he thought. But his reaction was just the opposite. The lack of words seemed to be creating a pressure inside him; his cheeks felt hot and swollen.

"What kind of work do you do?" he said, and his voice sounded strange to him, thick and smooth as turgid water, but Jaye Fisher seemed undisturbed by it, for he smiled and said: "Nothing very earth-shaking. I work for a photographer. Tammy Ellenburg. Do you know the name?"

"I'm afraid not."

"Well, there's no reason why you should. Unless your wife dragoons you into reading fashion magazines. But Tammy's all the thing at the moment. He uses white, waxy backgrounds, and makes his models look like dope addicts. It's really very bad stuff, I think. But it's deliberately bad, and maybe that's why it caught on. I do his prop work, get him places on time, listen to him when he's yelling about what fools art directors are, and so forth." Jaye Fisher was sitting on one of the studio couches facing Ford. There was a good-humored but apologetic little smile on his face, and Ford had the impression he found it embarrassing to talk about himself seriously. There was something whimsical in his expression which entered a modest disclaimer against the weight of his opinions. He had a nice face, Ford thought: humorous, sensitive, unguarded. And his eyes were good. He looked honorable, Ford thought. Was that an odd word? Honorable?

"How long did you know Clay?"

Jaye Fisher seemed distressed by the question. "I'm sorry—forgive me—I thought you preferred not to talk about him. The way you asked about my work, well, I decided you just wanted to keep away from Clay."

"I didn't mean it that way."

"I understand, of course. It's so damn hard to say anything at all at a time like this. I met him—oh, it was a month before Christmas. Well, that's not accurate. I'd met him at a few parties before that. Just to say hello to, and so forth. But it was the month before Christmas that we got to know each other. He was a magnificent person, warm and honest, and truly decent." Jaye Fisher smiled. "Maybe you think it's odd my telling you that. He always said you understood him better than anyone. I'll confess that made me a little envious, at times. . . ."

Outside Ford walked quickly through the falling snow. He walked quickly away from St. Luke's Place. The air was soft and cool on his hot face, and the streets were shining under the lamplights. All the buildings he passed seemed to be straining toward the sky, as if they were trying desperately to tear their roots from the ground.

He must have walked several miles before he stopped and looked about curiously, surprised to find himself at a strange intersection, with lights in his eyes, and people surging past him. He shook his head quickly, and pressed his fingertips to his temples for a moment. Then he took a cab to Pennsylvania Station and got on the seven-thirty train to Wilmington. He found a seat in the lounge car, and ordered a whisky when the train started up.

Until that instant one part of his mind had been attempting to reject the meeting with Jaye Fisher as pure fantasy while another part was struggling vainly to make some sense of it. He made an effort not to speculate on what must have happened to Clay at one point or another in his life. There would be plenty of time for all that later, a lifetime, in fact, to wonder about camp counselors and nurses and classmates, and what disappointments and failures he must have suffered in loneliness and guilt.

There would be time to think, too, that they both came from the same stock and background, and had been exposed in a thousand ways to identical pressures and influences.

Ford sat staring at the darkness beyond the windows, seeing the occasional bursts of light from factories, and bright necklaces of traffic strung along the New Jersey highways. He ordered another whisky and sipped it slowly as the train rocketed along through Elizabeth and Trenton and Princeton.

314

He wasn't sure just what he felt, other than a pity for Clay that that was almost physically painful in its intensity. He wasn't dismayed or revolted, he wasn't even shocked anymore. He did not love Clay any the less, but he was saddened to contemplate now how little he had really known him. He knew only that Clay must have killed himself because he couldn't resolve the demands of his body and his conscience.

But no one else knew even that much, he thought wearily. And had he known that before, would it have helped anything? It seemed to him the lessons in Clay's death were transparently clear: cling to what you found to love in the world, and to hell with the rest of it. Clay had sacrificed himself on a pointless rack of pain and frustration—clinging not to what he loved, but to what would only destroy him.

Ford realized that he did not want to go home. He couldn't bear to talk with Janet about Clay, or listen to their friends theorizing on his death. They didn't know anything about it. And if they did, they wouldn't understand it. They would interpret it with winks and nudges, or long, disapproving faces. None of them would be able to see the tragic truth in it.

As the train began braking for North Philadelphia, he told the steward to bring him another whisky.

And then, quite suddenly, the facts of Clay's death seemed to take on a new and vivid meaning for him. In understanding his brother's death, he had given it a certain dignity; but only what he did with the rest of his life could give it any significance. If he returned now to the patterns of a society he had come to detest, he would have missed the point and truth in Clay's death; he would be making a joke of it, turning it into a simple equation of mild ironies.

His thoughts were spinning so clearly and luminously that he wondered if he could possibly be drunk. He had had three drinks—no, four, counting the one in New York—and he hadn't eaten dinner. His head felt light, true enough, but he was certain his thoughts were calm and sober, despite the excitement they were generating in him. But he couldn't exorcise a suspicion that he was somehow playing a trick on himself; for translating his brother's death into terms that supported his own rebellious needs—made them damn near noble, in fact—looked to him more like the work of a juggler than a logician.

But there was a truth to be learned from Clay's death. And Ford had learned it. To find the doorway you could always enter happily and peacefully, the windows whose views did not fill you with pain and regret, this was the only search that made sense. . . .

The night was clear as he drove away from the Wilmington station, and the traffic was light. He made good time on the empty highways.

The dogs came slinking out from under Roby's trailer as Ford walked up the dark twisting road. They circled him with excited, tentative growls, and he was happy that they remembered him; it had only been two weeks, he thought, only two weeks. And she must have read or heard about Clay; she would know why he hadn't been able to see her.

The air was damp and cool on his hot cheeks; he was slightly dizzy, he realized, from four whiskies on an empty stomach. There was snow coming; he could feel it in the heavy, humid weight of the air. It was snowing in New York, falling gently on shining streets and darkened buildings. It would come drifting down the Atlantic coast tonight, blowing inland with the freshening winds from the east. It would be the last snow of the winter, and it would make for a green and early spring. But now the sky was still bright and clear and, as he picked his way across the muddy ground, he could see the half-moon floating serenely through the black branches of the locusts behind her trailer. It seemed caught in the trees, and his heart lifted at the sight of it. He felt he had come a long way, and that his search was over.

But when he stopped at her trailer and knocked on the door, he knew that something was gone; the metal panel was bitterly cold under his knuckles. No fire had warmed it for days. He knocked again, pounding his fist on the frozen, unyielding metal, and the sound was like the sudden quick beat of his

316

heart, frantic and somehow pathetic.

He backed away from the door and looked helplessly at the dark windows of the trailer. He spoke her name quietly and reasonably; he called to her softly; if she were somewhere near, he thought, she could explain this. He didn't quite know what had happened to him yet; he felt nothing but a lonely confusion.

A bar of light fell on the ground beside him, and he heard Roby calling, softly and urgently: "Mr. Ford? Is that you, Mr. Ford?"

"Yes. Where is she?"

Roby stood in the doorway of his trailer, the light behind almost obliterated by his big body. Ford walked quickly toward him, and said: "Where is she, Roby? What's happened to her?"

"Maria's gone," Roby said.

"What do you mean? When?"

"You better come inside, Mr. Ford. Come in out of the cold. She's gone a week or so, anyway. Come on in now."

They sat around a white-enameled kitchen table, with a bare electric bulb hanging brightly above their heads. Roby's wife, Martha, asked Ford if he wanted coffee, but Roby shook his head at her, and brought a bottle of whisky to the table. He poured Ford a drink and left the bottle near him.

"You don't know where she went?" Ford's voice sounded sluggish and thick; he had asked the question several times.

"No, like I told you. She came over one morning. About eight, wasn't it, Martha? She had her suitcase with her, and she wanted to know if I'd take her into Cottersville. I took her to the Shore Line bus depot. That's where she wanted to go."

"But didn't she tell you why? Didn't she say anything?"

"Oh, she talked, all right. But she didn't tell me why she was going, or where to. You know, she had a mind of her own I think that's the way she is. Once she got the idea of going, well, she'd just take off without any talk about it."

"But, Roby, she didn't have any money," Ford said wearily. "How could she just leave?"

"I don't know about that."

"Now you tell him," Martha said.

"What?" Ford said. "What?"

Roby looked uncomfortable. "She told me not to say anything to you. But she sold some of the clothes you brought her. But this whisky, she gave it to me. It's yours, I guess you can tell."

"I'm keeping you both up," Ford said. "I'm sorry."

"Now don't worry about that. Have another touch. I hope you don't mind me offering you your own whiskey."

"No, of course not." Ford poured himself a drink. He couldn't imagine ever being drunk again; he was clearheaded, cleareyed, and he knew he would stay like that for a long time.

"I'm sorry about your brother," Roby said. "I read about it in the paper."

"Did Maria know about that?"

"Well, yes she did. Everybody seemed to be talking about it. I saw him ride once, over at the Unionville Point to Point last year. He could of made that horse win just running on two legs, I think. It was a shame about him."

Ford drank another whisky. "Roby, if I were to find you the name of the best doctor in the country, and offer you all the money you'd need—would you accept it?"

Roby looked puzzled. "What for?" Then he smiled sheepishly, and fingered the long granular birthmark on his face. "This? No, I don't think so, Mr. Ford. It may sound foolish to you, but I beat this thing. I got it to the point where it's no more concern to me than a pimple or a razor scratch. That took some doing. And I'd be lonesome without it, maybe." He was smiling at Ford; he obviously thought he was drunk. "Now you O.K.? About driving home, I mean?"

"You're certain about the money?"

"I guess so. Hell, it ain't so bad, Mr. Ford."

Ford smiled at him. "You just tell yourself you don't give a damn, right?"

"You remember what I told you about that lieutenant, eh? It's good medicine, you'll find out."

Roby took Ford's arm as he stood up. "You're O.K. now?

You're sure?"

"Yes, thanks, I'm fine. Thank you, Martha."

Ford drove home slowly. He had nowhere else to go. The half-moon still sailed across the sky, and the damp wind was stirring the crowns of the tall trees on the Downs. He drove carefully along the quiet, curving roads, trying to dismiss the memories of her from his mind. You knew it had to end, he told himself; you knew this was going to happen some day. But he hadn't known how he would feel. He had thought of pain and regret and the unsatisfied needs of his body. Not this desolate emptiness. . . .

When he let himself into the foyer he saw there was a light in the study.

"Ford?" It was Janet's voice. "Is that you?"

"Yes," he said, and walked down to the study.

She was sitting on the sofa with a magazine in her lap. "Well, I'm glad you're back," she said. "I'd about decided you were staying over for the night."

"No, I came back," he said.

"You looked bushed," she said. "I think making that round trip to New York in one day is sheer masochism. Would you like a sandwich or something? Or a drink?"

"No, I don't believe so." He sat down slowly in a deep chair and looked at the wall. "Were there any messages for me?"

"Nothing important really. Harvey Shires wants to know if you feel like going on with the point-to-point arrangements. In his stout fashion, he said he could take over if necessary."

"I see."

Janet stood and walked to the bar. "I'm thinking nightcap-type thoughts. Sure you won't change your mind?"

"No thanks. I had a couple of drinks on the train."

"It's the only possible antidote against that dreary trip."

She was wearing a black dress and high heels, he noticed. She looked quite festive, with fresh make-up, and the soft lamplight shining on the waves in her gray-blond hair. "There's something I want to ask you," she said.

"Yes? What is it?"

319

"Well, will you be going over to New York regularly?"

"No, I don't think so."

She smiled at him and he realized that she was quite nervous; her eyes were too bright, and all of her careful grooming couldn't conceal the haggard lines of her worry in her face. "Well, I just thought I'd ask," she said quickly. "If you are— I mean, if you have business over there—it seemed to me we could just plan around it. That would be sensible, wouldn't it? I know your work's become more demanding. And I thought if you had to be gone a couple of days every week, we could simply—" She cleared her throat; her voice had trembled slightly, but the strained, intense smile was still fixed on her lips. "Truly, it wouldn't be too grim. If I knew what days you'd be gone, well, I'd just plan things, parties and such, for when you'd be home."

So she knew about it, he thought; Ellie would have told her, of course. But he was surprised by Janet's proposal; and his senses were not too dulled and lifeless to be touched by it. That surprised him, too.

"I have no plans to go back to New York," he said heavily. And because he owed her something for the pain he had caused her, he looked at her directly and said in a firmer voice: "I had a small matter to attend to on Clay's estate. But that's settled now. I won't be going back. There's quite enough here to keep me busy."

Janet's smile became tremulous. She looked quickly away from him, and said in a small breathless voice: "Yes, I know. The gardens, and those box stalls—" She stood up quickly, and went over to the bar. "If we're going to talk about what's to be done here, I need another drink." Excitement seemed to be running through her like an electric charge; her face was tense and bright. "You know, Ford, I always swore on the Holy Bible I wouldn't let the house get dreary and dull when the children went off to school. I know a thousand women who've done that—they just sit around like zombies waiting for the pad of great big feet at Thanksgiving and Christmas to cheer things up. But I haven't been much better, have I? But you just watch, my dear. I'm going to have a talk tomorrow with our dear, dark jewels, and they're going to buff and shine this house up until it looks like something from Tiffany's. And we do need some new things. But I won't bore you with any details." Her hand was trembling, so that the whisky she was trying to pour splashed erratically about the rim of the glass. "Look at me. I'm getting the shakes," she said, grinning at him.

"But, I'm serious, dear, this spring's going to be gay. We'll have tons of those small dinner parties you like. Where we can really sit down and talk to people. Oh please, Ford! Have a drink with me. Let's drink to it."

Before he could tell her he didn't want a drink, the phone began to ring. Janet started, and scooped up the receiver as if she hoped to stop its rhythmic, insistent demands before they could shatter this moment of excitement and happiness.

She said, "Why, yes, Wiley. Let me see." She covered the receiver with the palm of her hand, and whispered to Ford: "It's Wiley. Do you want to talk to him? I can say you've gone up."

"Oh, I might as well," he said wearily, and took the phone from Janet. "Yes, Wiley. What is it?"

"Hi, Ford. Damn, I'm sorry to be calling so late. You about ready for the sack?"

"No. What's up?"

"I'm not sure," Wiley sounded subdued and thoughtful. "I guess I drank too much beer at dinner. I fell asleep here in the den. Just woke up. You may think this is funny, but the reason I called is, I had a dream about Clay. It was so clear, Ford, so clear and—well, I just had to call you. It's already getting kind of fuzzy. But we were out together on the back nine of the Cedars. The weather was great, cool and sunny. And you remember, Ford, the way Clay grinned when he was getting ready to put a little something extra into a shot? Nice and easy, like he knew a joke you didn't, and then—pow! He'd smoke one down the fairway like it came out of a gun.

"Well, that's how it was—the way Clay was grinning at me in the dream. I don't know why it seemed important. But thinking about Clay, made me start thinking what friends are all about. It's a question of going on together, having some fun, helping each other that way. And this is no time for you to be moping around alone. I thought we ought to get out and start hitting some golf balls. And maybe make some plans to go shooting up in Canada." Wiley sighed heavily; he sounded confused and worried. "It seemed so damn clear in the dream," he said. "Life goes on, and it's friends that put sense into it. You think that's a funny idea?"

"We might get in some golf tomorrow," Ford said slowly. "It's not a bad idea. If that snow holds off, we might try it."

Janet looked at him, and nodded vigorously. She seemed very happy. She picked up the whisky bottle, and smiled tentatively.

"Just a tiny one?" she said. "Please?"

"All right," he said.

Janet hurried off with the tray. He heard her high heels clattering quickly and impatiently down the hall to the kitchen.

"Now you're talking," Wiley said emphatically. "And we'll see about some shooting, too."

"I wonder if I could still hit a bird in the air."

"You never forget that. Cover 'em all the way, and boom!"

Janet returned with fresh ice, and a bowl of salted peanuts. She made their drinks with care, smiling as she measured the whisky over large shining ice cubes.

"Seriously, things got woefully out of hand here this winter," she said, as Ford put down the phone. "I'll have a little talk with Catherine in the morning, you can be sure. I can't imagine what she thought you'd do if you wanted a snack. There's simply nothing. No mushrooms, no liver pâté, no cheese spreads, no anchovies, nothing."

Ford sat down and stared at the wall.

"Were you and Wiley talking about going shooting?"

"Yes. It might be something to do."

She gave him his drink and smiled as she held out the little silver bowl of salted peanuts. "Here, try some. They're all we have."

The irony in her words seemed dreadful, but only because it was unintentional.

"All right," Ford said. "Thanks."

CHAPTER 20

FORD and Janet decided to go to Europe that summer. This seemed both pleasant and practical, for neither of the children was coming home: Peter was leaving for the Army, and Ginny wanted to spend her vacation at a riding camp and to learn something of stable management.

Ford applied himself vigorously to making plans. He had no sympathy for travelers who returned with what they seemed to feel were comical stories of missed connections and inferior accommodations; to his way of thinking, there was something ludicrous and pathetic in the spectacle of grown men lowering their standards under the frowns of room clerks and pursers and transport clerks. For the money he was spending, he saw no reason why he and Janet should have, not only a pleasant time in Europe, but an uncomplicated one.

He put a map on the bulletin board in his outer office, and charted his itinerary with precise, heavy pencil strokes. He asked his travel agent for photographs of hotels they would be staying at, and for exact descriptions of their accommodations. He insisted on being above the noise of traffic in the larger cities of Europe, and in the quieter areas of the small towns, near fields or ponds or streams, if possible.

The details of the trip absorbed him. He instructed himself in currencies and customs, luggage allowances and motoring regulations. Friends added suggestions to his thickening file; he duly noted that it was against the law to bring firearms into Gibraltar; that England impounded dogs for six months; that

Brioni's in Rome was the place to buy suits.

Germany, France, Italy, and Ireland, these would be their main interests. He had no wish to go to Spain.

With the correspondence he was engaged in, and the need to keep an eye on the work going on in his gardens and barns, Ford passed his time interestingly enough.

One afternoon he turned in error down the road which led to the woods where the trailers had been parked that winter.

It was as if he had come on a familiar picture which unaccountably had been altered in his absence, for the trailers were gone, and a group of men were working in the trees with axes and brush-hooks. They were hacking out weeds and honeysuckle, raking up leaves and branches and other debris to heap onto the two large fires burning in the rutted tracks made by the trailers. The smoke curled up through the hot sunlight in thick, greasy columns.

Ford parked beside the road. One of Tony Marshall's farmers came over to his car, a thick, smiling, gray-haired man with dark arcs of perspiration staining the underarms of his denim shirt.

"Spring cleaning?" Ford said, staring at white ashes caught in the fires' draft.

"You bet, Mr. Jackson. Last week I spotted three trailers, squatting here on Mr. Marshall's land like they owned it. I told a big fellow in one of them he'd have to haul ass. He said he'd look around for somewhere else, and I told him to look fast, because I'd be back in the morning with a cat and snake them trailers to the dump."

He frowned at Ford, a puzzled and virtuous man. "Isn't that a hell of a thing? If property isn't safe, I'll be damned if I know what is."

Instead of returning home, Ford drove to Rosedale and parked in front of the Catholic church. The priest's name was Father Sandeman. He was stocky but wiry, with thinning red hair, clear white skin, and a prominent nose. Ford recognized him from the Sunday morning he had gone to his church to find Maria. In a black suit and ash-flecked vest, he seemed far less puissant and mysterious than he had looked on the altar framed within the ancient symbols of gold and wax and incense. Also he had a habit of staring about the top of his desk as he talked, which gave a suggestion of tension and uncertainty to his words. "No, I wouldn't have any record of the girl," he said. "Maria Ruiz? No, I'm afraid not."

"I see," Ford said.

They sat in the study of the priest's house, a spare and comfortless room, with only a crucifix to relieve the monotony of the white walls. The single personal note was the framed picture of an elderly couple which stood on the priest's desk.

"If she had been married here, or baptized a child here, then we'd have records of course. But since she was only a casual parishioner, coming to Mass and confession at her convenience, well, there wouldn't be any records of that." Father Sandeman switched his intent gaze over the surface of his desk, as if, despite his denial, there might conceivably be relevant information darting among his papers or lurking artfully behind the inkstand or tobacco jar.

"No, I'm sorry," he said sighing. "Lord knows, I'd like to meet all these people. But it's simply not possible."

Ford thanked him. They chatted of other things for a bit then; standing to leave, he was surprised to realize he had stayed nearly half an hour. Outside in the warm sunlight he hesitated on the sidewalk, and then turned and went up the steps into the church. He took a seat in a back pew, and there, in the cool, faintly damp gloom, rested for a while.

Before leaving for Europe he stopped in to see Father Sandeman on several other occasions. And after their talk, it became his habit to spend a moment or so in the quiet church. Father Sandeman evinced no curiosity at his visits; apparently he thought them the most natural thing in the world. But Ford knew, of course, that the priest was playing with him like an expert angler. He was wryly amused at an image of himself lying sluggishly but comfortably in the deep waters of agnosticism, while this patient fisher of souls exercised his wily skills to lure him upward to the shining light of faith. . . .

326

In a casual fashion, Father Sandeman gave him books and pamphlets to read; and no matter where their talk strayed among crops and weather and local news, it always returned, like the dominant theme in a symphony, inevitably and satisfyingly to the subject of grace and obedience, and their relationship to the paradox of divine mercy and divine will. The blind would see the light with grace; and the deaf would hear the faint roll of drums that announced He was near. . . . This was grace, a benison distributed whimsically by God. No need or point in trying to understand it. Obedience was simpler; you did what you were told, and no nonsense about it. But Father Sandeman had a full box of lures. He seemed to sense that Ford's interest was vaguely sentimental, and he attempted to tease him with pictures made up of mysterious and poignant generalities. He avoided the concrete and explicit, although Ford got an impression that he longed at times to prod him in the accents of a circus barker.

Ford felt guilty about taking advantage of Father Sandeman's professional zeal. Understandably enough, the priest had misinterpreted his visits. Ford was sorry about that. He should set him right, of course, but he couldn't do that unless he made up his mind to stop seeing him.

The truth was that talking to Father Sandeman made him feel close to Maria. His quiet vigils in the church served the same purpose. It was not spiritual truth or awakening he sought in that atmosphere of silence and incense and dull golden lights. It was simply that he could think of her there without distraction. The emptiness and lassitude of his spirits, which filled him with despair elsewhere, seemed to be complemented and annealed by the warm dusty gloom of the church.

He wanted a time and place to bear witness to his experience; to accept, deliberately and passively, the pain of it; and while he never succeeded in resolving anything in that way, the attempt reassured him that his memories were not false, and that for a time, at least, he must have been vigorously and intensely alive. . . .

In Paris, despite the humid heat of August, Janet managed to come down with the flu. Their suite in the Prince de Galle was transformed into a dispensary; a fussy French doctor pulled the blinds on its rose and golden elegance, and filled the languid air with an aroma of camphor and cough syrups. Maids tiptoed out with sheets saturated from contact with Janet's feverish body, and replaced them in an operation which entailed flipping her exhausted, cylindrical frame about with the rough dexterity of overworked nurses. The doctor said her troubles came from drinking iced water at meals. He amplified this theme until she became haggard with irritation at him. She was miserable with discomfort and embarrassment; to be vulnerable made her desperate.

She begged Ford to go over to Dublin without her for the horse show. He agreed to at last, because he knew she would only worry and blame herself if he didn't.

In Dublin he watched the jumping classes and the green hunters. He dined at Jammett's and the Russell, and found them very good. In the long, soft evenings he went dutifully about the city and looked at notable examples of Georgian architecture.

There were groups of British about everywhere, and Ford was puzzled by his reaction to them. He had never minded the British accent before, that he could remember, but now it fell tiresomely on his ear. Its connotation of privilege, and good form and good blood, irritated him. A stocky man with a red face and the look of the retired military joined him one afternoon in the lounge of the Shelbourne, and Ford found it difficult not to be rude to him. Escaping, he hurried into the lobby and nearly collided with Harvey and Dora Shires.

He was happy to see them. The encounter made them feel festive and special, even somewhat glamorous. They found a table and ordered tea.

"Talk about coincidences!" Dora said. "Not just bumping into you, Ford, though that's marvelous enough. But we had a letter from Alicia yesterday. Isn't it all wonderfully intricate? I wouldn't be surprised now if the Postons came charging in."

Ford had received one letter from Alicia since she had moved to New York. It referred to a business matter. He didn't even know her present address. The home on the Downs was on the market and so was the dairy. She hadn't consulted Ford on either of these steps. A firm in New York was handling her affairs, Vaughn and Restall. He had made inquiries about them, and found they were very good people.

"She seems wonderfully happy," Dora said. "I was mildly surprised—mildly shocked might be better. Harvey says it's none of my business, and then *he* goes happily on striking attitudes all over the place."

Harvey took the pipe from his square jaw, and grinned modestly; he took any comment about himself, regardless of its content or implication, to be flattering.

"I don't think it's your business, agreed. But my point was a general one. I don't quibble about other people's religious beliefs. There's something in that line about my father's mansions having many rooms which expresses my feeling well enough. But it seems to me she's just going way out in left field in getting married in a Catholic church."

"But he's a Catholic, dear."

"That's a particular consideration—a personal sympathy, if you will. All well and good. But I'm trying to see the general view."

Dora looked curiously at Ford. "This can't be news to you. You know Alicia and Delucca are getting married, of course."

"Why yes," Ford said untruthfully. "She mentioned something about that in her last letter." He glanced at his watch. "I'm interested in the jumping classes this afternoon, so I'd better run along. But supposing we all meet here for dinner?"

He walked to the porter's desk and borrowed paper and an envelope, and wrote a note to Alicia. Reading it back, it seemed stiff and formal; the closing "God bless you both" sounded clumsily pompous, but he couldn't think of anything else to add, so he addressed it to her home on the Downs, and gave it to the porter to send off.

When he and Janet returned from Europe in the fall, Ford

called Alicia from his office. He didn't call from home, because Janet had been stiffly disapproving when she learned of Alicia's plans. "What in heaven's name is she marrying him for? Why not just live with him? It's really quite hilarious to dignify all this barnyard activity with a ring and a veil—and flower girls, I wouldn't be surprised."

"Please don't talk that way," he had said, looking at her steadily, and she never did again—to him, at least.

A week or so later Ford went over to New York to see Alicia. She was living in a large apartment on Fifth Avenue which she had sublet from one of her friends. The furniture was in colors of cream and gold, and there was a view of Central Park. When Ford arrived lights were gleaming in the city, pale bright rectangles pressing against the smoky shade of early evening.

Alicia hugged him tightly. "This is just too wonderful," she said. "That letter from Dublin, then talking to you, and now you're here in person." She laughed suddenly, and there was a childish little catch in her voice. "But you should have let me know. I would have told George. He's got some sort of meeting tonight."

"The next time I will."

"Well, did you have a marvelous trip? And how's Janet?"

"Fine. We had good fun."

"Oh, I've missed you so. Your letter came on a gloomy morning, and it made the whole day cheerful."

She looked very good, he thought, but too thin and pale. In dark slacks and a white blouse, her body seemed childishly spare.

"Enough about the trip," he said. "I have no home movies, no color slides, no hilarious stories about the difficulties my rusty French plunged us into."

"Oh, I could listen to them for hours."

"You're out of your mind. When's the happy occasion?"

She looked at him steadily, the smile fading from her mouth and eyes. "Do you mean that, Ford? Do you think it's a happy occasion?"

"Yes, I do."

"Bless you. I've been so miserable at times. About everything. I know I failed Clay. And I'm terrified that could happen again."

Ford put his hands on her shoulders and shook her gently. "Now listen to me. I said it was a happy occasion. I meant exactly that. Don't think about anything else. Don't remember anything else. Will you do that for me?"

"All right, Ford. I'll try."

"Now—how's George?"

"You're a dear, dear person," she said, with a breathless little laugh. "Give me a cigarette, will you? I feel all shaky. Isn't that ridiculous? Do you want a drink or something?"

"No thank you."

"George is fine, just fine," she said, and Ford was touched by the sudden eagerness in her voice. "He's looking after a restaurant here for a friend who's in Europe buying wines. But he's found his new place! Ford, you must see it! It's a wonderful old mill on Long Island. It has to be completely done over, of course. Lighting, new kitchens, bars, power rooms. But his architect is blending all the new things in with the old. The millrace flows right through the first floor and they're leaving it that way. Imagine having your own private waterfall to look at while you're dining. And there's acres of parking space around the mill pond, and all the old flooring and beams are so thick and solid you couldn't budge them with bulldozers."

"Well, you put my name down for a reservation on opening night. I want a table close to the falls."

"Ford—if I wrote you, a little later, would you come over and see us? Not right away—but in a little while?"

"I'd be grateful if you would. You let me know."

The doorbell sounded in the foyer and Alicia turned her head quickly, a faint frown touching her forehead. A maid opened the door, and Ford heard the rumble of a deep, smooth voice. He felt a sudden coldness in his stomach; the reaction wasn't one of fear or guilt, but it was related to both these emotional states in some fashion; and he drew a deep breath to steady himself as George Delucca walked quickly into the living room.

He wore a dark and beautifully cut suit, and looked as if he had just left his gym or club; his thick black hair was damp at the temples, and there was a rough, healthy burn of color in his hard brown cheeks. He saw Ford, but paid no attention to him after one sharp, surprised flick of recognition; without checking his stride, he walked straight to Alicia, his eyes going over her face carefully and appraisingly. When she came to him he held her away for an instant, his big hands cradling her shoulders.

"Everything O.K.?" he said, and when she nodded quickly and happily, he took her in his arms and let her head rest against his chest. He rubbed her slender shoulder blades gently with the tips of his fingers, while his dark, intent eyes came slowly around to Ford, as ominously as cannons swinging onto a target.

"So what is it that brings the Downs back into our life?" he said gently. "What have we done to deserve this honor?"

Alicia said, "Please, George," in a worried, unhappy little voice, and the expression in Delucca's face changed subtly; he sighed and said, "O.K., baby, it doesn't matter."

"Ford just came by to wish us long life, good luck, and everything else on the happy occasion. That's what he called it, a happy occasion. And I haven't even given him a drink to toast us with."

"We can fix that," Delucca said quietly. "There's nothing we can't fix, remember that." He held her away from him and smiled into her eyes. She nodded quickly and tightened her grip on his arms.

They might have been the only people in the world, Ford thought, watching them. He felt tired and awkward, his very physical presence irrelevant and intrusive; they formed a perfect emotional circle, strong and inviolate. It was the simple thing Clay couldn't do for her, the simple, fundamental thing without which nothing else meant a damn—just to look at her and tell her with his eyes and presence that he was grateful she belonged to him.

Alicia was smiling at Delucca now. "But what happened to your meeting? I wasn't expecting you for hours."

"Hell, it's going to drag on till next week. So I sent the lawyer over. He's got a cast-iron tail. He'll sit there with an intelligent frown on his face and outlast everybody. I thought we'd drive out to the restaurant and look at the new work. They got the downstairs bar in today. Then we'll have dinner on the Island coming back. Feel up to all that?"

"Yes, it sounds wonderful." She was like a trusting child with him, radiant under his attention and approval. "I'll change. I won't be long."

"Good girl. No slacks in my joint. I seem to have made that point with you before."

She turned quickly to Ford. "Please stay a minute. Do have a drink. I'll be right back."

When she hurried from the room, Delucca took a narrow cigar from the breast pocket of his suit and began to unwrap it slowly and deliberately. "You want a drink?" he said, watching Ford with a faint smile. "We got sipping whisky."

"I don't think so. Thanks anyway. Alicia was telling me about your new place. It sounds exciting."

"Well, it won't be the White Hackle. But it's got its points." Delucca smiled wryly as he strolled to the windows and looked down at the bright threads of traffic twisting through Central Park. "It's odd how you can get attached to a chunk of real estate. It was just another good steak joint, I suppose, but I thought it had a nice tone to it. About this time of the evening particularly," he said, nodding out at the yellow lights gleaming through the blue haze above the city. "When everything was clean and shining, ready for the cocktail crowd. Bars, lounges, kitchens—not a lemon peel out of place in the whole damn joint, and just enough light outside so you could still see the meadows and ponds."

"Would you mind if I asked you a question?"

"Probably," Delucca said, turning and looking at him with

333

a small smile. "But go ahead."

"Why didn't you fight for it? Why did you give it up?"

"That puzzles you, eh?" The faint smile had hardened on Delucca's lips. "You haven't lost your talent for missing the obvious, I guess. You saw her! I'm still holding my breath for fear she'll flip completely. And she's better right now than she's been for weeks. She hurts for everybody, that's her peculiar cross. I'd have enjoyed breaking Wiley Poston and Tony Marshall over my knee. They'd have come out of a brawl with me looking like disaster cases. And it would have been nice and legal, too. But more than that I wanted her sane." Delucca sighed and rubbed his big hands together slowly. "Can you imagine what a brawl between me and her friends might have done to her? With the tactics they'd use? And the way I'd have to fight? So I let it go. I played victim, which is a role I'm not one damn bit cut out for. Because that was the only way I could see for us to make a clean break. And to give her enough anger and contempt to keep her alive during the transition. I had what I wanted out of the deal—I had her. I couldn't fight for a piece of real estate with that in the balance."

"I understand," Ford said slowly. "You had to take her away. It couldn't work down there. Nothing can, I'm afraid."

"That's typical of you. Root your head deeper into the sand. Let me tell you something about the Downs: you people are half-dead, and you like it that way. Because waking up and living is a chore. You're willing to let the Downs slide down the drain, because that's a hell of a lot easier than fighting for it. You're hiding in big houses with the doors locked and the shades drawn, and when you finally look outside you'll find that sweet stretch of country jammed from one end to the other with housing developments and used-car lots. And it didn't have to happen that way. That's the goddamn shame of it."

Ford frowned at him. "This just doesn't make sense to me. You talk as if you like the area."

"Don't you?"

"I detest it."

334

"So go ahead and sulk. You think what's wrong down there is the result of some natural law? Men made it. Other men could change it. But you won't, I'll bet on that. Hell, there's nothing wrong with big houses and open country. They represent human effort, and whether the effort was made by you or your great-grandfather is beside the point. I respect it. But I also respect the human effort in housing developments and the union movement. The world can't be all grand homes and rolling country and point-to-points. But it doesn't have to be a dreary stretch of cheap housing, and bad restaurants, and gas stations either.

"But you don't give one damn about the people who need those things, and may make a mess of the world trying to get them. But they care about you, and they're waiting to go for the jugular. And what are you fighting with? Values that were getting moldy fifty years ago when they were grafted onto you. You've got style and I admire style. But it's not related to function anymore. You've got attitudes instead of convictions, a pose instead of a posture. So you and your friends are going to go limping out of sight after the dodo."

"I've got the wrong kind of friends. Is that it?"

"I'd say you don't have the right kind of enemies. You'll go on playing golf and gunning with Poston and Marshall until they plant you all back of the Quaker meeting house. Because that's easier than making enemies and keeping them." Delucca made an abrupt, dismissing gesture with his hand. "To hell with it. We're counting angels on pinheads." He stared directly at Ford. "This is hard for me to say. But I'm glad you came over. It might help her. Now do you want a drink?"

Ford shook his head slowly. "Another time maybe. Will you say good-by to her for me? Tell her I'd had to make a train or something?"

"O.K.," Delucca said. "I'll tell her."

One afternoon at the close of October, Ford stood in front of his home marveling at the colors in the trees. The sun was brilliant and the maples and oaks looked as if gentle fires were burning in the branches. There had been no frost yet and the meadows were still fresh and green. From where he was standing he could see the swirling designs made on the surface of his pond by a sweep of buoyant fall winds. It would be a perfect day for golf, he thought, but as he was driving toward the Cedars he changed his mind and went to see Father Sandeman. Without understanding why, he resumed the visits he had begun before leaving for Europe.

One morning, Father Sandeman said to him: "Now see here, you always retreat from any notion of absolutes. Well, you've had experience with farming, and you know that you plant in the spring and harvest in the fall. And you know it takes a certain number of days for a cow to drop her calf. You aren't surprised at this. You don't anticipate any changes in these matters. For practical purposes, you take them as absolutes. Right?"

"For practical purposes, yes," Ford said.

One afternoon when snow was falling beyond the windows of the study, Father Sandeman looked directly at him, and this was so unusual it made Ford listen closely to what he was saying: "I think you've acquired some bad habits from your money," the priest said. "It's natural enough, I imagine. You're accustomed to paying for what you want. And you're suspicious of things without price tags on them. You tell me you want to find some place in a design that won't bend and twist under human pressures and considerations. You want to give yourself to something absolute. You want peace. Fine and good! But I'm not a shopkeeper with those things on my shelves. I have nothing to sell. You've got to sacrifice something for them. You've got to give up your own needs and vanities. It's the hardest thing in this world to understand, but you must suffer for God's love."

Later, thinking wearily of all this in the cold, quiet church, Ford decided there was no point in seeing Father Sandeman any more. His need for absolute values was as strong as his need for Maria had been; he had longed for God's grace, as he understood it, as much as he had ever longed for her. But there was no way to prove it existed—no way to prove he deserved it. For he had nothing to sacrifice, nothing to give up.

That winter Janet gave a number of small dinner parties, and they were very pleasant. Ford saw little of Wiley Poston and Tony Marshall that season. Somewhat to his surprise, he had gravitated toward the Cullinans and the Harrises and the Landons. The Cullinans usually had a baby-sitting problem, and Ford and Janet finally urged them to bring their two small sons when they came for dinner. The boys ate early in the study and watched television until they fell asleep, but until then their high noisy voices made a pleasant sound in the big house.

Tom Landon had a number of projects he was trying to interest Ford in; his mania for growth and expansion was still virulent, and he had a banker's flair for the scent of money in even such altruistic considerations as bookmobiles and day camps, although his steps were generally taken in the right direction. But occasionally it was difficult to keep him from losing sight of their goals in a tangle of profits and balance sheets. At the other extreme Sally Cullinan was even worse; unless he reined in her wooly-headed liberalism she was capable of sacrificing any realizable gain for a satisfyingly noble defeat. Ford tried to function as a balance wheel between Landon's compulsive canniness and Sally's compulsive impracticality; there were times when this seemed hopeless, and there were times he was tempted to call George Delucca and tell him so. But he never did. For despite some vexations, his involvement in these problems helped the day and nights to pass.

One night—a night he would always remember—Catherine looked into the living room to tell Ford he was wanted on the telephone. He excused himself to the Landons and Harrises, and took the call in the study.

"Mr. Ford, this is Roby. You remember me?"

"Why, of course, Roby. It's good to hear from you. How's everything?"

"Everything's just fine with us, Mr. Ford. Couldn't be better.

The reason I called is I'm pulling up stakes here. I wanted to say good-by to you before I left."

"I'm glad you called. Where are you off to?"

"Well, I'm going back home, where I was born and brought up. Cloverdale, Alabama. Bet you never head of it."

"No, I haven't."

"That don't surprise me. We got about a hunderd people and about two hunderd hound dogs in Cloverdale. But my cousin does all right with a little mill he's got on the Tennessee River—see, Cloverdale's just over the Tennessee border near Sheffield. That's our big town and you could put most of it in half Cottersville. He wants me to come help him out and that suits me fine. I liked wandering around in the trailer but it's time to settle down. Martha's going to have a baby."

"That's wonderful, Roby. And how is she?"

"She's fine, too. Just fine." Roby paused, and then continued tentatively: "Well, there's another reason I called, Mr. Ford. I've been wondering what to do for these last couple of days. I mean, about calling you. I got a letter from Maria, see."

"Maria," Ford said, and felt a little shock go through him; his knees trembled as he sat down on the arm of the sofa. "Maria?"

"That's right. I didn't know whether you'd want her address or not. She just said hello to me and Martha, and that she was working. She wants to keep in touch. She didn't say anything about giving you her address. Maybe she hoped I would. Maybe she didn't. I don't know. I sat up half last night trying to make up my mind. I didn't want to butt in where I wasn't needed or wanted. You see what I mean?"

Ford stared helplessly at the dark windows of his study. "Yes, I understand," he said. "Perfectly."

"Well, I put the address down where I can keep it. I've got a book for stuff like that. I got you in it, too. I'll write you from Cloverdale, and tell you what kind of a baby we got."

Through the windows of his study, Ford thought he saw a light playing on the meadow; and he felt a sound on the wind that made his heart beat faster.

338

"Mr. Ford? You want the address?"

Ford drew a deep breath in an attempt to steady himself; he felt like weeping. The equation was too merciless; the design too austere to have been drawn by human circumstances.

"Well? It's up to you, Mr. Ford."

"Would you hold on until I get a pencil?" Ford waited a moment, and then said: "All right, go ahead," and before Roby began speaking he placed a hand tightly over the receiver and stared at the windows.

He counted slowly to thirty before putting the receiver up to his ear.

"Mr. Ford? You got that all right?"

"Yes, I have it."

"I can read it again, if you want."

"No, that's all right. I have it. Thanks, Roby. Say hello to your wife for me, please. And good luck in Cloverdale. . . ."

Ford put the receiver down and pressed his hands against his face. He had given her up. . . .

Now he had done what Father Sandeman had said was necessary; he had given something up, made his sacrifice. And now he knew all about suffering. What he had learned before had been only an intimation of this. . . .

So now he was ready for grace, he thought bitterly. There was no love in him, no kindness or peace. But he had made the lonely, bitter bargain with God; he had given up Maria to search for something more lasting, more perfect. . . .

Janet called to him. "Ford, we're going in for dinner. Hurry, please."

"Yes, all right."

He walked slowly down the hallway to the foyer, where the small fire cast its leaping lights on the smooth pine flooring and the gracefully curved arms of the cockfighting chair. In the long mirror beside the grandfather's clock, he advanced steadily toward himself, a tall, insubstantial figure in the flickering illumination.

The wings of silver at his temples had become more sharply

defined in the last year, and there was a hard clarity in his eye which caught and held his attention; staring at his image in the clouded old mirror, he was reminded of pictures he had seen of the grandfather for whom he had been named, that irreverent, tough-minded rebel who had never traded substance for shadows, or reality for dreams, and who had stubbornly refused to quicken his pace toward the eternal, dissolving dust.

There was a new, cold strength in Ford. All right, he thought; the bargain was made, and he would keep it. He was pledged to search for something perfect, and he would make that search; but if the lights he sought were only marsh fires, and the sound that stirred his soul was nothing but the familiar wind in the trees, he prayed he would have the strength to realize it. Before it was too late to begin another search. . . .

"Heavens, what are you frowning about?" Janet asked him, as he came into the dining room.

"I was trying to remember the name of a town," he said, knowing sadly that the trial of strength had now begun. "Cloverdale. I just don't want to forget it."